Cold Moon

THE LUNATICS ~ BOOK THREE

A.M. LEONARD

Raven Song Press

Freeville, New York

Cover design: Cristiana Leone
Editors: Connolly Bottum

Raven Song Press
46 Hammond Hill Road
Freeville, New York, 13068
(607) 844-8706
www.RavenSongPress.com

Publisher's Cataloging-In-Publishing Data
Names: Leonard, A.M., 1956- author
Title: Cold Moon / A.M. Leonard
Description: Freeville, NY: Raven Song Press, (2025)
Series: The Lunatics
The Library of Congress Cataloging-in-Publication Data is available upon request
ISBN 979-8-9907544-4-7 (paperback) ISBN 979-8-9907544-5-4 (e-book)

First Edition October 2025
10 9 8 7 6 5 4 3 2 1

Dedicated to our granddaughter McKenzie, equestrian and long-distance runner extraordinaire. You are a force to be reckoned with.

~and~

To all who step up and play their part rescuing our world from the many forms of evil that never cease trying to overwhelm us.

One

Kellas was missing. Gone without a trace. And I was very close to losing it.

We were outside on our deck on the longest night of the year. Our solstice guests had left half an hour ago, and Dad and I had been readying ourselves for bed. I was shivering in my flannel pj's. In upstate New York, winter is cold. Not as frigid as North Dakota, where I used to live, but bad enough. It could also have been a reaction to Orianthi's news. "You're sure it was Erin you saw Kellas leave with?" I asked through chattering teeth.

"That traitorous Cait Sidhe collared him like a dog, then they disappeared into thin air." Orianthi's breath was freezing in small white puffs as she relayed what she had seen. Clad only in her nightshirt, the little dryad had come pounding on our back door, drawing my father and me at a panicked run, wondering who it could be.

Orianthi nodded vigorously. "Positive. Look." She grabbed my hand and led me to the edge of the deck where two different size footprints had trampled the snow, led away, then halted. "That's where they disappeared." She pointed, then shuddered, cold as well. "I would never have seen them if I hadn't looked out my window at that moment."

Dad knelt and examined the footprints. "It was definitely Erin?" he pressed, echoing me.

Orianthi tossed her head. "The wards are still up, aren't they?" she scoffed. "Who else could have come through them if not her? Besides, I know that evil Cait Sidhe queen well enough." She looked at me, worry writ large on her delicate features. "Why Kellas didn't immediately slay her after what she did to Raven, I don't know."

I was shuddering uncontrollably now, staring at the footprints like I'd seen a ghost. Erin had done her best to kill me... and Kellas had gone with her? Had he willingly left with Erin? Or had she kidnapped him? Not that either option was anything we'd want to happen, but if he'd left willingly... No. He'd never have done so. He loved me. I loved him.

"Inside. You too, Orianthi." Dad put an arm around my shoulders and ushered me into the house, where he guided me onto a stool by the kitchen island. Then he moved about the kitchen, preparing hot chocolate.

Orianthi clambered up on the stool next to me and wrapped her little kid arms around me in a hug. "We'll find Kellas, Raven. Don't worry."

I nodded, but without conviction. If I had learned anything from all the chaos lately, it was that nothing was guaranteed. Happy endings were rare as hen's teeth in the real world. I rubbed my hands over my goose-bumped skin. My heart ached.

Dad finished making the hot chocolate and set two steaming mugs in front of me and Orianthi before taking a sip of his own. He grimaced and set the mug down. "Raven."

Oh, gosh, here it came. The dad lecture. "Mmm?"

"You must not go off on your own to find Kellas." Clad only in his sleep pants, Dad leaned back against the sink, arms crossed over his bare chest. "We need to think this through. Plan, not go off half-cocked like you're in the habit of doing."

"Are you calling me impulsive?" His words stung... but if I was being honest, Dad had a valid point there. I don't make the best choices under pressure.

Orianthi giggled, eyeing me over the brim of her mug while blowing on her hot chocolate to cool it. Dad grunted in disgust. "Pretty much how you handle everything, fledgling." Orianthi, drat her, was nodding in agreement.

Annoyed, I tried a sip of cocoa and immediately burned my tongue. I set the mug down, grimacing. "Where do you suggest we start?"

"We alert the police. File a missing person report." Dad picked up his mug again and sipped, then frowned, set it back down and went to the fridge.

"Erin took him! The police will find nothing," I protested. Erin was a Cait Sidhe, fairy cat, able to shift from human to cat form and back at will. "She'll disappear into a parallel dimension." Kellas was a Cait Sidhe too, but he was nothing like Erin. I swallowed hard, the lump in my throat threatening to choke me.

"Nevertheless, it's where we start." Dad brought out the milk, poured some into his mug, then offered some to us. Orianthi immediately thrust her mug toward him. He poured some into her cocoa, and then into mine even though I hadn't asked for any. "I will bring the A-Team up to speed in the morning." He leaned both hands on the countertop between us and fixed me with an intimidating scowl. "You're for bed. Don't you even think of going anywhere alone. You're still recovering from the last time your impulsive behavior put you in harm's way. Orianthi will spend the night with you." He shifted his glare to the dryad. "Make sure she stays put."

"Can do." The feckless dryad nodded vigorously. Whose side was she on, anyway? Orianthi might only be five, but dryads have an impressive skill set. Even as young as Orianthi was, dryads are fierce warriors. Plus, Orianthi knew I would do anything for her, and she'd not hesitate to use that power. Dad could not have chosen a more effective person to ensure my compliance.

Dad relaxed against the sink counter and took a long slurp of his cocoa. "Archer has a month's recess from university. He can hang out with you when I'm at work." *Oh, joy! His brain was already figuring out the logistics of always keeping me under guard.* "Perhaps your mom can do her remote work here as well, instead of at her cabin."

I groaned. Dad tended to helicopter parent. I can kind of understand. I'm an only child, and yeah, I have gotten myself into some awful situations since coming into my magic last year at 16. Archer is the closest thing I have to a sibling. Mom works remotely as a lawyer, and she is in high demand. Mom and Dad have lived apart for a sizeable portion of my life, but recently Mom moved nearby so that she could be closer to me. Perhaps now she and Dad could put their marriage back together. I hoped so. At least they were finally talking through the issues that had caused them to separate. But Dad's fretful hovering by proxy was annoying.

He'd hover in person, I'm sure, but Dad works long hours; he's a doctor at the area hospital. As if that job wasn't enough to keep him busy, he also moonlights as a paramedic with his crew, the aforementioned A-Team. They're all retired special forces medics, and a quartet of powerful, scary-looking dudes. At least they are to someone like me: five foot six and 120 pounds dripping wet. Dad's always been overprotective. Since Mom and he split, he'd had his team take turns guarding me from the shadows. They, and Kellas.

Who is missing. Gods....

Panic, fear, loss flushed through me and surfaced as anger. "You can't tell me what to do." The words burst from me unbidden. "I'm not a little kid anymore."

Dad cocked his head to one side and fixed me with a frustrated glare. "What moon phase are you in right now, fledgling?"

I growled. He would have to bring that up. I get younger as the moon wanes, and older as it waxes. It's my biggest handicap, inherited from my dead

Nan, Dad's mother, the only person in the world other than me who'd been afflicted with this condition. She had called us moon-bound magic wielders "lunatics." A crazy way to live, for sure.

Dad laughed without humor. "Exactly. Your glamour may make you look 17, but physically you are maybe... six?"

I am only ever my true age at the full moon. The whole waxing and waning bit is problematic. Especially when the moon is "new." I disappear. It's a pain in the butt.

I huffed and got off my stool. "You're treating me like a child. I'm not." Orianthi reached for me, but I shook off her hand impatiently.

"Raven, you almost died." Dad gritted out. "If it hadn't been for Kellas..."

I'd started for the front door, but whirled on him. "Right! If it hadn't been for Kellas, I'd be dead, Dad! And now Kellas is gone, and you don't want me to go after him. How does that make sense?"

He exhaled a frustrated huff. "We'll find him. Together."

"And we need to go. Now. Tonight. Before she can disappear into the ether with him."

"She already has!"

"You don't know that." I turned my back and walked away.

Dad caught up and grabbed me by my left arm. It tugged painfully at my healing shoulder wound, and I winced. He noticed, of course. "You're still not healed fully."

"Nearly." I twisted in his grasp. "Let go!"

"No! Raven..."

From deep inside, rage flooded through my body, and I felt myself transforming into my Celtic avatar, the form that overtook me anytime I was under attack. Through the bloodlust that blurred my vision, blinding me to reason, I heard my father cry out in desperation. "Raven, no! You're my only daughter. I can't lose you, too!"

It stopped me. Snuffed out the anger like it had never been. My body changed back in an instant, and I collapsed on the floor, dizzy from the rapid change and horrified that I had been on the verge of attacking my father. I started crying.

He fell on his knees and wrapped his arms around me, holding me close. I could feel his heart pounding rapidly against my ear. "Raven, please. We must proceed with caution. Have faith that I want Kellas back as badly as you do. We'll get him back. On my honor, I promise. But you must trust me."

I swallowed my sobs and nodded shakily against his chest, feeling his relieved sigh.

"We'll come up with a game plan in the morning," he assured me. "Meanwhile, go to bed. You're exhausted, and so are we."

So, I went to bed. But come morning, I was going after my boyfriend and nobody was going to get in my way.

~

I started lucid dreaming the moment my head hit the pillow. Of course.

"So good of you to join me, Light Bringer," a man's voice spoke out of the total darkness that surrounded me. "I'd hoped you would."

"Where am I?" I had dimension-hopped while dreaming, an occupational hazard of mine. Where that was, however, I did not know.

"You are here, in my demesne. Where eventually I hope you will stay." His voice was smooth and sweet, like liquid caramel.

I had no intention of remaining here if I could help it! This pitch darkness was nothing I cared to linger in. To illuminate where I was, I called up a small light in my hand (after the craziness of the salt mine, I'd worked on that spell until I could cast it). It hardly made a dent in the pitch black; mostly it put a spotlight on me.

"Lovely as ever," the voice sighed.

His voice was vaguely familiar, although I couldn't place it at the moment. "Who are you?" I wished I could see who was speaking.

"Don't tell me you've forgotten already!" his deep voice mocked. "Not after I left such a lasting impression on you and your beloved."

Then I remembered, and it chilled me to the core. "Dub." God of Darkness... one of the three Old Gods who had tried their best to kill me on Samhain, my 17th birthday.

"That's me," he said.

I reached over my shoulder and put my hand on Fraegarthach's hilt. "Show yourself, you coward!"

A quiet laugh. "Difficult to do now. Thanks to you, I lack a physical presence."

"That's your own fault." I released my grasp on my sword. He couldn't hurt me in his current condition. At least I didn't think he could.

That elicited a deep sigh from him. "I see that now. I would like to make amends if possible."

Amends? Wait. What? This was the god who'd come close to killing Kellas, who'd assisted Dother in his torture. Who'd threatened me with... nastiness. "Are you kidding me?"

A deep chuckle: warm, even pleasant. "I could not be more sincere."

This was just nuts. "I don't believe you."

"Oh, for crying out loud!" He sounded annoyed at my attitude. "I can understand your reticence, Light Bringer, but I assure you of the purity of my intentions. As proof, I will tell you what my brother intends for you and yours."

"Which one, Dian or Dother?"

"Dother, of course."

I scoffed. "He's encased in stone and unlikely to be planning much of anything right now."

"Unfortunately for all of us, my elder brother has been freed and has joined forces with the red-haired feline. Together, they plot... mischief."

My heart sank into my toes. Dother had escaped? So soon? "Why should I believe a word you say? And why is your brother being freed unfortunate for you?" I said the last bit aggressively. He and his brothers were the reason my grandmother was dead! Unfortunate? For him? Really?

That made him growl. "I swear to you; I speak the truth! They have already taken your beloved Cait Sidhe. Sadly, they will use him to avenge themselves." He sighed, and strangely, it sounded like actual regret. "He will suffer the tortures of the damned. You would do well to steal him back as soon as possible."

I was silent, mulling over what he'd said. "Why are you telling me this? What's in it for you?"

A soft chuckle. "We got off on the wrong foot, you and I. The moment I saw you, I felt you were the only one for me. Hence, I attempted to kill the Cait Sidhe, and failed when I underestimated your fierceness in protecting him."

"You were... Are! Disgusting. The things you said and did..." I shuddered, remembering.

His voice became caramel again. "There was a time when domination was how a man courted a woman. What we wanted, we took."

I made a retching sound. "That's disgusting."

"Hmm." He sounded amused. "There are still many who would disagree with you."

I certainly hoped not! Unfortunately, he was probably right.

He continued. "In time, I hope you will form a far better impression of me than you currently hold. I will show you I can be your ally, your port in the storm, your rock. Eventually, I hope you will come to love me even more than your Cait Sidhe, that you will leave him and become my Queen, shining your light in my dark demesne for all of time."

No way I was going to let that happen. Done with this nonsense, I woke myself up.

People were shouting downstairs. Careful not to wake the sleeping dryad, I scooted out of bed and hastened down the spiral staircase from my room to the first floor. My brother met me in the kitchen.

"Stay here with me," Archer warned in an undertone, barring me from going into the living room with one muscular, outstretched arm. "The state police sent a detective over, and he and Michael are already butting heads."

I call Archer my brother, but we're not, really. We *are* related... my dad is Archer's great grandfather. Dad is distinctly atypical—about 1400 years of superannuated, which is better than saying he's older than dirt. It was one of the little things that caused issues between Mom (who is mortal) and him (he's not, obviously) back when I was little. Archer is *Gayogo̱hó:nǫ'*. He's almost 100% Native American, and maybe the best-looking guy I've ever laid eyes on... and he's also Two Spirit. Gay, that is. We pass as siblings because I'm half Native myself; Mom is Hidatsa; Dad's Irish.

"So, what's the problem?" I asked. "We're reporting a kidnapping. Why should there be any issues?"

He put a finger to his lips and beckoned me to a spot near the living room where we could hide yet hear everything that was being said.

"So, let me get this straight," I heard an unfamiliar voice say. "This young man, per your description of him: 5 feet 11 inches, 160 pounds, black hair, blue eyes, about 25... has only the one name: Kellas. Huh!" There was a meaningful pause. "And he's dating your daughter, who you tell me is 17? Are you sure you wouldn't prefer him arrested for being involved with a minor?"

Archer immediately pressed a hand over my mouth. "Shhh!" he hissed in my ear. I yanked his hand away but kept my mouth shut, seething.

"Kellas is an honorable man," I heard Dad say in a stiff tone. "We trust him."

"He disappeared without a trace, in the company of another woman. Doesn't sound trustworthy to me. In fact, it sounds like he was playing the field."

"We told you. He was kidnapped."

"But you didn't see this happen." The stranger again, his disbelief bleeding through.

Dad sighed heavily. "We didn't, but our neighbor..."

"Who is five. Really. Like you can trust a five-year-old to get the facts straight." The man's voice practically dripped with sarcasm. "They have active imaginations. I should know. My daughter is six."

"Jackass!" I whispered. Archer grunted agreement.

"I'd trust a five-year-old sooner than you, apparently!" Dad sounded heated. He wasn't any happier with the cop than I was.

Mom spoke up, and she sounded calm and reasonable. "Officer..."

"Detective!" he corrected.

"Sorry. Detective," she amended without rancor. "I can attest both to the observation skills of our young neighbor and to the solid character of our missing friend."

I shifted restlessly next to Archer. He put a restraining hand on my shoulder.

"And you are an expert because?" the detective demanded.

"I am a lawyer. My specialty is prosecuting sexual offenders of all stripes. I know the type entirely too well." How Mom could remain calm and collected in the face of the cop's belligerence was beyond me. "I assure you, Kellas does not fit the profile. I understand your questioning this as a possibly inappropriate relationship, but I assure you it is not. We are very concerned for his safety and would appreciate if you focused on that instead of their age difference." OK. So maybe she wasn't as calm as her tone of voice would show!

"Breathe!" Archer whispered in my ear.

"I am breathing!" I retorted in an undertone. Actually, I was snorting through my nose like an angry bull. I was furious! "How did that guy get in here, anyway?"

"Michael met him up by the road and brought him down."

So that was how this jerk got past my wards—the magical but invisible barriers I constructed to keep out people like the detective and safeguard our privacy. At least it wasn't because they had failed. Bad enough Erin had gotten through. My fault. I had neglected to rework the wards to exclude her after she'd shown her true colors on Samhain. Not that I had been in any shape to do so. I'd spent a week in the hospital following the attack on October 31st.

From the sound of it, things were wrapping up in the living room. Archer tried to pull me away, but I shook off his restraining hand and stepped in front of the detective as he followed Dad out of the living room.

The guy was big. Bigger than me, which, honestly, isn't hard. He hauled up short and gave me the once-over. OK, so what if I was still in my jammies? Full coverage: long sleeves, long bottoms, not at all suggestive, but not exactly the sort of garb one wears when confronting an officer of the law. My hair was probably a rat's nest, too. Not that I gave a hoot. Right now, I was sending the guy the sort of glare that should have had him going up in flames on the spot.

A muscle jumped in his cheek. "You're the girlfriend."

I continued the glare. "You know what they say about the word 'assume,' right?"

"To assume makes an 'ass out of you and me.'" The cop smirked. "This is my job, sweetheart. I know what I'm doing." He stepped around me, followed Dad to the door, and left.

"That utter jackass!" I exploded. Ignoring the fact Mom was right there and was stern when it came to swear words. "A fat lot of help he's gonna be!"

"We tried." Dad headed for the coffeemaker and started it up. "Breakfast first, then we build a plan."

Two

Dad's plan involved not much, it seemed to me. A lot of putting the word out, checking in with his network of street people. Having the A-Team keep an eye out while they were on emergency calls. Kidnapping involved much waiting for news and wondering about your loved one's return. In short, agony.

Which, in fact, was probably Erin's intention. I still couldn't believe she thought I'd stolen Kellas from her. I hadn't... he wasn't at all interested in her, and hadn't been for a very long time—hundreds of years, in fact. Not that anything would convince her of that detail.

Archer pestered me to go for a run with him after breakfast. "To get your mind off things for a little while," he said. My parents greeted his suggestion with enthusiasm. Maybe they just wanted to get me out of the house. I know I'm not the best company when I'm upset. OK, I can be a jerk occasionally, not to put too fine an edge on that. Sorry, not sorry.

My ugly mood didn't seem to faze Archer. He bundled me into his ancient Subaru and headed up Taughannock Park Road. In short order, we had parked and headed down the Black Diamond Trail, a long rail trail that led all the way into Ithaca. "If you make it all the way down and back, I'll buy you lunch at the bakery," he offered.

That was a 16-mile round trip. Not exactly easy, but I was angry enough to take on the challenge. However: "Dutch," I insisted. Archer was not flush with money. He was in college. 'Nuff said.

He shrugged and nodded.

We started out slowly, getting warmed up. Our breath came in white puffs in the cold air, and I was glad for my fleece leggings and the close-fitting half-zip top I'd received as a gift on Alban Arthan, the winter solstice. I'd donned a fuzzy ear band and mittens as well. Archer was less heavily dressed. In fact, his thin leggings and light top looked positively worthless against the cold. At least he had light gloves on his hands.

"Aren't you cold?" I asked as we got underway.

"A little, but I'll warm up fast." He grinned. "You're going to roast in that outfit, you know."

I snorted in disbelief. "I doubt it."

"Time will tell," he assured me. "C'mon. Let's pick it up a notch."

By "a notch" Archer meant increasing the pace from a relatively easy ten-minute mile to something more on the order of an eight-minute mile. Archer is an elite runner. I'm a wannabe. Not that I was going to let him leave me in the dust. I have my pride, after all. But for him, that pace was easy. For me, it was a real stretch. I was breathing hard in no time, and soon he had pulled out in front, running like water flowing: easy, graceful. How I envied his ability!

I did my best, but eventually conceded his superiority and dropped to a slower pace, getting my breathing and heart rate back under control. Archer continued increasing the distance between us; in the zone, not realizing I wasn't right behind him anymore. It was depressing, really, given how hard I'd worked to improve my running. Considering the last couple of months that I'd spent recovering from some serious injuries, though, it wasn't at all surprising I'd lost so much conditioning.

My thoughts reverted to my missing boyfriend. I wish I could have saved him from being kidnapped. I deeply regretted not killing Erin when I'd had the chance. She richly deserved to die for her betrayal of my family. My thoughts got darker and darker until, so overwhelmed with misery, I neglected to be aware of where I was putting my feet, stumbled hard and fell.

But I didn't crash on the gravel surface of the rail trail. I felt the disorienting shift of dimension travel, then landed on my face in the dark. It was a surprisingly soft landing, like I had fallen on a pile of pillows or a mattress. Once again, the small light spell came in handy. I scrambled up to my knees and called the light up immediately. Again, it did little to dispel the dark.

I was back in Dub's domain: darkness. With the God of Despair. Wonderful.

"Ah, you're back," Dub said from mere inches away.

I immediately rolled away from his voice, right off the side of the bed—where it seems I had landed—and flopped to the floor. I lay there moaning; the wind knocked out of me. Not a terrific situation, given whose demesne I was currently in.

"Tsk." There was a scuffling sound as Dub fumbled for something. A match flared. He lit a candle, then held it high as he looked over the side of the bed. "Whatever are you doing down there?" he asked, amused.

Oh, my gosh... Dub had his body back? Not good. I regained my breath and scrambled to my feet. "Not intentional, I assure you."

The candle did a better job of dispelling the dark than my small magic light. A quick look about revealed an enormous four-poster bed in a space far larger than the candlelight could penetrate. On the bed was a gigantic man, no longer just smoke, but not quite solid, either. Almost like a mirage, but one that looked very familiar.

"You look like Aquaman now?" I demanded, incredulous.

Dub levered himself up on one elbow and set the candle on the bedside table near me. "You like?" he asked. "I did some research before choosing this form. It appealed to me, and apparently it does to you as well."

"What are you talking about?" How could Dub know of my early teen obsession with the demigod?

He subsided onto the bed, lying on his side, head propped up on one hand, grinning. "Your dreams were quite informative."

"What do you mean, my dreams?" I was becoming distinctly uneasy.

The God of Darkness made a 'you know,' gesture with his free hand. "You found this form quite appealing... if your dreams are any indication."

I went cold with shock, then hot with anger. "You were mucking about in my dreams? How dare you! Those are private!" How in the name of all that was holy had this nasty god hacked into my dreams? And, omg, how much had he seen of my stupid fantasies, anyway?

"Pshaw." Dub sat up, the bedcovers falling to his lap.

I immediately slammed my eyes shut. "Cover yourself," I demanded in a tight voice.

"Why?" he asked, his voice all faked innocence.

As if he didn't know! That god was anything but innocent! "You're naked, and I don't want to see you that way."

"Could have fooled me, based on your dreams." He chuckled, a wicked undertone in it. There was a rustling sound as he moved the bedsheets about. "You may open your eyes, my dear. I am 'decent' now, as they euphemistically say in your world."

I cracked open one eye and saw that he had pulled the top sheet free and wrapped it around himself. When I opened them both, I realized my eyes were adjusting to the low light. The room was quite vast and opulent. The bedroom of a god, in fact. It made me feel distinctly uneasy. No, make that scared.

Jason Mamoa's Aquaman, or rather, Dub as he now presented himself, was quite the eye candy. I had been obsessed with Aquaman when I was 14, watching those movies over and over and dreaming about him in full color, picturing myself as his girlfriend... oh, all the usual kid stuff. He was a big man. Somewhere I'd read Jason was 6 foot 4 inches, 230 pounds of pure muscle. As Aquaman, he had tattoos all over his muscular chest, abs, and arms. That bit would have appealed to Dub, who in his old form—the one I'd destroyed for him—had been built like an MMA wrestler, inked with his weapon of choice: despair.

"What am I doing here?" I demanded. It really bothered me he'd been riffling through my dreams. Not that I had any idea how he could have managed that little trick. I felt... violated.

"You tell me." Holding the sheet around himself, Dub scooted off the bed and went over to a nearby dresser. "Look away, lest you see more than you care to. I'm putting on pants. Wouldn't want to offend your sense of propriety."

I did a fast about-face, putting my back to him. I heard his soft chuckle again. There was the squeak of a drawer opening, the swish of fabric, then the drawer shutting and the sounds of Dub putting on his pants.

"Safe to turn around now, little one."

I turned. Dub might have thought it was safe, but he was still bare-chested and fastening the top button of his jeans. The shock it sent through me was not at all what I should have liked. The man was seriously... hmm. Best not to go there.

"Come." He gestured toward the bedroom door. "We'll go someplace that feels less fraught with danger for you, shall we?" He stepped around me and opened the bedroom door, gesturing me through. I slid past him, careful not to touch any part of him, which drew yet another dry chuckle.

Dub led me deeper into his home. Lights came on as he snapped his fingers, invisible servants hurrying to light candles everywhere. They made soft squeaking sounds and rustled about like mice dashing for cover. "I have a lot of servants, none of whom care much for the light as you do," he explained. "You have nothing to fear from them, however. Shall I have something fetched for you? Something to drink, perhaps?"

Persephone in the Underworld immediately came to mind. No way was I going to endanger my freedom for a drink of water or a piece of fruit. "No, thanks."

"As you wish. This way." He showed a door that stood ajar. "My office. All highly proper and non-threatening to someone like you. Please." He waved me into a room that was decorated with a great deal of dark wood. There were miles of tidy bookcases filled with books. In front of a pair of windows (darkness beyond) was a large, ornate desk. The desk was empty except for a sizeable monitor, keyboard, and mouse, and sat facing a fireplace on the opposite wall. A fire crackled cheerily, sending off lovely warmth. Above the fireplace was an enormous TV screen. The space was overwhelmingly male. Despite Dub's description of his office as "non-threatening," it very much was. I don't think guys like him had any idea how intimidating they are to women, even when they are trying not to be.

Dub took a seat in the leather office chair behind the desk and gestured at a chair on the other side. "Please take a seat. You are my honored guest." I reluctantly did as he asked, and it brought a smile to his handsome face. "Do you like it?" he asked. "The room, that is."

"It's quite nice." I was being honest. "A little dark for my taste, but it suits you."

"Indeed." He leaned forward and pressed a button on the desktop that I hadn't noticed before. "Bring me coffee. And ask my brother to join us." He didn't bother to say 'please.'

I bolted to my feet. "Dother is here?" My heart was pounding in my chest. The God of Evil had maimed me, tried to kill me.

"No, no, relax. Sit down, little one." Dub waved me back down in my chair. "It's Dian. He and I do our best to stay out of our brother Dother's orbit. He has a—deleterious effect—on our personalities. We avoid him as best we can."

Dian, God of Violence, was not one I cared to hang around either, even less so than this oddly erudite and gentlemanly version of Dub, God of Darkness and Despair. However, I obeyed him and sat tensely on the edge of my chair.

Dub chuckled deep in his chest. "You have nothing to fear from my brother. Ever since you defanged that red-haired Cait Sidhe, he's been agog with your ability to commit violence. Perhaps you were not aware, but violence committed in the name of justice is far more potent than any other sort. Very empowering to one such as himself. He's a complete fanboy, keeps asking me when he might see you again."

Color me unconvinced. Dian was the sort to cut power to hospitals to see how many people could die in the shortest amount of time possible. Not exactly the kind I wanted as a fan.

"Hey! Hi!" And there he was, bouncing into Dub's office like a teenage boy, although he was more on the order of a man mountain. I stared. Dian could have been twins with Dwayne Johnson. As large as Dub-as-Aquaman was—and Dub was easily twice my size—Dian was even larger: several inches taller than Dub, deeper and broader, too. He probably tipped the scales at over 260, every bit muscle. Dressed only in gym shorts, his chest was bare and glistening with sweat, like he'd just come from a workout... and he was bald as a cue ball. There was a huge grin on his dark face, teeth perfectly even and white, but he looked happy and boyish, not at all like someone who took joy in hurting others, like he'd been the last time I'd seen him.

Dian dropped to a knee in front of me and grabbed my hands. "My muse! So glad you came to visit us! You are all Dub and I talk about these days. How are you doing? Are you fully recovered from your misadventures?" A slight frown put twin furrows between his eyebrows. "I want to apologize for how I behaved the last time I saw you. That wasn't my fault. Dother is a terrible influence. I'm actually a pussycat. Aren't I, bro?" He glanced over at Dub as though for reassurance.

I pulled free and shrank back into the chair, drawing my legs up under me. Words failed me. This was the guy I'd blasted apart with my sword barely two months ago. Now he was like an overly enthusiastic puppy.

Dian's face fell. He rose to his feet and backed away, then lounged on the corner of his brother's desk in as relaxed and unthreatening a pose as an alpha male like him could assume. "My apologies. I did not mean to frighten you."

I managed a tight nod, fighting back panic. "Why am I here? I was running with my friend, and suddenly here I am." And why did I keep ending up here, in Dub's demesne? Was it something I was doing? Or was Dub pulling some kind of nasty trick to draw me here?

The brothers exchanged meaningful looks. "You came here like anyone does: you're depressed," Dub told me. "All my servants are that way. They're always dropping in on me, making a nuisance of themselves until they either figure out how to get un-depressed, or take themselves off."

Depressed? Hardly! I was upset, certainly. Angry for sure, but depressed? No. Before I could respond, a muffled gunshot sounded in another part of Dub's mansion. I flinched, and could not repress a shudder. Guns. In a place like this? Ye gods...

"Like that," he shrugged. "Guns and drugs are the favorite methods. I have the others clean up after them. Gun suicides..." He shook his head. "Messy."

"How can you be so callous?" I exclaimed, horrified. "Those poor people!"

Dub had the decency to look abashed. He leaned back in his chair, making it squeak. "It's not that I don't care, child. It's a terrible waste. But it's also a fact of life, and ready access to the means to kill themselves makes it easier to do. For you..." He leaned forward again, and his expression softened with something like kindness. Kind! This guy? No way. Don't buy it, Raven. "...depression is a temporary condition, and we must take advantage of the time we have together," Dub said. "I guess you are upset over the disappearance of your lover..."

Heat flooded my body. "Boyfriend!" Why was everyone jumping to conclusions? All Kellas and I had ever done was kiss. Enthusiastically, yes, but... Dub-as-Aquaman inclined his head, acquiescing to my correction. His long curls fell forward over one shoulder, and that weird power surge shot through me again. My nose flared as I drew a deep breath. He smelled wonderful. Like salt air. And... why was I even thinking this? It made no sense.

"Boyfriend. As you wish," he agreed. "The Cait Sidhe's disappearance has you in a tailspin, and lacking any proper way to extract him from your enemy's clutches, you lose hope. Thence, depression." He sent a glance Dian's way, and his brother nodded in agreement. Dub continued. "For an ordinary mortal, I would agree: all hope is truly lost. Your Cait Sidhe is at the mercy of some truly heinous characters and would not, under ordinary circumstances, emerge alive. But for you, and fortunately for him, I have a solution. And in return for us helping you, you can be of assistance to me and Dian." He fell silent, regarding me with a calculating gaze.

I waited for the explanation, but he just sat silently, a Cheshire cat grin slowly widening over his face. OMG, those eyebrows! I was most definitely not 'over Aquaman.' I gave myself a mental shake. It made absolutely no sense. I loved Kellas. This guy was a user. Why was I having these thoughts at all? Disgusting. Shame on me!

Dian broke the impasse. "Ah, c'mon, bro, tell the little lady what you're proposing! Don't keep us all in suspense."

Dub's grin widened, and an emotion I could not identify glittered in his eyes. "She must ask nicely."

That rankled, but I was seriously curious. If it were something that could save Kellas, I could swallow a bit of pride. I shifted in my chair. "Please tell me your plan."

The grin turned into a dazzling smile as he leaned forward onto his desk, and my heart thudded hard against my ribs. Ye gods, Raven! Get yourself together! He was magnetically beautiful, yes; but terribly, infinitely dangerous. All the alarm bells were going off at once. Danger, Will Robinson!

"I propose we work together as allies in this matter," he said. "The red-haired Cait Sidhe is no friend of ours, and she works with our brother in hideous ways. We prefer not to cooperate with such. Dian and I will help you take her out once and for all, rescue your beloved, and Bob's your uncle."

Bob was not an uncle I was aware of, and Dub's plan had some enormous holes in it. Like, actual details. "How?" I demanded.

He waved that off as unimportant. "We'll figure it out as we go."

"Details, Dub. I need a plan," I snapped. He was infuriating vague, and I was losing patience.

He tossed his head back and laughed. Damn. Even his laugh was beautiful! "Since when? I thought you were a seat of the pants kind of gal."

And now he was making fun of me! Drat him anyway. Dad had said much the same thing earlier. After how awful he had been last year, he didn't seem like the same god, and I wasn't at all sure how to interpret that. All I knew was I wasn't afraid of him anymore. No, just annoyed. "Stop playing games, Dub. I won't take chances when it comes to saving Kellas."

Dub leaned back in his chair. "OK. You start. What do you propose?" Dian was doing his best not to smirk as he listened to his brother verbally spar with me.

The ball was back in my court. The problem was I had nothing. No idea at all. So, I shrugged. "You're the god, Dub. I was hoping you had some ideas."

A muscle twitched in his cheek. "I do. But they depend heavily on your knowing where to find your boyfriend."

The insinuating way Dub said 'boyfriend' was not lost on me, like he was suggesting Kellas and I had been lovers. It made my face flush with irritation. A faint smile flitted across his face. Perhaps annoying me was what he had intended all along. "See? You can still feel emotions other than despair. Fear. Anger. Frustration. All feelings that can create action. So, what action shall you take? After all, you have a unique connection with the fairy cat." Dub pointed to a small cat tattoo just above the inside of my right wrist, my one and only tattoo. "My ink. Your cat. It links all three of us irrevocably. Or did you not realize what that marking signifies?"

I touched the tattoo. The small black cat Kellas had inked above my wrist sat up, blinked, yawned and sent me a sly sideways look. Kellas' look, the one that always made my heart jump into my throat. "I... don't, actually. Kellas gave me this to extract your poison after Erin stabbed me with it." My tattoo linked the three of us? Not wonderful. In fact, it was deeply concerning. What hold did Dub have over me and Kellas? Was this why I kept ending up in the God of Darkness' demesne?

His expression darkened. "A point of contention between the red-haired one and me. She had no right to take what was not hers. However, that mark is not one a Cait Sidhe would normally place on anyone." He fell silent.

Dian stirred restlessly, as though this back and forth was annoying. "Will you just make your point already, bro?"

Dub sent him a dark glance and returned his full attention to me. "It gives you a far greater connection to him than anyone else. I suggest you use it to find him wherever it is the red-haired one has spirited him off to."

Hope surged through me. "I can do that?" I suddenly felt lighter.

He nodded. "You can. But it's on you to find out exactly how. And when you know, Dian and I will aid you."

My heart jumped for joy... and I abruptly found myself back on the Black Diamond Trail. Archer was running back toward me, calling my name.

Archer ran up to me, a panicked expression on his face. "Where did you go? I turned around to run back to you, and you were nowhere to be seen. Until you were! Not here, and then suddenly here. What happened?"

Shaking my head to clear it, I drew a deep breath. "I inadvertently hopped dimensions. But at least now I know how to find Kellas!"

"How can you do that?" There was a worried scowl on my brother's face.

Hunger was making my belly growl. "C'mon." I tugged at his sleeve. "Lunch is calling me. I'll fill you in as we go."

Energized, I fairly flew down the trail, Archer matching me stride for stride while I explained (between panting breaths) about the parallel dimensions I could move between by dint of my moon magic. Before this, I'd only done so while unconscious or asleep; This was the first time I had made that step-between while awake. But that was how my magic worked. Useful, but often unpredictable.

"So, you can use that tattoo to find Kellas?" Archer demanded. "How?"

Dang him, he wasn't even breathing hard. But his question was a good one. I hadn't figured out the answer yet. "All I know is it's a connection I can use. How? Dunno. But I'm gonna find out."

Archer was unhappy. "Look, sis. You always ending up in that god's demesne is not healthy! He's a user. I don't want you anywhere near the guy! We can find Kellas on our own." He sped up and ran backwards in front of me. *Show off!* "What will keep you happy and out of that dude's clutches?" he demanded.

"You're gonna trip and fall on your can if you keep it up," I cautioned him. Then he did, and I burst out laughing.

Archer bounced to his feet and dusted his rear off, a wide grin on his face. "Hey, I can play the part of a buffoon if that's what it takes to keep you happy, Raven."

I gave him a shove, not that it moved him much. Archer might be lean as a wolf, but pound for pound, he was incredibly strong. "Don't be dumb, bruh. We'll get this figured out. Hopefully, we won't need Dub's help, but I'm not ruling anything out right now. Saving Kellas is more important." I wiped snowflakes off my eyelashes. It was snowing harder now. "Come on, let's get home before this storm gets any worse."

"Catch me if you can," he teased, and took off running. I scoffed and started after him, knowing there was no keeping up. I was deeply grateful to my brother and his concern for me, though. He had my best interests at heart... but I knew the only way to accomplish my lasting happiness would be to rescue Kellas. For that, according to Dub, I would have to forge an uneasy alliance with two gods who, until a short while ago, had been my immortal enemies. I wasn't sure that would be advisable or even possible. It would be like playing with fire, knowing the likelihood of getting burned was extremely high. But if that was what it took to save Kellas, I'd do it.

Three

It was nearly one in the afternoon when we got back from our run. I took a quick shower and went to my room to dress in fresh clothing. A bit chilled after our cold run, I chose black leggings and a fuzzy cobalt blue sweater to put on over a lacy set of matching bra and panties. I flopped down on the easy chair in my bedroom, rested my stockinged feet on a footstool, and stared mournfully through the French doors that led to the tiny deck outside. It was still snowing, slowly piling up in fluffy white drifts on the deck. The sky was gunmetal gray; The lake below reflected the low clouds. Trees were bare, black silhouettes occasionally disappearing when the snow shower intensified. The world in grey-scale.

"Peaceful." The Morrigan appeared without warning next to the French doors, looking out on the scene below. The Celtic Goddess of Death was fond of showing up at unexpected times, but I must have been getting used to it, because I hardly flinched. My immortal guardian turned away from the view and gave me the once-over through narrowed eyes. "You look like death warmed over," she said at last.

I merely grunted. She was trying to be funny. Wasn't working. Besides, the Morrigan was one fetching lady: petite, with raven black hair that floated artistically around her lovely face, her lips blood-red and her eyes so dark they seemed like they could look right through you. Death warmed over couldn't look all that bad if that is what Death herself looked like, right?

She started strolling about my bedroom, looking around with curiosity. I was glad I'd tidied up a bit earlier. "Very nice," she commented, then her eyes narrowed. "Well, isn't this interesting," she muttered under her breath, and a moment later snatched something out of the air and crushed it between thumb and forefinger.

"What was that all about?" I asked.

She turned, and there was a heavy scowl on her face. "Someone has bugged you," she said. "I just destroyed it, but there will be more. I must find them."

"Bugged? As in actual insects or listening devices?"

"As in, someone has been watching you."

I jolted up from my chair. "What?!"

She folded her arms across her chest in annoyance. "Some lowlife has eyes on you. Mechanical flying insects with cameras sending pictures of my champion someplace unknown. How dare you!" she demanded as her gaze darted around the room. I was pretty sure it wasn't me she was talking to. Then she focused on me. "Also, I think I know who it is."

"I've been being watched?" I asked, horrified.

She glanced my way. "If I know him, he's had you followed everywhere. I wouldn't put it past him."

"In here? With me... naked?" OMG, that was just... awful.

The look the Death goddess sent me was as close to pity as I think I've ever seen from her. "Indubitably."

Oh, gods, no. No! "Am I being watched now?"

The Morrigan made another snatching motion with one hand, then held something close to her face, inspecting it. "Yes." She spoke right at the tiny metal insect she held trapped between thumb and forefinger. "Cease and desist, you old pervert, or I won't be responsible for what I do to retaliate." Then she squashed the bug flat.

I was in shock, not quite able to believe this was happening to me. Spy cams happened to other girls—in locker rooms, at bed-and-breakfasts. Not here in my home, my bedroom. "Who?" I asked in a faint voice.

She sent me a get-real glance. "Take a guess."

Then I just knew who it was, and my heart sank to my toes. Anybody capable of hacking into my old dreams was more than capable of sending mechanical bugs to spy on me. "Dub?"

"Right on the first guess."

Horror was being rapidly replaced with fury. "If I get my hands on him, I'm gonna gut him!" I was pacing back and forth, rage coursing through every nerve in my body. "Tear him limb from limb." How could I have entertained the notion of working with Dub in the first place? Disgust at his actions, and also with myself, for having entertained the notion of allying with him. And, there was a lingering sense of shame at how I'd found him... attractive. No more! I had his true measure now.

"Calm down." The Morrigan was studying me through narrowed eyes. "Stop. Look at me for a moment."

This being the Goddess of Death, I did as she bade me. "What?" And yes, that came out rudely. Just because I was cooperating didn't mean I was going to be polite about it!

"I'm curious to know why Dub is spying on you," she said. "Is there something you should tell me?"

I swallowed hard, remembering the conversations I'd had with the God of Darkness. "I think he wants me to... be with him." The mere thought made me go hot and cold all over. The oddest combination of attraction and revulsion juxtaposed each other. "That jerk and his brother mucked around in my old dreams and picked new bodies from the guys I used to be crazy about when I was younger. They chose Aquaman and the guy from Jumanji, the big guy. Dr. Bravestone."

She nodded at my explanation and almost smiled. "Let me guess. Dub chose Aquaman."

I nodded. "He's a dead ringer. And Dian looks a lot like Dwayne 'The Rock' Johnson."

A delighted smile flooded across her face. Not the reaction I thought she'd have to the news about my hacked dreams. Not after her rage over my bedroom being bugged! She pushed my footstool closer to me and shoved me down on it. "Sit. We need to think this through." Her hands remained on my shoulders, fingers kneading the tight muscles on either side of my neck. I sat ramrod straight, every nerve on edge. (Hey, how many people can stay calm when Death has her hands on them? For one thing, her fingers were freezing.) "I think we can turn this to our advantage, you and me."

"How?" I asked through teeth gritted against the pain she was inflicting on me.

"Tell me about Aquaman. What kind of man is he?"

"Demigod, you mean." I hesitated briefly, then decided I might as well be frank. "He's seriously gorgeous. And hunky, and he's got more tattoos than you can shake a stick at, so I'm betting that's why Dub chose Aquaman, since he needs tattoos for his nasty poison ink."

"Is that why you were dreaming about him? As a younger teen, that is. Obviously, you're not anymore," she added, almost as an afterthought, but there was a note of derision in it, like she knew the demigod's beauty still affected me.

I squirmed under her hands. There had been those odd electric shocks I'd gotten just looking at Dub in his new form. Not that I was going to admit that to the Morrigan. "Aquaman was just a decent, likable guy. Kinda tenderhearted. Sweet, too. The kind you want to see have a happily ever after, you know? The same with Dr. Bravestone, Dwayne Johnson's character."

"So, they're men of excellent character. Possibly a high moral code?"

"I guess so. I mean, I wouldn't have liked them otherwise, right? If they'd been awful people, I wouldn't have liked them just because they were... hmm."

"Sexy. It's ok. You can say that to me. I understand." But she was practically vibrating with excitement. "Dub may have outsmarted himself this time," she mused aloud.

Her thumbs dug into a tight muscle at the base of my neck, and I about passed out. "How?" I groaned. "Ow! Not so hard, please!"

She gave my shoulders a pat and started strolling around my bedroom again, deep in thought. "He chose Aquaman as his new body to appeal to your fantasies. His intention is blatantly obvious: to lure you into a relationship with him."

Not sure I liked her pointing it out so bluntly, even though Dub had said much the same. It made me feel sick to my stomach.

"Not one I would recommend, however," she continued. "He's the sort to love you, then leave you. I should know." There was a bitter edge in her voice that brought my attention squarely back to her.

"You were with Dub?" I startled to my feet. Her revelation had unnerved me.

She sent me a rueful glance. "One of many, but he was my favorite... at least he was until Dother corrupted him and Dian. That's when we parted. When you are immortal, there is no such thing as happily ever after."

And just like that, I felt sorry for her... one of the most powerful, feared goddesses of all time. "That's terrible!"

She huffed as she came to a halt in front of me. "Comes with the territory." She might have brushed it off, but I could tell it still saddened her. "Back to what I was saying before we got sidetracked. By adopting the form of a decent demigod, he's possibly cornered himself into being decent himself. Not free to commit whatever dark act his nature would otherwise allow." She made a pointed gesture and resumed her pacing. "Like when he tried to murder Kellas so he could take you as his own?" A satisfied smirk twisted her cherry-red lips. "Aquaman's moral code would never allow that. But…" She swung around to face me. "We must tread carefully. The extent to which we can count on his new form changing his baser tendencies is still uncertain. He may be like Aquaman one moment, and his Dother-corrupted self at another."

"I see what you're saying." It worried me, though, as I had a feeling where this was leading and I wasn't at all sure I liked it. I went over to stare out the French doors at the snow falling outside. It had really started adding up, at least an inch, just since the Morrigan had arrived. "What about Dian?" I asked.

The Morrigan considered my question. "I would think the same would apply to him, with the same caveats. They are not at all domesticated—near feral, in fact. But of the two, Dub is infinitely more dangerous."

She'd come over and stood next to me, her lovely forehead furrowed in thought. "He is?" I pressed. "I would have thought Dian was. After all, he's the God of Violence."

Her laugh held no humor. "Dian's simple. If it's violence you need, he's your god. Compared to Dub, he's an open book. Beyond conflict, nothing really matters to him." She sighed and grimaced. "Dub is 'still waters run deep.' A thinker, a plotter, a planner, and a schemer. He invented the dark web, you know."

It was news to me. I shook my head, knowing little about the dark web other than the name.

Death took me by the shoulders and made me face her. "Make no mistake, my champion. Dub is extremely dangerous." There was no missing the warning in her voice. "He can search deep into your psyche, ruthlessly hack your memories, plunder your thoughts like a pirate… all the while with the sweetest smile on his face." The Morrigan dropped her grip on my shoulders and wandered away again, back to searching for spy flies and apparently not finding any. "He is the patron saint of hackers everywhere. All work in anonymity. In darkness." She glanced briefly over her shoulder at me. "As you found out, he can hack into your dreams. He's a master's master." Her hands fluttered in a gesture like a bird's wings. "He does it all on a lark. To see if he can. It was all fun and games for him..." her voice hardened in anger, "...until Dother corrupted his brainchild and turned it into a way criminals could avoid detection."

I wondered if this might be what Dub had been referring to when he said he and Dian preferred to avoid their brother. But the Morrigan had already moved on to another topic. She stopped prowling around my room and fixed me with a level stare. "What you must do next is risky, but worth it in the long run, I think."

I shifted uneasily. "What do you mean?" If the Morrigan thought it was risky, I wasn't at all sure I wanted to try.

"You will return to Dub's domain and enlist his help in your quest to free the Cait Sidhe from Dother's grasp." She nodded decisively, as if she'd decided this was the best course of action. "You are to make an ally of despair."

y heart sank. After the last trip to the God of Darkness' *demesne*,
I wasn't all that pumped about returning. "But... Orianthi said
Erin took Kellas!"

The death goddess shot me a pitying look. "That pathetic excuse for a Cait
Sidhe would never have managed it on her own. The bond between you and
Kellas is far too strong for the red-haired one to tear asunder. No, she had help.
And if I had to make a guess, I would say that help came from the God of Evil
himself."

"And you're sure about that?" I demanded.

"Absolutely. Without a shadow of a doubt."

My heart sank to my toes. So... Dub had not been lying. If Dother had
Kellas, what hope did I have of saving him? Nan, who had far more powerful
magic than I, had failed in trapping Dother. Had died trying, in fact.

My face must have blanched with fear, because the Morrigan rapidly closed
the distance between us and put her hands on my shoulders again. "Which is
why you must recruit Dub and Dian to your cause." Her voice was gentle. "On
your own, there is no hope. You must make allies of Dub and Dian if you are
to win this fight. So." She gave me a little shake. "Pull yourself together and get
going, before it's too late." And with that, she was gone.

I hadn't the faintest idea where to begin, and it was threatening to plunge me into despair again. Dub's demesne was tugging at me. I fought against its pull, using my fury at the dark god's spying to fend it off. He'd said it himself: anger, fear, frustration could all counter his influence. I sure felt all of those right now. I could not allow despair to stop me from finding Kellas. Especially if I were to enlist the God of that awful emotion to help me!

I needed Nan. She'd know what to do... except she was dead. My throat swelled and my eyes stung with tears, thinking how she'd sacrificed herself to save me. We'd had so little time together. There was so much more I should have learned from her. But, wait! She was dead only in this dimension. I'd dreamed about her, alive and well in Tír na nÓg. I could go to her! Then that hope collapsed. The time difference between our dimensions would cause delays in rescuing Kellas. What were a few moments there amounted to days or weeks in my dimension. Cerridwen's kidnapping of me lasted a week there, but nine long months passed here. I could not risk it. Also, what if I could not locate her? It was not a tiny dimension. Like looking for a needle in a haystack.

Frustrated, angry, sad... so many unhelpful emotions battled for supremacy, leaving me struggling to gather my thoughts. At this rate I'd never figure out how to save Kellas. I plopped down on my easy chair again, absentmindedly playing with the medallion I wore around my neck. My grandfather's medallion, one that helped me speak languages other than English. He'd given me a magical lute as well. A lute that was also Fraegarthach, the Unbeatable Sword of the Tuatha dé Danann. Could the lute/sword help me find the answers I needed?

I pulled my lute from its hiding spot behind my back. Hidden away in a dimension only I could access, this kept both forms of my magical armory close at hand and safe from anyone stealing them. It was also extremely useful, because both forms Fraegarthach assumed were bulky.

I tuned my lute and plucked the strings absentmindedly, thinking about the whole sorry situation. My fingers started pulling a melody from the strings, one I'd been practicing lately—a hopeful little tune called "Up From The Ashes." I'd found it on the internet, played on a fascinating instrument called the Chapman stick, and worked hard to adapt it to my lute. The tune lifted my spirits. Music always did, and this lovely tune was helping lift me from the ashes of my despair over Kellas.

A deep voice startled me. "Well, my dear, you certainly have continued your studies!"

I jumped to my feet and whirled around to face... Taliesin. Who was standing inside my tall bedroom mirror looking out at me—a reflection that was not a reflection.

"Keep playing," he ordered. "The music has connected us."

"*Seanathair!*" I exclaimed. A word I instinctively knew: grandfather.

Taliesin's eyes grew misty. "I had never thought to hear that from your lips." His voice was husky with emotion. "No! Play!" That was in response to my quick motion toward him. "Otherwise, we'll lose the connection." A flash of recognition crossed his face when he spied the huge leather-bound book on my side table. "Ah, you have inherited my book from Amaris, I see." He brought his attention back to me. "You seem upset."

'Upset' was an understatement! I hastily filled him in on my life. "Kellas is missing, and I need to find him. Can you help? Is there any way I can reach him through this?" I flashed my tattoo at him in between notes.

My grandfather's eyes widened in surprise when he saw the tattoo. "The magic between you two has certainly grown!" His forehead wrinkled in thought. "Have you tried that book?" The old bard gestured toward my side table.

I felt a flash of irritation. "No. I can't read a thing in it." The language was foreign, and I couldn't make sense of any of it.

Taliesin smiled. "That was intentional on my part. I encrypted the thing to keep its secrets from anyone who should not be reading it. But, think. You have the means and the ability to decode it." He sent me a chiding look, the sort you give someone who is being particularly dense.

So, that book had been Taliesin's? Still playing, I walked over to my bedside and examined the massive book, the heavy leather cover beautifully embossed with Celtic symbols, a perfect copy of my medallion carved in its center.

There was a knock on my door, and Dad's voice called through. "Raven, a moment."

"Come in." I was grinning in anticipation of his reaction as he stepped through the doorway. Mom was right behind him.

Dad stiffened in surprise when his gaze fell on his father in the mirror. "We heard Raven talking to someone," he choked, his voice husky with emotion. "I sure wasn't expecting you, Da!"

Taliesin's face twisted in an expression of pain mixed with joy. "Boyo."

Dad strode across the room and laid his palms on the mirror glass. Taliesin brought his own up to match Dad. The two stood silently for a long moment, looking at each other, before Dad broke their silent exchange. "Long time, Da. Missed ye." The Irish lilt Dad's voice always carried had intensified.

Taliesin nodded, as though he didn't quite trust his voice. "You're lookin' grand," he said finally.

"There's someone I want you to meet, Da." Dad half turned and beckoned urgently to my mother. "Meg, this is my father." He looked back at Taliesin as Mom came to stand next to him. He wrapped an arm around her shoulders and snuggled her close to his side. "My wife, Margaret."

Taliesin bowed his head. "Pleased to meet you." Then to Dad: "She's a ride, boyo."

Mom looked confused, and Dad chuckled as he pressed a kiss to her forehead. "He just called you a creature of great beauty, Meg."

Mom struggled with the compliment, forcing a small smile, but nothing else.

I walked over and leaned close to the mirror, saying in a loud whisper I meant for her to overhear. "Don't mind her. Mom's shy."

Mom snorted in derision. "Just surprised to be talking to someone in a mirror."

"Which must end soon, or you will overdo the magic tricks once again, Brannaugh. Questions for me? No? Then, *slán go fóill*. Until next time." And just like that, he faded away.

I stopped playing, and my legs turned to jelly under me. Dad jumped over and caught me under the arms before I fell.

"Easy, fledgling. Sit." He guided me into my chair.

I slid my lute away behind my back and dropped my face into my hands, my head pounding with a nasty headache. "Oh, gods…"

"Perhaps one of you would be so kind as to explain what just happened?" Mom asked. There was an edge in her voice. No surprise, as she was unaccustomed to the world of magic intruding into her carefully orchestrated life and was only just beginning to accept that her husband and daughter were distinctly atypical.

I pressed a thumb in the corner of one eye, hoping to ease the pain point that throbbed there. "That was unintentional," I told her. "A magical form of video call, I guess. My music called it up."

"Do you do this a lot?" she demanded.

"First time," I admitted.

"Was it worth it?" Her words were harsh, but the concern on her face was real.

I didn't have an answer to that, so I stayed silent.

"You were talking to your grandfather for quite some time," Dad said. A statement, but there was a question in it. He stood before me, arms crossed over his chest, looking stern.

I grimaced. "At first, it was a social visit from the Morrigan."

Mom went pale. "What did she want?" She'd stepped close to Dad and was regarding me, worry deepening the furrow between her eyebrows, her arms crossed over her chest like she was cold. Her fear was obvious, understandably so given our recent experiences.

"She wants the same thing as the rest of us do: to save Kellas." I gestured in frustration. "But she discovered spy cams in my room."

That brought a flurry of upset and questions. I did my best to answer, none of which gave my parents any assurance. If anything, they were more horrified by Dub's peeping Tom behavior than I was myself.

Mom was particularly upset that the Morrigan would even suggest working with Dub and Dian after all they had done. "There's no way I will countenance that!" she declared, her face set in hard lines. "You can count on a pedophile to re-offend given the opportunity. I will not allow you to put yourself in such danger, Raven." Her lips thinned into a tight line. "No. Absolutely not."

Unfortunately, I didn't think either of us had much say in the matter. From the dismayed expression on Dad's face, I knew he was thinking the same thing as me and feared Mom's wrath if he challenged her. To be fair, Mom's wrath was fearsome indeed. I didn't blame him one bit.

I stepped into the breach. "I don't think we have any other choice, Mom. If it helps at all, I have dealt with both before. They're not unknown entities.

I know what they are capable of and can expect the sort of antics they might throw my way. Nor am I defenseless. And, like it or not, it's our best chance to rescue Kellas."

"No." She was stubborn. Like me, to be honest. Probably where I got it from.

I shrugged helplessly. "Mom. It's not your call. It's mine. And I'm making it."

She folded her arms across her chest again, but it was as much a protective mechanism as a way of showing her lack of acceptance of my decision. "No!"

"Mom..." I sighed heavily, then drew a deep breath. "I'll show you then. I'd hoped never to have to do this in front of you, but... don't freak out, OK?" Reaching over my back, I drew Fraegarthach.

The ceiling in my bedroom is about nine feet at the highest, so I had to scrunch down as I grew into my warrior avatar, clad in leather and dwarfish steel, my sword sparking with blue electricity the length of its deadly sharp blade. I knelt on one knee in front of her, sword point pressed against the wooden floor, both my hands on the hilt. Leather and steel vambraces covered my lower arms. I wore staggered metal plates to protect my shoulders, a tooled leather breastplate across my chest, and three daggers holstered at my hip. Leather and steel greaves encased my legs from the knees down. Although I couldn't see my back, I instinctively knew something covered it. Fraegarthach's sheath lay fully visible now, across my back.

Mom shrank back, her mouth opening in a gasp, eyes wide. Behind her, Dad gripped her upper arms, pulling her close against his chest. "It's all right, Meg. She's still our daughter."

I spoke in my hoarse avatar voice: mine, but not quite. "I'd hoped to spare you this. But now you know: I'm not as helpless as you might think."

"You know how to use that... thing?" Mom asked in a faint voice.

I nodded. She meant Fraegarthach, I was sure. And she was not happy about it, either. Not that I blamed her. In this form I could be... somewhat unhinged, to put it mildly.

"Elias worked with Raven before he left, teaching her how to sword fight," Dad said.

"The sword does a lot of the work for me, too." I thought about the were-wolves and zombies I'd battled in Tír na nÓg and sent a brief vote of gratitude to my magical sword, which hummed in response. Careful not to cut anything by accident—Fraegarthach was razor sharp—I slid my sword back into its sheath and felt myself return to my normal size again. Shrugged. "Say hi to the new me." Feeble joke, Raven!

"I don't know what to say." Mom kept staring at me as if I'd grown horns.

"There's not much to say," I agreed. "It takes a bit of getting used to. I'm still trying."

She nodded and leaned against my father for support. "Did you know this was something Raven could do, Michael?" she demanded.

Dad wrapped his arms around her, and she brought both hands up to grip his wrists. I swallowed hard, recognizing the unspoken connection for what it was. It gave me joy and pain in equal measure; My parents drew closer, while my love...

"Since she came back from Tír na nÓg with that magical sword," he told her.

"I have no say in the form I take; it just happens," I said, blinking against the sudden wetness in my eyes and the pounding in my skull. It felt like bongo drums at my temples. Pressing my fingertips against the throbbing wasn't help-ing all that much.

"Maybe take some ibuprophen and lie down for a half hour," Dad sug-gested. "C'mon, Meg, let's give her some quiet."

I followed them downstairs, took Dad's advice about the painkillers, then retreated to my room, where I curled up on my bed under a lap quilt. Daylight was already fading, the heavy clouds blocking what little light there was. I reached over to my bedside table and turned on a mercury glass light that resembled the full moon. It had been Nan's. Dad had given it to me after she died. The soft silvery glow was just enough to push the darkness back. The pain pills were knocking down the headache. I drifted off, my tears for Kellas soaking the pillow under my head.

Five

When I awoke, my headache was gone. Sounds from below let me know my parents were downstairs in the kitchen, preparing supper. I went to join them, hesitating by the wall that defined the space between living room and kitchen, watched them, unobserved. Mom was washing something in the sink. Dad was bent over, looking into the oven, with the door held open. As I watched, Mom snapped a towel in a practiced flick so that it cracked hard against Dad's rear. He straightened in a hurry, letting the oven door close as he turned and snatched away the towel, then pulled my mother into an embrace, laughing down at her. "You'll pay for that, my lovely!" He bent to kiss her, but Mom had caught sight of me. She ducked away from his kiss, but I saw her pat him on the chest. Clearly a promise.

"Raven! Are you feeling better? Supper is almost ready. Hungry?" She was pink, just the faintest blush. Maybe because I saw her flirting with her husband? Well, seeing their parents behave like that might embarrass some kids, but it didn't embarrass me. Any sign at all that they were making progress toward getting back together was hugely welcome.

"Starving, actually. What's in the oven?" I asked, sniffing appreciatively.

"Scalloped potatoes and ham. And your dad made an apple pie for dessert."

Yummy! "I'll set the table." I pulled the everyday dishes off the shelf and turned to go to the table. Stopped. Someone had already spread a dark green tablecloth and put tall beeswax candles on either side of an evergreen and red roses centerpiece. I put the everyday plates back and got out the bone china: white with a gold leaf pattern around the border, the ones that had to be hand-washed and therefore rarely got used. Obviously, my parents planned this to be special. I would not spoil that with ordinary tableware. I added heavy silver on folded linen napkins, then washed the dusty crystal and set that out as well.

We worked like a practiced unit, moving around one another easily, as if this was something we did every day. Soon everything was on the table, and we sat down together. It wasn't until we'd all finished dessert that my parents exchanged the sort of meaningful glances that confirmed my suspicions: they had ulterior motives for all the fanciness.

"Raven..." Dad started.

I wiped my mouth a final time with my napkin and laid it carefully next to my empty plate. Patience, Raven! Must not jump to conclusions. "Yes, Dad?"

I must have projected my reservations in the manner I responded, because his mouth quirked in a grimace. "Your mother and I are concerned."

"As you should be. You're my parents." That prompted another quick look between the two of them. "But don't let me stop you. Please continue." I fixed my face in a pleasantly bland smile and propped my chin on one fist, elbow planted on the table.

Dad dropped his head and waggled it back and forth in mock dismay before looking up at me again. "That's your 'you can talk all you want, but I'm gonna do it my way anyway' look, fledgling."

"Observant!" I drawled, and smirked at him.

He scoffed, but my snarkiness was met with a brief twinkle in his pretty blue eyes. "We are deeply concerned that you're going to take Dub up on his offer to help rescue Kellas."

Well, that was straight to the point!

Dad wasn't done. "We all want Kellas back safe, but risking your life in the process is not acceptable, and accepting help from those two..." He fell silent for a long moment, pondering something. The twinkle was well and truly gone when he spoke again. "We can only guess why the Old Gods were spying on you, and it scares the dickens out of your mother and me. Is there something you aren't telling us, and should?"

Yes, there was. And it involved assisting the gods in some unspecified way in the future. What that was, I hadn't asked. I should have. But I couldn't tell my parents that. "Are you suggesting that I have secrets I'm not sharing?" That came out a bit tartly, as it was only recently I'd discovered just how much the two of them had been keeping from me. Dark, important things I should have been told about years ago, but hadn't been. It still rankled. Yet, here I was doing the exact same thing. I felt sick to my stomach for lying to them, but if I shared this, they'd forbid me to go.

They exchanged glances again. I rolled my eyes, knowing too well how secrets could cause more problems than they solved. I shared what I could. "My tattoo links me to Kellas," I said. Held my arm up and gave Kellas' image a poke, so Mom could see how it moved; not exactly your typical sort of tattoo. She blanched, and I felt a little sorry for her. "Apparently, I can use this to reach Kellas, find out where he's being held, and go to him. I simply don't know how yet. Taliesin suggested I could search his book of magic to find ways, but it's encrypted and I need to figure out how to break the code. I just haven't had a chance yet. I intend to do so right after dinner."

"Will this involve Dub and Dian?" Dad asked, his reservations about that collaboration clear.

I shrugged. "That I don't know yet, either. The Morrigan thinks I should. I haven't decided." Yeah. That was a lie, too. It was a wonder my nose wasn't growing like Pinocchio's.

Mom was shaking her head in dismay. "I really don't like this!"

I reached over and put a hand on her arm. "I'm not thrilled about it either, Mom. But I don't see a better way. Yet. That could change." Yeah, maybe. Probably not, though.

"Michael?" There was a pleading note in my mother's voice. She knew Dad had better luck convincing me than she did when I needed to change my behavior. Maybe it's a mom-daughter thing. We butted heads. Fiercely, in fact.

Dad closed his eyes and drew a deep breath. When he opened them again, he fixed me with a steady stare. "I don't see a better way either, fledgling. But promise me you will tell us your plans before you do anything, so we can support you in any way we can. Although my magic is the learned sort, it is considerable. And your mother is highly capable in other ways that can also assist you. Team effort, Raven. You don't have to go through this on your own."

I nodded. "I promise. As best I can, but please don't be upset if I can't always. Sometimes things happen fast, and I just gotta go with it. It's not that I don't want to warn you..."

Dad was nodding. "But there isn't always an opportunity to give us a heads-up. Understood."

Mom didn't look happy, but remained silent, biting her lower lip. She rose and gathered the plates, signaling the end of our conversation. I began to help them clean up, but Dad took away the glasses I'd gathered and glanced at the ceiling. A clear dismissal. I had more important work to do.

I looked back as I started up the stairs to my room, and saw how Dad had pulled Mom into his arms, resting his chin on top of her head. Her shoulders were shaking as if she were crying. Gritting my teeth, I continued up. There was nothing I could do to fix that problem. Dad would have to deal with it on his own.

When I reached my room, I moved Taliesin's book to my desk and sat looking at it a moment, before lifting my medallion over my head and holding it next to its twin on the cover. They were even the same size. Puzzled at the coincidence, I placed the medallion gently over its carved image on the cover of the book, and stifled a gasp of distress as it sank into the cover and disappeared. The odd script on the cover twisted and reshaped into words I could understand. Book of Spells, it now read. Digging at the cover with my fingertips, I pried the medallion from the cover, and immediately the script reshaped itself into odd, meaningless characters. Shock and embarrassment about overwhelmed me. What an idiot I was! My medallion was a passkey that unlocked the book's contents, and I had been totally unaware of it until now. I replaced the medallion, this time leaving it in place, then opened the book and started reading.

~

I found the spell for dimension travel the next morning and about kicked myself for being such a dunce for not figuring it out before. Yes, it required magic—combined with my inherent ability to lift out of the here-and-now in my mind, daydreaming. I suspect everybody has done something similar: gone for a long hike or run, got thinking about something else, and regained their senses only to find themselves miles further along than when they had last taken measure of their surroundings. Easier to do while asleep, because the mind does this in dreams naturally. In the times I'd tumbled into Dub's dimension, it had always been while preoccupied with Kellas missing and feeling deeply distraught. The dimension hop there had been facilitated by being linked to Dub by his ink. To go to Kellas, I had to put myself in that state of suspended reality and focus solely on being where he was. This was exactly what I had done when I'd time traveled to find him, when he'd needed a cure for Dub's poison. I did not need to be in my dark moon phase, either. The time I'd done so last year, it had just been coincidental.

I galloped down the stairs to find Dad and tell him the news. He was in Nan's old office, doing paperwork. He listened to my hurried explanation of the technique, nodding in understanding. "Good work." He gave me a tired smile. "This makes sense. But remember the time you dragged all of us along to where you were battling Famine? Is there an explanation of how you did that? Can you do that again and take me with you? Bring Kellas back?"

My excitement died like a balloon popping. "That information wasn't in that spell. I'll go see if there's a spell for transporting others. Honestly, I didn't remember any of you being there until you told me you were, though." I looked around. "Where's Mom?"

"She went back to the cabin to work on a case."

"Ah." I shrugged, acknowledging this. "Back to work for all of us, then."

He nodded, turning back to his paperwork as I started out of the room.

A sudden blast of pain slammed through me. I cried out in agony and fell to my knees, left hand grasping my wrist over the top of Kellas' icon. *'Brannaugh!'* His desperate scream ripped through my brain. Through a reddened haze, I saw my father bolt to his feet, but that faded as the room disappeared around me.

Six

I regained my senses in a darkened space that smelled of mold, rats, and excrement. A cold, damp stone floor was under my hands and knees, the iron bars of a prison cell just to my left. A long hall led away from the cell, illuminated poorly by a single torch hanging at a drunken angle from the wall. The sound of approaching footsteps warned me to hide. I plastered myself against a nearby wall, called up my chameleon spell, and blended as best I could against the stone.

Two men, guards, were dragging another man between them. He was barely conscious, staggering along between his guards as if he needed their support to remain upright. They passed the torch, and light fell on his face. Kellas. The blows he'd taken had battered and bloodied his face. His clothing was torn to ribbons; blood streamed down his chest. I bit back a sob as they reached the cell door, opened it, and thrust Kellas through, then yanked the cell door shut and locked it.

Kellas staggered and fell to his knees, then keeled over to lie utterly still on the stone floor. I waited until the guards had disappeared around a corner, then flitted to his side and knelt there.

"Kellas?" I called to him in the barest whisper, so as not to alert the guards if they came back. "Kellas, it's me." I could barely make him out in the pitch dark and risked calling up my magic light.

My Cait Sidhe was barely breathing, his back a mass of deep cuts and bruises in so many places I hardly knew where I could touch him. And he was unconscious, probably a blessing, considering how badly injured he was. I cleared a spot on the floor and attempted to roll him over. Not happening. He was very heavy.

"Allow me," a quiet voice said.

I startled, then focused on Aquaman's hulking form in the dim light. "How did you get here?"

"I followed you. Remember, my ink connects the three of us." Dub knelt next to Kellas and lifted him up in his arms, cradling him like a child.

Kellas' head rolled back limply; his eyes closed. I pressed a hand against my mouth, suppressing a sob. Merciless claws had torn him. The Cait Sidhe's shirt lay in ribbons. Blood welled from multiple deep cuts down the side of his face, across his chest and belly.

"The red-haired one," Dub said quietly.

I managed a nod, remembering Kellas' remark on how Erin liked to fight claws out.

I drew in a deep, shaking breath, and pulled out my lute. "Keep watch," I warned, then played.

Fraegarthach must have had a volume control somehow, because I could barely hear the music that I summoned from its wooden heart. Considering it could also sound loud enough to fill an entire arena, that was remarkable. Magic. What can I say?

The tune that I played now sounded very familiar; perhaps it was the same one I'd played when I'd dragged Kellas and Taliesin back from death's door after the werewolf attack. Words formed in my mind, and I breathed them out in a soft whisper. Now-familiar silver strands formed in the surrounding air, swirling and swaying as, one after another, they entered Kellas' body, easing first the pain, and then knitting his torn flesh back together.

"Remarkable," Dub said quietly. "Your healing magic is more powerful than I've seen in all my years."

I ignored him, instead watching Kellas, looking for signs that he was recovering enough that we could move him. We could not remain here long, nor could we move him before he was well enough. I realized how close he had been to death the moment I started singing... an integral part of my healing magic. Had I arrived a few minutes later, he would have been gone forever.

He finally stirred in Dub's arms, and those beautiful blue eyes opened, met mine. "Oh, gods, no." His voice was a breathy whisper. "Brannaugh, go! Leave now. Before they find you."

"Not without you." I got to my feet, meeting Dub's gaze. "Let's go."

"I can't." Kellas gestured at the iron collar locked snugly around his neck. "It... stops me." Realizing then that he was being held in another's arms, he sent a questioning look up at Dub, then at me. "Aquaman?" He stirred restlessly. "You can put me down. I'm OK."

Saying nothing, Dub set Kellas back on his feet, then, when the Cait Sidhe wobbled, helped him sit down, his back against the stone wall of the cell.

"He's helping us." I supplied, clambering to my feet. "We need to get you out of here!"

Kellas shook his head again, touching the iron band clamped around his neck. "Until this is gone, I'm stuck here. You must leave. Find out how to rid me of this collar and then come back."

The distress on his face was almost more than I could bear. "Kellas, no. You nearly died! Don't make me leave you." Hot tears ran down my face. I was devastated by what he'd told me, and horrified that I wasn't able to take him with us. "I can't just leave you here!"

"You have no choice, Brannaugh. Leave now. But be careful. Something possesses Erin. She's far worse than you can imagine."

Oh, I could imagine! No problem. But there were noises in the hall outside, footsteps approaching.

"Go!" Kellas whispered urgently.

I didn't move, but was suddenly in motion anyway. Dub had a hard grip on my upper arm and was dragging me away. I wrenched myself free and fell to my knees, straddling Kellas' lap, my lips pressed against his in a desperate kiss. Felt something gush out of me into Kellas in a torrent of desperate longing. I began to black out... then was dimly aware of being cradled in Dub's arms as he ran, Kellas' despairing cry echoing in my ears.

∼

I woke up in a darkened room, bundled under piles of blankets, shivering uncontrollably, aching from the top of my head to the soles of my feet. I was freezing. There were voices. I could only catch snatches: *'Kiss of Life. Nearly killed herself. She does not know. We barely made it out in time.'* It made no sense. I tumbled down into darkness again.

The Morrigan was there when I woke again, one cool hand on my forehead, a deeply concerned expression stamped on her pretty features. "About time, moon child!" she snapped as I took a deep breath and clumsily levered myself up on my elbows to look around.

"Where am I?" I asked. I sounded half-drunk even to my own ears. "What happened?"

"You're in Dub's bed. Don't worry, I banished him to the sofa in his office, not that he liked the idea." She fixed me with an irritated scowl. "To answer your question, you do not know how powerful you are, and you overextended yourself. A terrible habit of yours, I might add. It will get you killed one of these days."

I struggled unsuccessfully to free myself from the piled blankets. She yanked them off me with a disgusted grunt. I sat up then, and nearly fainted, when a wave of dizziness crashed over me.

"Go slow," she cautioned gruffly. "It'll take some time to regain your equilibrium."

With the way my head pounded, she wasn't far wrong there. How I wished for some pain meds! "I don't understand. Healing with my music has never affected me like this before."

Her answering snort had me looking at her in astonishment. "It wasn't the music, my champion. It was that kiss, and the life-force deprived environment you were in when you gave it. You transferred too much energy to Kellas, with no way to replace it. You could have died." Her scowl was intimidating as she prowled back and forth. "Like it or not, you now owe Dub for your life. And trust me, that is not something either of us would like to have hovering over you. Who knows what he'll require as payment." She was snippy about it, but I could see the concern lurking in the back of her eyes.

I owed Dub. Gods. Even I knew that couldn't be a good thing.

He chose that moment to come barging in. OK, so it was his bedroom, but couldn't he have at least knocked first?

"Good. You're awake. You need to see this. Now!" He grabbed my upper arm and ungently manhandled me off his bed and through his darkened home to his office, where he unceremoniously dumped me in his own chair before grabbing a remote off his desk and clicking it at the giant TV across the room.

"I left some spy bugs behind," Dub explained grimly. "There are so many insects in that awful place, the Cait Sidhe will never notice a few more. This first." He started a video. The Morrigan had followed us and taken up a position by his elbow, slender arms folded across her chest.

In the video, Erin stood in front of Kellas, now chained to the prison wall by both wrists, forced either to stand or hang by his arms. The camera angle shifted so that we could now see both their faces. Erin's imperious. Cruel. Kellas with more life in him now, his color back... and defiance clear on his strong features.

"I grow weary of your fantasies regarding that mere girl. Has she come to save you?' Erin demanded. "She's a coward, through and through. You and I are among the last of our kind. We will be together whether you wish it or not. You shall give me kittens!" She leered in a distinctly unpleasant way as she said that, and it made no sense to me. Kittens? Why in the world would Erin want Kellas to give her kittens? And why that expression? She looked like she was propositioning him, for crying out loud.

"No." Kellas' face convulsed in pain with the word, but he fought it off.

"No, what?" she asked coldly.

"No... kittens. No, to all of it," he said, and gasped. His head fell against the stone at his back, his face chalk white.

Erin started laughing softly. "It's kittens or the Colosseum, Kellas. Hardly a tough decision to make. Live with me, or die horribly."

"Then I shall die horribly. You will never have kittens from me, Erin." A groan escaped him, and he sagged in his restraints.

Fury twisted Erin's face into an ugly mask. She raised one hand, claws sprouting from her fingertips, and raked them across his bare chest, slicing him open again. Kellas' face went tight from the pain, but that eased almost immediately as his torn flesh knitted itself back together, healing in seconds as we watched. From the expressions on both their faces, this was completely unexpected. They stared at one another for a beat, then Erin threw her head back and laughed mirthlessly.

"This is quite an unexpected turn of events." But it was not Erin's voice that emerged from her mouth. It was Dother's, God of Evil. Erin leaned forward and sniffed the blood that still trickled in streams on Kellas' healed chest. She licked his blood in one languorous, seductive motion as he cringed away, then closed her eyes, tasting it.

"The moon child has been here." Dother's voice said from Erin's body. "She has not only healed him, but imbued his body with the ability to heal rapidly. However, in doing so, she has also left us her signature. Which we shall use, my kitten. Use it to torture her beloved, and her, until they beg for death to take them, just to end it all." And Erin tipped her head back and laughed in Dother's voice, joined almost immediately by Erin's tinkling giggle. Two spirits, one body; together, but separate. An abomination.

Dub stopped the recording and turned his dark gaze on me, where I sat transfixed in horror in his chair, barely able to breathe. "Out of the frying pan and into the fire," he stated, his tone flat.

"I don't understand," I whispered.

The Morrigan exchanged a meaningful glance with Dub. "What part of that mess don't you understand, my champion?"

The most ridiculous part first. "Kittens? Why would Erin demand kittens from Kellas? Can't she just get her own from the SPCA?" My voice was barely louder than a whisper.

Dub closed his eyes and shook his head despairingly before fixing me with a pitying look. "You can be such a child. It's another euphemism. She demanded that he create babies with her."

Shock and disgust jolted through me, but I chose not to comment. "Why did it look like it caused him pain to refuse her? And stop calling me 'child.' I'm not a little kid anymore." One of his expressive eyebrows quirked up at my 'little kid' comment, and I felt a flash of annoyance. "My lunar tendencies aside, Dub!"

A small smile touched his lips and was quickly gone. "That band around his neck is a collar of compulsion," the God of Darkness explained. "It forces the wearer to do the bidding of the one who clamped it on. The collar inflicts pain anytime he defies her."

Oh, my gods. The horror of Kellas' situation left me gutted. I had to get that monstrosity off him. Somehow. I did not know how. I had more questions, though. "How did Kellas heal like that? What did Erin—Dother—mean by 'having my signature?' Why should that matter? What could they possibly do with that?" I was confused and scared and it didn't help that the expression on the Morrigan's face was the grimmest I'd ever seen on her.

"It means they can use your unique life signature—your DNA—to recreate your image on anything they desire." Dub said. He was fiddling with the remote, tossing it back and forth between his huge hands, tension in every line of his body.

I blinked, even more confused than before. "How?"

The Morrigan growled, annoyed at my thickheadedness. "Think. How could they use that against you? Against Kellas? That ill-considered kiss has rendered both of you horribly vulnerable. Yes, it has also given him the ability to heal rapidly, but at a cost beyond what we first thought: a shadow of your power runs through his veins."

"But now he can heal quickly. Isn't that a good thing?" Surely some good had to come of my kiss. But judging from the Morrigan's continued scowl, that was apparently not the case.

She exchanged a long look with Dub. He answered her unspoken question with a slight nod. She took a deep breath and sighed it out. "With Dother taking a taste of your power into Erin's body, he now holds the reins. We now have no choice but to destroy Erin and, by extension, Dother, if we are to free the two of you from his torment."

We did? My heart sank. Even my incredibly powerful grandmother had not managed to stop Dother. What chance did I have against him? I had meant nothing with that kiss but to leave Kellas with my promise to come back for him. As much to feel his lips against my own, in case everything went south. I did not know I was transferring power to him. Was that what I'd felt? That gush of something?

"Magic is not something you can splash around like so much holy water and get away with it, Light Bringer. There are consequences." This from Dub, with an unreadable expression on his face. Closed. Hard. "You need to see the next recording, too. Then you will see exactly what those two are doing with the power you gifted them with." He clicked his remote again.

This time the TV lit up with bright sunshine, the ground shimmering in the heat of a summer day. High stone walls, too high for a man to jump even if they hadn't been topped with wire mesh, surrounded a large oval space the size of a football field. Above that, people dressed in clothes that looked like something out of the movie Gladiator crowded the rows of stadium seating. Behind them was a series of horrifyingly familiar stone arches.

"The Colosseum in Rome," I whispered. It was in perfect shape.

"Indeed. At the height of the Roman Empire, besides," Dub confirmed. "The games are at their most vicious. Man against man, man against animal. Watch."

A blast of horns and pounding drums signaled something was about to happen in the arena. Someone thrust a young woman into the arena from one opening, and she stumbled to her hands and knees. She scrambled up in a flash and threw herself at the already closed door, beating on it, crying and screaming. Dub's spy fly swung low, drew close. Focused on her face.

My face.

I must have gasped, because the Morrigan's hand gripped my shoulder. "It only looks like you. It's some other hapless victim. Not that Kellas will know."

Another door opened across the arena, and Dub's spy fly zoomed over. A man in gladiator armor walked out, a sword gripped in his right hand, a small, round shield on his left forearm. His head was bare. The wind gusted messy black hair back from his face. Kellas. Barely recognizable as my Kellas, his eyes narrowed against the bright sunlight, face taut with anger, teeth bared in a snarl. He faced the end of the arena where the Caesar and his Senate lounged in state. Clashing the side of his sword against his shield in defiance, he turned slowly, taking in the crowd, tension in every line of his body. They screamed; catcalls, jeers, derisive howls. Howls that became louder as a gate opened on the far side, and a lion paced out, jaws hanging open, yellowed teeth long and viciously sharp.

Kellas must have noted the girl with my face, because he positioned himself between her and the lion, then clashed sword against shield again, drawing the lion's attention to him. The giant cat threw its heavily maned head back and roared, then leapt toward the Cait Sidhe at a run. Kellas was roaring too, sounding much like his panther self as he lifted his sword and ran at the lion.

They met in the middle, Kellas laying on with his sword like it was an extension of his arm. The lion took advantage of its longer reach and heavier body to knock Kellas back, tear at him with razor-sharp claws, long teeth reaching for his throat.

I couldn't watch after their first contact. I squeezed my eyes shut, my fingers stuffed into my ears, trying to block out the roars of the combatants and the screams from the crowd. Clenching my teeth against the moans that tore from my center, I rocked back and forth on Dub's chair.

At some point, the sound of battle stopped, and I peeked up at the screen in time to see Erin float down from the Caesar's box, grab the girl—me—by the hair and set a knife to her throat. "Gladiator!" she yelled, triumph in her voice. Across the arena, a bloodied and torn Kellas climbed to his feet, the dead lion sprawled nearby. Horror crossed his face, and he jumped into a run toward the two women. Erin laughed... and slashed her knife across the girl's throat.

The crowd roared its approval, drowning out Kellas' despairing cry. I was barely aware of it, because it felt like Erin's knife was slicing fire across my throat—as if she were killing me. That was the last I knew.

I woke sometime later, back in Dub's bed, hearing whispered voices arguing about something, my throat on fire, despair heavy in my heart.

"No more. She cannot watch that. The cruelty alone will destroy her." It was the Morrigan, and she was furious.

"She needs to know what that horrible woman is doing. What my brother is doing." Aquaman's voice. Dub, then.

"What are you trying to do, Dub? Cause her so much despair she can never leave your demesne? Because I will never allow that."

A growl from low in his chest. "You saw that red-haired witch. She will use these decoys as voodoo dolls until the moon child dies. Raven felt it when that knife sliced across the girl's throat. You know she did!"

"And watching will not help one whit. We need her strong. She needs to fight."

"Agreed. And soon. They won't fight the Cait Sidhe again soon, but no one knows when he'll be forced back into the arena. If he heals as fast as he did before, it may be far sooner." Dub paused, then added in a thoughtful voice, "Most gladiators only fought a few times a year. They were far too valuable to their owners to risk frequently; they were prized as breeding stock."

Breeding stock? What the heck did he mean by that?

"Don't remind me." The disgust in the Morrigan's voice was clear. "You and Dian keep watch over your brother. I'll do what I can to put my champion back on her feet."

I couldn't lie there listening any longer. I had to go back for Kellas right away. Rid him of that hideous collar. So far, the only lead I had was Taliesin's

Book of Spells, and I needed to get going on that immediately. No time to waste. I rolled off the bed and landed hard on both feet. "You two stand there chatting if you like, but I have a Cait Sidhe to rescue," I snapped at two very startled gods and shot like a rocket back to my dimension.

Seven

I landed where I'd taken off—in my dad's office. He was on one knee, a hand gripping my shoulder. "Raven! What happened?"

Time warp. It was moments here, far longer away. Useful information, and not in a good way. It meant I had no time to waste, because every minute here might translate to hours, possibly days, where Kellas was. "I found Kellas, but I can't get him out. Erin put a collar on him that prevents him from leaving."

Dad looked stunned. "A collar of compulsion." He helped me to my feet.

"You know about that?" That surprised me, but it probably shouldn't have. After all, he'd lived for millennia.

"Unfortunately." Dad was scowling, part fury, part concern. "And if it stays on him for long, even if we remove the collar, the compulsion might remain."

I felt sick. "How long do we have?"

He put a reassuring hand on my shoulder and squeezed lightly. "It depends on the individual. Some have stronger wills than others. Kellas is stubborn." Dad gazed down at me; His eyes were serious. "Any idea how long he's had it on?"

"Since the solstice. It's how Erin compelled him to leave with her."

"And how long where he is?" Dad was aware of how time varied between dimensions.

"Where Kellas is, it's been a couple of weeks. Maybe more?"

My father closed his eyes, grimaced, and then nodded.

I gestured toward the stairs. "I'm going to check Taliesin's book, see if I can find something to get rid of that thing."

Dad nodded again. "Quickly, now. No time to waste."

No kidding...

But I could find nothing in Taliesin's book. Nothing at all about how to remove a collar of compulsion. That made little sense. How could the wisest man in the world not know that detail when he knew absolutely everything else? It was high time to talk to the man directly. I pulled out my lute, sat down on the floor in front of my mirror, and played.

When Taliesin finally showed up, he was yawning widely and digging sleep out of his eyes. Apparently, I'd hauled him out of bed, a risk one takes when there's no way of telling time from one dimension to another. I apologized for waking him and went straight to the heart of the issue: that collar Kellas wore.

Taliesin settled into his chair by the fire, now fully awake. "A collar of compulsion. Are you sure? They are very rare." His brow furrowed in concern.

"That's our best guess." I felt my throat swell, remembering. "Every time Kellas denied Erin, he felt severe pain."

Taliesin scowled. "Then it likely is. It's surprising your young man allowed it to be put on him."

"What do you mean, he allowed it?" Shock jolted through me at that revelation.

"Not something a Cait Sidhe would normally agree to. Cats and collars don't mix. Especially wild cats. I'd have thought he'd fight it." My grandfather scowled, puzzling over this. "To work as intended, a compulsion collar cannot be forced onto the wearer. It must be freely accepted. You need to find out why he allowed it to be fastened on him."

"But how do we get it off?" I was getting impatient. "Why he allowed it in the first place is immaterial, right?"

"On the contrary, my dear, it's very important. It's key for getting it off him." Taliesin was tapping his chin, pondering the situation. "If someone lied to Kellas about its purpose, you can easily get it off by telling him the truth." He leaned forward, his expression serious. "However, if he accepted it out of love for you—if he thought doing so would protect you—then it becomes almost impossible to remove. His love and sense of duty keep him a prisoner of its power."

I almost stopped playing at that revelation. "How do we find that out?"

"You ask him." Pity shone in my grandfather's eyes.

"And if he did it because he loves me?" My voice was the barest whisper.

"Then the only way to free him is for him to stop loving you," he breathed. "I'm so sorry, my dear."

~

Three guesses where I ended up when that struck home. This time I landed right in Dub's lap where he was sitting at his desk, leaned back in his chair.

"Well, hello again!" he exclaimed, wrapping his arms around me in a close embrace. "Dian, the remote!"

There was a scrabbling sound as his brother grabbed the remote and clicked off the TV. With the sounds of a terrible battle cut off, the room was abruptly silent.

"Are they fighting him again?" I asked through a tight throat.

"You don't want to know the answer to that," Dub told me, cuddling me close like a doll, his breath soft on my cheek. He felt like—safety. Weird.

"Yes, they are." Dian said. He was standing nearby, thick arms crossed over his chest, face lined with tension.

"Is he okay?" I had to know.

"Yes," said Dub.

"No," said Dian.

I looked up at Dub, his face inches from my own, then over at Dian. "Somebody is lying."

"Not it," Dian grunted.

I pushed back from Dub's embrace. He reluctantly released me so I could scramble to my feet. I'd ended up in the arms of despair far too often. "To get that collar off him, I need to know why he let her put that collar on."

The brothers exchanged meaningful glances. I looked from one to the other. "OK, out with it." I planted my fists on my hips. "You know something, and I am going to get it out of you. So... spill it!"

That totally empty threat brought faint smiles to their faces. Like I could force those two to tell me anything!

"What would you do to us if we didn't?" Dian asked, some of the tension leaving his body, as if he was enjoying our spat. His brown eyes were twinkling.

Now I was on the spot! I crossed my arms over my chest, lifted my chin, and glared at him. "I won't be your friend anymore."

Both brothers burst out laughing. I stood there feeling incredibly foolish, unable to take back my stupid elementary-school threat.

They did eventually stop hooting at my inanity. "Does that..." Dub started chuckling again, and struggled to regain control. "Does that mean we *are* friends, little one?"

"Maybe. Maybe not." I raised my chin defiantly. "Are you going to tell me what you know about that collar?"

That banished the remains of their laughter, and the brothers exchanged somber glances yet again. "We will tell you, even though it will be nothing you want to hear," Dub told me. "We are your allies in this matter, Light Bringer." He got up from his chair and approached me.

I took a single step back. He was too magnetic. I could not afford to let him get too close.

Dub stopped, acknowledging my need for space, but a dark look crossed his face. "You are our last hope of defeating our brother and regaining control over our own destinies, girl. You alone possess the ability. And the unbeatable sword, Fraegarthach." He clenched his fists and growled under his breath, dealing with some unnamed internal struggle. When he spoke again, it was with barely constrained violence. "That young man is your bodyguard. Your protector. He took that collar on to keep you safe, not only out of a sense of duty, but out of love for you. Love, Light Bringer!" His eyes closed, and he shook his head as though to rid it of pain before fixing his electrifying green gaze on me. Seizing me by my upper arms, he shook me hard, once. "The Cait Sidhe is doubly bound by his sense of duty and his love for you. And nothing will free him of our brother's miserable collar except his death or he no longer has any connection to you. His love and sense of duty must be severed. Do you understand now what that red-haired devil cat has done?"

I swayed on my feet, feeling faint. Dub tightened his grip on my arms to steady me. "How do I get him out of there?" If losing his love was the only way to save Kellas, then I would do just that, no matter the cost to myself.

"We," Dub corrected. "Together, *we* will get him out of there. The collar keeps him by the red-haired one's side. She must die, and then we will remove the collar and bring him out of that demesne. Not before. But first, you must improve your ability to fight. Become a master of that sword you bear."

I looked from one god to the other, a cold, hard determination rising from my core. "When do I start?"

"Right now," Dub told me. There was a glint of something I could not identify in his eyes.

Instantly, the Morrigan swirled into a visible form, standing by my side. I guess she'd been waiting and listening in. "Not so fast, Dub. First, we ask the parents. She's still underage. They must grant permission, or the school will never consent to train her."

School? They wanted me to go to a *school* for this?

Dub scowled. "Then let's ask. It's a formality anyway. We all know it's the only way the Light Bringer will defeat the cat woman while our brother possesses her. We go now."

We went, landing in our dining area next to the kitchen. Mom and Dad sat at the kitchen bar, conversing in low tones. Archer was at the counter pouring himself a mug of coffee. Considering the four of us suddenly materializing in their midst, I had to admit my parents were astonishingly chill. Archer didn't do nearly as well, spilling his coffee over one hand, and cussing under his breath as the hot liquid scalded him.

Dad took it all in with a single glance and slid off his high stool. "This way, please," was all he said, leading the way to the living room. "*Fáilte roimh aíonna onórach,*" he said, his Gaelic impeccable. "Welcome, honored guests. Please sit down." He motioned to the easy chairs arranged in a conversational group, then extended a hand to Mom. She took it, standing close to his side, eyeing the three gods with open distrust. Once they took seats, Dad eased down on the couch, a gentle tug on Mom's hand encouraging her to join him.

I didn't sit. I was too tense. Some sixth sense let me know Archer was right behind me: backup if I needed him.

"Meg, let me introduce you to our guests," Dad told her. "The lady is the Morrigan, Celtic Goddess of Death. Dub, the Greek God of Darkness, is the man who looks like Aquaman. Dwayne Johnson's look-alike is Dian, Greek God of Violence."

"Hello," my mother said quietly, holding it together, but I saw how she clung to my father's hand. Mom was doing her best not to let the sudden appearance of the three gods shake her.

"May we ask the reason for your visit?" Dad asked, sounding very formal, but not wasting a single moment.

"We have located the Cait Sidhe who has been your daughter's body-guard," Dub said, taking the lead. "Magic has trapped him, binding him to the red-haired feline in another dimension. That would be bad enough, but Dother... that's the God of Evil," he added that for Mom's benefit, and she went even paler than before... "has possessed the one you call Erin. To res-cue him, we must defeat them both. And to do that, we need to train your daughter how to fight. She possesses Fraegarthach, the only weapon capable of killing him."

"No!" Mom exclaimed immediately, starting up from her seat. Then, as Dad squeezed her hand: "Michael, no. I will not allow it."

He tugged her back down next to him. "Please explain your reasoning," Dad requested, his gaze steady on Dub, but tension was clear in every line of his body. Staying calm was costing him.

Dub nodded, then conveyed all the details about Kellas's situation and the dimension he was trapped in. "To effectively compete against these odds, your daughter must learn how to fight, and fight well, with as many techniques as she can absorb in a short amount of time."

"How long?" Mom wanted to know.

"Where?" Dad demanded. The undercurrent of anger in his voice sug-gested he suspected the answer and did not like what he was about to hear.

"Fight school," Dub said, and the sheer relish of how he said it made my heart sink in dismay. "Four days in your time."

"I am familiar with the place." Dad grimaced. Apparently, he was not fond of it; why he felt that way remained to be found out. If my tough-as-nails Dad disliked the school that much, what awfulness might I encounter? I was not nearly as strong as my father. "How long in Kellas' current dimension?" he asked.

"Forty days," Dub responded. The two had focused solely on one another, their locked gazes shooting daggers.

"And for Raven... at the fight school."

"400 days," Dub said.

Mom jumped to her feet. "No. No, you can't. Michael, she mustn't go. That's over a year for her!"

"One year, one month, 4 days." Dub said, pondering the math with a thoughtful expression on his face. "Enough time to train her decently, while not keeping her away from you for too long and not leaving the Cait Sidhe fighting for his life for an excessive amount of time." He sent my parents a calculating look. "Doable!"

Dad stood. "My wife and I must discuss this privately. If you will excuse us?" He led Mom out of the living room. And yes, I followed. Hey, this affected me too! Archer was right on my heels.

As soon as we were out of the hearing range of the gods, Mom pulled on Dad's arm, stopping him. "What is this 'fight school,' Michael?" she hissed in an undertone. "You act like you know something about it."

Dad nodded, a dark expression on his face. "It's weapons and mixed martial arts training for those who would fight professionally. It's brutal."

"And you know this how?"

"I survived training a while back."

Survived. Gods... My stomach churned.

"Anything else you want to tell me... us?" Mom had noticed Archer and me, and included us in the conversation. I was grateful.

"They take roughly 20 immortal trainees per session. Maybe half of those make it to the end." He stopped, scowling.

Twenty immortals? I was stunned. There were that many in the universe? I exchanged a startled look with Archer, who shrugged and made an 'I dunno' face.

"And?" Mom pressed. "What happens to those who don't make it?"

Dad just shook his head.

"Do they... die?" she asked.

"A few have over the years," he told her. "Most are just too broken to continue and drop out."

Gods. This was just getting better and better. Not! And Dub wanted me to go there?

Mom was shaking her head. "Not what we want for our daughter, Michael."

Dad's head briefly dropped forward, chin on chest, before he raised it to gaze at my mother again. "What choice do we have, Meg?" He palmed Mom's face with one large hand. "You heard the situation with Kellas. We can't just leave him there. As Dother continues to gather strength, he will become increasingly difficult to overcome. Right now he doesn't have a body, which is why he's occupying Erin's."

Mom backed away from Dad's caress and crossed her arms, hugging herself. "This is insanity."

A grimace flashed across my father's face and was gone. "No argument there. However, if they can take Erin out, even as empowered as she is by Dother's possession, he will suffer another setback." He sighed heavily. "It's a chance we must take. Raven has recruited some serious firepower to our side as it is. Those three in there?" he gestured at the living room where the Morrigan, Dub and Dian waited. "You don't know them like I do. They're formidable. Somehow, Raven has enlisted them all to our cause. I'm unsure how she managed that bit of magic." He shot me a glance that said he wasn't thrilled about it, either, before turning back to Mom. "The Morrigan has saved our daughter's life and now claims her as her champion and warrior. If the Death goddess thinks this is necessary, then we accept that fight school is where Raven needs to go."

Mom's face set in stubborn lines, but she said nothing.

"I'll go too." Archer stepped to my side.

Dad hesitated. "It will be dangerous."

Archer just shrugged, keeping his face neutral. "She's my sister."

Mom looked worried. "What can Archer do?" she protested. "He's mortal. Aren't the trainees all immortals, like you said?"

"He's the closest she has to a brother," Dad said, gazing thoughtfully at Archer. "I'm not thrilled about Archer going, too, but it could make all the difference." Mom looked at him dubiously. He took her by the shoulders, attempting to reassure her. "Brother-sister bond bears a special sort of magic of its own, Meg. His presence alone could tip the balance of power in Raven's favor."

Mom stood quietly for a long moment, head bowed, before she looked up at my father again. Nodded. "All right. Since you see no other way."

Dad dropped a kiss on Mom's forehead, then pulled Archer and me into a fierce hug before abruptly releasing us. *"Dul. Ár mbeannacht oraibh.* My blessing goes with you both."

Archer laid an arm around my shoulder. "Time to go, little sis," he murmured, and led me back to the living room.

My parents followed us. "I'd like a word with you alone, Dub," my father said in a low voice.

The God of Darkness followed him out of the living room. They stood facing each other in the kitchen, where I could see they were talking to each other, but Dad must have used a silencing spell, because we couldn't hear a word they were saying. I could see Dub's face, however, and something Dad had said must have really upset him. "Tell me something I don't know, Love God!" he yelled, breaking the silencing spell with his anger.

Love God? Whatever did Dub mean by that? Not that I had a chance to question either my father or Dub about that detail, because the God of Darkness was already stomping back into the living room. "We leave now," he declared, and beckoned us closer.

We had no time to pack anything. If the gods were surprised Archer was going with us, they didn't show it. The dark triumph on Dub's face concerned me, however. Like we'd walked into a trap of some kind. If it hadn't been for the Morrigan's calm acceptance of the situation, I might not have agreed to go. Dian just looked like he always did. Stoic, thoughtful. Impossible to read.

Dub rubbed his hands together, then reached for mine and his brother's on his other side. "Join hands. We'll trip this one together. On three..."

Archer and the Morrigan barely had time to grab our hands and close the circle before Dub reached 'three' and our living room dropped away in a blaze of white light.

Eight

Dub was far more capable of transporting across dimensions than Kellas and I had experienced at the hands of the Celtic Gods back in August. We floated gently to earth like thistledown, arriving by an elaborate fountain centered in a grassy courtyard. An enormous mansion loomed nearby, four stories of stone facade, with multiple rounded towers and intricate rooflines soaring high above us; a lavish display of wealth. However, the music here immediately overwhelmed me: a foreboding, dark minor key suggested things were not as they seemed. I felt my stomach clench.

"Home sweet home," Dian sighed happily and started toward the wide stone steps that led up to what looked like the main entry to the mansion.

"Nice try, *greadadh*," the Morrigan snarled at Dub.

He merely grinned at her like he'd accomplished what he'd intended by nearly leaving her behind: irritating her. "You're still quick with the name-calling," he teased. "Come, let's get the Light Bringer enrolled in fight school. This way," he said to Archer and me, and we followed Dian's departing figure.

We entered the mansion through a set of double doors, thrown wide to warm summer breezes, and crossed a parquet floor toward a broad desk, polished to a shine. The smell of lemon wax hung in the air. A man and a woman sat behind the desk, busily scribbling in large ledgers, while a small group of people waited in line in front of the desk.

"Go sign in." The Morrigan instructed me. "They will give you a room and paperwork to complete. If asked, your sponsor is me."

"What about Archer?" I asked.

"They will not allow your brother to enroll," she said simply. "He must pretend to be your servant."

Having Archer pose as my servant did not set well with me at all. "And why can't he enroll, too?" I demanded.

"He's not immortal," she said.

I made a face that said clearly what I thought of that uppity crap. "Archer has mad skills. Too bad you fancy-ass immortals can't seem to accept that you aren't the be-all and end-all."

The Morrigan hid a smile. Dub just scowled. "Get in line," he ordered. "Don't forget you're one of those fancy-ass immortals, too."

I scoffed, but took up my place at the end of the queue. It wasn't moving along all that quickly, so I looked around.

We were in a vast space, two stories high at least, with a massive oak balcony that ran the length of the room along the second story. There were people up there too, some carrying baggage, all looking like they had also recently arrived: a bit harried, tired, and more than a little anxious, judging from the jittery music that I could hear coming from them, even from this distance. One young man stood by the railing, looking down at the activity below. Maybe he was waiting for someone.

The people in line in front of us seemed similarly anxious. The only female was a tiny, beautiful Asian girl about my age. At the head of the line, a large Black teenager had just finished signing in. Impatiently, he hefted a large duffel bag to his shoulder and pushed past the rest of us as if we were a bother. He might have thought he was being all tough, but I sensed the same thrumming tension in him, his music discordant as he strode by me with barely a glance. A slender youth followed shortly after him, a shock of unruly sandy-blond hair hanging down in his eyes. Haunted eyes, like he'd seen things no one should ever see. He gave me a startled look as our eyes met, then scowled, and stalked toward the staircase that curved upward to the balcony.

Wow, friendly place!

We waited another ten minutes as the two boys still ahead of us got signed in: a redheaded white kid whose music felt deeply ominous, and another darker-skinned black-haired youth who I was positive was Native. They left for the stairs as well, just as tense, just as unfriendly as the two before. That left me in front of one registrar behind the desk, with the Asian girl in front of the other.

She alone seemed at ease with the process of signing in to fight school. Despite her small stature, she exuded the quiet confidence and hauteur befitting a princess, but there was something about her music that wasn't quite right. I kept darting sideways glances at her, trying to figure that out as I answered the registrar's questions. (They were all the usual sort: name, age, parents, address, sponsor, and so on.) The Asian girl was barely five feet tall, with sleek reddish-black hair that flowed like a silken river to her rear. A tight, sleeveless red dress draped effortlessly around her curves. I felt sloppily dressed next to her, in my now far-too-warm sweater and leggings, and wished I'd had time to change—not that I had anything nearly as stunning as the clothes she was wearing.

"Like my dress?" she asked quietly as we waited for the registrars to finish up our applications. There was a small smile on her face.

"It's gorgeous," I admitted. "And you look great in it."

Her smile widened. "Why, thank you!" She extended a slender hand. "The name's Kit."

"Raven," I supplied, meeting her hand with my own. Her hands were fine-boned, delicate, but her grip was firm. She didn't have the look of a warrior... but here she was at fight school. Curious.

"Those people with you?" she asked, tipping her head toward my brother and the gods.

I glanced at them. The Morrigan and Dub had drawn to one side and were conversing in undertones. Archer's steady gaze remained on me, watchful. Dian was nowhere in sight.

"That one's my brother," I told her, indicating Archer. "The goddess is my sponsor. The god..." I hesitated. "He's extra." How could I explain Dub's presence to anyone? I'd have to figure that out soon.

"Your brother's gorgeous," she breathed.

"He's Two-Spirit," I cautioned.

Her face fell. "Such a shame."

It was nothing I hadn't heard from heterosexual women before, but it still rankled. "I doubt his boyfriend thinks so."

Her lovely eyebrows arched in amusement. "Firmly put in my place," she murmured. "Nicely done."

I'd corrected her rather sharply, and she'd appreciated it. Huh! I was going to have to keep an eye on this one, and it wasn't just because of the edginess of her music.

"As the only two females in this year's class, you two will bunk together," the lady who'd signed me in said, handing me a set of keys. "First door on the left at the top of the stairs," I nodded and turned away with a glance at Kit. She grabbed a small backpack and joined me to walk toward the grand staircase.

"Oh, but I truly wanted the bedroom to the *right* of the stairs!" Kit mourned quietly as we climbed them.

I sent her a quizzical look. "Kidding, right?"

"Stupid to specify the room on the left, when the room on the right is the entry hall two stories down, don't you think?" she scoffed.

I grinned and nodded. When we reached the top of the stairs, I unlocked the door to our shared room for Kit, then paused briefly to look over the balcony to where Archer and the Morrigan were talking to the registrars. I hoped they would come up with a room for Archer that wasn't too far from mine. A mortal among immortals was at a serious disadvantage, even if he wasn't participating in classes, and I wanted him close. I had no idea how my fellow students would treat anyone they felt was inferior, but if they mistreated my brother just because he was mortal, I would not let them get away with it.

I followed Kit into what was going to be our digs for the next year, then stopped and stared. The bedroom was enormous; opulent to an obscene degree. Heavy velvet draperies hung at the windows. Elaborate oak moldings framed windows, floors, ceiling, and doors. The floor was red oak, polished to a shine, with large, dense rugs scattered about. Two enormous beds spaced well apart from each other sported fluffy white coverlets and multiple pillows.

I heard a toilet flushing. Shortly after, Kit came out through a door I had not noticed immediately. She hooked a thumb over her shoulder. "Bath and toilet that way, in case you were wondering," she said. Walking over to the bed closest to the windows, she picked up her backpack from where she'd tossed it earlier. "I'm taking this one."

"Fine by me." I headed for the bathroom door. I didn't need to use the toilet yet, but I liked to familiarize myself with my surroundings. The bathroom was every bit as over the top as the rest of our room: a huge clawfoot tub, a separate glassed-in shower, dual sinks, gold faucets, lots of mirrors. The single window had obscure glass. At least I wouldn't have to fret about anyone peeking in that one! One especially nice feature: the toilet was in a separate, closable cubicle, so it remained available while someone else was in the bath.

I went back to the bedroom where Kit was putting away a few things she'd brought with her. "Where's your stuff?" she asked as she put a book on her nightstand.

"I didn't have time to pack." None, in fact! "Kind of a last-minute thing."

"Well, hopefully your sponsor will see fit to provide you with something," she sniffed. "Mine certainly has!" She opened a door opposite the end of her bed, revealing a walk-in closet overflowing with anything a young woman might want, especially if she was the sort to kick immortal backsides. Besides clothing and accessories, there was an entire wall filled with weapons of all sorts.

I went over and gaped through the doorway at the sheer quantity of everything she had to work with. Envy started its ugly crawl around my belly.

"Your closet is that one." Kit pointed.

I went over to the door, convinced I would find an empty closet. Opened it to utter darkness.

"Light switch on the wall to your left," Kit drawled with barely suppressed humor.

I snorted, flipped the switch, then stared. "Wow." I'd never seen such a vast assortment of clothing in my entire life. And yes, I also had a wall full of weaponry, not that I had a clue of how to use any of it... well, the swords, sure, but I already had one of my own.

"Totally dope!" Kit was standing next to me, her head barely as high as my shoulder. "Your sponsor really likes you! I thought I had nice rags, but yours are something else!" She stepped into my closet and started pawing through the dress rack. Didn't even ask for permission, not that it bothered me. They weren't really my clothes. "Prada. Christian Dior. Completely lit! Oh, will you look at this one. It's Oscar de la Renta." She held up a shimmering blue silk dress. "This shade of blue will look stunning on you." She put it back and continued searching through the rack. Held up dress after dress, all vivid colors and drapey fabric. "Your sponsor enjoys seeing a lot of you, I think," she remarked, sending me a wry look. She held up a brilliant red floor-length dress that left very little to the imagination. The dress featured a low neckline, a peekaboo gap from breast to bellybutton, an open back down to the hips, and two slits up the front, exposing the wearer's legs to the top of her thighs.

"That one's a hard no," I groaned. This had to be Dub's work. "Do I at least have some workout clothing? I doubt we'll be spending much time prancing around in fancy clothes." I backed out of the closet and plopped onto the end of my bed.

"Shapeless sweaters more your style?" she teased. "You'd do that dress justice, though." Done with the dress rack, she turned and admired the weaponry. Whistled. "Sweet!" She took down a double-ended ninja sword and gave it a practiced swing, missing all the fancy clothing, although not by much. "Lovely weight and balance." She put it back and came out of the closet, closing the door firmly. "Hey, anytime you want to share clothes or hardware, just say the word. You've got one slay gig there."

"Sure," I grunted. "You'll look better in that stuff than I ever will." I was studying the schedule the registrar had given me. "It says here there will be a welcome dinner at six p.m. in the formal dining room, wherever that is. Formal wear required." I groaned at the thinly veiled order and looked around for a clock. Found none. "Do you know the time?"

She glanced at a delicate gold watch on her wrist. "Pushing five. Guess that means we should get a move on, don't you think?" Her eyes sparkled. "How about that red dress, yeah?"

Clothing was not my first concern, however. I needed to find Archer, to make sure he was okay. Jumping to my feet, I pointed at my closet. "Help yourself to anything you like in there. I gotta go find my brother."

I scooted out of the room to find the entire balcony deserted. Walking down the length of the balcony, I could hear male voices rumbling behind closed doors. At the far end of the balcony, I found one door that was slightly ajar and heard the Morrigan's voice coming from inside the room. I knocked quietly. Archer pulled it open. "Hey! I was wondering how you are making out," I said.

He stepped back and waved me into his room. It was hardly larger than my walk-in closet, windowless, with a tiny cot hardly long enough to accommodate his six-foot frame. A repurposed broom closet, no doubt.

"You're kidding me!" I gasped. Anger surged in my belly, sending a red flush to my face. "This is so not OK!"

Archer sent a wry glance at the Morrigan. "I told you she'd be upset." He turned to me. "Really, Raven, this is fine. I'm used to far rougher digs, really. You should see my dorm room at school."

"They are being insulting! Just because you are mortal? Not on my watch." I would have stomped out right then to make a scene, but Archer grabbed my shoulder. "Wait. Your Morrigan has already come up with a solution. Are you ready for this?"

I grumbled, but stopped my headlong rush. The Morrigan sent me a small, secretive smile. "If anyone steps into Archer's room, this is what they will see. Exactly as they intended. However..." she snapped her fingers, and the space was suddenly as opulent as my room, complete with en-suite bathroom and large closet. Through its open door, I could see clothing and weapons as impressive as mine.

I squealed in excitement. "Yes! That'll show them, the arrogant stuck-ups!"

The Morrigan smoothed her dress with a smug expression on her face. "Your brother will escort you and your roommate to dinner. Be ready." She waved at Archer, then walked me out of his room. "Be sure to make a big impression, my champion," she cautioned. "Now is not the time to be shy about how you dress. Be bold, get noticed. Your roommate will be very helpful in that regard, I'm sure. Kitsuné foxes are not shy."

"But, why?" I demanded. "Aren't I here to learn how to fight? Why do I need to get noticed at all? Wouldn't it be better to fly under the radar?"

The Morrigan sent me a disgusted look. "When you and the Kitsuné are the only two females in this class? You'll get noticed. Just make sure it's spectacular."

Nine

Kit proved to be a lifesaver. She had curled her hair and was braiding the sides back by the time I got back to our room. "All okay with your brother?" she asked, then when I nodded, she pointed imperiously toward the bathroom. "Shower, shampoo. You smell like old sweat."

"Bossy much?" I snorted, but knew a shower was in order. That cared for in double time, I came back out wrapped in a towel, my hair done up in a towel turban, then stood in my closet, at a loss of what to wear. Kit came over, in the process of zipping herself up in a strapless, skin-tight black minidress that shimmered with sequins.

She sidled up to me and raised one arm. "Help me get this all the way up."

It took both of us tugging and pulling to get the zipper all the way closed. "You look fantastic," I told her. "But how can you breathe in that thing?"

"Fashion isn't designed for comfort, Raven," she told me, her voice strained. "I'll adapt. Meanwhile, you need to get ready."

She had already applied her makeup, and her smoky-toned eyeshadow and brilliant red lipstick made her look even lovelier than before. At least, those were the elements I recognized. I had never owned makeup in my life and had zero idea of how to go about applying it. "Umm..." I started and fell silent.

Kit gave me an appraising look. "Something wrong?"

I grimaced. "Would you help me? I've done nothing like this before."

A feral grin spread across her face. "Love to!" she declared. "I've been itching to from the moment we met downstairs." She took me by the shoulders, fixing me with a stern look. "Do you trust me?"

I bit my lower lip. "Don't I kind of have to?"

She chuckled, dragged me over to her dressing table, and shoved me down onto the stool with a great deal more strength than I would have thought possible in such a slight body.

"First your hair, which will have to be simple because we are running out of time." She dried and brushed my hair, then sorted out two sections on either side of my temple, then started twisting them, pulling them to the back of my head, fastening them together with a clip. "This white streak is especially nifty. Born with it?"

"Tortured with it. Long story. Tell you later." It was fascinating how she made this all seem so effortless, all the while wrapped up tight in a straitjacket of a dress.

She left the rest of my hair free to cascade down my back and started on my face. I discovered there is a great deal more involved with makeup than a touch of lipstick and some eyeshadow. Kit carried on an entire conversation about the various steps as she went about her work, applying an even layer of something she called foundation, then chiding me to hold still as she dragged a tiny brush along my eyelids. She drew around the outside of my lips with some sort of pencil, then finished with a different color using a soft brush. Blush on my cheeks, then eyeshadow... and she went after my eyebrows with a tweezer.

"Ow! What are you doing?" I demanded, pushing her hand away and ducking.

"Bushy eyebrows are fine and good; they're even making a comeback lately, but yours needs a little shaping," she insisted. "Stop being such a baby." She pulled a few more while I grumbled. "There! Finished." Kit sounded satisfied. "Open your eyes."

I almost didn't recognize myself. My eyes seemed larger, more luminous. My eyebrows were expressive dark wings above. Wow, my lips were incredible. A movie star stared back out of the mirror at me.

"See why I had to get my hands on you?" Kit demanded, her hands on my shoulders, face next to mine as we looked in the mirror together. "You're stunning. We just had to get you past your farmer look." She cocked her head to one side, and a sneaky smile crossed her lips. "So, here's the thing. I know you said no to the red dress, but that is absolutely what you must wear tonight. Or else I will refuse to help you anymore. You'll be on your own, understood?"

I glared at her. "You wouldn't!"

She folded her arms across her chest and gave me the hairy eyeball look. "Try me." She glanced at her watch. "We have less than five minutes. Decide quickly!"

I rolled my eyes. "Okay. You win. But don't get used to my being so easy to convince."

She gave a wicked chuckle and dragged me to my closet. "Now the farm girl becomes a princess," she declared, and without further ado, hustled me into that very revealing red dress.

When a knock came on our door a few minutes later, I was wobbling coltishly on three-inch stilettos, barely able to walk. Kit had clipped a pair of diamond earrings onto my earlobes. She'd given up trying to pry my medallion off me, but I'd agreed to replace the leather thong with a delicate filigree gold chain. "Accessories are essential," she said, before I could protest. "Be grateful I'm not making you wear long gloves." She left me teetering on my deeply unfamiliar heels and went to open the door for Archer.

"Come in," she invited, as my brother stood in the doorway and stared at me like he was seeing me for the first time.

"What have you done with Raven?" he demanded faintly when he regained his power of speech.

"That is what your sister looks like when she's dressed like a woman instead of a kid," Kit declared, deeply satisfied.

Archer looked down at the Kitsuné and grinned. "Your work, I take it? Raven is clueless about such stuff."

Kit wrapped her small hands around his elbow and smiled coquettishly up at him. "You can thank me later, tall, dark and handsome," she said. He blushed. "Don't worry. I know you're involved with somebody already. Your sister warned me off. But that doesn't mean we can't have a little fun at everyone else's expense." She turned her attention to me. "Raven, get over here!"

I nearly pitched onto my face with my first step, barely catching myself by grabbing the closet door frame. Archer gasped. Kit burst out laughing. I growled, sending a glare at Kit, and, drawing a deep breath, made my way over to where they stood without further mishap.

"Atta girl," she said approvingly. "Slow is good. Be sure to let those lovely hips of yours sway. You'll drive the boys crazy. I can't wait 'til they all start killing each other over you."

"Not at all bloodthirsty, are you?" I remarked, sending her a wry look. "Let's see if I can get down those stairs without killing myself first."

She laughed with delight. "You will be the belle of the ball tonight. Wait and see."

There was a crowd of people in the great hall below as we began our descent down the stairs... slowly, because of my unfamiliarity with high heels... but Kit was all for that. "The more time they have to stare," she whispered in a deeply satisfied tone. And stare they did, students, sponsors, and faculty alike. I could feel my face heating as we went, and was never so happy to reach the bottom of a set of stairs in my life.

"How nice of you to join us finally," a deep voice drawled next to me.

I looked up at a giant white man, stone-faced, thin-lipped, his salt and pepper hair clipped short.

"You're late," he continued, irritation obvious in his voice. "From now on, you'll receive a demerit for each minute you're late. Come, I will escort you to the dining room." He took my free hand and unceremoniously yanked me away from Archer.

I struggled to maintain my footing as he hustled me along. "You're delaying," he snarled at me.

"Stilettos," I muttered. "You try walking in these things!"

"You will keep a respectful attitude, young lady. Or else." He'd tucked my hand into the crook of his elbow but retained his grip.

"Or else what?" I tried to pull my hand away.

"Or else," he whispered, again. His hand clenched over mine so hard I thought my bones would shatter. The threat was unmistakable.

"You're hurting me!" I gritted through clenched teeth, and tried to pull away again. Not that I succeeded. He just gripped my hand that much harder.

"That was the point, half-breed," he retorted, a self-satisfied smirk on his face.

It made me gasp. Half breed. One pejorative I had not heard since leaving Kestrel over a year ago. I felt the helpless anger it caused all over again. "How dare you!"

"I dare plenty. Something I advise you to be aware of in the next few weeks... if you even last that long." His smile was not the nice sort. "I hold all the power here. Don't you forget that."

We went the rest of the way to the dining hall in silence, where he stopped at the head of the table and waited for the others to arrange themselves along both sides. Then he pulled out the chair directly to his right and unceremoniously thrust me onto it. "You may be seated," he announced dispassionately, and took the chair at the head of the table himself.

Cradling my injured hand in my lap, I glanced around the room. A young man, who looked like a younger version of the bully to my left and was just as large, had seated Kit catty-corner across from me. He kept glancing furtively in my direction. Possibly a son or grandson, I decided. To my right was the Native youth I'd seen at registration, his dark eyes slitted with distrust. The Morrigan sat across the table, several people down from me, with Dub to her left. Further down the table, I saw youthful competitors mixed in with older individuals, probably their sponsors. Perhaps 50 immortals in all. I could not locate Archer, however, and that worried me.

"If you are looking for that mortal you arrived with, he's eating in the kitchens with the rest of the peons." The big man's voice dripped with disdain.

I turned to glare at Mr. I-Hold-All-The-Power with murder in my eyes, then flinched as '*Wait. Our time will come*,' sounded in my brain. The Morrigan. Communicating with me telepathically, like Kellas and I did. She caught my startled look and just barely shook her head. I swallowed my anger and vowed vengeance on the big man.

Freezing him out was currently my best option. I turned so that my shoulder faced him. He made a derisive sound low in his chest. It was obvious that he recognized my stiff posture for what it was. Thankfully, he didn't bother talking to me, mostly addressing the other gods and his son, who was now doing his best to avoid looking at me.

The painfully slow dinner consisted of one tiny plate of elegantly prepared food after another, most of it unidentifiable and barely edible. I picked at my food, not hungry. The whole ostentatious ceremony was incredibly tedious.

"Not enjoying your food?" The boy on my right side had leaned over and spoken directly into my ear.

I drew back a little. "Not really."

"You should eat," he urged in the same undertone. "You might not get fed this well for a while again."

I poked at a molded, jelly-like blob of something on my plate. "Ugh."

"That's aspic, and it's really pretty good. Maybe a few more vegetables than I'd like, but it's tasty. Try it."

I sent him a dubious glance, but picked up a bite-sized piece on my fork and tried it. Hmm. It wasn't awful. I took another bite. From where he sat a few chairs down across the table, Dub noticed I was finally eating and sent me an approving nod.

"Name's Loki," the boy said, offering a half smile. "Not the Norse one, though."

From what I'd heard about the Norse god Loki, that was a good thing. "What sort are you?"

"*Diné*," Loki said, and went back to eating.

So, the Native name for Navajo. "Raven," I whispered. "*Nuxbaaga*. Some say Hidatsa."

He just nodded, and the corner of his mouth twitched. "Figured it was something like that. The cheekbones give it away."

Not much got by that kid. Good to know.

We finished the aspic and leaned back to let the servants clear our plates. "They will require you to dance, you know," Loki drawled, not looking at me.

I sent him a droll look. "Only if they want their toes completely trashed. I'm a terrible dancer."

That brought a wide grin to Loki's face. "Let mine be the first to get trashed then," he said, and fixed me with a golden-eyed stare. "Seriously, this whole thing is a setup. It's less about how skilled you are and more about who you make allies with. We're the only Native people here, other than your currently banished escort." He fixed me with a measured look. "Or is he your lover?"

I blushed bright red. "Heck, no! He's my *brother*!" Gross. Why did people always assume I was in an intimate relationship when I'd never gone beyond kissing?

"Yeah, well, it's easy to get confused," Loki said, looking relieved. "Some of the other guys have brought comfort women with them, so I guessed bringing a plaything along was fair game for girls, too. Well, good! You're unattached. Glad we got that bit clarified. So maybe we can be allies, then?"

Comfort women? Plaything? What the heck was that supposed to mean? Sure, I could guess… and if I was anywhere near correct, the idea that other students had bought prostitutes with them was just plain disgusting. Certainly I hoped that his 'unattached' comment wasn't suggesting I would be open to anything like that, despite the dress I had worn to dinner. There was no chance to respond to his "allies" question, however, as dessert came out at that juncture. I had no trouble eating that, as it was a small slice of incredibly dense, rich chocolate cake with a dab of vanilla ice cream alongside. Yummy.

With the scraping of chair legs across the floor, dinner was abruptly over. Mr. I-Hold-All-The-Power yanked me to my feet and dragged my injured hand over his arm again. There wasn't any point in protesting. He had deliberately hurt me once, and no doubt would do so again without remorse.

After announcing that we were to retire to the ballroom, he pulled me along with him. Everyone else followed along behind. I avoided tripping in the miserable heels, wondering how other women seemed to navigate so easily in such incredibly painful footwear. A string ensemble started playing as we entered the ballroom, and the big man swung me around, a hand on my back, clasping my right hand in his left. "Left hand on my shoulder," he growled. "You know how to dance, don't you?"

"Not especially," I retorted, then gasped as he clamped me tight against his chest with enough force it drove the air from my lungs.

"You'll just have to figure it out as we go, then," he declared, and swung me into a waltz.

Fortunately, Dad had taught me the waltz as a little girl, so I did all right, although handicapped by the ridiculous height of my heels. Any time

I staggered, my partner gripped my waist even harder and set me back on my feet again. His eyes slit in amusement at my awkwardness. "Maybe I should start a ballroom dance class for inept students," he muttered in my ear.

I flinched away. "Don't put yourself out on my account."

"Oh, but my students might appreciate not having to rescue you as often as I've had to," he breathed. "Not that you don't make a lovely armful, but this is hardly dancing, the way you galumph around like a baby giraffe."

"What's your deal, anyway?" I snapped at him. "If you find me so disgusting, why don't you simply leave me alone? Or do you like being a domineering jerk?" I tried to push away, but it was like being bound in iron.

A wolfish snarl parted his lips. "Relax, sweetheart. You're not going free until I let you. I have my reasons, none of which you need to know."

I flushed deep red and turned my face away from his, only to feel his silent laugh a hot breath on my cheek.

"Anger becomes you, my dear. But alas, our dance is done, and there are many others here who would like to make your acquaintance." He'd brought me to the edge of the dance floor and set me on my feet next to Loki. "Your turn, young man. Watch out for your toes. She's dangerous." He laughed, as though he found my being dangerous an absurd concept.

Loki barely looked at the man, instead offering his hand instead of grabbing mine like Mr. I-Hold-All-The-Power had done. I reluctantly placed my hand in his, then flinched when he gripped it. He immediately loosened his hold. "What's wrong?"

"My hand. It feels broken." I pointed at the slender, long bone from my middle knuckle to my wrist. "Cracked, maybe?"

Loki immediately cradled my hand as if it were made of glass. "What happened?"

I grimaced. "The big man happened."

Loki's face darkened with anger. "He's a bully." He paused, considering something, then decided. "We'll make sure not to make things worse for you, then." Wrapping a gentle arm around my waist, he pulled me closer, but not squashed against him like the head dude had done. "I see you're having a little trouble with those sticks you're wearing. I'll try to help you with those, yes?"

I sent him a look of gratitude that had his eyes widening... beautiful, golden-brown eyes rimmed in black... before he shuttered them again into his more customary slits. "Careful who you look at like that," he muttered, and swung me out onto the dance floor.

"How was I looking at you?" I asked, confused.

He avoided my eyes. "Like I mattered to you. Never mind. Just dance, okay?" He grunted in pain as I clumsily stepped on his toes. "Ouch. Concentrate."

I got better at dancing in those heels as the night wore on, cautioning my partners about my hand, which was quickly becoming less of an issue than my aching feet. Some of my partners were shy, barely able to look at me. Others practically devoured me with their eyes. It was a bit much to deal with. OK, so Kit and I were the only girls here, but why all the attention? Kit was being kept as busy as I was, but it seemed she wasn't having to deal with the same intensity of male regard. It was deeply uncomfortable, and it made no sense to me.

I finally refused to dance, sat down, and pulled my shoes off, moaning softly as I massaged toes that felt like they had blisters on top of blisters.

"Last dance," a gruff voice announced, and a hand appeared in front of my face. "This one's mine."

I looked up at the blond giant who had escorted Kit to the table earlier. The one who looked like a carbon copy of Mr. I-Hold-All-The-Power. "I'm done dancing," I told him. "My feet hurt."

"Then I'll hold you off your feet and do all the work," he told me, put his huge hands on either side of my waist, and levered me to my feet like I weighed nothing.

"Let me go!" I pushed against his broad chest. Not that it did me a smidgen of good.

The giant laughed in my face, gray eyes dancing with humor. "Not a chance, sweetheart. You're mine now." He swung me onto the dance floor, my feet not even touching.

I fought, but it was like fighting an immovable object. My breath came in gasps, my heart pounded like a frightened rabbit's. Panicky, I pushed against his chest again, vainly attempting to break free, but his arms just tightened viselike around me.

"Tell me you don't like this, darling," he whispered in my ear. "Why else would you dress like a tramp if you weren't on the prowl?"

Dub's words echoed in my brain... that some women liked this patriarchal domination crap. And how this dress, this ridiculous dress, had made me look like I sought that sort of attention.

Well, if it was a tramp he wanted, maybe I could give him what he thought I was. I slid my hands up his chest into his hair and fisted them in his curls— flinching a little as my right hand protested. Then I purred: "Oh, so you're a lover, are you? Think you're man enough for me?"

His eyes widened in surprise, then narrowed again, a smile twisting the corners of his mouth up. "Oh, I am that and more, my lovely."

"You think so, huh?" I untangled my hands from his hair and slowly glided them down his neck to where his neck met his shoulders, as he bent his face close, mere inches from my own.

"I'm more than man enough for you, sweetheart," he whispered against my mouth. "And I'll prove it to you tonight."

"Really?" I whispered back, then, to distract him from what I was doing with my hands, I suppressed my gag reflex and kissed the jerk. My thumbs found the carotid sinus on either side of the base of his thick neck—and I pushed down hard. I held that kiss for five long, miserable seconds, waiting for the "off switch" Dad had taught me to kick in. I fell on top of the giant as he collapsed senseless to the floor, then scrambled to my feet, ignoring the cries of surprise around me. Gathering my long skirts in both hands, I ran barefoot from the ballroom.

Ten

By the time Archer and Kit came charging into my room, I'd stripped off the offending red dress, mashed it into a ball and thrown it in a corner. They found me collapsed in a heap in the middle of my closet, a blanket wrapped around my shivering body.

"Hey, hey, none of that now, sis." Archer knelt next to me and pulled me into his arms, palming my head against his chest and rocking me.

I dug my fingers into his dress shirt and clung to him like I was drowning, sobbing uncontrollably.

"Shh, shh... it'll be fine. Deep breaths, kid. You've got this." It took some time, but I finally regained a little self-control and let go of my death grip on his shirt. "Better some?" he asked.

I nodded shakily.

"Want to tell me what happened?" he asked gently.

I looked up into his dark eyes. "You didn't see it?"

Archer's lips thinned. "They banished me to the kitchens. Your roommate came and got me."

Kit knelt next to me. "I didn't know what else to do. You were so freaked out."

"So... what happened?" Archer demanded again.

"You mean after she dropped The Barbarian on his ass, or before?" Kit snorted. "Short version: It was a feeding frenzy, and your sister was the dish du jour." She gave me a concerned look. "I'm so sorry; I did not know that would happen."

"Oh, didn't you!" a new voice cut in from the doorway. I looked up; It was the Diné boy, Loki. A furious scowl furrowed between his heavy black eyebrows. "Why did you gaudy her like a call girl and send her into the lion's den if you didn't want to stir up trouble, eh, vixen?" He came to the doorway of the closet. "You knew exactly what would happen, Kitsuné. What I'd like to know is why you'd betray another woman like that." He looked at me, a concerned expression on his face. "I brought your shoes," he said, and tossed them to one side.

Kit jumped to her feet, advancing on him aggressively. "I didn't betray anyone, dog boy! What are you doing in here? Get out of our room!"

"Don't call me that!" he growled.

"Dog boy!" she snarled back.

Archer let me go and scrambled to his feet. "Hey! You two want to fight, take it outside." The two moved away from each other, but neither offered to leave.

I struggled to get to my feet, hampered by the blanket I was wrapped up in, unaware that it had slipped off one bare shoulder. "Loki, what are you saying?"

The Diné boy looked at me and then away just as quickly. "Your blanket," he choked.

I glanced down. The blanket had fallen far enough that it bared one breast, scantily clad in a barely-there pushup bra. I hastily snatched it back up over my shoulder, my face hot with embarrassment. "Loki, what are you suggesting Kit did?"

"She made you an object to distract attention from herself." His expression was pained. "She deliberately made you the target of tonight's over-the-top machismo."

"I did not!" Kit protested. "Raven needed help to get ready. I helped her."

"Oh, is that what you call it?" Loki was unimpressed.

I remained confused by Loki's attitude toward Kit. "She did, Loki. Help me, that is. I've never used makeup before... well, lip gloss, but that hardly counts, right? And I know nothing about fashion." All I knew for sure was that I didn't want them fighting over this. I needed allies, and so far, they and Archer were all I had.

Loki shoved his hands into the pockets of his dress pants and scowled at the floor. "The fox girl is not worthy of your trust," he insisted.

"Oh, and you are, coyote? Trickster?" Kit spat.

"Look who's calling the kettle black," he snarled back.

Archer made a motion as if he were ready to toss them both out of the room. I caught his eye and shook my head. "Can we just calm down and figure this out?" I asked deliberately, pushing between the two combatants. "Just looking for a little clarity here. Come on, let's go where we can sit down at least. My feet are trashed."

Kit stormed out of my closet and flung herself onto the middle of her bed, arms crossed defiantly across her middle. Archer and I sat side by side on the edge of my bed, his arm around my shoulders. Loki sprawled on my dressing table chair, legs stretched out, arms crossed over his chest, with his customary scowl firmly in place.

"Do you two have a history I should know about?" I asked. "Because it might shed some light on why you seem to hate each other already."

"Kitsuné fox goddesses and Coyote gods don't get along, period," Kit stated, glaring at Loki, who ignored her.

I looked between the two of them. "Have you even met before?"

"Before tonight, you mean?" Loki asked, and at my nod: "Barely."

"Yes!" exclaimed Kit hotly, her face going pink. "Yes, we have, and he was a total jerk then, too!"

"But why continue a traditional hatred? When it might not be in your best interests in the long run?" I asked softly. "Can you find a way to put aside your differences for now?"

Loki glanced at me, and then away. "After what she did to you, you would defend her?"

"I did nothing to her!" Kit snapped.

"Quit it!" I was tiring of their go-nowhere squabbling. "My sponsor told me to make a big impression. That horrible dress did the job, not that I enjoyed the kind of attention it attracted, but apparently my sponsor felt it was necessary. Maybe in time I'll understand why." I blew out a frustrated breath and softened my tone. "You both have been very kind to me. I need friends like you here. The gods know we need all the help we can get, because after tonight, I'm realizing the situation at this academy is not all it seems. Can you move past this—garbage history—and we all join forces? Because you know the others will, and allies would be good to have." Archer briefly tightened his arm around my shoulders. He approved. "So, what will it be?" I demanded. "Can I count on you both?"

Loki raised his head and put that golden gaze on me. "You can count on me."

I looked at Kit and was surprised to see fear flash across her lovely face, fear she quickly concealed when she saw me looking. "Of course," she sniffed. "Just... don't expect him and me to be besties while we're guarding each other's backs."

Loki growled low in his chest. "Besties? Ha! Fat chance of that happening! But I'm willing to ally with you both."

Looked like this was as good as I was going to get at this point. "Great, we'll leave it at that, then," I said lightly. "If you are both okay with this, we should probably all go get some sleep."

Kit glanced at her watch. "Especially since it is past midnight, and the wake-up call is at 5 a.m."

~

During the night, I dreamed. I moved like a ghost through tunnels of stone, past cages that held wild animals that paced the confines of their prisons: tigers and lions, mostly, but a few smaller cats: ocelots, jaguars. Farther on, the cages became prison cells, stone on all sides except the one facing the hall, that side secured by iron bars. Within the cells, men lay on cots, or leaned on the bars of their prison, gazing out with haunted eyes... men whose scarred bodies were often bloody, with dirty bandages poorly applied to their wounds. I moved onward until I could hear voices, the occasional crack of a whip. Easing around a last bend in the corridor, I saw Kellas hanging from his arms, chained against a wall, dark head slumped over his chest. Before him stood Erin, a short whip in her right hand. The wooden handle had multiple leather strips attached.

"Ready to swear allegiance to me yet?" she was demanding. Kellas said nothing. I wasn't even sure he was conscious. She lashed the whip against his abdomen, eliciting a groan. "Answer me!" she shrieked. When he didn't, she slashed her whip at him again, cursing. This time he didn't even groan, just hung from his bonds, unmoving.

"My dear lady, stop. With more of this, he will be unfit to fight on the morrow. He's healing much more slowly these days, and we've already lost the ability to replicate the girl's face on others." An olive-skinned man in the garb of a centurion stepped out of the shadows and laid a hand on Erin's arm. "We stand to win far more if he's ready to fight. Come on, my lovely, let us retire to our bed."

"Let him hang there all night then," Erin said, letting the man take the whip from her hands.

"Why not let the physicians look after him? He's worth too much to us in one piece," the Centurion urged.

Erin hesitated. "Only because you make a good argument for it," she responded, and made an imperious gesture to someone outside of my view. "Take him to the infirmary. Tell the medicus to make sure he can fight tomorrow or I will have their heads."

They left, and two guards came into view, released Kellas from his bonds, then dragged him away. I followed them to a room that stank like death, with a single table at its center. The guards lifted Kellas' limp form onto the table and stepped back to stand on either side of the door. I went to him, leaned over him, laid a hand gently on his battered face.

He didn't respond, so I took time to examine his wounds. As before, the cuts laid open on his body were closing, healing before my eyes... but as the centurion had said, far more slowly than before, as if his ability to heal was wearing thin.

"Brannaugh..." it came out in a sigh so soft I almost didn't hear it.

"Kellas!" I clasped his face between my hands. "I'm here. Tell me what to do, I'll do it."

A single tear pooled in the corner of one closed eye. "Brannaugh..."

~

Someone was shaking me violently. "Raven! Wake up! You're dreaming! Wake up!"

I awakened with a gasping sob. Kit was leaning over me, small hands on my shoulders gripping me with unnatural strength. "Finally! Sheesh. Do you have any idea how hard you sleep? What were you dreaming about, anyway? Who is this 'Kellas' you keep calling for?"

I pushed against her lower arms with my own, and she released me so I could sit up. "Nightmare," I muttered and rubbed my face, trying to rid myself of the horror I had just witnessed. Was it merely a nightmare or had I dream-walked? Hard for me to tell sometimes. It had felt authentic enough. My face was wet with tears, too.

"You were moaning and thrashing about like you were fighting demons," Kit said. She slid off my bed and went back to her own.

"Yeah, well, close enough." I sent her an apologetic half-smile. "Sorry I messed up your sleep."

She shrugged. "Small matter. I wasn't sleeping all that well to begin with, and it's almost time to get up as it is. I've got first dibs on the shower."

I went to my closet while she was in the bath, determined to make a full accounting of what was in it, and then have a bit of a talk with the Morrigan and Dub about the uselessness of the clothing they'd saddled me with. When I snapped on the light, however, it was to find a vastly different assortment of garments than what had been hanging there before. Yes, there were still evening gowns, but they were far fewer of them and nowhere near as daring as the red dress had been. Instead, there was more workout clothing and casual wear: a stack of blue jeans in various colors, a denim jacket, a few sweaters, T-shirts. Also (thank the gods...and more than likely the Morrigan!) underwear that wouldn't cut me in half up the middle like last night's thong had. Phew.

As the itinerary we'd been given at registration stated we would not be training on our first day, I hurried into a blue boat neck tee over a modest running bra, a pair of boyfriend jeans that felt like an old friend, and white

Converse sneakers over white ankle socks. By the time Kit exited the shower, I was in front of my dressing table, pulling my hair into a single French braid.

She fixed me with a wry smile. "More your usual style, eh?" She disappeared into her closet, emerging after a little while dressed in a far more fashionable athleisure wear ensemble than mine: a closely fitted short sleeved jersey shirt that just skimmed the top of her wide banded black pants. White stripes down the outside of her sleeves and pant legs were the only relief to the all-black outfit. She looked stunning.

"Got me beat!" I told her, admiring.

"We'll work on your signature style," she promised.

"Nah. This is me."

"Your choice!" She scoffed, then ran a brush through her long black hair, left it loose and flowing, and added just a touch of makeup to her eyes. "Ready?"

I sighed. "As I'll ever be," and stood up.

"Sure you don't want to do up your face a bit? It's obvious you've been crying."

I glanced at my face in the mirror. "Not much I can do for the bloodshot, puffy-eyed look, is there? They'll have to get used to me as I really am." I headed for the door.

Loki was at the door, one hand raised, ready to knock when I opened the door. His eyes widened as he saw me and Kit, and he immediately stuffed both hands into his jeans pockets. "Morning, ladies. I thought I might walk you down to breakfast?"

Kit made a dismissive huff and pushed past us out onto the balcony, headed for the stairs.

I gave Loki an apologetic grin and shrugged. "Maybe she's not a morning person? Breakfast sounds great, though."

His answering smile was small. Kit's snub obviously rankled.

"Give her time," I suggested, and tipped my head toward the stairs. "Shall we?"

Breakfast was in a different room from the fancy hall we'd had our meal in the night before. Smaller, more intimate, with small tables scattered about. On a long table set up against the wall, food was already waiting in steam trays. Not all that different from a breakfast buffet at a quality hotel, although far more elaborate. I piled my plate high with bacon, eggs, and a toasted sesame seed bagel liberally spread with cream cheese, then took it to where Kit already sat with a small bowl of what looked like oatmeal. Instant, no sugar, skim milk. Gross. Something like Mom would serve herself.

She looked at my own loaded plate with something like envy. "How can you eat like that and not gain weight?" she demanded.

"Got a tapeworm, apparently," I joked.

She looked puzzled. "A tapeworm?"

I took a bite of my bagel and nodded. "A parasite in the gut that keeps you from gaining weight."

She scowled. "Please don't talk with your mouth full. It's rude. A parasite, though? Can I get one?"

I snorted inelegantly and swallowed my bite. "I don't have an actual tapeworm. It's not something you want either. It's just something my dad says when I'm eating a lot."

Loki came over then, his tray loaded with breakfast things. "May I join you?"

Kit's answer was a surly "No."

"Sure!" I countered and sent Kit a frowny look. "Now who's being rude?"

She scowled. "Fine." But it sure didn't sound like she thought it was fine.

I smiled up at Loki as he hesitated and shoved a chair out with one foot. "Don't mind her. Apparently, my roommate is a grouch in the morning. Take the weight off."

Loki and I made small talk over our food as Kit silently ate her miserable little breakfast. She finished before us and got up to leave, but I hooked my foot under the front rung of her chair to stop her. "What's the hurry?" I glance at the clock on the wall over the buffet table. "We have a few minutes before we're due at assembly." That detail had been on the schedule we'd gotten at registration.

Her eyes widened as she looked behind me, and she abruptly sat down. That was odd, not the sort of reaction I'd expected, especially as a sweet smile then bloomed across her face. "Why, good morning!" she greeted someone who had walked up behind me. She freed her chair from my toes and rose gracefully to her feet, extending one slim hand.

"So much for not being a morning person," I heard Loki's wry comment as I twisted in my chair and looked up at a tall young Asian man, his muscular chest encased in a skintight black T-shirt. He had a thin mustache above beautiful full lips, a bit of scruff along a firm jaw. Dark eyes held a hint of blue and green... very unusual. And—he was gorgeous. Wow!

He took Kit's hand and bowed over it; very formal, very correct. I glanced at Loki in time to see his disgruntled look, then back at the Asian guy. Sadly, I could not stand as Kit had, because said gorgeous guy was partially blocking my chair.

"Please do not get up on my account," he said, his voice as cultured as he looked. "I merely came over to make your acquaintance."

Loki grunted at that, his annoyance loud and clear.

"I'm Yaeko Kitsuné," Kit told him, gracefully reseating herself. "My friends call me Kit."

He smiled and executed another graceful bow. "Hàorán Qīnglóng. I do not have a nickname." He looked at Loki. "Good morning, roommate. We've yet to exchange names. You came in a little late yesterday evening."

"Loki," the coyote god said grumpily, and fell silent.

Hàorán inclined his head, as though Loki's less than polite manner was perfectly acceptable. "And you need no introduction," he addressed me, stepping to one side so that I no longer had to crane my neck to see him. "My father told me about you."

Kit and I exchanged startled glances. "He... has?" I asked.

"Yes! I would have thought... ah. Language barrier. Yes. *Qīnglóng* means 'Blue Dragon.' Father tells me you met in another dimension recently. Something about being one of your... nightmares?" His voice lifted slightly in confused surprise.

All color must have drained from my face, and I jumped to my feet. "Shen Long is your father?" And yes, we had met in Tír na nÓg, when I had called all my most feared nightmares down on the Celtic Underworld in one fabulously fantastic mistake. I had cleaned up my mess, but the Blue Dragon was one that truly had not deserved to be feared. Scary, yes, and downright dangerous, but not anything to fear. Unless you were in his bad books. Like Cerridwen. She'd done her best to murder him.

Hàorán bowed again. "Indeed. My father. Your singing ability impressed him."

Huh.

He went on. "He hopes to hear you sing again. Since he is an instructor here, we hope we can arrange it."

I bit my lower lip and nodded, stunned silent. Only, wasn't this fight school? How much singing and dancing would be required, anyway?

Hàorán looked up at the clock and jerked his chin down in a decisive nod. "It is time we proceeded to the parade ground. Shall we go together?" He extended an arm to Kit, which she took without an ounce of hesitation, and they started off. Loki and I exchanged raised-eyebrows looks and followed.

The parade grounds were in a central area surrounded on three sides by the stone castle of the fight school. It was a large, flat space covered with closely cropped grass. Scattered around were various odd bits of construction. One, a climbing wall, was familiar, but I did not recognize the purpose of the others. Students were gathering in front of a raised platform where a group of older men were standing. We went over to join them. Another group, mostly older men, waited to one side. The Morrigan and another woman who looked strikingly like Kit were there as well. Possibly the sponsors.

The large man who'd escorted me to dinner stepped forward and raised his hands for silence. "Good morning, fellow instructors, sponsors, and new students. Welcome to the 500th year of fight school training for gods and demigods. We have a long and illustrious history…" On and on he droned until I thought I would fall asleep from the monotony of it all.

A slight motion caught my eye. Archer was at my elbow, giving it a squeeze. He whispered in my ear. "I can't stay. The Morrigan sent me to give you this." He shoved a note into my hand and left silently. I tuned out Mr. I-Hold-All-The-Power (I would miss nothing important anyway!) and surreptitiously opened the Morrigan's note.

"You are to tell the others that I am your sponsor. Feign ignorance of Dub or Dian. They are instructors and technically may sponsor no one, not that this has stopped a couple of the other instructors. Remember that you are in your waning stage as the moon phase approaches darkness. They will believe you are weak because you will increasingly become so until after the moon waxes again. Plan accordingly. Do not tell anyone about your magic until you have met your teammates, then tell only them. Fraegarthach is unavailable to you in sword form, say nothing about it to anyone, but they are unaware of its lute form's effectiveness as a weapon. The dragon's son is an ally; use him. The same goes for the coyote. Be careful around the

fox... she is like her mother, seemingly a friend at one moment and a foe at another, but once she's convinced you are worthy of her trust, she will be an ally forever. Do not openly defy the big man; avoid him if you can. He's dangerous. When asked what your skill set is, tell them you are a singer, nothing more. It's best they under-estimate you, see you only as they first regarded you, just a pretty girl in a red dress, not powerful enough to be a threat. They will not realize your singing ability is in fact an impressive weapon. They will pretend that your training here is fair to all. It is anything but. Stay alert. Never let down your guard."

I folded the note, shoved it deep into my jeans pocket, and returned my gaze to the platform before us. The big man had wrapped up his boring speech and was finally getting down to the real deal.

"There are 20 of you in this class. We have instructors in five disciplines: wrestling, mixed martial arts, archery, swordsmanship, and equestrian skills. We expect you to improve your overall fitness with a variety of workouts. You will be in groups of four. Your instructors have selected leaders to oversee each group. State one good reason for your selection. The leaders will make their choices accordingly."

By my elbow, Loki groaned. "High school sports teams all over again. Gods."

All too well acquainted with the system of the "in" kids being selected first, I had always been one of the "weirdos" left until sorted onto a team by default, the kid no one wanted. But this time, we all had to state why we were "special." Cringe!

The big man's son stepped forward first. "As a wrestler, I have never lost a bout." He stepped back.

The Black boy I'd seen at registration stepped forward. "My skill with a broadsword is unparalleled."

The red-haired kid: "I hold black belts in jujitsu, Tae Kwon Do, and aikido."

So it went down the line until it was Hàorán's turn. "I compete internationally in all forms of mixed martial arts and swordplay. My specialty is the *jiàn*."

Loki grunted. "Figures he'd be skilled with a gentleman's sword."

Kit's turn. "I'm clever and quick," she said, and stepped back into line. I heard snickers, barely suppressed.

Loki's turn. "I can outfox the fox," he declared, scowling. More laughter, louder this time. Someone clapped.

I hesitated until someone mocked. "What can the other girl do besides step all over her dance partner's feet?"

My face must have turned a deep shade of red. Loki gave me an encouraging nudge with one elbow. "Just spit something out. Nobody cares about us. We're just the slummers they hope to wipe their fancy blades on."

The Morrigan wanted me to seem undangerous. Not that I felt in the least bit dangerous, at least not in comparison to the abilities the others had announced. I took a deep breath and took the Morrigan's advice. "I'm a singer."

My announcement was greeted with laughter and catcalls. "How is singing going to save your ass on the battlefield?" one kid yelled. "Hopefully she's a better singer than she is a dancer," someone else jeered, and that set the bunch of them off. My face grew hot, and I wished I could just sink into the ground.

A large bird landed on my shoulder, shaking her wings out as she settled herself. '*Well done, my champion. They will rue the day they underestimated you.*'

"Umm. Why do you have a bird on your shoulder?" Kit was leaning forward, looking at me and the Morrigan with wide eyes.

"She's my familiar," I lied, working hard to keep a straight face.

"Your familiar?" Kit was stunned. "Does that mean you're a witch?"

"I've been called that a time or two, though not usually nicely. So, I guess, maybe?"

Loki was snickering. From the look on his face, he knew my feathered friend was not your run-of-the-mill raven. A muscle twitched in Hàorán's cheek, the only sign he'd been paying attention to our little back and forth. Then the leaders were called forward: the Barbarian, also known as Leonidas; the Black boy, named Morien; and Hàorán, plus two others whose names I did not catch, and team selection began. I ducked my head and tuned out, knowing where I stood in the pecking order... only to be startled out of it.

"I call Raven Callahan," Hàorán said clearly. He stood at parade rest, chin up, looking straight ahead, his face an unreadable mask. Loki chuckled and gave me a shove. "Reckon he likes singers," he muttered in my ear. I hesitated until Hàorán turned his head and looked right at me, a slight frown on his face. I stumbled forward and stepped in behind him. There was muttering going up and down the line, mostly disbelief, but a few less-than-savory suggestions about how Hàorán was looking for a little "action." He did not twitch a muscle, although I was certain his hearing was every bit as good as mine. Still perched on my shoulder, the Morrigan merely chuckled to herself.

The other leaders made their first choices: all men. When it was Hàorán's turn again, he chose Kit. That brought an even louder burst of derogatory comments until Shen Long stepped forward and sternly warned everyone to silence.

Yet another round. Loki was now standing separately from the remaining youths.

"Loki." Hàorán's voice was determined. I heard Kit groan softly. The other leaders greeted his choice with astonishment, as the other unchosen all seemed like stronger competitors. Hàorán's team appeared weak compared to the others. However, the raven, still perched on my shoulder, was chortling in glee. What role had the Death goddess played in this?

As the finished groups pulled away from each other, Hàorán finally allowed himself to relax, the ghost of a smile flitting across his face. Perhaps a touch of relief as well? It was hard to tell with someone who carefully cultivated his ability to maintain a stone-face. "I have my dream team," he told us. "Fortune has smiled at me today."

"You're kidding, right?" Loki asked, his dark eyes narrowed in suspicion. "Of the four of us, you and I are the only ones who have any hand-to-hand fighting experience."

I wasn't about to correct him... I had never been all that successful at fighting.

Kit looked worried. Of all of us, she was the smallest: slender-boned and fragile-looking.

"Appearances can be deceiving. I happen to know each of you has a unique and invaluable skill set." Hàorán led us toward a small shed on one side of the field. "This morning is merely introductory. We meet each instructor who will explain his field of expertise, maybe do a short demonstration with a helper. Then we move to the next, and so on. Let's start with my father." He pointed at the Dragon Lord waiting by the shed, an assortment of blades laid out on a blanket nearby. "He will instruct us in sword play, daggers, and the like."

Oh, lovely. Right off the bat, I had to face the one instructor to whom I owed an apology. But Shen Long seemed not to pay any attention to me, instead dropping a fond hand on Hàorán's shoulder and congratulating him on his team picks. Then he turned to the rest of us. "Who here has any experience with a sword?" he asked.

Loki shook his head. "Knives only," he admitted.

Kit volunteered she knew her way around a dagger. From the dangerous glitter that entered her eyes when she said that, I had to wonder what she was hiding.

I shrugged. "I've had some instruction."

Shen Long gave me an appraising look. "As you probably already know, we don't allow magical weapons here. You will practice with a blunted sword like the others."

Eleven

"What magical weapon?" Loki demanded immediately, eyeing me with suspicion.

I said nothing. The Morrigan had specifically warned me not to say anything about Fraegarthach. The coyote was astute, though, quick to size up a situation and ask pertinent questions. I wondered if Hàorán's choices for teammates had been more than a little canny. Probably directed by someone in a position to know more about the strengths and weaknesses of various students. Like his father. Good old nepotism at work. No doubt the Morrigan and Dub had put in their oar as well. I'd seen how the three of them had seemed extra chummy at the welcome banquet.

I ignored Loki's question and nodded to the Dragon Lord. "Understood." The Morrigan's warning about things not being exactly fair resonated in my head. Fraegarthach and I likely were more than a match for anyone else here. Not that it was anything I could claim credit for. My sword more than made up for my shortcomings in the skill department. But it would be great to gain more ability of my own. I just wasn't sure I'd measure up. Everyone else seemed like they'd had years of training. Except maybe Kit. Her comment about daggers had me concerned. I still wasn't sure what her skill set was.

Shen Long explained the selection of weapons he expected us to become familiar with and outlined how he intended to instruct us over the coming year. Then it was time to move on to the next group.

Unfortunately, Mr. I-Hold-All-The-Power led it. At least I learned an easier name to call him by: Antaeus, son of the Greek sea god Poseidon and earth goddess Gaea. He ensured we knew this, as if expecting us to be impressed. I was going to have to brush up on my pantheons and all their gods if I was to keep up. He was as large a man as Dian, but lacked Dian's easy-going pleasantness. That sounds like an odd thing to say about the God of Violence, but it was the truth.

Antaeus ignored Kit and me, instead addressing Hàorán and Loki as though they were the only ones he intended to instruct in the varied ways to wrestle. This did not sit especially well, and I would have spoken up if it hadn't been for the Morrigan pecking my cheek hard enough to draw blood. *Hush!* she warned as I hissed in pain.

We moved on.

Dian was instructing mixed martial arts, or, as he explained it, ways to take your opponent apart with just your bare hands. He was so jolly about it, one could almost lose sight of the fact that he was explaining how to hurt people in the most exquisitely violent manner. I walked away after his demonstration, shuddering. Kit didn't seem in much better shape than I, and no wonder. She was even less of a physical threat to the men gathered here than I was. Or at least she seemed to be. That dagger comment, though...

Dub was instructing archery, not that this was a particular surprise. His favorite way to deliver his poison was with bow and arrow. He made a point of introducing Archer as his teaching assistant. Archer stood quietly to one side as Dub explained what we were going to be doing, including shooting from horseback. At full gallop. At multiple targets. Sheesh. At least I knew how to ride a horse, and the thought of being on horseback didn't appear to concern either Loki or Hàorán. Poor Kit looked aghast at the idea.

The last area of instruction was horsemanship, which was being taught by the Greek twins Castor and Pollux. Instead of ignoring Kit and me as Antaeus had done, the twins seemed to direct all their attention at us, virtually ignoring the guys. It was creepy. Both gods were overly familiar, repeatedly resting their hands on our shoulders or attempting to loop arms around our waists. Kit and I avoided the worst of their caresses by sticking close to our teammates.

Lunchtime finally arrived, and we filed past a table heaped high with bag lunches and bottled water. Grabbing our share, we headed for the closest patch of shade we could find. The noonday sun was getting intense. I regretted having chosen jeans.

"That was unpleasant. I hope those two don't paw us like that every day," Kit fretted as we settled onto the grass.

"I'll ask my father to talk to them," Hàorán assured us. "You shouldn't have to deal with harassment."

"What's on tap for the afternoon?" Loki asked as we worked our way through elaborate meat sandwiches, a generous handful of nuts and an apple each.

"I'm told they will assess our physical fitness," Hàorán said. "Speed work, endurance, weightlifting, horsemanship, quickness… you get the idea. Anything they can think of, they plan to throw at us. It's finding out where our weak spots are."

And I was wearing blue jeans. Gods.

Kit moaned and flopped back onto the grass, gazing at the sky. "I'm dead," she declared.

"I seriously doubt that," Loki said. "Sure, you're not a guy, but you have strengths of your own."

"And why are you being nice to me now, dog boy?" she snipped.

Loki scowled. "Good question." He turned his back on her. "Ruddy vixen," I heard him mutter, too low for Kit to hear.

"Done?" Hàorán rolled to his feet in one smooth motion and extended a hand to assist Kit. I clambered up with my usual coltish clumsiness, while Loki gained his feet with the coiled grace of his coyote heritage.

We joined the others on an oval-shaped running track where a stern-looking blond woman dressed in scanty running clothing assigned lanes for each team. I doubted she had an ounce of fat on her. "You will take turns running a relay as a team, handing off the baton to the next member of your team until all have finished. I will note your individual times for the quarter mile, but this is also an assessment of how you work together as a team. Questions?"

"Yeah," Loki drawled. "Do we have to stay in our designated lanes, or can we switch?"

"After the first turn, you may change lanes," she answered. "Good question. Any others?"

"What if you drop the baton?" Leonidas asked with a smirk.

"Then you pick it up," the woman stated, a small frown of annoyance furrowing her forehead. "I advise you not to drop it, however, as it will cost you time. Any more questions? No? Good. Decide your running order and line up, please."

Hàorán pulled us to one side. "Do any of you know how fast you are in the 400?" We answered his question with shrugs and head shakes. "OK, so we're going to wing it. Kit, you go first. I'll go next, Raven, you're third, and Loki, you're our best hope. Ready?"

We were not the fastest team, but we did okay. I was the least fleet of our group, although I tried my best. Kit and Loki were among the fastest of the entire class, a detail that I saw the other students noting with annoyance. Hàorán was not far behind them. I was the snail that slowed our overall performance down. My jeans did not help. Live and learn, I guess. If my teammates minded I was a slug, they didn't let on.

When it came time to ride horses, Kit was too terrified to get on what seemed an otherwise placid pony. When it was my turn to mount up, the handler brought me a horse that had a wild look, the whites of its eyes showing. I spoke to him softly, trying to communicate that I was not to be feared. When the handler got impatient with my "stalling" (as he called it) I gathered the reins and stepped on. It was like straddling a powder keg. The tension in that horse could have fueled a volcano.

Our instructions were simple. "You will ride to that far post, go around it and return," Castor told us. "Do whatever gait you are comfortable with. We will assess your level of expertise no matter how fast you go."

My mount had other ideas. The minute the others started, my horse was crow-hopping under me. The only way to handle vertical energy was to substitute horizontal energy. Yelling "go-go-go!" I thumped my legs against his ribs as though they were a drum, and he took off at a dead run. A barrel racer had nothing on that horse's acceleration rate. I bent over his neck, clinging to the saddle horn in a death grip, pushing the reins forward. The pole we were to navigate around came up fast. I dragged the reins against his neck, leaning in toward the pole. Felt it hit my shoulder, hard, and then we were speeding back the way we came, approaching the watching crowd at a dizzying rate of speed. They must have realized the peril they were in, because there was a stampede in either direction to get out of my way. Not that I was about to let anyone get plowed over. I sat down in the back of the saddle, slammed my feet down hard in the stirrups and briefly shortened the reins... and the horse dropped its butt nearly to the ground, planting all four feet and sliding to a halt. I dismounted, breathing hard, and slapped my mount on its sweaty neck. "Nice, dude," I muttered. The horse snorted like it had not only understood but had appreciated my wild ride.

Its handler came up and snatched the reins out of my hands. "You're a crazy witch, you know that?"

Wow. Language, jerk! I got right up in the groom's face. "You want a fancy riding demonstration next time? Give me a horse that hasn't been driven crazy from being cooped up too long." I stalked away from him, rubbing my shoulder where it had smacked the pole. Bruised for sure.

My teammates joined me, having finished with their much more sedate rides. I was the only one handed a fire-breathing dragon. "Is it just me, or does anyone else think they gave you a dangerous horse on purpose?" Loki asked, his usual scowl firmly in place.

"The horse wasn't the problem," I assured him. "The way they managed him is. One should never leave a horse with that much fire in a stall for very long." Still rubbing my shoulder, I asked, "What's next?"

Next was weightlifting. I did my best, but the shoulder injury didn't help my performance. Quickness followed that, and my teammates excelled. I was so-so. Endurance was last. By then, we were all teetering on the brink of exhaustion.

The class set off as a group, around the track in endless loops. The sun was relentless, sucking moisture out of every pore. They didn't give us water, either. I was getting dreadfully dry. One by one, people started dropping out, flopping onto the grass in the middle of the track and laying prone, chests heaving. When assistants started distributing water to the drop-outs, the rate of attrition spiked. However, Loki and Kit trotted alongside each other like the canines they drew their lineage from, seemingly tireless. My shoulder was aching miserably. I wanted to rub it continually... not a good way to run. Hàorán had fallen in next to me, preferring to match my pace than push faster. "Won't anybody beat those two," he observed. "The question is if they will concede to one another or if they will have to declare a draw."

"They'll run each other into the ground rather than concede, I think," I said. "The tension between those two is tight as a bowstring."

"Hmm." Sounded like he agreed. "I'm willing to quit if you are."

Not that his offer registered. I was far too hot, and my mind was blurring. Abruptly, I was straddling two realities: endlessly circling the track in one, and thrust into the sand arena of the Roman Colosseum in the other. Kellas was battling several armor-clad men at once, his face a rictus of anger and suffering. Blood ran down his almost useless left leg as he balanced precariously on his right and fought three attackers at once. He'd backed up to a wall so that they could not get behind him, but it was taking everything he had to keep them at bay.

"Hey, you!" I yelled, jumping up and down and waving my arms, trying to distract Kellas' attackers. Couldn't do much else—I was unarmed, just a kid in street clothes, unable to draw Fraegarthach because I was barely there. The distraction worked, though. Two of the men turned, startled out of their focus. Kellas took advantage, slashing the attacker who hadn't turned away across his face, and then stabbing one of the distracted guys in the back. The third man spun to meet Kellas' attack.

That was all I saw, as my back suddenly felt ripped to pieces. I screamed and pitched forward onto the track/sand of the arena, still straddling realities. My back was on fire. Hàorán was exclaiming in horror. Dimly, I could hear shouts as people realized something was happening. Then something struck me again. I felt as if knives had ripped me apart.

"Zhèlǐ dàodǐ fāshēngle shénme!" I heard Hàorán yell as I curled into a ball, sobbing. He was shaking me. "Come back, come back, you can't stay in between!"

Somewhere, I could hear Kellas yelling. Then his feet were on either side of my body and I heard the clanging of steel on steel as Kellas fought off my attacker. Blood was coursing down his injured leg, splattering the ground with red gore inches from my face.

Then, Loki and Kit were there. "She's stuck between dimensions. We need to pull her back!" Hàorán's voice.

"Act first and apologize later," Loki growled, and he slapped my face hard once, then again. I felt my lip split and tasted the sharp iron tang of blood. Then he hit me a third time, this time with his fist... and everything went black.

I woke up in the infirmary, face down on an operating table, while doctors worked to stitch the wounds on my back together. Someone warned that I had awakened and slipped an anesthesia mask over my mouth and nose. Everything went dark again.

When I finally clawed my way back to consciousness, I was face down on my bed. Voices were talking around me. Gradually I could pick out the Morrigan's voice from the murmuring, then Dub's. My teammates. Archer. I twitched, trying to pull myself out of the black void further.

"Raven?" It was Kit, bending low, her face within inches of mine.

I groaned, tried to push myself up on my elbows, and instantly regretted the motion when my back protested loudly. My mouth felt like cotton wool. And the thirst? "Gods..." My voice was unrecognizable gravel. "Water?"

Archer was there immediately, holding a bottle with a straw to my lips. I sucked in gratefully. "Better?" he asked. I managed a nod and slumped back onto the mattress. He briefly laid a reassuring hand on my cheek.

"OK all, now you've confirmed she's alive, go back to your rooms. Give her space to recover or you'll be continuing as a threesome." Dub's voice, needlessly strident. Why he was here? Weren't we supposed to pretend we didn't know each other?

"This is my room," Kit protested.

"Go visit the boys." Dub wasn't having her excuses, apparently. "It's nearly mealtime, anyway. Go together. Guard each other's back. And tell the others nothing, do you hear me? Nothing!"

Muttering protests, my teammates and Archer filed out of the room. I heard the door close quietly behind them. The bed sank as the Morrigan sat next to me.

"What happened?" she demanded. "Where did you go?"

I groaned. "It was like I was in two places at once... on the track and with Kellas in the Colosseum. Then I hurt."

"Understatement." Dub had crouched down next to the bed so I could see him without moving. As moving anything hurt like the dickens, I appreciated the gesture. "A large cat apparently clawed you. Twice. Your back is a mess. It took the school doctors an hour to stitch you back up." He reached up and gently touched the corner of my left eye. I winced. "You have a shiner there. Loki hits hard."

"'Act first and apologize later.'" Talking hurt too; I had a fat lip where he'd split it with his open hand. "I guess I owe him thanks for getting me back, huh?"

"It worked, although it wasn't the best possible way to pull you back to this dimension." The Morrigan. She sighed. "You need to sleep. In the morning, we'll find out what your fate will be. There is talk of expelling you, not that I'll permit that."

"Why? Because I got hurt?" As if that made a ton of sense!

"They're scared," she said, then laid a gentle hand on my head. "It's highly unusual to have anyone straddle dimensions like you did. Sleep. We'll figure it out in the morning."

Twelve

I dreamed. Strange dreams that made little sense: Kellas, his hands cupping my face, blue eyes gazing seriously into my own: '*Brannaugh. You must not try to reach me anymore. It's too dangerous. It would ruin me if you got killed trying. Best forget you ever knew me.*' Shen Long, studying me with a frown of concentration on his face: '*How can someone with so much innate ability know so little about her own power?*' Antaeus, talking to several others, all of them scowling: '*The witch must die. She is a danger to us all.*' My father's voice, urgently repeating over and over: '*Watch your back, fledgling. Watch your back...*' The Morrigan: '*They will pretend that all here is fair. It is anything but...*' And winding throughout, the now familiar sound of my lute, and my voice singing "*leigheas na scars, maolú ar an bpian, 'go dtí nach bhfuil fágtha ach cuimhne...*" Heal the scars, ease the pain, 'til only memory remains...

I awoke feeling much better and slid out of bed, hardly noticing any twinge from my injured back. Kit was already gone from the room. I washed my face before remembering Dub had mentioned a black eye. It had faded to green and yellow hues, practically gone, and my split lip had healed, just a lump on the inside, a lingering bit of not-quite-better. Strange. I dimly remembered that Loki had hit me. Ow! That guy packed a wallop. I pulled my nightshirt up and examined my back in a mirror. Red lines crisscrossed my back, fragile looking, but obviously well on the way to healing. Huh! Maybe the singing in my dreams had done the trick? All I knew for sure was that my belly was complaining noisily about being empty, and a look at the wall clock Kit had found for us confirmed that breakfast was already well underway. I had to hurry or I would miss out on food.

I tossed on workout clothing... sports bra, T-shirt, sneakers, running shorts, (not making the jeans mistake again!) ...and headed downstairs at a run. My teammates were eating breakfast together, heads bowed over their food. I bounced over and dropped one hand each on Kit's and Loki's shoulders, startling them, and smiled at Hàorán where he sat on the other side of the table. "Hey, hi! Good morning. What's for breakfast?"

From the stunned looks on their faces, I was the last person they'd expected to see this morning. Incredulity replaced even Hàorán's normally unreadable expression.

"R-raven?" Kit stuttered after they had all stared at me for a long moment. "How are you even vertical?"

I shrugged. "Hungry, I guess! I'll be right back. There's a waffle calling to me."

They were still muttering in disbelief among themselves when I came back balancing two plates overflowing with breakfast. They weren't the only ones—other students had taken notice and were whispering to each other. Eh! Let them. I was in a very fine mood and not about to let a little whispering behind my back bother me.

I dragged a chair up between Kit and Hàorán and plopped down. "I'm so hungry I could eat a horse, although thankfully I don't have to. Pass the syrup?"

Kit wordlessly complied and watched in something like awe as I started devouring my breakfast like I hadn't eaten in a month of Sundays.

"Your breakfast will not run away, Raven. You can slow down," Loki said faintly.

I nodded, not looking up. "Yeah, but we're due out on the parade grounds in five, so I figure I have little time to waste if I'm going to get this all in." I abruptly changed the topic. "How did things go after things went all weird on the track?" I shoveled some egg-over-easy into my mouth and closed my eyes, savoring it in delight. Food had never tasted so delicious.

"You mean after I decked you because you were between dimensions and an unseen demon was hacking you to pieces?" Loki demanded, his eyebrows quirking in disbelief. "That bit of crazy?"

I nodded, because my mouth was full.

"As in the entire faculty descending on us and wanting to know what the hell game we were playing? That bit?" Loki's voice was rising, and more people were looking our way. "Because, Raven, none of us knew what was happening. The instructors seemed to think we knew something we didn't. Maybe, since you are apparently no longer on the brink of death—which we all feared you were, based on the stripes that demon laid on you—you should tell us what the hell game you are playing?" the coyote demanded without drawing breath.

It drew my focus away from breakfast. "Wow, Loki. Impressive breath control!" I sent him a wide grin. "Relax. I'll fill you in as soon as I get done eating."

"Girl!" He lurched to his feet, his chair spinning away and crashing to the floor behind him. He glared at me, fists clenched at his sides. "Are you insane?"

I laughed at him. "If I don't eat, I'll crash and burn before lunchtime. When I use that much..." I twirled my fork in the air, not wanting to use the word magic, "It takes a lot out of me, and food is the only way, well, food and sleep, that I can put the energy back."

Hàorán bent to grab Loki's chair and set it back up, then unceremoniously shoved the coyote boy back into his seat. "Sit, Loki. You're drawing too much attention this way. She'll tell us, eventually."

"That would be nice!" Kit was staring at me through slitted eyes. Distrustful, that look. It worried me.

I swallowed quickly. "On the way to the grounds, I promise I'll tell you as much as I can. Okay? Just I gotta finish this." I groaned as the buzzer sounded, signaling the end of breakfast, warning we had a short three minutes to get to the parade grounds or get team demerits for tardiness. Hàorán snatched my unfinished plates of food away and tossed them in the trash before I could protest, then grabbed my upper arm and rushed me out of the breakfast room, Kit and Loki on our heels.

"Talk!" Kit punched me on my shoulder as we strode out of the building.

"Ouch!" I exclaimed. "Remember, I am a singer? Well, I can heal things when I sing. I sang myself better last night. In my sleep. Cool, huh?"

I was not expecting Hàorán's hand to clamp over my mouth, nor to have his hot breath gusting in my ear. "Keep it down!" he hissed. "Nobody but us must know that. Are you crazy?"

I pulled back from his hand, sending him a hurt look. "You asked!" I glanced around. "Nobody's close enough to have heard me anyways!"

"You can't announce that kind of thing to the entire world," he scolded. "You want a target on your back?"

Confused, I stared up into his eyes… eyes that were swirling with dark clouds and lightning. He was a dragon lord… like his father, he would command the storms. "I don't understand," I whispered.

Then Hàorán said something that sounded eerily familiar: "How is it you know so little about the consequences of your own power?"

I continued to stare up at him, waiting for an explanation, but he ignored me.

"We'll be late." Dropping his hold on my upper arm, he grabbed me by the hand instead, dragging me after him at a run. Kit and Loki were already ahead of us, running.

The buzzer rang as we barely made it into line at yesterday's platform.

"That will be two demerits for lateness for Team Dragon," I heard Antaeus say, his voice smug.

What? We weren't late! But apparently, being just in the nick of time was tantamount to being late, at least if you were on a team competing against Antaeus' son's team, and he was determined to stack the deck against you. I seethed, but kept my big mouth shut.

We received our schedules for the day and headed out to our first class. Archery. My brother was there and immediately pulled me into a gentle hug.

"What happened yesterday?" He muttered in my ear.

"I saw Kellas. They'd sent three men against him." I whispered.

"Is he...?"

"Badly hurt, but he defeated them."

"The rumor is that you were demon-attacked."

I shrugged. "Something got me. No idea what."

"Gods, Raven." He laid his cheek against the top of my head. "You were terribly injured. I've never seen so much blood. How is it you're here at all?"

"Tell you later." I pushed back out of his arms and turned to face Dub.

The God of Darkness was standing with his legs spread shoulder-width apart, arms folded over his chest, one eyebrow arched in wry amusement. "Now I have the young lady's attention, perhaps we can get underway?"

I blinked. "Sorry."

He smirked and started instructing us in the proper way to hold a long-bow. I was the only one who had never held one before, so once again I was playing catch-up. This was really getting old!

We did finally get to shoot some arrows. I could hit the target sometimes. However, the bullseye didn't like me, and I never even got close. Archer came over after the last arrow sailed over the top of the target and buried itself in the ground well beyond it.

"Here," he said, and wrapped his arms around me from behind, his hands folding over mine on bow and bowstring after I'd nocked another arrow. "You're trying to strangle the thing. Loosen up, breathe deep. Then draw..." He lifted the bow just a fraction, then helped me pull the bowstring back to my ear. "Here. Just the very tips of these fingers. Breathe out... and release." He let go of me just as he said release, and I had no choice but to let the arrow fly. It thunked hard just on the edge of the bullseye. "Well done!"

I turned to him, grinning widely, just as Antaeus' son Leonidas and his team walked by. "Bravo for the witch," Leonidas clapped mockingly. "Maybe someday you'll be able to manage that without being folded up in some man's arms?"

I went cold and then hot all over. "Jealous much?" I snapped.

"Of your *brother*?" He snorted. "You'll be begging to have my arms wrapped around you soon enough, woman! Just you wait."

I was not aware of my hands forming fists, or even that I'd surged toward that sneering oaf, until abruptly stopped by muscular arms grabbing me and lifting me off my feet. "Cool your jets, Raven." Hàorán had his mouth by my ear, a note of warning in his quiet voice.

I struggled, though it didn't do me a lick of good. "You're gonna regret that, Barbarian! I will take that sneer right off your lousy face!" I fought against Hàorán's grip unsuccessfully.

"And yet... there you are, wrapped up in yet *another* man's arms, moon witch. I think that proves my point." Leonidas was scowling, almost like he was at war with himself. Leonidas' teammates were roaring with laughter.

My response was a wordless snarl. Hoots and catcalls followed us as Hàorán half-carried me further from my tormentors. "Ignore him. He's just trying to get you riled," he ordered.

I could still hear Leonidas' mocking laughter and the careless taunts his teammates sent my way, and struggled again to free myself. Hàorán merely tightened his hold until I was gasping for air. "Let... me go!"

"Promise you'll calm down."

"Can't... breathe. Not joking!" His grip loosened, and I gasped for air.

He set me gently back on my feet and stepped away, one hand sliding up my arm to touch my face. "Got this now?" His dark gaze met mine, and I got one of those deeply unsettling shocks that made it crystal clear how my body felt about gorgeous men. Entirely too vulnerable to male beauty, that's me. It made no sense at all, especially since I already had a boyfriend. I needed to get myself under control. *Now!*

Thinking about Kellas settled me faster than an ice water plunge. "Got this," I gulped, and looked hastily away. "Sorry. Leonidas... pushes my buttons."

"As long as you realize that's the game he's playing," he said simply, and turned me back to where my teammates were watching, their faces solemn. "What's next?"

Kit harrumphed, and Loki looked resigned. "Guess it's swordplay, unless our crazy lady goes off the deep end again," the coyote grumbled.

"What are you saying, Loki?" I demanded, stung.

"You're a bigger hothead than I am, and that's saying a good bit," he snapped. "Now, who's ready to get sliced and diced?"

The Dragon Lord was a deliberate and thorough teacher, and I found I really liked his manner of instruction. Something about his calmness and the deep timbre of his voice settled my frantic brain and focused it on what he was teaching us. After we had practiced basic moves solo, Shen Long paired Loki and Kit to practice the series of moves he'd demonstrated with Hàorán, then had me take his place opposite his son. "We'll do this in slow motion," he told us. "We are training your bodies as much as your minds, developing muscle memory for the attack, parry, attack. Ready?"

I felt odd, facing someone for whom this was so basic, but Hàorán did not seem to mind, instead coaching me. "Stretch higher!" when I did not raise my sword enough, then "lower that crouch, deeper on your back leg... yes, like that."

Shen Long watched us briefly, then turned his attention to Kit and Loki. I was grateful. Having a master watching so closely was unsettling, especially because the god's eyes were distinctly reptilian and a glittering gold color.

"OK, this is too easy for you. Faster now," Hàorán teased, a twinkle in his eyes as he picked up the pace. Something like joy flooded through me, and I met his attack with a flawlessly executed parry, then went on the attack with a series of moves that we had not practiced at all, but which felt utterly natural to me. Elias' careful training and Fraegarthach's skill were taking over. I could feel my magic sword's abilities thrumming through my muscles as I went after Hàorán, feinting to the left before delivering a sharp thwack across his backside with the flat of my sword. His eyes widened in surprise, then a wicked grin crossed his face. "You've been holding out on me!" He laughed breathlessly, effortlessly parrying another of my attacks. "Come on, *bǎo bèi*, lay it on me!"

I grinned wolfishly and tossed him a line from Shakespeare's *Macbeth*. "'Lay on, Macduff. And damned be him that first cries, *hold, enough*.'" I twirled my sword with a practiced twist of my wrist. "On guard, dragon!"

His strange eyes lit up with savage glee, and he threw himself at me, his sword moving so fast I could barely see it. I parried his attacks and then went on the offensive, raining blows on him as fast as I could. He met my attacks with a set of lovely parries, then went on the attack again. Back and forth we fought, neither of us gaining the upper hand.

I redoubled my efforts, but he was without question the better swordsman, and I was tiring fast. Moments later, his left arm was a hard band around my middle, my back yanked up against his heaving chest, sword pressed against my throat, his laughter soft in my ear. "And just like that, you're dead, darlin'. You're superb, but I'm still better than you are!"

I huffed, pushed the sword away from my neck, and then twisted away from his grip. Turned so I could see his laughing face, a wide grin on my own. "Perhaps, godling," I mocked as we stood there, panting from our efforts. "For how much longer, d'you think?"

"Eh, we'll see about that, shall we?" Hàorán dropped his sword so that the tip dragged against the ground, and slung a sweaty arm around my neck, turning us back to look at the others.

His father and our teammates were studying us through narrowed eyes. "That was an interesting demonstration of skill, Light Bringer," Shen Long said quietly. "Who was your instructor?"

I swiped sweat out of my eyes with the bottom of my T-shirt before answering, my voice coming in quick pants. "Cait Sidhe. Elias."

I heard Loki hiss in surprise, and Kit leaned close, whispering in his ear. "Later," he warned her in an undertone.

"Ah, yes. I've seen that one fight." The Dragon Lord nodded thoughtfully. "It explains your technique. He is a formidable swordsman. Many of the cat fae are. Not to mention their battle skills while in cat form." Then he turned his gaze on Hàorán, and a shadow crossed his face. "No matter how taken you are with this young lady's abilities, you will not forget your duty, *fùqīn*."

Whatever it was Shen Long had meant caused Hàorán to go rigid by my side. He immediately released me and stepped away, bowing formally to the

Dragon Lord. "As you command, Father." Hàorán's face had instantly become closed, unreadable, and there was a rigid coldness in his bearing that hadn't been there before. It felt… awful.

"We have finished here. It is time to move on to your next practice block." Shen Long turned his back on us and walked away.

Hàorán strode away without a word to any of us.

"Hey, wait!" I dropped my sword and started after him, but Kit grabbed my arm.

"No. Let him go." Her voice was serious.

I stared after our teammate's departing back, completely at a loss. "What did his father say that upset Hàorán so badly?"

Loki made a derisive snort. "The Dragon Lord reminded Hàorán of his duty to family. The dragon's son is pledged to another, Raven. That has always been so with his kind. Influential families maintain their status through alliances formed by betrothing their children from infancy. They have promised Hàorán to the next empress."

Hàorán's engaged? I felt sick. "Does Shen Long think I was trying to…" I couldn't finish the thought.

"Seduce his son?" Loki shook his head. "I seriously doubt it. More likely, he thinks Hàorán is in danger of becoming too fond of you."

"But…" We were friends. Just friends. Teammates. Weren't we?

Kit grabbed my hand. "Come on, the next class starts soon. We'll talk about this later."

I went through our mixed martial arts class in a daze. Dian kept shooting me questioning glances, which I evaded. He finally shrugged and showed the others more advanced punches and kicks. Once again, my teammates had far more training that I had, and my rudimentary grasp of the techniques had me struggling to keep up. When we moved on to practice sparring, I was pathetic.

Kit knocked me prone on the mat far more than I was on my feet, and she finally took pity on me. We stood to one side, watching Loki and Hàorán look like they were beating the crap out of each other.

I groaned after watching Loki land a kick to the dragon's core that had him doubling over and falling to his knees. "There's just no way."

Kit shrugged. "Kinda how I felt watching you and Hàorán sword fight."

I felt myself go hot, then cold. Sword fight. Kit's comment reminded me of what Kellas was being forced to do just to stay alive. Every moment I spent here, being schooled in the many ways to tear another person apart, was another moment he had to spend on his own, defending himself against all odds. It wasn't right. It wasn't fair, and I was wasting precious time by being here.

"I'm so done with all of this!" I whirled and started for the school, determined to leave immediately.

Kit's yell barely registered over the roar in my ears as I broke into a run, my eyes blurring with unshed tears. I had to get to Kellas before it was too late. Maybe I was just tired. Maybe I was overreacting, but I needed to get out. Now. I didn't care that Dub thought I needed more training.

I crashed blindly into a large body, stumbled and fell to one knee. Above me, Dub's face furrowed in concern. "Where do you think you're going?" he demanded.

I scrambled to my feet. "Out of here. I never should have come." My breath was coming in quick gasps, like I'd run miles instead of mere meters. "You gods are all crazy, you know that?" I demanded. "Making sport out of tearing each other into tiny little pieces. It's disgusting, and I won't have anything more to do with it. Kellas needs me. Get out of my way!" I had started out in a normal voice, but now I was shouting at the top of my lungs. There was a definite hint of hysteria in it. Maybe unintentional, but give me a break already. Kellas was in deadly danger and I was stuck at fight school playing make-believe. I couldn't do it anymore.

"Light Bringer." Dub laid a hand on my shoulder, his voice calm, like he was trying to steady a frantic horse.

I shoved his hand away. "Stop calling me that! This isn't real. None of this, not any of the insanity that has been my life for the last year. I can't take it anymore! I just can't..." That came out in a sob, and I tried to push past him, but he just caught me around my waist with one arm and hoisted me off my feet, effortlessly squashing me up against his chest. A surge of anger pulsed through me, and I fought to get free. This whole yanking me off my feet thing was getting old. I was not a small child!

Sternly, Dub told me, "You're not going anywhere, Light Bringer. You belong here, with those charged with watching over mortals. You came late to the circus, but are one of us. There's much you have to learn..."

"I need to go to Kellas," I protested. "He'll die before I can learn anything worthwhile to help him." I continued to struggle uselessly against Dub's grip, then slapped both hands hard on his broad chest. "Put... me... down!"

He shook his head, long curls swishing. "Not until you calm down."

Shoving hard against his chest, I threw my head back and roared my rage... and my body transformed into my avatar. I broke free of Dub's viselike grip and dropped to my feet, then tossed the God of Darkness aside like he was nothing more than a toy. "I leave now." My voice was a low growl.

Dian stepped into my path. "Light Bringer..."

"Not you too!" I snapped at him.

He looked almost apologetic. "You can't leave."

"Try stopping me!" In my avatar form, I was even bigger than he was, and that was saying something. I tried to push past him, but he blocked me with one muscular arm. Shook his head.

"Don't make me do something we'll both regret," he whispered.

I threw the first punch.

The next few minutes were a confused blur. I remember hitting Dian so hard, he staggered and fell. Dub tried to drag me to my knees. I flipped him over my head and body slammed him onto the ground. Dian scrambled to his feet and threw a roundhouse kick that I caught under one arm, trapping his leg against my side, then thrashed him with multiple punches to his core until he collapsed. Dub recovered and came at me again, lifting me up over his head and throwing me. I flipped in midair and landed on my feet like a cat, only to have them both rush me and drag me to the ground, spitting and snarling.

So... I didn't immediately lose, but it took Dub and Dian together to overwhelm my larger size and blood rage. They wrestled me face down on the ground and held me pinned, both holding my arms, while a third god sat all his weight on my legs and struggled to clamp shackles on my wrists and ankles.

"Raven!" Archer flung himself prone next to me. "I know you're in there somewhere. You must stop fighting. If they can't control you, they will kill you, do you hear me? *They. Will. Kill. You!* And if you die, I will lose my only sister. Please, Raven, listen to me! It's your only chance!" He pressed his forehead against mine, laid an imploring palm on my battered cheek. "C'mon, sis. For me. Please." A desperate whisper only I could hear.

The fight went out of me as abruptly as it had roared its way in. My body collapsed back to normal size. Suddenly, the combined weight of the gods on my arms and legs was excruciating. I cried out, but no one moved off me until I felt iron shackles bite down tight on my wrists and ankles.

"She's bleeding."

"Get her up."

Too dazed for it to register who was talking, I nearly passed out from the pain as they hauled me to my feet with a rattling of chains, steadied between Dub and Dian. Both were breathing hard.

"We nearly didn't manage that, brother," Dub muttered. Dian just grunted agreement.

Shen Long stepped around to face me, having been the one to secure the irons. "What now?" he asked in an undertone.

"We take on an angry mob," Dub said.

Thirteen

They marched me to a room that looked like a lecture hall: folding cushioned seats on tiers that stepped upward to the back of the room. In front was a low dais. Shoved to my knees in front of the dais, Dub and Dian held me in place. Shen Long stood to one side, a hand resting on the hilt of his sheathed scimitar. I could hear people filing into the room behind me. The other instructors and sponsors walked in up front, gathering in a silent, unfriendly semicircle facing me. The Morrigan was not among them.

Antaeus was the last to arrive. He stopped in front of me, glaring down at me. "You are a menace."

I drew breath to respond, but about fainted from the crushing grips Dub and Dian immediately administered to my shoulders. Bruises later, for sure.

"And you two! How dare you bring an untrained Berserker into my school?" Antaeus growled. "Are you crazy? Are you trying to get us all killed?"

"Be grateful she is untrained, Antaeus," Dub snapped.

"I am grateful she has not done more damage than she has. We will not allow her to remain. I will not be responsible for training a Berserker in the art of war." Antaeus was practically spitting nails, he was so angry. "It took the three of you to bring her to her knees, as it was. Imagine the damage she could wreak if she knew what she was doing!"

"I can imagine it." Dub retorted. "It's why I brought her here. Untrained, she is a loose cannon. With instruction, she will learn to control her abilities, focus her intent, chose her battles wisely. Win." His voice was shaking with the intensity of his feeling. "We must train her, or else she will be a mortal threat to us all."

I was a threat? A loose cannon? Is that what he really thought? Was I truly that dangerous? Surely not!

"Then why not cut off her head while she kneels there bound in magicked iron? A dead Berserker cannot kill," Antaeus sneered.

Fear roared in my ears, left me reeling. He would kill me? While I was unable to defend myself? What kind of monster would do such a thing?

There was a heavy flapping of wings, and the Morrigan in her raven form landed heavily on my shoulder, atop Dub's hand.

'The Light Bringer is my champion. I have claimed her as my own. You shall not hurt a single hair on her head, any of you, or you will answer to me. Lest you forget: I. Am. Death!' The Morrigan's voice echoed in my head, and I could see from the startled expressions on the others' faces that they had heard her just as clearly as I. *'She is young and foolhardy, but she is bright and will learn quickly. You will forgive her passion; She loves one whose life is in mortal danger, and her only wish is to free him. Alas, without training, she will fail, and they will both die. She must learn, and quickly. There is no time to lose. Free her now. I will take responsibility for her actions henceforth.'*

Oh, gods. Even the Morrigan thought I would die if untrained. And if I wasn't allowed to continue, that meant Kellas would die too... That my guardian was willing to take responsibility for my actions stunned me. She had that much faith in me?

There was a moment of silence as that promise settled over the hall, then:

"As will I," Hàorán called in a clear voice.

"And I," Loki declared.

"And I as well." Kit, more quietly than the young men, but still determined.

There was the sound of approaching steps, then Hàorán, Kit and Loki were there, standing beside me.

"Why would you pledge such a thing?" Antaeus demanded. "Do you know the consequences if she loses control again?"

Consequences? What consequences? I felt my stomach clench.

"She is our teammate. We stand together," Hàorán declared. "If she fails, we fail, and our lives will be forfeit."

No! I twisted violently under the gods' restraining hands, and about crumpled under the crush of their grips. "You mustn't! I can't let you..." I gritted between teeth clenched against the pain. I tried to catch Hàorán's eye. "Please don't do this."

"I accept your terms." Antaeus said, a cruel smile on his lips. He sneered at me, enjoying my distress. "You will keep restraints on her so she cannot transform into her avatar. Get the witch out of my sight. We're finished here."

As they dragged me from the room, my gaze fell on Leonidas and one of his teammates, the sandy-haired boy. The boy had his arms around Leonidas, and was whispering urgently into the Barbarian's ear. Leonidas met my gaze, and he swallowed hard, his face a mask. 'Sorry,' he mouthed silently at me, then looked away, his mouth twisting like he was in pain.

～

They escorted me to my room in irons. Once the door shut the rest of the world out, Shen Long removed the shackles but substituted two wide gold arm bands that circled my biceps. "These are suppression cuffs. It gives me no joy to bind you with these," he told me. His golden gaze held pity. "They will prevent you from calling up your avatar and its power. The bands will tighten and crush your arms if you try. Left long enough, they will take your arms off entirely. You must learn to manage your rage. You must not lose control. Not even for a moment. No matter how badly others may goad you. Do you understand?"

I bowed my head, sickened and ashamed. "I understand." The consequences were too dreadful to consider.

A gentle hand touched my jaw and tipped my head up so our gazes met. "You are entrusted not only with the life of my eldest son and heir but also with the lives of a Kitsuné goddess and a Diné god. That is no small thing. You must rise to the challenge." Shen Long looked around at the others in my room: Dub, Dian, the Morrigan, my brother, my teammates... my friends whose lives were now in my hands. "We should go, let these young people talk among themselves."

The Morrigan lingered as the other gods exited. "Look at me, my champion." Reluctantly, I obeyed. "This was inevitable, foreseen by myself. Do not despair, Light Bringer. Out of darkness comes greatness. You and your friends shall prevail. This also I have foreseen." She bowed her head briefly, and a smile touched her lips. "You will need a bath and someone to bind your wounds. Then you all must plan. This would be a good time to tell each other everything. Here," she added, pressing a thumb drive into my palm. "Watch this video together. Show your friends the whole thing; hold nothing back. It will explain a lot to them." And with that, she was gone.

~

Kit came into the bathroom with me over my protests. "Don't be stupid; you're busted up bad. You will need help to get out of those clothes."

She was right. My cuts had reopened and blood had glued my T-shirt to my re-injured back. It took soaking to get it unstuck. Kit ended up fetching scissors and cutting the shirt free of my bruised shoulders and arms as I winced with every little motion. She gave my shirt a disgusted look as we eased it off, blood soaked and filthy from the dirt I'd been rolling in. Carrying it between thumb and forefinger, she stalked over to the trash and dropped it in.

I could slide out of my shorts and ditch sneakers and socks on my own, but the hooks of my bra were a bridge too far. Kit undid the fasteners for me, and I peeled that off, wincing as it stuck to one of the cuts on my back.

The shower hurt my cuts, and despite Kit's gentle ministrations, it was almost more than I could bear.

She patted me dry with multiple towels that all came away stained with blood. "You are black and blue all over," she muttered. "Men and their brutish strength. They should never have beaten you like that."

"I don't think I gave them a lot of choice. Do you?" I said ruefully.

"Corner a wild animal, expect to get bitten," she snapped irritably. "And now they bind you with magic for fear you will bite them again. That would be the least they deserve for the way they have manipulated you from the start."

I tried a smile, but my damaged face protested, and it was more like a grimace. "Careful, Kit. I almost get the feeling you're on my side!"

She snorted, but did not deny it. She helped me slide a white terrycloth bathrobe up over my aching arms and wrapped it around me before belting it tightly around my waist with a bit of unnecessary force. "We'll get Hàorán to dress those cuts. He has more experience with treating knife wounds than I. When I stick a knife in somebody, he's dead. No need to patch anyone up." A vicious glint came into her dark eyes. "Now, sit so I can do your hair."

I fell into a daze under her ministering touch, because she didn't just brush and dry my hair, but ran her fingers through it, pulling it into a series of braids that she then curled up into an elaborate bun at the base of my skull. "There.

You look a little less like a punching bag," Kit said at last and stepped away. "We've kept the boys waiting long enough, I think."

I followed her out to our bedroom. Archer and Hàorán were cross-legged on the floor, playing a game of Mancala. Loki had slumped against the end of Kit's bed, eyelids closed, his eyelashes almost impossibly long and dark against his golden skin. The mattress supported his thrown-back head, exposing the strong column of his throat. Dozing. In repose, his face had relaxed into peacefulness, the resentment and anger that so often lined his features gone. He was very good looking, I thought, with a start of surprise. Funny that I was just noticing. Next to me, I heard Kit draw in an involuntary breath as she saw him, too.

I glanced down at her. There was something raw there in her face, a hunger that she had kept well-hidden except for this single moment when surprised. Huh. Perhaps the fox was more taken with the coyote than she let on? Well, I wasn't about to share her secret.

Archer looked up from his game, and his face crinkled into a smile. "That's much better, sis. You're still gonna have to play some music, though. You're looking the worse for wear."

Hàorán came to his feet in one graceful motion and bowed. I sent him a quizzical look. "Don't look so surprised, Light Bringer. It is my training to rise in the presence of a lady."

I felt my face get hot. A lady, was I? "As it's not something I am used to, you will forgive me if I act awkward about it."

"You don't like to be treated like a lady?" A muscle quirked at the corner of his mouth. Like he found this amusing.

I shook my head. "That's not it. It's just that our cultures have raised us differently. Mine is not so formal."

"And yours does not treat a woman with respect?" The humor had quickly changed to confusion.

I bit my lower lip and looked at Archer for help. "We lack the graciousness of your culture," Archer explained. "No doubt Raven and Kit both appreciate your excellent manners."

Loki had roused himself as we were talking. He looked between Hàorán and me, no doubt taking in the heightened color in my cheeks... well, the color that wasn't because of the bruising that I could feel darkening one side of my face, that is. He got to his feet with the same liquid grace as Hàorán. But it was Kit he spoke to. "Maybe I should take instruction from the dragon?"

She lifted her chin defiantly. "Maybe you should!"

A slow smile crept across Loki's face. "Fancy that."

I glanced at Hàorán and saw the same flash of understanding cross his face that I had felt earlier. Something beyond the age-old battle between fox and dog was brewing between those two.

"How are those cuts from yesterday?" Archer asked. "I imagine they might not have fared well during that fight."

"They're a mess," Kit responded for me. "Many have broken open." She had not taken her gaze off Loki. A muscle bunched in his jaw, and he looked away.

"Will you allow me to take care of those for you, Light Bringer?" Hàorán asked.

I looked back at him. "Please call me Raven. Light Bringer sounds so pretentious."

He smiled. It softened the hard planes of his face. "Raven, then. Although the honorific is yours as well."

I nodded and looked at the floor, suddenly uncomfortable. "Thank you."

Hàorán excused himself to fetch bandages from the room he shared with Loki next door. Archer helped me arrange my clothing to expose my back without also baring my chest, his dark eyes somber as he took in the extent of my injuries. My brother said nothing; he didn't need to. I knew how my wounds affected him.

Loki took one look at the extent of my cuts and bruises and stalked out of the room without saying a word. "He's... seen so much," Kit explained, looking awkward. "Violence against a woman... upsets him."

"Go," Archer urged. "We can take care of things here. Just make sure he comes back here with you when he gets over being upset."

Kit nodded and left to follow Loki.

And yet, it had been Loki who'd punched me when I'd been suspended between dimensions. I wasn't sure what to make of that. It was obvious there was far more history between those two than they'd let on.

When Hàorán returned, I sat cross-legged on a rug, a pillow clamped tightly over my front, the terry robe down around my waist. He knelt behind me. "Let me know right away if anything I do hurts you."

I managed a single nod and braced myself.

I heard him hiss softly as he took in the extent of damage to my back, and felt his gentle touch as he dabbed at the blood that continued to ooze from my cuts. "Some of your cuts stayed closed, but others have reopened. I can butterfly them closed, but you must try not to reopen the cuts or you will scar badly."

"She can heal herself; just match up the edges well." Archer shifted position so he could watch what Hàorán was doing.

"This is what you mentioned this morning after breakfast, isn't it? It really is healing magic?" Hàorán asked as he worked.

I waited for Archer's nod before replying. "Yes."

"Then yours is potent indeed to have done so much in such a short time." Hàorán worked in silence for a beat before asking, "Can you heal others as well?"

I nodded again.

He made a soft huff of approval. "We are fortunate in our choice of ally then."

"Even though I've put you all in danger?" I demanded, feeling sick to my stomach that I'd done so.

"Nonsense," Hàorán scoffed. "We're all here for each other. That's what teammates are for." He fell silent and continued to butterfly my injuries closed.

Loki returned with Kit after Hàorán finished taping me back together, my bathrobe once again hiding my cuts and bruises. He and Kit sat on the edge of her bed as Archer helped me climb up onto mine, and then my brother dropped cross-legged onto the floor next to Hàorán.

"Time for your music, sis," Archer prompted.

With my back as stiff as it was, it was difficult for me to pull my lute around from its hiding place. I could not bring myself to look at the surprise on Kit's and Loki's faces as I did so. It seemed like a secret I should have shared much earlier. "I should have told you about this..."

Hàorán was shaking his head. "You didn't know any of us well enough. However, I must confess I already knew about your lute. My father told me how you summoned him with your song. He told me he could not resist your call at all. Not something a god of his stature is accustomed to being subjected to, by-the-way." He shot me a rueful glance. "The sheer temerity of it, summoning a god like he was a dog! He thought you must be a Siren at first, but changed his mind about killing you after seeing how the Moon Goddess was also trying to kill you. As he says, 'the enemy of my enemy is my friend.'"

The Dragon Lord had intended to kill me? Yikes. Good thing I hadn't known that at the time! I tuned my lute and plucked the first of the arpeggios that accompanied my healing song. "I'm grateful he changed his mind."

Hàorán chuckled softly. "So am I."

He looked at me with such tenderness I felt the heat rise in my face again. I bowed my head so he would not see it. Sang: "*Leigheas na scars, maolú ar an bpian, 'go dtí nach bhfuil fágtha ach cuimhne...* heal the scars, ease the pain, 'til only memory remains..."

"Can you target your healing?" Kit's question was so abrupt, I paused playing.

"What do you mean?" I asked.

"Can you choose where to send your healing?" she persisted. "Can you fix some things and not others?"

I shook my head, confused. "Why would I do that?"

"Because," she continued, her voice hard, "You should leave your bruises as testament to your toughness, as well as shame those who hurt you. You should dress tomorrow so all can see what those brutes did to you and hold your head up high." Her pretty mouth turned down, her distress clear. "Besides, if you heal everything, it will arouse suspicion. Healing magic is rare indeed, and those who fight covet healers. Do you wish to be forced to work for those who value you only for your ability to patch them up?"

Loki nodded. "Kit's right."

I was aghast. "Somebody would force me to heal them?" But it made sense that some power-hungry god would do just that. The possibility of being forced against my will to use my magic sickened me.

"It's why I hushed you earlier," Hàorán said. "When you came to breakfast as though nothing had happened to you the day before. If certain individuals were to find out about your ability to heal, you would become a prize. Enslaved. A tool to be used."

"Now, isn't this grand?" My accent mimicked my father's. Of course, it was anything but. No wonder the Morrigan had warned me not to be fully open about my abilities with anybody but my teammates! Fighting back nausea, I went back to singing, directing the silver strands my music manifested to my back only. The newly blackened eye, the freshly split lip would have to remain. However, I wasn't above sending healing energy to my friends' aching muscles and ridding Archer of a massive headache. How did I know he had a headache? His music was off key. And sore muscles were common to all of us at this point. We'd been working hard.

When I finished, everybody acted like they were coming out of a dream.

"That felt awesome," Loki said, stretching luxuriously. "I did not know I was so messed up. Thanks!" The others made noises that showed they agreed.

"So!" Hàorán said louder than necessary, and I flicked my gaze at him in surprise. He avoided my look. "Raven has her healing music, her Berserker strength when not in shackles, her ability with a sword. Anything else we should know about you, lady?"

"You really want to know?" I mumbled. "Because it's also my biggest handicap."

"Just spit it out already," Kit snapped irritably.

So, I let my glamour fade and let them see the three-year-old I was now.

Fourteen

When my friends recovered from shock, I apologized. "It's the price of my magic. Everything I can do—my music and healing, the Berserker form I assume when I draw my sword, depends on the power I draw from the moon. I have learned how always to look my true age, but it's a glamour I assume, so I feel less like a freak. My age, and my strength also, is bound to the phases of the moon."

"What happens when the moon is dark?" Loki demanded immediately.

I might have guessed the coyote would ask that question. He always seemed to cut right to the key aspect.

"I vanish," I told them, and tried not to cringe at their stunned reactions. "Though I remain, I exist only as pure energy, vulnerable to attack because I cannot fight back. I'm a total liability to you all once a month for about 24 hours."

"We'll figure it out," Hàorán reassured me. "But you should know what your allies here are capable of as well. You know about my skill with a sword. Like my father, I can also assume the form of a dragon, summon storms and rain. And a few other little things." He shrugged. "That's pretty much it."

Loki scoffed. "Such modesty, dragon!" He fixed his dark gaze on me. "I am Coyote clan, which I figure you understand at least a bit, being part Native yourself."

I nodded. "You are a shapeshifter, as well. Coyote is wisdom and foolhardiness, creator and destroyer, hero and fool."

He grimaced. "Succinct. Such fun having my life summarized in a handful of words."

I smiled at him. "I think you're awesome. Coyote has always been a favorite of mine. You stole fire from the gods so humans would not be cold. Raven stole sunlight. My namesake is not so different from you."

He managed a tight smile, then looked down at Kit. "Your turn, Kitsuné."

Her head bowed, Kit stared blindly at her hands fisted together in her lap.

"Kit? What's wrong?" I asked.

She looked up at me, her lovely eyes swimming in tears. "As you know, I am a Kitsuné. Fox clan. I am the youngest daughter, the designated assassin of my clan. Sent by my mother to seduce... so I can then murder... certain men."

Horror left me shuddering. No wonder her music had felt "off" to me. Hàorán's face was a mask. Loki was staring at the ceiling, the only "tell" being the way his Adam's apple bobbed as he swallowed his distress.

"I didn't want to tell you," Kit whispered. "I am ashamed. I hate what I am made to do and wish I no longer had to do as my mother orders."

"Have you been instructed to kill someone here?" Hàorán asked, his eyes slitted with suspicion.

Kit shook her head vigorously. "Mother wants me to get stronger. She wishes to send me against another clan, murder their alpha. I'm not fast enough to succeed, yet. But I don't want to. He's not a bad man. He's just standing in the way of what Mother wants."

"Then you shouldn't go, Kit. Follow your heart. Otherwise, you have nothing to be ashamed of." Loki spoke with such passion it startled all of us.

"We are all victims of our heritage. Pawns in the hands of the ones in power. You do what you must, and if it rids the world of a few awful men, so what? It benefits all of us." He took Kit by the shoulders and addressed her as if the rest of us were not there. "You are the fox. Your quick and clever mind has a unique ability to control another's thoughts. You can create an entire army of warriors if needed." He stopped then, and a look of determination crossed his face, like he had decided something important. "Yes, you are beautiful. Alluring. Desirable. But it is your unswerving courage and generous heart that draws me to you."

Seriously? I hadn't seen that coming! Neither had Kit, from what I could see. She was staring at Loki as if she were seeing him for the first time. Then his head was dipping down, his lips were meeting hers...

I looked away to give them their privacy, exchanged a smile with Archer, then caught sight of Hàorán. The raw envy on his face caught me by surprise.

He glanced at me, saw how I frowned in confusion at him, and he quickly schooled his face into a smirk. "Love blooms right under our noses and we didn't see it!"

I nodded. There was something going on with Hàorán, however, and I was going to find out just exactly what. And, apparently, the backstory behind Loki and Kit was far more involved than either had let on. Someday I was going to find that out, too.

"I saw your sponsor give you something earlier." Hàorán was obviously deflecting, but he was also right to bring it up.

"A thumb drive," I said. "She says we should watch the video together."

"Then let's do that." He rose to his feet and scooped up the drive from where I'd left it on my bedside table before my shower, then he crossed the room to where a large picture hung on the wall, inserting the drive into the frame. The picture disappeared, now showing a menu of choices available.

"That's a computer?" I asked, startled.

Loki chuckled and led Kit over to her bed, where they sat down together. Hàorán sent me a questioning look. "You did not know what this was?"

"I thought it was a painting!"

Hàorán's eyebrows quirked up. "I see." He turned back to the monitor and touched the screen over the icon for the thumb drive. It took a moment to load, and then the triangle that showed "start" showed up in the middle of the image. "Shall we?" he asked, then joined me and Archer on my bed, a clicker in his hand.

I had a decent idea of what we might be about to see, based on the initial still image of Kellas. His face was bloody, blue eyes wild, teeth bared... and it chilled me to my core. "Probably better."

Hàorán frowned at the reluctance in my voice, then hit the start button.

It was every bit as awful as I'd thought it would be: a collage of fight scenes from the colosseum, edited for time. The one I'd already seen, where he'd fought the lion and the girl with my face was murdered; another where he fought men armed with swords while he had nothing but his fists; one where he was pitted against a pack of jackals while in panther form, and last, the one from yesterday, where I'd straddled dimensions and been clawed by a giant tiger. Erin, no doubt. Then there were scenes from the dungeon, including the one where Erin had whipped him; how he was kept chained and left filthy and bloodied from his fights; one where I'd kissed him, giving him the ability to heal rapidly, and how I had collapsed afterwards, then snatched up by Dub and disappeared. Oddly: a brief clip of me dancing, alone, in my bedroom. And last, one of me and Kellas kissing passionately in my father's kitchen. That was it.

I was stunned. Dub had spy cams on me for a very long time. I was unaware that I was rocking back and forth until Archer pulled me into his arms. "Easy, sis."

I leaned against him and let the tears slide silently down my face.

"The gladiator in those videos—that's the Cait Sidhe, Kellas." Hàorán's voice was quiet. "In Rio de Janeiro, he won multiple gold medals at the games, the only immortal ever to beat me with the *jiàn*." He faced me. "*Kellas* is your boyfriend? The one the Morrigan told us was in mortal danger? The reason you are here at fight school?"

"Pretty obvious from that last scene that the two of them are an item, dragon." Loki drawled. "Also obvious to me why she went ballistic earlier today. I think I'd lose it too, knowing my sweetheart was being forced to fight in the Roman Colosseum. The question is, how much time do we have to prepare before we go in and get him out of there?"

I was stunned. They would do that? For me? Oh, gods. Not only had my friends immediately figured out what was going on, they were offering to go in after Kellas with me without the slightest hesitation on any of their parts. It brought tears of gratitude to my eyes.

"What is the time difference between his dimension and here?" Kit asked.

"One of his days is ten of ours here," Archer told them. "They're making him fight frequently from the look of these videos."

Hàorán was nodding. "Not that we want to leave Kellas there any longer than necessary, but it gives us some time to bring Raven's skills up. How fast can you learn, Light Bringer?"

I mopped my face on the sleeve of my bathrobe and clenched my jaw; determined. "Just tell me what I have to do, dragon."

I beat everyone down to breakfast the next morning, and was done and out on the parade grounds before any of the other students. I saw Dub near his training area and went over.

"A word if I may," I gritted between clenched teeth.

He looked at me over his shoulder, then faced me, eyes narrowing as he saw the extent of the bruising that my very brief camisole top and extra-short shorts left uncovered. I had taken Kit's suggestions to heart. Let the gods see the damage their violence had done! They'd done plenty. I was a mass of cuts and contusions all over my body. And those horrible arm cuffs were on full display.

"Go on," he said, his face tight.

"You've been spying on me for a long time, haven't you? Even before Nan died."

A curious combination of emotions flitted across his handsome face and were immediately banished.

"Don't deny it, Dub. The Morrigan shared a whole compilation of videos that I know came from surveillance tapes that only you could have made. That video of me kissing Kellas..." I swallowed hard, missing Kellas so badly it hurt. "That was before the whole fight in the salt mine on Samhain. On my birthday. Kindly explain yourself."

He continued to look at me, expression still tight, closed.

I drew a deep breath in through my nose, but before I could say anything, he raised one hand, stopping me. "Yes. I have been. Since my brother killed the tree nymph, I've had spy flies on you." He took a deep breath and exhaled. "At first it was because he ordered it. Then later, after your grandmother died defeating him, I continued to do so, even as 'barely there' as I was." Dub looked down for a moment, like he was trying to gather himself. When he looked back at me, his green eyes glinted with something I couldn't quite place. "Dother never realized just what you were. I did. I saw it immediately. Your fire. Your passion. I was... entranced." Pain flashed across his face and was gone as quickly as it came. "There were videos I kept from him. You healing the Cait Sidhe of his burns was one. Dother would have never left you alone had he seen that one. He'd have made you his slave forever." Dub's mouth tightened, and he shook his head. "I didn't want my brother anywhere near you. I wanted you for myself. But when I saw how you despaired when your beloved was dying from my poison..." He stopped speaking and looked away, like he couldn't bring himself to face me any longer. His next words sounded distraught. "I followed you on that utterly dangerous trip through time that you made with no training whatsoever, just because you loved him. I watched every single kiss you shared with him. It made me insanely jealous. I swore I would kill him." His throat bobbed as he swallowed hard before returning his gaze to my face. When he spoke again, it was in a whisper. "And then... I knew I couldn't. Because I knew how it would devastate you. Instead, I stopped the red-haired one from killing you and carried you out of the cavern just before it collapsed... and then I left you with him, because I couldn't... bear to hurt you anymore."

Oh, gods. Dub thought he loved me. I drew a breath to speak, but he motioned with one hand, cutting me off.

"I admit I tried to woo you away from him by remaking myself into a form you once cared for. Not that it has worked. Any of my efforts. You remain faithful to Kellas, determined to rescue him, despite being utterly unprepared."

I stared at him in stony silence for a long minute, my mind warring with itself, angry at him, but also feeling sorry for him. "You worked hand in hand with Dother. Tortured my father. Threatened me with... violence, remember?" I suppressed a shudder. "You put your hands where they had no business going. Choked me when I broke your nose for doing that! And you expect me to believe your infatuation with me caused that?" I was reminding myself of everything he'd done to hurt me, trying to rid myself of those confusing emotions.

"Not infatuation!" Dub roared, his eyes blazing. "*Love.*" He closed his eyes then and rocked back on his heels, breathing hard, struggling to regain some measure of self-control before looking at me again. "I played a role so Dother wouldn't realize what you meant to me. It had to look and feel real. When he tortured you, I wanted to kill him myself and couldn't. I am really, truly sorry."

I closed my eyes, willing the tears not to fall.

He stepped closer and laid gentle hands on my arms. I opened my eyes and looked up at his face, now close to mine. "We need you, Dian and I," he breathed. "I know fight school is nothing you would choose. You don't have a cruel bone in your body. Everything you've done, even the violence, has been from a place of love. You have no idea what a rare and beautiful thing that is." One hand crept up my arm, and he touched my face gently, sincerity in every line of his. "But Dother won't care about that. He is evil. And he will bind Dian and my wills to his own, making himself even more powerful. Help us get free of him, Light Bringer. Set us free once and for all. And by doing so, save yourself and your beloved from our brother before it is too late. Please."

It took my breath away for a long beat before I could draw a shaky breath. "You... have a way with words, God of Darkness." I gazed at him through a blur of tears. "I will do everything I can to help you break free of Dother. But there is something you must promise me in return."

"Anything." He brushed the back of his fingers against my cheek. "Just say it."

"You've got to stop taping me when I kiss Kellas. Anytime I'm with him. Give me that small gift of privacy, please? I... suspect you are still watching me around the clock." I drew a shuddering breath. "There are things you should not have known about me, but do. Dian, too. I can kind of understand why you are doing it, but it feels... like I'm living under a microscope. Nothing is sacred or secret. Can you understand how that makes me feel?"

He sighed, and then reluctantly nodded. "I promise."

I gave him a small smile, feeling how the smallest stretch of muscles pulled on the hurt areas. I saw him notice how it hurt me to smile, and a look of pain crossed his face.

"I am so sorry," he said. "I never meant to hurt you."

I stepped in close, and tugged on his arm, pulling him down, then kissed him lightly on his cheek. "I know. Try not to do it again, hear?"

He traced a gentle fingertip down my nose, the only part of my face left unharmed. Smiled. "I won't. Anyone who tries to hurt you will answer to me."

"Bloodthirsty god," I teased. "Let's hope it doesn't come to that." I jerked a thumb back toward the school. "Just gonna go visit the ladies before classes start. Wash my face." Starting the day with a mashed-up face was bad enough; having my eyes all puffy from crying would only make the look even worse.

He nodded. "Make it quick. Roll call in ten."

Heading for the bathrooms at a trot, I ducked in before any of the other students had emerged from breakfast. I splashed cold water on my face, accidentally soaking the front of my camisole. I tried (unsuccessfully) to dry myself off, then gave it up as a lost cause. It was hot out and I'd dry quickly, anyway. I left the bathroom, tugging the wet fabric away from my chest... and ran into someone. A very large someone.

"Oh! Sorry," I started, backing up a step, then looked up into Leonidas' scowling face.

"Moon witch."

"Barbarian." I drew myself up to my full height and still wasn't tall enough for the top of my head to reach his chin.

His frown deepened. "I came to warn you. You have made an enemy of my father. My teammates and I have standing orders to harass you. Make you angry. So those horrible things..." he pointed at the gold bands on my upper arms with a grimace of disgust, "cut your arms off." His lips thinned. "We may have our differences, witch, but..." a pained look crossed his face. "I don't want you to lose your arms."

I hadn't expected that. After all the cruel teasing, the taunts, this was a side of Leonidas I hadn't known existed. "I don't understand."

Leonidas sighed heavily, and seemed on the verge of saying something as he lowered his gaze. His eyes widened.

Looking down, I realized I had been holding my damp camisole out far enough that my breasts were clearly visible from his greater height. My hands flew to my chest, covering myself, as I blushed furiously. "I got water on myself. I wasn't showing off!"

His startled look gave way to a sheepish grin. "Not that I minded. I mean... sorry." He ran one hand through his curly hair, laughing shakily. "Phew. OK. Just be careful. Better yet, don't go anywhere without your teammates from now on. You'll be safer that way." He started to leave.

I grabbed his sleeve, stopping him. "Why warn me?" Then the glint of something around his upper arm caught my eye. I pushed his sleeve up. Leonidas had armbands just like mine, binding his biceps. I stared up into his eyes... gray, bitter. He stared stonily back. "You're cuffed, too," I whispered, aghast. Someone had bound him as well. The horror of it must have shone on my face, because a grimace that might have been pain flitted across his face and was gone.

"You mustn't tell anyone, witch," he gritted out. "I've risked everything coming here to tell you this."

"Why do it then?"

He looked bleak. "Why, she asks." He closed his eyes and blew out a frustrated breath before fixing his gaze on me again. "Because I can't stop thinking about you since you kissed me at the dance... then effortlessly dropped me on my ass like I was so much dead meat," he growled. "It makes no sense. I should hate you for that. But... I don't hate you, and I don't know why. What are you, anyway? Why do you affect me like this?"

The buzzer signaling the end of breakfast went off behind us, and he gently pulled away. "Just watch your back, moon witch." Then he turned and practically ran from me.

I followed more slowly, deep in thought. Somebody had bound Leonidas just as I had been, but why? Leonidas' father Antaeus had it in for me from the start; I had figured that out early on. His behavior at the welcome dinner had made that obvious. Why he hated me was unclear, however, and why his son was bound in the same way as I made no sense to me, unless Leonidas was a Berserker as well. I'd ask the Morrigan when I saw her next. Not that she hung around a lot, but she could not be too far away and she would know things like that.

Following Leonidas out to the parade grounds, I saw him greet the sandy-haired boy. The two embraced like sweethearts. Oh! Maybe they were? No time to think about that now, however. I broke into a run and joined my teammates just in time to avoid yet another lateness demerit. Hàorán had our daily assignments in hand already and after roll call led the way to where Dian was waiting.

Kit gave my ensemble an approving glance and winked. "Nicely done. You're catching on finally." She was scantily dressed in a midriff baring tank top over her running bra and a pair of cutoff jean shorts that showed off the lower curves of her backside.

Loki made a derisive sound, and Hàorán merely smiled to himself. Kit giggled. "I can't wait to see how the boys react to us today."

"Pretty clear how they will react," Loki scoffed. "Any of them that aren't gay, that is."

"We get the idea, coyote. Say no more." Hàorán smiled at me, warmth in his dark eyes. "I can't say I would blame any of them for losing focus, the way you ladies look."

We had reached Dian by then. His reaction to the bruises that patterned my arms and legs was nearly identical to Dub's, but he said nothing. "We won't scrimmage today. Form only." He didn't say why, but it was obvious. I was already in bad enough shape. But as he went about demonstrating the proper form for various blocks, I noticed something. Dian was bigger. Stronger. Faster.

My teammates had observed it, too. Kit and Loki were muttering together, their dark heads close. Dian finally realized we weren't paying proper attention and stopped what he was doing. "Something I should know, Team Dragon?"

"Sir." Hàorán was, as always, polite. "We could not help but notice you seem... stronger today. May we ask why that is?"

Dian half smiled. "As the son of the Dragon Lord, I would have thought you would know why."

"I suspect only, sir."

"Then I will tell you, as much for the benefit of your teammates as to confirm what you suspect." A corner of his mouth quirked up. "Violence strengthens me. Any form, but especially..." he broke off and looked at me apologetically. "Hers."

I stared at him, feeling a cold, hard lump forming in my gut. "Is that why you wanted me here? To strengthen you?"

He looked aghast. "No. My reasons are the same as Dub's. You must become a better fighter so that you can defeat our brother. Free your beloved from the God of Evil."

"As well as freeing you and Dub from his influence," I added softly.

He nodded, grimacing. "That, too."

Loki had been looking from Dian to me and back again. "Wait. Am I to understand you are planning to send Raven up against your *brother*? *That* god of evil?" Dian nodded, his forehead furrowing. Loki snarled. "You aren't asking much of her, then! Not to mention we've promised to help Raven rescue Kellas, meaning we'll be going up against your brother as well. Would have been nice to know before now!"

Hàorán moved closer and put a protective arm around my shoulders. "Sir. Is this true?"

Dian dropped his gaze to the ground and nodded, then brought his head up and looked from one to the other of us. "It's the only way."

Kit sidled up to Loki, pressing herself against his side, fear in her eyes. He slid an arm around her waist and held her close.

"Sir. With your permission, I would ask that you give us a few minutes." Hàorán again, waiting only long enough to see Dian's nod, then he led me away to where a clump of trees lent some protection from curious looks. Kit and Loki followed.

Hàorán took me by the shoulders and gently turned me face him. "How long have you known about this? That you are going up against evil incarnate to rescue Kellas?"

I shrugged helplessly. "A while now." I heard Kit moan softly, and chanced a quick look her way. She was clinging to Loki like he was a lifeline. He'd bent his head and was whispering in her ear.

Hàorán stared at me, his face a riot of conflicting emotions: fear, astonishment, concern. "You know your chances are practically slim to none?" he asked softly.

"Yes. It changes nothing."

He was shaking his head slowly. "I wish I had someone to love me like you love the Cait Sidhe."

"And why wouldn't you?" I demanded.

"Arranged marriages rarely produce that sort of devotion, Light Bringer."

"And you would settle for less?" I stepped closer and looked up into his somber face. "I will fight for my love against the odds. You must fight for yours, too."

"How?" Despair battled hope for the upper hand on his face.

"I'll help you," I said, then fisted his T-shirt with both hands and gave him a little shake. "Deal? You help me learn to fight better, I'll help you win your empress. If that's what you want, that is."

"You would be my Mazu?"

"I do not know who that is."

"She is our goddess of love, benevolence and integrity... and a fierce warrior." Hàorán managed a slight smile. "Not so different from you, then. Alright, it's a deal."

I told my friends what Leonidas had told me by the bathrooms, and they agreed there would be no more going off anywhere without at least two of us always being together. As Loki and Kit were quickly becoming more to each other than mere teammates, it seemed natural for me and Hàorán to pair off. Not that I minded. The more I got to know the dragon, the better I liked him.

We moved on to wrestling after lunch break. Where most of the looks I had gotten that morning from fellow students had been sympathetic, even admiring, Antaeus' glare was anything but. He stood in front of our team as we awaited his instruction, his gaze openly hostile. No question in my mind about that! When his scrutiny finally reached my face, I stared back at him with every bit of defiance I could call up. No anger, though. Leonidas' warning echoed in my ears. His father was trying to rile me. I could not permit that.

Antaeus merely sneered. "Today we will learn proper takedowns, one pair at a time." He gestured at me. "The moon witch will assume the defensive position. Dragon, you will take the upper stance."

I heard Loki's sharp intake of breath. Hàorán looked shocked. "Sir!" he protested. "Wouldn't it be better if the girls…?"

Antaeus ignored him. Instead, the God of Wrestling was glaring at me. "On your hands and knees, moon witch."

I sidled closer to Hàorán and whispered. "What is he asking me to do?"

Hàorán's answer was to step toward Antaeus. "Sir, with all due respect, this is not appropriate. I will not allow my teammate to be subjected to humiliation, nor will I wrestle someone so much smaller and less experienced than myself. I object."

Antaeus swelled like a tom turkey. "I am in charge here, not you, dragon. Lest you forget, this is my school, and this is my class. You will follow directions."

"Sir! I object!" Hàorán's strident voice carried across the parade grounds. Not that he yelled; no, he projected his voice in a timbre so powerful you could have heard him a mile away.

Antaeus lunged at me. Hàorán moved faster than an eye-blink, now in an aggressive crouch between Antaeus and me. *"You will not touch her."* Still in that carrying voice that had every head turning to see what all the fuss was about.

I looked around wildly. Kit had her arms wrapped around Loki, preventing him from jumping into whatever this was between Antaeus and Hàorán. If looks could kill, the one Loki was shooting at Antaeus would have murdered him on the spot.

The other instructors came at a run. Shen Long reached us first, followed closely by Dub and Dian. "What seems to be the trouble?" The Dragon Lord asked in an undertone.

Hàorán opened his mouth to answer, but a quick motion of his father's hand silenced him. "I'm asking Antaeus."

"I am attempting to instruct in my field of expertise," the god answered, glaring at Hàorán.

"Son?" Shen Long prompted.

"He planned to humiliate the Light Bringer," Hàorán said evenly, straightening up from his crouch, returning Antaeus' glare with every bit as much antipathy as the god of wrestling was sending his way.

"How so?" Shen Long asked. "Stand back, son." Hàorán bowed his head and stepped back next to me. His hand reached for mine, clasped it.

Dub and Dian had taken up positions on either side of the Dragon Lord, their heavily muscled arms crossed over their chests, watchful.

Hàorán never took his eyes off Antaeus. "He would have me take the upper position over her on hands and knees, sir." A muscle in Hàorán's cheek bunched. "It is not honorable. I will not agree with this. Sir."

Both Dub and Dian seemed to swell with rage, but they remained silent, merely scowling, letting Shen Long handle the situation. I saw Kit release Loki, pat his arm. The coyote remained tense, coiled, like he was still ready to spring, but had himself back under control.

The Dragon Lord fixed his narrowed gaze on Antaeus. "And why would you pit *my son*, who is much heavier and stronger, as well as trained in the art of wrestling, against a much smaller female opponent who I suspect has zero training in this sport?"

"How else is she to learn?" Antaeus snapped.

"Perhaps by pairing her with the other woman in this team? A fairer pairing, and less fraught with *unacceptable salacious overtones* than the one you propose?" Shen Long's voice had taken on a dangerous note.

"This is my class, and I will run it according to my rules," Antaeus retorted angrily.

"Then you leave me no choice but to remove Team Dragon from your oversight." Shen Long turned his back on Antaeus and addressed Dian. "God of Violence, would you take over training my son's team in Antaeus' stead?"

Dian bowed his head immediately. "I would be honored to, Dragon Lord."

"Then we are agreed," Shen Long stated, shifting his focus back to Antaeus.

"I have not agreed, Dragon Lord!" Antaeus exploded. "You forget whose school this is."

"I can hardly forget when you are constantly referring to it as such." Shen Long turned to Hàorán. "Take the others and leave. We will handle this." He obviously meant the situation brewing between instructors. Hàorán nodded, tugged on my hand, and hurried me away. Loki and Kit followed close behind. As the only class still in session was the equestrian one, and Castor and Pollux had their students off galloping around the track, the remaining students crowded around, asking questions. Hàorán tried to brush them off, but Leonidas stopped him. In a moment, they surrounded us. Hàorán pulled me close against his side, one arm tight around my waist.

"What happened, dragon?" the Barbarian asked quietly.

I saw Hàorán's lips tighten, how he closed his eyes a moment as though to collect himself, to push down his anger.

"I know what he had planned, dragon. You didn't permit it, did you?" Leonidas pressed.

Hàorán hesitated a moment, then shook his head. No.

Leonidas drew in a deep breath. "Good." He raised his voice then. "Alright, everyone, we can go back to practicing now. Don't need the instructors for that. Move on!" Then, as the other students started drifting away, he looked down at me, forehead furrowed with concern. "Do us both a favor, Light Bringer. Stay far away from my father. Stick with the dragon."

Not moon witch. Light Bringer. You could have knocked me down with a feather.

"Why?" I whispered. "What changed your mind?"

His smile was a little crooked, but his eyes twinkled. "Let's just say… I saw the light, shall we?" Then he winked at me—winked!—then turned and jogged off, the sandy-haired boy by his side.

OMG, he didn't mean what happened this morning? Nah. That was just too much. Well, yeah. That probably was what he meant.

My teammates were as stunned as I was. Hàorán released his death grip on me and was looking at me, a thoroughly puzzled expression on his face.

"What the hell did you do to him, Raven? Flash him a little boob?" Loki asked.

I turned beet red and shoved him.

He threw his head back and laughed out loud. "You did, didn't you! Damn, girl, you're getting more like Kit every day."

"It was an accident!" I protested.

"Yeah, like a wet T-shirt kind of accident. I saw you flapping the front of your top all the way across the grounds this morning. I bet at least half the guys here noticed." He grinned down at me. "Well done."

Somehow, we got through the afternoon with no more mishaps and I could join the others for dinner, something I'd missed out on two evenings in a row because of ending up hurt both nights. Although we still had to dress up, the meal was far more relaxed than the welcome dinner. The tables were scattered instead of being pushed all together, and students sat with their teammates. We served ourselves from large serving dishes of food in the middle of each table. Archer, no longer banished to the kitchens (I'd have to ask Dub who to thank for that) joined us at our table. I ate every bit as much as the boys, to Kit's envy and all but Archer's surprise.

After dinner, we all went to the rec room. The space was outfitted with an abundance of comfortable seating, an enormous TV, a pool table, and other games. Archer and Hàorán started a table hockey game. Kit and Loki curled up together on a couch and had their heads together, whispering. I was happy to cuddle down in a cushy armchair and watch the others through sleepy eyes. Somebody turned on a popular music station, and soon I was humming along, my eyes drifting shut, letting myself go with the music.

"Hey," someone said right by my ear, causing me to lurch upright in fright, my eyes popping open.

Leonidas backed up, both hands raised at his shoulders. "Easy there. Didn't mean to scare you."

I shook my head and huffed, settling back in my chair. "You startled me, certainly."

"Sorry." It looked like he meant it, too. "Herakles and I," he nodded at the sandy-haired boy who stuck to him like glue, "we wanted to ask you. Remember, you said you are a singer? And you've been humming for, like, ten minutes anyway. Would you be willing to sing for us?"

I sat up, suddenly aware that I was the center of attention.

"Please," he added.

"I guess... if you really want me to."

"She's great," Kit piped up. "You should hear her sing in the shower."

There was some chuckling, and one smart aleck remarked that he'd like to *see* that for sure.

I sent Kit a scowl. "Thanks a lot, fox!"

Kit just snickered. "Sing 'Unbreak My Heart,'" she ordered. "I bet you'd kill that one."

I just stared at her. That vixen never missed a trick. She had something up her sleeve for sure. "Why that one? It's such a sad song!"

"Just sing it, girl. Do you trust me?"

After a moment's hesitation, I nodded. Somebody pulled out a karaoke machine, found the Toni Braxton song and started it up. I accepted the mic from the sandy-haired boy—Herakles—and listened to the opening notes of the song. The lyrics were up on the TV, but I didn't need them. I knew this song a little too well, having discovered it as an early teen, practicing it endlessly in my bedroom. To my silly younger self, the song—about a dead lover and the singer's heartbroken grief—seemed incredibly romantic. Right now, the message cut a little too close, with Kellas torn away from me. I closed my eyes and let the music take over.

I poured heart and soul into my singing, my voice throbbing with loss, my gestures showing my grief. Stood, head bowed as I finished, the mic hanging at my side. Slowly aware that all was unnaturally silent around me, I became alarmed. I hadn't transported some place, had I? But no, I was still in the rec room, surrounded by fellow students, all of whom were still as statues, staring at me.

"Is everything OK?" I asked hesitantly. "I didn't overdo it?"

"Hell no," somebody managed in a choked voice.

"Will you have my baby?" Herakles breathed. He looked—entranced. Like he was hypnotized or something. Uh, oh. What had I done now?

"Get in line, buddy. I saw her first." Leonidas took one step toward me.

And then things went just a little crazy. Boys from all sides mobbed me, and I could feel myself starting to panic. They were just too close. It wasn't until Hàorán fought his way through the crush and wrapped his arms around me that things calmed down. "Back off, all of you!" he ordered, and despite some grumbling, the others slowly obeyed.

"You okay?" he muttered against my ear.

"Wobbly," I admitted in an undertone. "Was I doing magic?"

"Possibly." A hesitation. "Probably."

Gods. Magic. But what sort? Not healing magic, like my one song, but something else. Why had the others reacted so strongly? Not to mention... "I feel like I'm about to pass out."

He nodded; I could feel his head move against my own. "Let's get you out of here." Hàorán kept me wrapped up in his arms as we made our way slowly through the crowd, out of the rec room and through the dining room while Archer and Loki ran rearguard.

Kit came up beside me. "Are you okay? Should I get your sponsor?"

"Probably should. She doesn't feel right." Hàorán. "We'll get her up to your room."

I remembered little about that trip up the stairs, or being helped into bed. The Morrigan was at my bedside nearly as soon as I'd gotten there and was pressing a drink in my hand. I dutifully took a swallow, then gagged as the liquid burned its way down my throat. I started coughing and could not stop. Someone, I think it was Kit, handed me a glass of water.

"Dub! Did you put something extra in this?" the Morrigan demanded.

"Tsipouro. I tried to tell you!" Dub said, sounding aggrieved.

"You irresponsible maniac!" she snarled.

"Here, take mine. I've added nothing to it." Shen Long handed me his glass.

The Morrigan urged me to drink. This time, it didn't burn on the way down. In fact, it tasted a lot like cherry juice. I drank a bit more and felt more myself. Finally able to sit up straight, I looked around at my friends and four gods, all gathered around my bed for the second evening in a row. "What is that stuff?"

"Vissinada ambrosia." The Morrigan was snippy about it. "Nectar of the gods. Something to prevent you from having to sleep for a week! When are you going to figure out you can't be working magic when you're about to go into a fade?"

I was feeling woozy from the hard liquor Dub had spiked his ambrosia with and dug the heel of one hand into my temple. "Is that what I was doing?"

That elicited an exasperated sigh from my sponsor. "You really are an infant! Didn't your grandmother teach you anything about your singing magic?"

"She wasn't a singer. It's likely she didn't realize. I'm sorry to put you all out. I really didn't know my singing would have this effect."

"How about the time you worked transport magic in Tír na nÓg with your singing?" the Morrigan demanded. "This was a love spell, but still amounts to overdoing magic when you are about to go into dark moon phase. At least this time, I was here to offset the consequences of your foolhardiness." She turned to face the others. "Which brings me to the next issue. She will need to be guarded every minute she is invisible. There are too many here who would take advantage of her vulnerability."

Archer stepped forward. "I'll take first watch. Spend the night."

"You have no magic," Hàorán objected, shouldering past the others to stand next to Archer. "What if someone attacks?"

"Kit will be here too," my brother pointed out.

"And you and Loki are right next door as it is," Dub added. "He can pound on the wall if needed. And no one will question if her brother spends the night in her room. Having you stay with her is more… awkward." He scowled at Loki and Hàorán.

Archer wasted no time jumping up on my bed and shoving pillows around so he could lean back against them in comfort. "C'mere, little sis. You're about to… all right, there you go."

Now feeling quite drunk from Dub's liquor, I'd abruptly lost the ability to maintain my glamour, suddenly regressing to toddler size and fading away at the same time. Archer scooped me up into his arms, settling me onto his lap as I disappeared entirely from sight. "Go to sleep, kid." He dropped a kiss on top of my invisible head as I cuddled up against his broad chest and fell sound asleep.

Sixteen

I dreamed I was in Kellas' arms. We were kissing, touching each other. I was running my hands over the hard muscles of his back, tangling my fingers in his hair as he ran kisses down my neck and on my throat, setting me on fire with desire. But every time I made it clear I wanted more, more, he would ease my hands away, kiss my eyes, my lips, and whisper by my ear. 'Not yet. Remember, I promised...'

I woke slightly and heard Archer and Kit whispering.

"She cries in her sleep every night. She won't ever talk about it in the morning, though."

"Hmm." Archer sounded sad.

"What's he like? Her boy, Kellas. Is he nice?"

"He can be a bit of a blockhead, but he's a good man. We've been friends for a long time."

"Does he love her?"

Wow! Nosy much, Kitsuné? But I could not rouse myself enough to say so out loud.

"To the moon and back." Archer said softly.

"I wish someone would love me like that," Kit said. Her voice was throaty with emotion.

"Doesn't Loki? I mean, it sure looks like you two are an item."

"Loki." The frustration in her voice was obvious. "That one keeps his heart locked away. He talks a good line about falling in love with me, but... well, a girl knows. He's not, really."

"Are you with him?"

"Good question." Her tone made it clear the conversation was over.

They stopped whispering then, and I drifted back to sleep.

Morning came, along with a bunch of awkward maneuvering to get me out of the room and down to breakfast while under guard. I hated that my friends had to accommodate my dumb disappearing act, lying about how I wasn't feeling well to the others who came up to them at breakfast, asking about me. Then they chivvied me out to the parade grounds, once again making excuses at roll call to the instructors who were not aware of my little secret, namely Antaeus and the twins. Castor and Pollux didn't seem concerned, but Antaeus looked like he didn't believe a word they said. Not that it mattered. As far as we were concerned, he was relegated to the minor role of taking attendance.

We had Dian the entire morning for both mixed martial arts and wrestling.

"Sir, I've been thinking." Kit addressed Dian at the beginning of class. "Wouldn't it be a good idea to show Raven what Antaeus wanted her to do yesterday, so she knows why Hàorán objected so strongly? She really doesn't know what that was all about."

"Kit, I don't think..." Hàorán started.

"The vixen is right," Loki interrupted. "I'll take the defensive position."

Hàorán's hands went to his hips, and he glared off into the distance.

Dian nodded, gesturing for them to proceed.

Loki dropped to hands and knees. Hàorán growled low in his chest. He reluctantly knelt on one knee, wrapped an arm around the coyote boy's middle, hand flat on Loki's stomach, and put his other hand on Loki's elbow.

"You will act as though you do not know how to counter Hàorán's take-down," Dian instructed Loki, and got a nod in return.

I couldn't see Hàorán's face, but his tension sounded to me like the drumrolls played before an execution.

"And... go," Dian said.

It happened so fast I couldn't follow how, in an instant, Hàorán had Loki pinned on his back and lay sprawled aggressively over his prone body.

Oh, my gods. Now I understood the Dragon Lord's allusion to salacious overtones. Although I personally would not have considered what Antaeus planned to be mere "overtones." Had that been me underneath, it would be closer to call it obscene and abusive. Beyond the mere domination, every cut on my back would have reopened. It left me shaken. Antaeus didn't want just to humiliate me. He wanted to hurt me.

Hàorán rolled to his feet and pulled Loki up with him. He looked in my direction, knowing I was tucked close to Kit's side so she could feel my energy field. The misery on his face was raw, agonized. "I could never..." he gritted out, and then turned his back, head bowed, chest heaving as he struggled to get himself back together.

Dian did not comment on the takedown, but immediately moved the instruction on, putting Loki and Hàorán to work on standing takedowns. They both had a great deal of training in place already, and it was eye opening just how much strength, tactics, and speed played in. Although Hàorán was taller and Loki was more muscular, they were evenly matched. It really was beautiful to watch, although the harder takedowns made me cringe.

"You understand that what Antaeus attempted was not just to be cruel to you, right?" Kit's sudden question startled me. I couldn't answer her, not that she needed me to. "He fully intended to humiliate the Dragon Lord by putting Hàorán in a compromising situation. Honor is all important to us Asians. It would have been a blotch not only on Hàorán's honor, but his entire family.

It very well could have caused his engagement to be called off by the empress' family. A serious infraction of their agreement."

Yikes. That was far worse than I could have imagined. The maneuvering of the gods was beyond my ken.

Leonidas and his team joined us for mixed martial arts. Dian matched Kit with a boy from Leonidas' team, a smaller kid with the cocky attitude of a banty rooster. Hàorán took Kit's place next to me, somehow tucking an arm around my small self in such a manner that it just looked like he was relaxing. It felt nice... like I was safe. Although he was sweaty, he smelled good; a mix of the soap he used and man musk.

"This should prove interesting," he said in an undertone. "What Rooster there doesn't know is that Kit is a master in the art of taking a man apart into tiny little pieces."

How I wished I could ask how he would know that, when she and I had been the only ones to spar during practice. Maybe it was some of that "insider knowledge" the gods had with this sort of thing.

Dian had them spar, and although the others were impressive, it was Kit I could not take my eyes off of. She didn't let Rooster too close, backing away, feinting, then easily dodging his blows. Then she attacked, raining kicks and punches on her opponent, driving him back until he was forced outside the fight circle, ending the bout.

Dian would have ended it there, but the boy protested, insisting it had been a fluke that the girl had bested him. Dian shrugged and indicated they should try again. This time, everyone stopped to watch. It took longer this time, but once again, Kit's superior speed and sneaky tactics forced her opponent out of the fight circle.

Hàorán sighed. "I hope her skill doesn't make her a target."

I had a feeling it would, though. Male ego and all that.

"Let me try." Another of Leonidas' team stepped forward aggressively; the red-haired, mean-faced kid. His music always gave me a feeling of dread. It suggested that he was far more dangerous than his small size would show.

"I don't think so, Eramos." Leonidas blocked the smaller boy with one thick arm. "I think the Kitsuné has more than shown she's a match for any of us in a fair fight." Then he looked over at Hàorán, a small smile on his lips. "Just like the Light Bringer." He sent a significant look at where I sat hidden against Hàorán's side, and nodded once before turning away. To anyone watching, it was just one team leader acknowledging another's excellent choice of teammate. But it sent chills through me.

Hàorán drew a deep breath. "He knows about you," he muttered. "He knows you're here. How?"

I did not know, and that made me distinctly uneasy.

～

Kit and I returned to our room at day's end to find it tossed: sheets ripped off the beds, our clothing torn off the hangers, weaponry dropped carelessly to the floor. Someone had strewn Kit's cosmetics around the room. Fortunately, whoever had done this hadn't poured out the contents, just had thrown the bottles and packets all over. Kit was beside herself, raging about the room, gathering her things. I felt myself resume form as she was picking up and started helping. The boys came in as we worked, ready to go down to supper, and found us still in workout clothes.

"Did you have a tornado go through here?" Loki demanded, looking around at the mess.

"A human tornado or four," I supplied, as Kit was still cursing a blue streak in Japanese. "Nothing spilled or broken, but it's going to take time before we get things back to rights."

"It can wait," Archer said. "You need to change out of yesterday's clothes and get something to eat. You must be hungry after your fast all day." He was right. My stomach was being extra grumbly about it, too.

Kit continued to gather her scattered underclothes. "If I find out who did this... who put their grubby hands all over my panties..."

Loki gently took the underwear from her and set the pile on the end of her bed. "Go get dressed, vixen. We'll help you put things right after supper." She growled, but nodded and disappeared into her messy closet.

Hàorán gave me a little push. "You too, Light Bringer."

We went down to supper only a little late. I must have eaten half again as much as the boys; I was that hungry. At least I could restrain myself from gobbling it as fast as I could. The others must have been getting used to my unusual appetite, because no one commented. Archer sent me a wry smile, but that was it.

Finished, we started for the front hall, only for Leonidas to accost Hàorán. "You aren't joining the rest of us in the rec room tonight, dragon?"

Hàorán sent him an expressionless stare. "We have a mess to take care of upstairs, Barbarian. Perhaps you have an idea who caused that?"

A bitter smile touched the other boy's face. "I'll just say it was not an order I could defy. I trust you'll find nothing missing or broken, at least."

Kit cursed and made a sudden move toward him. Loki stepped between, stopping her. "I'm doing you a favor, Barbarian. The vixen is not best pleased with you or your men."

Leonidas' bitter smile only deepened. "She is not alone in feeling poorly, Coyote. I would offer an apology, but I doubt she would accept it." He nodded at Kit and me and walked away, Herakles a half step behind, as usual.

We returned to our room, all three boys helping tidy up. "This had better not get repeated," Kit grumbled.

"It won't be," I assured her. "I can ward the door so they won't be able to get in here again." She nodded, pleased. "Leonidas is a Berserker," I blurted. That brought everyone to a standstill, and they stared at me. "He has bands on him, too. I saw them yesterday. He keeps them covered with his shirt."

"Interesting," Loki drawled.

"I suspect he doesn't have full control over what he does," I said. "I think he's forced to follow orders." At Loki's skeptical look, I added. "Just a guess. Underneath it all, I think he's a decent guy. He just can't let his father know he helped me. But if he'd refused to trash our room... that would let Antaeus know he's trying to help us."

Hàorán took a deep breath and went back to sliding my dresses back onto their hangers. "That would explain a fair amount, actually."

"You mean his split personality?" Loki grunted. He'd finished replacing the sheets on Kit's bed and was arranging the blanket.

Kit was fussing at her dressing table, arranging her cosmetics the way she wanted. "I don't care. He's a bully."

"I don't think he wants to be, though." I helped Archer draw my coverlet into place. "Remember, he warned me yesterday, before Antaeus tried... that bit." I couldn't bring myself to say it. "That's when I saw his armbands."

"I wonder why," Hàorán mused, expressing what all of us were thinking. "I'd have thought his father would want him to use his Berserker strength."

We finished tidying the room shortly after that. Archer excused himself and left. Kit and Loki decided they were going to take a walk. Yeah, right! Maybe as far as some quiet corner where they could make out. Hàorán left briefly to go to his room and was back in short order, carrying a laptop. He settled onto the chair by my dressing table and put the laptop down on its otherwise empty surface. "You don't have any cosmetics?" he asked, genuinely puzzled.

"I have little use for them," I told him. "Besides, Kit has enough for an army."

He chuckled, then opened his laptop and signed into an email account. I plopped down at the end of my bed, wondering what I could do. Nothing, I guess. I was bored.

A soft grunt from Hàorán drew my attention. "Bad news?" I asked.

"Not really. Look." He turned the laptop so I could see what was on the screen. It was a picture of a lovely young woman, slaying that fit for the photographer, posing by a waterfall.

I slid off the bed and sat on the arm of his chair. "Oh, sheesh, she's stunning! Who is she?"

Hàorán hummed. "That's my betrothed. The Empress Mèng yáo."

I swallowed hard, hating how seeing his betrothed bothered me in a way it really should not have. After all, I loved Kellas, right? Why would I feel envious of the empress? "Did she send you that picture?"

He nodded. "We've been emailing back and forth a little."

I glanced at the email, but it was all in Chinese characters, beyond my ability to translate without actively cueing my medallion. As it was private correspondence, I didn't think that was a good idea. "What do you talk about?"

He scoffed. "You've been hanging around Kit too much."

"Sorry, I didn't mean to be nosy." I began moving off the arm of his chair, but he clamped one muscular arm over my leg, stopping me.

"Maybe you can help me," Hàorán said, and something in his voice made me look at him closely.

"What do you mean?"

"Well..." he hesitated. "I'm supposed to be wooing her, but I don't seem to make all that great an impression."

"How could you not?" I was genuinely surprised. "Look at you! You're accomplished, drop dead gorgeous, really sweet..."

"Stop!" Hàorán had turned bright red. "Raven!"

"What? You think you aren't?" I gave him a gentle shove. "News flash, dragon boy, you are one hot number. Does she have a picture of you?"

He shook his head, still pink from my compliments. "She's been asking for one. I just have nothing to send her."

"Well!" I exclaimed, impetuously ruffling his thick black hair and making his face flame red all over again. "We're just going to fix that! Tomorrow, Kit and I are taking pictures of you, and tomorrow night we'll send her some. OK?"

He leaned his head against the back of the chair and closed his eyes. "I take awful pictures!"

Yeah, and if I'd had a functioning smartphone, I could have taken a fine one of him right then. And... right there I needed to stop. Even thinking this way felt like a form of betraying Kellas. I didn't have a phone because they don't last long when carried on my person for any length of time. Something about my magic was hard on electronics. I fried their circuitry rather quickly. I chuckled deep in my chest to cover the confusion I was feeling. "Oh, but just you wait. I will take great ones of you. Now. What are you going to write back?"

He grumbled, but eventually translated what she had written to him. Pretty innocuous stuff: she described what she had been doing that day, where the picture was taken, and the dreariness of standing for fittings. My boring life, she'd said. I hope yours is more interesting. Please tell me what you are doing. He wrote something, and I demanded he translate that as well. He might as well have been writing a train schedule for all the excitement it held.

I laughed despairingly. "Oh, gods, no wonder she finds you dull, Hàorán! You haven't told her anything about what you are truly up to! Here, write this!" I dictated what he should write.

He groaned (of course) and protested, but I insisted. I had him write about the fight school and his teammates. "She needs to know you are the only leader with two women on your team," I scolded him.

"Kit is a bad influence on you," he grunted, but reluctantly agreed to add that information. Then I ordered him to tell her how he'd defied an instructor. "Gods, Raven. Not that!" he protested.

"She needs to know you're a man, not a mouse," I scolded. "That you protected me, even though it put you at risk. It will whet her interest. Trust me."

"OK, Kitsuné!" he grumbled, and added that as well. I was thinking maybe he was getting into this. He wrote a bit more, then I stopped him.

"That's enough! Don't tell her anything more; she's going to have to wait 'til tomorrow for the next installment!" Then I hit the send button before he could stop me.

Seventeen

The following day, I borrowed Kit's smartphone and took dozens of pictures of Hàorán, careful not to hold on to the phone for too long and ruin its circuitry. Kit jumped into the project with both feet, taking a bunch more photos whenever I was busy with lessons. We had to be sneaky about it; if he knew someone was taking photos, Hàorán stiffened and truly took an awful picture. At lunchtime, when he'd wandered off to discuss a new takedown technique with Dian, Kit and I poured over her phone. The best photo by far was one I'd gotten of him leaning back against one of the climbing structures we'd been having to clamber over: shirtless, muscular arms crossed over his equally muscular chest, his face crinkled in a smile as he joked about something with Loki.

"Gods, if this one doesn't make her sit up and pay attention, the empress is an ice maiden," Kit breathed. "Hàorán looks good enough to eat!"

"The challenge will be getting him to send it to her," I agreed. "He's incredibly shy about things like this."

"What are you two whispering about?" Loki snuck up behind us and snatched Kit's phone away before she could stop him. He sprawled on the ground next to her and studied Hàorán's picture, eyebrows raised, then handed the phone back to Kit with a smirk. "Doing the paparazzi thing? Don't you two get enough of an eyeful of the dragon just hanging around him every day?"

Kit sniffed. "One would think you were jealous, dog boy. But for your information, this is for Hàorán's empress. She wanted a picture."

Loki gave us a calculating look through narrowed eyes. "That one would do the trick, I think." A pause. "I take it you two are playing matchmaker now?"

I glanced over to where Hàorán continued to talk with Dian. "He needs a little help in that department. He's rather clueless."

That elicited a disgusted snort from Loki. "He's not the only one. You're pretty oblivious yourself."

I stared at him, astonished. "What are you talking about?"

His answer was to jerk his chin at Kit. "Show her that picture you got of the two of them earlier. Surely you caught it."

Kit scowled at him. "Maybe that's not such a good idea."

"Don't you think she should know?" he retorted.

"What picture?" I asked.

Reluctantly returning her attention to her phone, Kit scrolled through her picture file, paused, then selected one. "This one," she murmured, and handed me the phone.

It was a shot of Hàorán and me as we'd finished a scrimmage. He'd just helped me to my feet, and his arms were still around me. I had my head thrown back, laughing, and he was looking down at me with an expression of longing on his face. It sent a shock through me so strong that I gasped.

"See what I mean?" Loki rolled to his feet. "Better delete that one, Kit. Wouldn't want the wrong people to see it."

"Sad to, really. It's such a nice shot," Kit said, then hit a couple buttons. "There. It's gone."

I could not get the image out of my head, though, and I fretted about it the rest of the day. This was just so messed up! Hàorán was promised to an empress. I loved Kellas, but there was this undeniable attraction I felt for the dragon, which was just all wrong. It felt like cheating, especially since the whole reason I was here was to learn how to save the Cait Sidhe. I was so confused, so unhappy.

My mood must have been obvious, because Dub held me back after class and demanded what the matter was. I just shook my head at him and tried to walk away, but he caught me by one arm.

"Something is troubling you, Light Bringer." I tried to tug free, but he merely tightened his grip on my arm. "We're alone. You can tell me."

I stood, head bowed, trying to come up with some way of telling him without sounding weird. "I think Hàorán has a crush on me."

He laughed softly. "So do half the boys here. Hàorán's not made of stone."

I looked up at the God of Darkness, tears blurring my eyes as I thought about how wrong my feelings for Hàorán were. How messed up it was that the dragon felt it too, when he was promised to another. "He can't, though! He's promised to an empress. What would the Dragon Lord say if he knew his son was... you know."

Dub's eyes softened, understanding. "I think he fully understands his son's attraction to you. I think he's even encouraged it, to a degree."

That about stole my breath. "What! Shen Long knows?" That was seriously messed up. Why? It made no sense to me.

"I think he was counting on it, to be honest. He encouraged Hàorán to choose you first." Dub drew me close and bent his head down so he could whisper in my ear. "The Dragon Lord has reasons for his maneuvering, which may become apparent in time. Or they may not. He had every reason to expect that Hàorán would fall for you. After all, what god worth his salt could resist falling in love with a moon goddess? I know I was incapable of resisting you."

We were mere chess pieces in a game played by the gods, and it made me faintly nauseous. I had no idea why my presence seemed to affect guys like that. After all, I wasn't *trying* to attract attention. The whole idea that I somehow did, even if unintentionally, made me deeply uncomfortable. This was so confusing. "But I love Kellas!"

He released me then. "True. But it's rather obvious you have feelings for Hàorán, too. You just haven't allowed yourself to admit it yet." He smiled sadly at me. "You don't hide your emotions all that well, Light Bringer. Be glad of it, though. It's the only thing holding the others back from mobbing you."

"It's wrong, though!" It was deeply disturbing to find out that guys found me... irresistible? Ugh! And Dub was affected too. Gods.

"Is it really?" he asked gently. "Perhaps you haven't discovered the full extent of your immortal skill set yet. You will eventually, I'm sure. Go on, now, your teammates are waiting."

My immortal skill set? What was that supposed to mean? But Dub was already walking away.

~

The empress must have been on her smartphone when we messaged Hàorán's pictures to her that evening, because she wrote back right away. An "OMG" and an animated emoji of a Chinese girl peeking through her fingers comprised the entire message.

Hàorán was confused when he showed us her text. "What does she mean by this?" he asked, frowning.

After Kit and I got over laughing, Kit explained. "It means she's so stunned by your gorgeousness that she can hardly bring herself to look at you."

That confused him even more. "That makes zero sense. You like how somebody looks, wouldn't you want to look at them more?"

"Oh, she's definitely looking at you," Kit assured him. "She's probably showing all her friends as well, and they're all going cray-cray over you."

"Gods, I hope not!" Hàorán exclaimed, blushing bright red.

Oh, he was just too sweet. I squashed the swirling jealousy that threatened to overtake me. That girl had better deserve him!

Loki, sprawled on Kit's bed, resting, started chuckling deep in his chest. "You're hopeless, dragon. That's what you want to have happen. Get a whole gaggle of girls swooning over you so that the empress simply must make sure she stakes her claim on you. Now, if her girlfriends all thought you were a dog... well, that would be bad."

"No chance of that," Kit said confidently.

"I feel like I'm on the meat market," Hàorán mumbled.

"Aren't you, though?" Loki scoffed. "So, what's the next step, ladies? What should the dragon say to his admirers?" For someone who'd teased us hard about doing Hàorán's wooing for him, he seemed quite interested in the dance steps, as Kit called it.

I curled up on my bed, leaned up against a pile of pillows, listening to Kit instruct Hàorán on what to say, and when to say it. She'd had extensive instruction on the topic. Part of her training as an assassin of dirty old men had been about how to lure them in. It was eye-opening, to say the least, and very much like a dance, with the push and pull, dip and sway. A song started playing in my head, and I was humming along until I just could not hold the words back any longer. Ed Sheeran's 'Shape of You.'

"Gods, Raven, that's perfect!" Kit exclaimed. "Have you seen that video on YouTube? The one of Pasha and Daniella dancing to that song? It is seriously the sexiest thing I've seen in, like, forever!" She went to the big picture on our wall and touched some nearly invisible buttons on the frame. Within a minute, she'd found the video she'd mentioned and got it going.

I'd stopped singing and watched in awe as the duo went through their calligraphy. Envy clawed at me. What it would be like to dance like that!

"You should do that, Hàorán. You and Raven," Kit said as the video ended.

"Oh, no. I can't dance. I'm a complete klutz," I protested.

Hàorán had watched the video thoughtfully. "Why not?" he said. "Obviously you like to dance, if that video of you dancing in your room meant anything. This dance is basically a samba. I know the form. Once you practice the moves individually, it's a matter of putting the bits back together." He fixed me with a thoughtful stare. "What say you, Light Bringer? Care to dance with me?"

I protested, but in the end let the others bully me into trying. Because, well, I *wanted* to move like that. First, however, I had to overcome my embarrassment over touching Hàorán suggestively, running my hands over his face and chest while he was pulling me up against him, pushing me away, spinning me, lifting me. We did the whole dance in slow motion. I stepped on his feet more than once, one time upsetting our balance so much that we fell. I landed sprawled on top of him, my face against his hard chest.

"Way to get the dragon horizontal, moon witch!" Loki chortled. He and Kit seemed to enjoy my clumsiness far too much, judging from their laughter and catcalls. I think my face must have been beet red the whole time.

Hàorán didn't seem to mind my awkwardness, however. He rolled me off him and rose to his feet, pulling me up in one smooth motion. "Again," he whispered in my ear. As he'd plastered me up against his body with one hand splayed over the small of my back, my right hand trapped in his left, I did not have any say in the matter. "Your other hand belongs on my chest, woman," he added in a sexy growl that sent heat waves shooting through my body.

Oh, gods. I was lost then. All I could think about was him. Feeling him, moving in rhythm with him, heat flaming through me like an inferno. It was as though someone had thrown a switch. My awkwardness fled, my hips and spine moved in liquid grace. And when, with the last move of the dance, he whirled me up against the wall and buried his face by my neck, my fingers tangled in his hair and I held him there, gasping. His heart was pounding against my chest; he was breathing as hard as if he'd run a six-minute mile. I wanted him to kiss me more than anything... and then we were... kissing, that is... and I never wanted it to stop.

"My gods, we have created a monster!" I heard Loki exclaim in mock despair. "Kit, my dear, I feel the need for some of our own snogging. Come on, let's give those two a little privacy and seek our own, yes?" The quiet opening and closing of my bedroom door was the only tell that they had left.

When we finally broke away from each other's lips, mine felt bruised and swollen in the best possible way. Hàorán's eyes were closed, his heart still pounding a mile a minute against my own. He buried his face in my neck again.

"I've wanted to do that since the first minute I saw you," he said finally. He drew back just far enough so we could look into each other's eyes. "You looked so small and lost. All I wanted to do was protect you, keep you safe. You'd walked into the lion's den, and I feared you would be devoured."

I kissed him gently. Felt the heat rise in me again, and the response in his own body where it pressed against mine. All I wanted to do was to tear off his clothes and make love to him... but that would be wrong. No matter what the God of Darkness thought, it was wrong to love two men at the same time. This was unfair to Kellas and unfair to Hàorán, whom I could never be with since he was promised to another.

I reluctantly pushed him away. "We mustn't."

He swallowed hard, the pain in his eyes so great I almost lost my nerve. I closed my eyes so I could not see it. "We mustn't," I repeated in a whisper.

His hand cupped my face. "Open your eyes, Light Bringer." I obeyed reluctantly. His desire was evident in every line on his face. "I would hold you in my arms for the rest of eternity, given my choice. I have never known a braver woman than you. You make my heart race just by saying my name. Now that I know you care for me, too, how could I ever bring myself to let you go?"

"But you must," I told him, tears starting in my eyes. "Hàorán, our relationship was doomed from the start. No matter how we feel about each other, you're betrothed to the empress, and I love Kellas, too. We each have another to think about. What we have…"

"Is undeniable, Raven. Incredible. Beautiful. Perfect." His voice was thick with emotion.

"And forbidden," I whispered, my tears threatening to spill.

He swallowed, hard. "We have each other for a brief time only; please don't push me away."

I couldn't deny him… me… us… even though I realized how badly we would regret it later when we finally had to part. Maybe it was weak of me, but I pulled him close and kissed him. Let my hands wander all over his body, and relished how his hands roamed freely over my own. I unbuttoned his shirt and slid my hands over his broad chest; he pulled my tank top up over my head and tossed it on the floor, my bra joining it moments later.

But when he tried to unbutton my jeans, I stopped him. "Gods, Raven." It was a groan against my neck. "You want this. I want this. Why?"

I lifted his face and kissed him softly. "Because I am not your empress. And you are not my Kellas." There were tears in his eyes, and mine as well.

This was so messed up. I shouldn't want him, but I did. It was wrong, and I had to stop. Somehow. Before this went any further. But, gods, it just hurt so much…

"I wish…" Hàorán started.

I stopped him with a finger pressed to his lips. "Shh." I wrapped my arms around his neck and pulled him close. "Me too…"

We stood like that for a very long time until he finally relaxed his arms and let them fall to his sides. "I should let you get some rest."

"Ditto." I started buttoning his shirt for him.

He caught my hands. "Best not."

My eyes blurred with tears, but I nodded and looked away.

He brushed an errant lock of hair behind my ear with a gentle hand. "I am your champion, Light Bringer. For as long as you need me, I will stand at your side and protect you until we free Kellas."

I caught his hand in mine and pressed a kiss onto his palm.

I dream-walked that night, guided by my connection to Kellas, and found him in very different circumstances than he'd been every other time I had sought him out. He was still bound by a leg chain attached to a nearby wall and that dreadful collar of compulsion was still around his neck, but he was clean. What little clothing he wore was whole, his many wounds carefully dressed. The remains of a generous meal lay on a nearby table, and he rested on a clean and comfortable bed. He was asleep, dark eyelashes long against tanned cheeks. His hair had grown long and now fell in tangled locks across his pillow, but he had neatly trimmed his beard. His body was both leaner and more muscular. Fading bruises and mostly healed wounds marked the parts of him not covered with bandages. I ached for him, for how he had suffered.

"Kellas..." I breathed.

His eyes fluttered open, and I lost myself in their blue depths. "Brannaugh." He blinked himself further awake and sat up in bed. "Am I dreaming, or are you truly here?"

"We're both dreaming," I told him. "I dream-walk, you sleep and dream of me. Tell me, how come you're being treated better now?"

Misery etched my beloved's face. "It is not kindness, *grá geal mo chroí,* light of my heart. It is a devil's bargain, made so that I might live long enough for you to come rid me of this collar. I am treated no better or worse than the stallions in the Caesar's stable."

"What do you mean?" I was confused.

His beautiful eyes closed. "You don't want to know."

The sound of a door unlocking behind me drew our attention. A moment later, the door opened and a leering Roman soldier thrust a scantily clad young woman into the room. "Your dessert, gladiator. Be sure you get her with child this time." The door locked again.

I whirled, staring at Kellas in horror. "They would use you... like that?"

A muscle in his cheek flexed. He nodded.

I felt sick, then rage flooded through me. "I swear to you, Kellas, they will pay in blood. They are dead men." My anger cued the golden bands wrapped around my upper arms, and they clenched tighter, heating as well, burning me. I cried out, clutched at one band, tried to tear it off. The pain yanked me from my dream walk, awake and in terrible pain.

I groaned in agony as the bands punished me for my rage, panting heavily as I pushed my fury down into a hard knot in my gut, felt the bands loosen as I regained control. Sweat drenched me; I shook uncontrollably, the burns under the golden bands fiery and raw. No way would I be able to sleep after this. But why had I not awakened Kit with my cries?

But she was not there, her bed not even slept in. Alarmed, I scrambled out of bed, dragged on a pair of jeans under my sleep shift, and ran out of the room barefoot.

I pounded on Hàorán and Loki's bedroom door until I heard feet hit the floor and running footsteps. I threw myself into Hàorán's arms the moment he yanked open the door.

"What?" He'd been asleep, his hair mussed. "Raven! What's the matter?"

"Kit's gone."

He half turned, looked over toward Loki's side of the room. "The coyote isn't here either. Ha! They're probably making out somewhere." He turned back to me, grinning.

Lord, he looked good… all broad bare chest, sleep pants hanging low on his hips. I took a deep breath to settle myself. I wasn't letting myself go there! "At this hour?"

"Raven, it's not even midnight. Not everyone goes to bed as early as you do." He was chuckling as he ran his hands up my arms, over my armbands.

I hissed in pain.

"Are you hurt?" All humor left Hàorán's voice.

"A little. I got angry in my sleep, and the bands got tight and burned me."

"The gods be damned." If curses could kill, his would have. "In your sleep? What were you dreaming about? Wait. Not out here. Come in." He took my hand and pulled.

"Shouldn't we be looking for Loki and Kit?" I protested as he drew me into his room and closed the door.

"Those two can take care of themselves. You need to tell me what happened… and we need to look at those burns now." Hàorán turned on a small table light near the door and bent to inspect my arms, then cursed under his breath. "Those are bad." He straightened and pulled me after him to his bathroom. "We've got to get those burns cared for right away. You're going to blister."

"Under these bands?" I asked, dreading what that meant. No doubt it would be unpleasant.

Hàorán just grunted agreement and dug a medical kit from a drawer. He picked me up like I weighed nothing, sat me down on the sink counter where the lighting was better, and went about treating my burns. Not a simple task, given how snug the arm cuffs were. He was very gentle, but it still hurt. He hissed in sympathy every time I flinched. When he finally finished, he was scowling, furious. "I will have a little talk with my father about this!"

"Please don't fight with him, Hàorán. Not because of me," I begged.

He gazed at me with eyes dark with sorrow, jaw muscles clenching as he gritted his teeth. "If I don't fight for you, who will?"

I gave him a stern look. "I am not helpless, dragon."

He dragged me into his arms with a groan. "You are unfairly bound!"

"True, but can you blame them?" I huffed out a pained laugh, then reluctantly pressed my hands against his bare chest, pushing away, putting some space between our needy bodies. "I fought Dub and Dian almost to a standstill."

"They hurt you." He ran gentle fingers over my fading bruises. "How can you forgive them for that?"

"I lost my head, Hàorán. Losing control like that is something I can't afford. To stand half a chance against the God of Evil, I must stay clearheaded." I couldn't help myself, tracing one of his eyebrows with the tip of a finger, then running it down across his cheek and across his full, expressive lips. His eyes closed at my touch. Gods, he was beautiful... "It may be a nasty way to teach me control, but it was maybe the only way I was going to learn quickly enough. Like Loki said: I'm a worse hothead even than him."

"You forgive far too easily, Light Bringer." Hàorán lifted me down from the counter and pulled me into his arms, laying his cheek against the top of my head. "Something made you angry enough that you momentarily lost control. In your sleep, even! What could do that?"

I remained silent, just wrapped my arms around him and held him. How could I tell one man I adored how another love was suffering?

"Raven?" His voice was very quiet.

I shook my head against his chest. "I can't tell you."

"You can tell me anything."

I groaned, thinking of how Kellas was being used. "Not this. It's too awful."

"Hmm." Hàorán pulled back a little, and I released him. "You need your sleep, bǎo bèi. I'll tuck you in and stay with you until the Kitsuné returns from her tryst with the coyote."

I let him lead me back to my room. "How can you be so sure that's what is going on?"

He just chuckled. "You are such an innocent, Raven. Come, out of those jeans and into your bed. I'll hang out here on the end of your bed until Kit comes in. You're too tiny to reach down this far, anyway."

Then, as Kellas had once done, he sprawled across the bottom of my bed, guarding me. I knew when he fell asleep; his breathing went deep and even. Somehow, I couldn't sleep, even after Kit crept into the room with Loki, and they crawled into her bed together, falling asleep soon after. I floated on the edge, wishing I could sleep, but the moon shining through my window was keeping me awake.

Moon goddess. That's what Dub had called me. Irresistible. But why? He'd said it was a part of my "skill set." How? I'd sung a love song, and the guys had circled around like moths to a flame. But it seemed to happen even when I didn't sing. Like they were all moon struck.

Then it hit me like a runaway truck. Gods, I was so dense. How often did songs talk about the moon and falling in love under the moon's influence? So many songs about that. Too many to name, in fact. And Dub had called my father "Love God." I was a moon goddess, a daughter and granddaughter of moon goddesses, and, like the pull of the moon on the ocean causing the tides, I was an irresistible force. A love goddess, whether I wanted to be or not. It truly was my fault, all these lovestruck immortals. Even Hàorán... he'd been drawn to me from the start, before I'd even noticed him, he'd felt that pull, had wanted to protect me. I was a fool. How much of his love for me was my moon influence? And had I done the same to Kellas?

I felt sick to my stomach. If he and Hàorán been drawn to me against their will, did they truly love me or was it just my moon magic? And how would I even know?

"Don't be so hard on yourself, my champion. Of course they love you." Somehow the Morrigan had intruded into my dream. And it was a dream, I realized. "It's not just your influence. Think about it: maybe the silly boys here all gather round, but who do you love in return?" Her laugh was barely more than a soft chuckle. "That's the key. Some you have mere affection for, and they may wish for more than that from you, but that is not on you, moon child. The ones you love, for whom you feel an answering pull, that is love in its true form, never fear." Then her voice changed, became harder, angrier. "Love is the key to freeing yourself from those cuffs. Think about it. Love is a force to be reckoned with. How can you wield it, Light Bringer? How might you free yourself and anyone else you care about, for that matter? Use your power! Love cannot be bound. It will always find a way." And with that, she was gone.

I awakened, knowing what I must do.

Eighteen

I went looking for Dub after breakfast and found him and the other instructors, minus Antaeus, still at breakfast in their private area around the corner from the students' breakfast room. The Morrigan was there as well.

As Hàorán had predicted, my burns had blistered. Several had burst, the clear fluid within running down my arms. I didn't mop it up; I wanted them to see what their bindings had wrought.

"When were you going to tell me about Kellas?" I addressed Dub, not even saying hello. I stood, hands on hips, legs straddled, glaring at all of them.

Dub set his fork down with a sigh and looked up at me with a resigned expression on his face. "You've been dream-walking."

I nodded. "And I saw what they are forcing Kellas to do. As you can see, that made me just the tiniest bit upset." I gestured at my draining blisters.

Dub scowled down at his plate, as if it displeased him. "The Cait Sidhe is only doing what he needs to survive. You cannot be angry with him for that."

I scoffed. "Who said I was angry with him? No, I'm angry with your brother for being a cruel monster. And I'm angry with *you* for not telling me about it!" I felt my rage surge and hastily tamped it back down as the cuffs tightened and popped a couple more blisters. More clear fluid ran down my arms. A bit of blood as well, which did not go unnoticed. Shen Long looked sickened. Dian's lips thinned, and his dark eyes flickered with what appeared to be distress.

However, the Morrigan had a smug smile on her face. "I told you, Dub, you gain nothing by keeping secrets from my champion."

I nodded agreement. "Secrets are unhelpful." I addressed Dub. "I need my grimoire. Taliesin's book. You know the one. And I need it today. You will fetch it for me."

"You dare order a god?" Shen Long lunged to his feet, reptilian pupils slitted dangerously in his golden eyes.

I glared coldly back at him. "I dare anything, Dragon Lord. *Anything*, if it saves the man I love. Do *not* get in my way. Oh! By the way..." I reached under one gold cuff and ripped the thing off, leaving the skin beneath torn. Blood coursed freely down my arms. Dark spots speckled my vision as the pain came close to overwhelming me. I tossed the bloodied and broken cuff onto the table with their breakfast dishes. Dian sprang to his feet with a horrified curse; Dub looked like he was going to lose his breakfast. I tore the other one off my left arm, this time unable to stop the groan that escaped me as I did so. I threw that cuff down, too. "Don't you *ever* try to bind me again," I gritted out. Blinking away the darkness that threatened at the edges of my vision, I turned to stalk away, then whirled back and addressed them all, hardly recognizing my voice, altered as it was by pain. "I will meet you outside shortly." My tone brooked no argument. "You will teach me how to kill the God of Evil and will do so with the utmost haste, because I will not have Kellas stay a minute longer than necessary under that devil's control." Then I stormed out.

Hàorán met me outside the instructor's breakfast room, where I had asked him to wait, catching me as my knees buckled. "I'm taking you to a medic." He supported me through the breakfast room, where our fellow students responded with alarm at the sight of my torn and bleeding arms.

"Wait." I tugged against Hàorán's grip. He stopped and held me steady. I pointed at Leonidas; beckoned. "You need to come with us."

He pushed another kid aside and came over immediately. Herakles was right behind him. "Where are we going?"

"To get those things off you," I said. Then, my knees abruptly gave out from under me. Hàorán swept me up in his arms and carried me.

The medic on duty took one look and shook her head. "Not you again," she muttered, and immediately started gathering the things she needed to treat me. "This is becoming a terrible habit, young lady!"

"Tell me about it," I muttered, then hissed as she started cleaning my wounds. Leonidas looked pale around the gills, and Herakles shoved him down onto a chair. Hàorán hovered until the medic sent him a disapproving glance.

"I know what I'm doing, dragon. Kindly give me a little space to work."

He backed up then, but was never more than an arm's length away.

The antiseptic she applied burned like crazy, and it took everything I had to keep from crying out. "What is that stuff?" I panted, sweating from the pain.

"This is a new product we just got in. It's a combination of antiseptic and skin replacement. Normally we're not supposed to use this on such a large area, but you persist in getting torn up, so..." She let the rest go unsaid. She wrapped soft gauze gently around both injuries and taped it in place. "I advise against any activity that would require the use of your arms for more than eating today. Not that I expect you to pay any attention to that, but I must say it at least. If the area becomes the slightest bit hot or the redness increases, you are to come to me immediately, and I will administer an antibiotic. Questions?"

I shook my head and thanked her. She just huffed and left the exam room. I turned my attention to Leonidas. "Ready to get rid of those things? Before you end up like me?"

He and Herakles exchanged a glance that confirmed what I had already suspected. They were more to each other than just teammates. Most likely lovers.

I slid down from the exam table and went up to him. He stood as I approached. "Now, what I must do next may feel awkward to you, and I'm sorry for it, but it is the best way to administer the amount of magic to break those cuffs off you. Ready?"

A small smile twitched at the corner of his mouth. "I am at your command, mighty witch."

"Then bend down where I can reach you, Barbarian."

One eyebrow twitched up, and a faint smile touched his lips. "Like this?" He leaned over, hands on his knees, his face now level with mine.

"That will do." I don't think he expected what I did then. I don't think any of them did. Taking his face between both my hands, I kissed him on the lips. Rather passionately.

The cuffs on his arms broke open and fell to the floor with a resounding crash.

I released him and stepped back, breathing hard. Love magic is a bit... well. It's emphatic. I'll say that much. I hadn't been sure my fondness for Leonidas would be enough to free him, but I'd wanted to try at least. It wasn't romantic love, but there were many forms of love. He'd risked a lot to help me, and despite our rough start, I cared about him. And he cared about me.

The stunned look on Leonidas' face was priceless. It took several seconds before he could draw a deep breath, then he shook his head and managed a shaky grin as he straightened up. "Yeah. Wow. Didn't see that coming! At least you didn't dump me on my can this time."

Ah, yes. Our last kiss had been under very different circumstances. "I know girls aren't your thing..." I started.

"I'm bi," he interrupted. "Girls totally are my thing. I just like guys, too." He glanced at Herakles, who was nodding.

"Can I get a kiss, too?" Herakles asked.

I declined. "More of that, and the entire school will be demanding kisses. No, that's enough love magic for one morning." I wavered, lightheaded from doing magic and the pain in my arms.

"Love magic?" Hàorán asked. He stepped close and slid an arm around my shoulders. Possessive. My girl, his actions said more clearly than words.

I leaned against him, put my arm around his waist—gingerly, as it hurt to have anything touch my wounds. "It's what we moon goddesses do best."

We left the clinic and headed for the parade grounds. We'd be seriously late, but I don't think any of us cared.

"So, you're a Berserker, too?" I asked Leonidas. "Is that why you were bound?"

He shook his head. "Not me. Herakles is."

I sent Herakles a wide-eyed look. That stripling, a Berserker?

Herakles just smirked. Leonidas chuckled. "People are always underestimating him, but wait until you see Herakles transform. Father bound me in suppression cuffs to control him. He couldn't get them on Herakles, so he used the threat of hurting me to control my boyfriend."

I scowled. "Yet another reason for me to tear that god into little tiny pieces."

Herakles growled low in his throat. "Get in line, moon witch. Get in line."

As my arms hurt badly from the burns, I ended up following the medic's advice and just watched the day's lessons. You can learn quite a lot just from observing. I learned Dub was hurting... not physically, but I was sure something was wrong. Dian was in his element, loving every minute of practiced violence. Shen Long was conflicted and brooding, and he kept scowling at me. Kit and Loki were happy as two puppies, relaxed with each other, playful. Hàorán hid behind his stoic mask. Leonidas and Herakles were ecstatic. Antaeus's anger hid an old hurt so large, he'd never been able to overcome it. It lurked in the back of his eyes. I spotted it once, when he'd glared at me a little too long.

After dinner, we went to the rec room to hang out with the others. I tucked myself under Hàorán's arm and snuggled close, one hand on his knee as we sat together on the couch.

"Dragon?" I whispered.

"Hmm?"

"Please don't be sad."

He made a soft sound. "Why do you think I'm sad?"

"Because you are. And it makes me sad, too."

He pulled me closer and kissed me on the top of my head. "Then I won't be sad. We have now, right? Why spoil now with what the future holds?"

I smiled up at him, but it was shaky around the corners. He leaned down and brushed my lips with his own. Settled back against the cushions with a sigh.

I guess there's no help in being sad sometimes.

Dub came in with my grimoire while we were cuddling. "Any particular reason you need this now?" he asked, handing me the book and sitting on an easy chair opposite us.

I shifted from under Hàorán's arm and quietly thanked Dub, running a hand over the tooled cover. "Still hoping to unlock that collar Kellas has on. Since I was able to remove my own bands, maybe it's something similar? I thought to check to see if the book has anything to say about that."

He sighed. "That could prove difficult."

I nodded. "Taliesin said as much. Something to do with his reasons for submitting to it."

His expressive eyebrows quirked. A wry smile touched his lips and was quickly gone. "There will most likely be some nasty repercussions after you remove the collar," he said.

I gazed at him. The god was holding out on me, and the best way to get it out of him was to wait.

I heard Hàorán scoff quietly. I smacked his leg. "He'll tell me eventually, dragon!"

That brought a small smile to Dub's face. "We could do this for hours, you know."

"I guess that depends on how long you want to spend like this." I said that nonchalantly, but felt anything but. I didn't want to admit it, but I still adored looking at Aquaman, and Dub made a very convincing Aquaman.

"I could look at you forever, Light Bringer," he murmured. "Not that it would gain me anything. All right. The trouble is, if you remove that collar, he will probably hate you for it. He might even try to hurt you."

My stomach clenched, even though I already knew this was a possibility. "Taliesin said as much."

"And you're at peace with this?"

"If the only way to free him is to let him go? Absolutely. Besides, I won him once. I can win him again."

"Harder this time, I think."

I shrugged, swallowed hard against the lump in my throat. "It is what it is."

I knew what was bothering him. Dub had followed my every move for quite some time, gone to great lengths to win me. And if Kellas hated me, well, it smoothed his path. No doubt my relationship with Hàorán wasn't anything Dub was excited about, either. The problem? Dub now cared enough to want for me what I wanted for myself. And I wanted Kellas. Being good friends with Hàorán was as far as that affection could go. As the Morrigan had said not so long ago—for immortals, there is no 'happily ever after.' "I'm so sorry, Dub. I never meant to hurt you."

Dub gazed at me for a long moment, his sea-green eyes sad. Then he looked down and shook his head. "Not your fault, Light Bringer." He grimaced in pain and then slapped both knees. Stood. "Let me know if I can do anything else to help." He left.

"He loves you." There was wonder in Hàorán's voice. "That old god is as nuts about you as I am."

I groaned. "It comes with the territory, I guess."

"And that would be?" he asked.

"She's a love goddess, you dope!" Kit plopped down on the chair Dub had just vacated. "You know... moon, romance? All that lovey-dovey crap? That's her bailiwick. You didn't know?"

"Hadn't a clue." The shock on Hàorán's face was priceless. It probably echoed the one on my own. Kit had known this about me when I hadn't even realized it myself? How?

"I didn't either until Kit gave me a heads up, and then I couldn't stop seeing the signs." Loki parked his rear on the arm of Kit's chair.

"I knew it the minute we met at registration," Kit sounded triumphant. "Guys are so blind. And I also knew she was the key to busting up the good old boy war machine. Which is why I made sure she went down to the welcome dinner dressed to kill."

"An immortal battering ram, that's me," I grumbled, feeling an odd mix of fury that Kit had known all along, had used me to shake things up, and hadn't bothered to tell me... and annoyance at myself for being so clueless all this time.

"Smashed down the gates just like I'd hoped," Kit announced with glee. "Got the warmongering gods in disarray from the get-go. Antaeus tried to wrestle control back, but the damage was done. You had made the first move, even though you didn't realize it, and it has completely rewritten the game here. Love, not war, is going to win this round."

"But it is war we are preparing for, Kit," I said quietly.

"Ah, yes, but the stakes are far higher than most. We go to defeat hate. We go to see that love wins." Kit said that with relish. "And win we shall, moon goddess. Win we shall."

How the fox could be so certain was baffling, yet oddly reassuring at the same time.

Kit was on a roll now. "While we're at it, guys, there's going to be a change of language around here. 'Witch' is a slur used by powerful men to badmouth strong women. Not OK. Raven is a goddess. Not a witch. No more calling her a witch, got it? And if you hear another guy calling her witch, even jokingly, cut 'em off. Correct them. Make them use the right nouns: Raven. Goddess. Light Bringer."

And, just like that, I wasn't angry with Kit anymore. She may have used me, but she was most definitely in my corner.

"How about 'gorgeous,'" Hàorán asked, a small smile on his face.

"'Gorgeous' is an adjective, dragon," she retorted a bit snippily. Although she was a teensy bit wrong there. 'Gorgeous' was often used as a noun, too.

Loki rolled his eyes, and both boys laughed. I felt the lump in my throat ease a little, listening to them joke and tease. I had friends, good friends. Friends willing to go to war with me, fight alongside me, just because they believed in what we were fighting for. I'd never had friends like these my entire life.

"I love you guys." The joking abruptly stopped, and they all looked at me. I shrugged self-consciously. "'Ain't never had friends like you.'" I paraphrased from the Disney movie *Aladdin*. "Thanks."

Kit slugged my thigh. "No getting mushy on us, goddess!" But she looked damp around the eyes.

Nineteen

We started for our rooms shortly after that, but didn't get far. As we exited the rec room, Shen Long stepped out of the shadows. It felt like he'd been waiting there.

"A word with you, Light Bringer," he said, his voice tightly controlled, like he was struggling to contain anger.

I could feel the tension in Hàorán's body, how his arm tightened around my shoulder at his father's request. I glanced up and saw his concern.

"I will not eat her, Hàorán!" the Dragon Lord snapped.

I patted Hàorán's hand where it gripped my shoulder. "It's OK. You go on. I'll be right up."

"I'll wait here," Hàorán said. There was no arguing with him, based on the stony look on his face.

"We'll wait," Loki added. Their lack of trust was clear; the Dragon Lord's face revealed his recognition and annoyance at their distrust.

I followed him out the front doors, open to the warm summer night, down to where the fountain splashed into its basin. I stopped. "This is far enough, sir."

Shen Long growled under his breath, but halted and turned to face me. "You have become strong, moon witch."

201

"Goddess," I corrected. "Not a witch. Goddess. 'Druid' works too, if you prefer that. Kit reminds me that 'witch' is a slur used by powerful men to badmouth strong women. She's right. So, you will not use the word 'witch' to describe me from now on." I drew myself up and glared at the dragon, willing myself not to show fear. "Now, what is it you wanted to speak to me about?"

He stared at me as if I'd grown two heads, then a slow smile touched his lips. "Fair enough, goddess." Was that admiration I saw on his face? "I need to talk with you about my son."

I nodded. "OK."

He growled under his breath like my borderline snippiness annoyed him, then hesitated, like he was struggling with finding the right words. "You do understand that Hàorán is engaged."

I took a deep, shaking breath and steadied myself. "I know this, yes."

He scowled at me. "You know? Then why are you toying with his affections?"

"Not toying," I said, my expression hard. "He loves me. I love him back. We know it's doomed, but we cannot help feeling what we feel, and it's as much your fault as it is ours..." I stuttered to a halt, then took in a deep breath and continued "...for throwing us together like you did. What I want to know is why. *Why* would you do this to your son, to me? Do you hate us that much?"

He looked stunned. "I don't hate you or my son."

"Then why?"

He was silent for a long moment. "You're a love goddess. I thought you could help him."

This was beyond belief. Shen Long had known this detail too? Why was I the last to learn this about myself? And no one had felt it important to tell me. It felt like betrayal. "Help him how?" I asked, my voice rising, a faint edge of hysteria creeping in.

"Help him win his empress. Wait! I'm not finished," he added quickly, because he could see how I was about to explode in anger. "Mèng yáo, his empress, is a wild child. She runs with a fast crowd and has a new boyfriend every week. Her parents are concerned. They hoped to have her settle her affections on my son more firmly."

My anger settled into a cold, hard knot in my belly. "So that your place in the hierarchy remains safe, not so?" I demanded. "What about what the empress wants? What Hàorán wants? Doesn't that count for something?" I was speaking in a low, angry tone, and I could see from his expression he recognized it.

"Do not judge us, goddess!" he snarled. "It has ever been so."

"And maybe that needs to change?" I challenged, taking an aggressive step toward him.

He huffed, and small jets of steam exited both nostrils.

Dragon. I'd angered a ruddy dragon! Living dangerously, Raven. "Look," I said, struggling to calm myself and deescalate the situation. "Your son and I have done nothing to endanger the contract you have made with the empress' family. I certainly hope you know what I mean by that, since you are so adept at insinuating otherwise." I took a deep breath and steadied myself again. "Your son understands his familial duty and that an alliance with the empress' family is desirable, even necessary. He's willing to go through with the arrangement, but honestly, Hàorán's unsure how best to do so. Probably because failure on his part would be catastrophic. Kit and I have been helping him as best we can and we figure to do more, but recent events," I pointed to my bandaged arms, "have slowed our progress down. Meanwhile, he and I must also deal with how we feel about each other... and not to put too fine an edge on it, Dragon Lord, it hurts. A lot."

Shen Long stood statue-like, still huffing clouds of steam, glaring off into the distance. "I know he spent the night in your room—and you expect me to believe that what the two of you were doing was innocent?" The last bit came out in a roar. He turned his head and glared at me.

If I were a dragon, now I would breathe fire! "Are you calling me a liar, Dragon Lord?" I snarled, my hands clenching into fists at my sides. "Yes, we danced, we kissed, we held each other close, but that's all." Then I willed myself silent, knowing that more words would not improve the situation. The dragon's ideas of appropriate were rather old fashioned... he'd freak out if he ever walked though the halls of a human high school. Not that I liked all the PDA's I'd had to walk past in my time at Kestrel High School, but...

He struggled with that for a beat, finally drawing in a deep breath, exhaling, forcing his shoulders to relax. "I owe you the benefit of the doubt, at least," he conceded gruffly.

I knew that was as good as I was going to get from a god as proud as the dragon. Suddenly, all of it was just too much. I looked up at him standing there, looking so like his son Hàorán, who I loved despite my better judgement, and felt my face crumple. I threw myself at him and buried my face in his shirtfront, sobbing. After a stunned moment, he put a careful arm around me and made soothing noises, patting me awkwardly on my back. I do not know how long we stood like that, but I finally got myself under control. Feeling the shift in my emotions, he released me, steadying me with gentle hands on my shoulders, careful not to touch my bandaged spots.

"Better?" he asked, concerned. Also, maybe a bit more than surprised and alarmed at my actions. Perhaps he wasn't used to unhappy girls throwing themselves at him?

I nodded a bit shakily, feeling incredibly dumb for my emotional outburst, scrubbing my tears away with the heel of my hand. "Hàorán is incredible. If his empress doesn't see his amazing qualities, she's unworthy of his love, and he shouldn't marry her. He would be miserable his entire life. I cannot imagine you or his mother would want that for him, right?"

Shen Long looked sad. "Hàorán's mother died years ago."

I huffed. "That explains a lot."

He looked at me like I needed to explain myself, but I just didn't care to. A mother would have put a stop to her husband's manipulations. I knew mine would have, at least.

"Look. We've got this. We know the rules, and we'll play by them as best we can, but please just stop telling us what to do, OK?" I swallowed hard, fighting the tears that threatened to fall again. "Not helpful, Dragon Lord, and likely to mess us up even worse. Are we clear?"

"Crystal," he said.

I left him in the garden and hurried back to rejoin my friends. Hàorán and Loki were there, but Kit was missing. "Where's the fox?" I asked.

"She went to the ladies a while ago now," Loki said. "She's taking her time, I guess."

"I'll go get her." I headed to the downstairs washroom, just a short distance away, around a corner and out of sight of the grand entryway.

"Kit?" I pushed open the door into the ladies' room. "You here?"

There was a scuffling sound, and Kit appeared from behind the bank of cubicles, held tight in Antaeus' arms. One of his hands was clamped across her mouth, the other cruelly twisted her arm up behind her back. Above his hand, her eyes were enormous with fear and pain. Taped to her body were things that looked like batteries. Little, button-sized batteries. There was one by her left eye, one taped to her throat, another on the wrist I could see.

"You were looking for the vixen?" he asked, and the look of triumph on Antaeus's face sent a cold shock through my gut.

"Let her go," I breathed, horrified.

The god laughed, short and without humor. "Not happening. You may have access to your Berserker strength again, but I know you will do nothing to harm her, and so she gets to suffer a little. Understand?" His smile was cruel. "You don't want her hurt, and I know many ways of doing just that. Therefore, you will do as I say quickly and without hesitation." His eyes narrowed as he glared at me. "And if you defy me? I will take it out on her." His eyes glittered with a crazed light. "Kapow."

I felt faint. Those button things were bombs. "Why are you doing this?" I had to delay him as much as possible. Eventually, the guys would realize something was awry and come after us, ladies' washroom or no.

"You have to ask, moon witch?" he sneered. "After all you have done to destroy what I have built? How dare you remove those cuffs from my son?"

"How dare you use him to control another?" I countered.

"It was an effective way of getting what I wanted." A cruel smile twisted his thin lips. "And look! Here I am doing it again. Obviously, it's effective."

"What is it you want?" Not that I cared, but I needed to keep him talking.

"This is my school. My domain." Antaeus's face darkened with rage. "You waltz in and try to change the rules here? You're a lousy moon witch! Here, as it should be everywhere, men call the shots, men say how it will be. Not a woman. Never a woman."

Oh. Misogyny in its loveliest form. Ick. "I never tried to interfere." I hadn't. Not intentionally, at any rate.

He laughed, but the sound was bitter. "You interfered by being here, just by being what you are, Love Goddess." He sneered at the title. "You waltzed in here, a proud little she-bitch, charming all the boys with your looks and your love magic. Confusing them. You should never have been brought here, and the God of Darkness shall pay for doing so." He twisted Kit's arm higher between her shoulder blades, and I heard a soft popping noise. Kit's eyes rolled back in her head, and she sagged, moaning, in the wrestling god's arms.

I gasped, horrified. "Stop! Don't hurt her!" Gods, this was simply awful. "What do you want from me?"

Antaeus's teeth bared in a sardonic grin, and he showed me a small device strapped to his wrist. "This is the detonator for the bombs I have placed on the vixen." He shifted Kit's weight in his arms, as the Kitsuné could barely stand on her own. She moaned. "We will go out to the parade grounds where you will publicly resign from the school and confess your sins. And if you don't, I will tear her to pieces."

Nauseated, I gestured violently, cutting him off. "Enough with your threats! Let's get this over with, shall we? Kit should not suffer for things you hold against me!"

His eyes narrowed. "There's a microphone on the sink over there. Put it on. Don't try anything clever, moon witch."

"Dub, you had better be watching this," I muttered under my breath, snatching up the small microphone and clipping it to my shirt front. I led the way outside, through a door that was hidden from the entry hall where the boys waited.

Once we were out in the middle of the grounds, Antaeus released his grip on Kit's arm and punched her in the face, knocking her unconscious. He turned to me with an awful smile on his face. "On your knees, witch." I hesitated just long enough that he reached for his detonators. "Remove your shoes first," he said as my knees bent. "It will make running away harder."

Not taking my eyes off him for a second, I complied. There was no other viable choice. I could not reach him in time to prevent him from setting off the bombs he'd placed on my friend. With my shoes off, I knelt on the damp grass, chilly in the darkness. Until it wasn't dark any longer. The stadium lights had blazed to life. I blinked, temporarily blinded.

"Even better!" Antaeus exclaimed. "Motion detectors have turned on the lights. Now everyone can watch as well as hear." He was chuckling, an evil sound. "Now, repeat after me: 'I am only a woman. It is not my place to tell any man what to do.'"

Dub! Where the heck are you? I thought desperately. "I am a woman. It is not my place..." My voice boomed over the loudspeakers, amplified many times over. It horrified me. No way anyone was going to miss hearing me.

"No, you missed a word," Antaeus corrected with a leer. His voice sounded over the loudspeakers now, too, not that he seemed to notice. Or maybe he had planned it that way. "You are *only* a woman. The key word is 'only.' Women are less than the lowest man, and it will always be so. Start again."

Keeping a wary eye on the hand he was hovering over the detonator, I dutifully parroted his hateful words.

His eyes half-closed. "Much better." His voice was oily, poisonous. "Now say, 'My only role in life is to make a man happy. To serve his every whim and every desire immediately and without question.'"

I rolled my eyes at him.

The God of Wrestling moved a finger onto one of the detonator buttons, teeth bared in a snarl. "I will destroy her face first, witch."

I repeated his misogyny, choking on the horrible words. Our voices were so loud anyone within the compound would be sure to hear. It humiliated me, diminished me, made me wither up inside. No doubt that was the whole point of this insanity.

"And now you confess to how you charmed all those foolish boys. Obviously, the Dragon Lord's son is under your love spell." His voice boomed over the loud speakers. No one could possibly be missing any of this anymore, least of all Hàorán. "Of all of them, the dragon should have known better. Tell them your secret, love goddess. Admit to your deviousness. Take your punishment. Quickly, or I take the Kitsuné apart bit by bit." He gestured at the detonator on his wrist again, the disgusting leer back on his face.

Nauseated, I could not look at him. He was laughing softly, enjoying his twisted idea of power. Confess? To what? Apologize for being who and what I was? That was insane. He was insane. And I could do nothing about it.

Then Antaeus wasn't laughing any longer. An arrow thunked into his torso, then another an instant later, this time through his throat. Blood gushed bright red from his severed jugular; blood mixed with an oily black substance. He staggered, fell to his knees, then onto his face.

I leapt onto his out-flung arm, pinned it to the ground, and tore the detonator off his wrist. Jumping to my feet, I distanced myself from his prone body. Not that he was going to follow me. He appeared to be quite dead. But he was a god! How could that be?

The next few minutes were a blur. Hàorán and Loki were suddenly there, then Archer and Dub arrived at a run. Loki dropped to his knees next to Kit's inert body, gently removing the bombs, one at a time. Hàorán wrapped one arm around my shuddering body and pulled me close. Gently, he removed the microphone from my shirt and clicked it off, then took the detonator out of my nerveless hand. Archer stood over Antaeus' body, his face set, hard, long-bow in his hands, an arrow nocked and ready.

Dub bent down and casually flipped Antaeus' body over, like handling dead bodies was commonplace for him. He wrenched the arrows out of the dead god's body and handed them, still bloody, to Archer. "He's dead, son. Put them away. Beware of the tips, though."

Archer nodded and lowered his bow, carefully sliding the arrows back into his quiver. Laying his bow down, he turned to me. Opened his arms. "Sis..." His voice shook.

Hàorán released me, and I threw myself at my brother. Archer's arms wrapped convulsively around me, one hand cupping my head against his chest. He was breathing fast; his heart was pounding. "Too close, baby sister. Just. Too. Close." I clung to him, shuddering uncontrollably.

Hàorán went to help Loki remove the rest of the bombs from Kit's body, piling them on a handkerchief.

A gusty sigh from Loki had me pulling back from Archer's arms. "Twenty!" the coyote exclaimed. "That bastard put 20 bombs on my girl." He looked sick with rage and horror. Ever so gently, he brushed her hair from her lovely, battered face. "Kit, wake up. Please, sweetheart." She didn't move, didn't respond. He made a small, animalistic sound, lifted her into his arms and staggered to his feet. "I'm taking her to the medics."

"You go on, all of you. I'll dispose of the bombs and body," Dub ordered.

Hàorán gathered up the handkerchief full of bombs and handed them and the detonator to the God of Darkness. Dub reached down, grasped a handful of Antaeus' shirt, and simply disappeared, taking the dead body with him. At least I hoped it was a dead body. I still didn't know if gods could ever fully die. Dub and his brothers sure hadn't.

Kit recovered consciousness as we walked back into the mansion, but couldn't say anything that made sense. The medics gave her a shot for pain before putting her shoulder joint back in its socket, then strapped her arm to her chest to hold it in place while she healed.

Dub came into the clinic as we finished and called Archer away to report what had happened to the other instructors. My brother left reluctantly after securing my promise I would let him know if I needed anything.

We took Kit back to our room, where I helped her into her nightgown. Loki lifted her into bed, then refused to leave. He curled up next to Kit, his arms wrapped around her, guarding her.

I was exhausted, but it was obvious Hàorán needed to talk. We went out on the balcony and shut the door behind us so as not to disturb the others.

He immediately pulled me into his arms. "Talk to me."

I wrapped my arms around his middle and laid my head on his chest. "There's not much to say. It was Kit he harmed, not me." Not the whole truth, but I needed it to be true.

"Gods, Raven!" he groaned. "That incel hurt you! He threatened you with violence, he publicly humiliated you... and you have nothing to say?" He gently brushed his fingertips against my cheek, tucking a stray lock of hair behind my ear.

I hunched my shoulders defensively. "He's gone now, isn't he? Why should I waste another moment of my life thinking about his awful behavior?"

"Because what he did was wrong, and maybe you're feeling hurt? Angry? Scared?" Hàorán pried my head up, forcing me to look at him. His face was dark with rage and sorrow. "Which is it, Raven? Pretending that this was no big deal might not be you being strong, but you hiding just how shaken you really are. Talk to me, let me carry your pain."

Shaken. He had that right. The experience had left me shaken to my toes. I just shrugged again.

He sighed heavily. "When you're ready to talk about this, I will be here for you, Light Bringer." Hàorán gently traced my eyebrow, then left his hand there, fingers caressing my face. "Dub ran from his rooms to tell us what was happening. How could he have known?"

A hysterical laugh forced its way from my throat. "Dub's spying on me. Every minute of the day and night, he has at least one spy cam following my every move. I thought the Morrigan got rid of them all, but apparently he just put more back."

"What?!" Horrified, Hàorán pushed me out at arm's length. "You're kidding me. All the time? Since when? Does your sponsor know this?"

I shrugged and grimaced. "Pretty sure she does now. Those clips on the thumb drive the Morrigan had me share with you? Some of them are already from last year, and some are very recent." I pulled away and put my hands on the railing, staring out over the expanse of lawn behind the mansion... the parade grounds where just an hour earlier... I stopped the thought and shuddered. When I spoke again, it was in a whisper. "I guess I should be grateful."

"So... was he watching *us* last night?" he asked, joining me at the railing. "This would end my betrothal if that video saw the light of day."

I nodded, not looking at him. "But Dub would not expose you. He and your father are friends."

He sighed. "Let's hope. But he's stalked you all this time! Maybe I should cut him into little pieces." He sounded like he'd be happy to do it, too.

I shook my head wordlessly.

He threw his hands up in frustration. "Tell anyone who will listen about his perfidy?"

I shook my head again.

"Beat him to a pulp for you?" Hàorán demanded. "I would be more than happy to do that."

I didn't respond.

He made a low growling sound deep in his chest. "Will you tell me one thing, then?" Something in the dragon's voice had changed, like instead of being upset for me, he was unhappy for himself.

I sent him a sideways glance. "Of course. If I know the answer."

He groaned and then leaned his forearms on the railing next to me. "Antaeus suggested you put a spell on me..."

I closed my eyes and shook my head. "Hàorán, no. I would never do such a thing. Not intentionally, anyway." I rubbed my temples, fighting a pounding headache. "I had no idea why I seemed to affect others like that... until recently. Even though others, your dad for one, seemed to know it. He thought I could help you with your empress. It's why he wanted you to choose me."

Hàorán scoffed. "I would have chosen you anyway. But the singing you did in the rec room? The effect it had on everyone. What was that?"

"It was unintentional. An accident! I didn't understand the impact of my singing." I threw my hands up in the air, my face crumpling as I tried not to cry. "Hàorán, I never intended to lure you on, or anyone else for that matter! I'm here for only one thing: to learn how to fight so I can rescue Kellas. That's it. Everything else that has happened has been..." I couldn't finish.

Hàorán drew a deep breath, straightened, and turned toward me. "I believe you. Tell me what you want me to do, Light Bringer. Anything at all. I need to do something."

I held out my arms. "Please, just hold me."

So he did, all night, in my bed. But holding me close was the only thing he did, because that was what I needed—and because anything more than that would have been a colossal mistake... and would hurt us even worse when we inevitably had to separate.

Twenty

When we went out to the parade grounds the following morning, things were very different. For one, it was the Morrigan who addressed the students in cold, clear tones.

"I am now in charge of this school," she informed us. "I am certain that you are all aware of the death of one of your instructors, having witnessed it yourselves. Antaeus richly deserved to die for deliberately injuring one student and threatening the health and safety of another. Who, may I remind you all, is my champion." She paused, waiting for her threat to sink in. "Consequently, the situation here is different now. If you continue your education, there will no longer be teams working against one another. You will act as a unit, together, advancing your individual skills and no longer pursuing the ones you have no talent for. It is foolish to waste time in areas that will not benefit the team."

She raised her voice further. "Let me assure you this is for your benefit: those who continue here are preparing for war against one of the most capable and cruel of gods: Dother, God of Evil. We cannot assure victory, and if you fail, those who chose to join the Light Bringer in her fight will all die horribly. Do I make myself clear? *You. Will. Die.* Those of you who do not wish to remain under these conditions are free to leave and will do so immediately after I am done speaking. Questions?"

Her words struck terror in my heart, and from the looks on the faces of my fellow students, they were feeling much the same.

One hand shot up. "And what unescapable influence has the Love Goddess inflicted on us? Why should we think any of this is free choice, when she has so obviously used her powers to sway our thinking?"

The Morrigan glared. "Antaeus has poisoned your mind with lies. The Light Bringer's power can place a suggestion within your heart to be receptive to love, but love and dedication will only grow in the hearts of those who feel an honest connection. A heart as hard as yours, Eramos, will never be swayed by love in any form."

And with those few words from the death goddess, all my worries about my love powers evaporated. I would have hugged her right there in front of everyone, had I dared.

"Yes, ma'am," he responded, trying to appear chastised by her words. But a smirk of something that looked very like satisfaction briefly crossed his face. Had I not been looking at him then, I would have missed it. Not that I had any time to ponder that.

"Any other questions?" the Death Goddess challenged. Silence. "Very well then. Make your decision to stay or to go. You have five minutes. Those of you leaving will pack your bags and be off campus in a half hour or less." She turned her back on the students and went to talk with the remaining instructors on the dais with her. Shortly, Castor and Pollux left the dais toward the school, leaving only Dub, Dian, and Shen Long remaining with the Morrigan.

From the looks of things, it would not take five minutes for our fellow students to make up their minds. One after another, they peeled off and headed for the mansion. My teammates remained with me, together with Archer, who trotted over after the Morrigan had issued her ultimatum. Soon, Leonidas and Herakles joined us. I sensed Hàorán and Loki step closer to me as they approached. Watchful. Tense. Not trusting.

"Eramos and the Rooster left," Leonidas said simply. "We're throwing in with you, if you'll have us."

From his and Herakles' expressions, I could tell they were unsure of their welcome. I extended my hands to the Barbarian. He took them in his own, then surprised me by dropping to his knees, head bowed. I heard Loki grunt in surprise. Hàorán shifted slightly next to me, but did not move to interfere.

"I am so sorry, goddess. I did not know what my father had planned. If I had, I would have warned you and the Kitsuné." Leonidas looked up at me, a pained expression on his face. "I'd have done everything in my power to stop him."

"We both would have," Herakles added. He briefly laid a hand on the Barbarian's shoulder. "There was no love lost between us."

"I know." Embarrassed that he was on his knees, I tugged on Leonidas' hands. "Please get up!"

He got back on his feet but did not let go of my hands. "Can you forgive me... us?" He glanced at Herakles, who was nodding in agreement.

I gave him a half-smile. "There's nothing to forgive, Barbarian. You are not your father's keeper. I know you would have warned us had you been aware of his plans. We are grateful for your and Herakles' support. Can't say I'm sorry your teammates left, though."

Leonidas pressed an impulsive kiss on my cheek and whispered. "I promise you won't regret this." He let go of my hands and stepped back next to Herakles.

Loki took a deep breath. I sensed Hàorán relax slightly.

"No substantial loss, having them gone," Herakles grumbled. "Those two are a couple of punks. So, we're off to fight the God of Evil, eh? Sounds like fun."

"You have a strange definition of fun, Berserker," I muttered. Herakles just grinned at me and cracked his knuckles, looking like he was very much looking forward to a fight. The sadness that had surrounded him since the beginning had fallen away since I'd freed Leonidas from his shackles.

The large Black boy had joined us during the exchange with Leonidas and Herakles, and he stuck his fist out at me. I returned his fist bump with a questioning look. "The name's Morien," he said simply. "I'm with you." He scowled. "What Antaeus did? That was seriously messed up."

I could only nod in acknowledgement. He had that right.

The sponsors had apparently received notification of this meeting, because Kit's mother was striding across the field at us. As soon as she was within speaking distance, she made her intentions very clear. "You are coming with me, Yaeko. I will not have you risk your life on such a foolish endeavor."

Kit stiffened and sent a frightened glance at Loki.

He just frowned at her. "Your life, Kit. Your choice."

Kit stood there, silent, shuddering just the tiniest bit, like an aspen leaf in a light breeze. Her mother grabbed Kit's unbandaged arm. "Now, Yaeko!"

It broke whatever indecision Kit might have had. She yanked herself free. "No, Mother, I will not go with you. Not now, nor ever again. Find somebody else to kill your dirty old men for you. I am *so* done with that life." She stepped over next to Loki and looped an arm around his waist. He put his arm around her shoulders. Together they faced Kit's mother, who was anything but pleased with her daughter's defiance.

"You would choose a dog boy over your family?"

"I believe that's exactly what I have done, Mother." Kit raised her chin defiantly.

"You will regret this."

"I seriously doubt it."

"Don't come crying to me when you get hurt."

"I promise I won't."

They stared at one another for a beat, then the older woman spun on a heel and stalked off toward the school building. Kit turned her face into Loki's chest and cried. He held her close, stroking her hair and murmuring in her ear. I looked away. Maybe Kit thought her 'dog boy' didn't completely love her, but she was wrong. He very much did.

It did not take five minutes to clear the field. Other than my teammates, Archer, Leonidas, Herakles, and Morien, no one else stayed. I guess I should not have been all that surprised. There's a significant difference between merely training to fight and knowing that you might be fighting to the death.

We were clustered together, waiting, when the instructors joined us.

"Do any of you have questions about how we are going to proceed?" This time it was Shen Long asking. When none of us spoke up: "No? Then I will ask what each of you believe you can bring to this fight, because make no mistake, it will be a fight. Our skills will need to complement each other. Morien, you first."

"I pledge my sword to the cause," he said without hesitation. "On my honor as a knight."

"My strength," Herakles spoke softly. "I know what faces us."

"My courage." Leonidas.

Shen Long smiled and nodded his approval.

Hàorán: "My sword and my dragon."

Loki: "My cunning and strategy."

Archer took a deep breath. "My skill with a bow and arrow."

"Whatever is needed most," Kit murmured. "Anything I am capable of."

They looked at me. I regarded each of them, memorizing their faces, scribing this moment deep into memory. "My heart and my sword," I said at last. "Words cannot describe what your support means to me."

"Show them, my champion." The Morrigan ordered. "Show them what you bring to this fight."

I hesitated, then nodded. Reaching over my shoulder, I drew Fraegarthach from its sheath with a resounding hiss. Felt my body transform, my body clad in its dwarfish armor.

My friends fell back, alarm and astonishment on their faces. "I'm still me," I reassured them. "I couldn't show you Fraegarthach before because fight school rules forbade it."

"So, is that really the unbeatable sword of the Tuatha dé Danann?" Loki demanded once they'd recovered from their initial shock. I nodded. He laughed outright, almost a bark. "Ha! Maybe we won't all die after all."

No one spoke for a beat, then a slow smile crossed the Dragon Lord's face. "With your skills and ours," he gestured toward the Morrigan and his fellow instructors, "we have a team worthy of any battle." He drew a deep breath. "As we will fight in the Roman Colosseum, we will start by studying the battle tactics of the time. We will preemptively plan how to overcome any challenges we face. Play to our strengths and our enemy's weaknesses. Because make no mistake, even the God of Evil has weaknesses. He just hides them very well indeed. We will start in the classroom in 30 minutes. Dismissed."

Our instructors and the Morrigan left, and my friends gathered around me, all asking questions at once. I did my best to answer them all, telling them how I'd come by Fraegarthach, how it was both sword and magical instrument. Told our new allies about my ability to heal myself and others. About my inherited magic—and its cost. Leonidas knew about my age problem; Antaeus had told him, hoping to have his son use it against me. They'd all seen me in Berserker form before, but this was the first they'd seen of me in armor, wielding a magic sword. Their glee was infectious.

When we started toward the lecture hall, the same place where Antaeus had ordered me bound with the repression cuffs, Herakles held me back. "You can control your size," he told me. "Just like I can. You neither need nor want to go to the full size of your avatar all the time. The bigger you are, the slower you'll be. I'll show you how to do that, yes?"

I sent him my brightest smile. "I'd love that," I told him, and he rewarded me with an answering smile.

~

That afternoon, when we went out to the parade ground for sparring practice, there was a horse grazing in the middle of the track oval. Several of the hostlers were trying to catch him, but he kept dodging their clumsy attempts, snorting in annoyance, and moving off just far enough to avoid their ropes.

I recognized him as he lifted himself and leapt gracefully 20 feet in one bound. "Knight!" I yelled and ran toward him. He lifted his head, let out a high stallion squeal, and bolted toward me, plunging to a halt just as he reached me, rearing, tossing his lovely fine head so his mane flew. I threw my arms around his neck as he came down on all fours. "Ah, yah beauty!" I exclaimed. "Where have you been keeping yourself? I've missed you!"

He just snorted and gave me a rough push with his nose. He'd missed me, too.

"Your horse?" Hàorán had joined me next to Knight. "He's truly a fine one."

"Oh, you just made a friend with that comment." I stroked the dark horse's silky neck. "He's vain, this fellow."

Knight stretched his neck out and sniffed the dragon. Snorted, as if Hàorán's smell had tickled his nose.

"He says you're not half bad yourself, dragon."

A half-smile lifted the corner of Hàorán's mouth. "You understand him?"

I nodded. "Mostly. Sometimes we get our wires crossed."

"What happens then?"

"He dumps me on my can."

He laughed. "Really!"

"Uh-huh. Really."

"Why is he here, then?"

I didn't know, but I bet the demon spawn did, so I asked him. "He says I need to learn to fight from horseback."

Knight blustered and shoved me again, knocking me back a step.

"And apparently, he wants to start immediately." The Dark Horse was uncanny like that. He always seemed to appear exactly when he was most needed. It made his often arrogant behavior more palatable. Mostly. He could still be a complete donkey at times.

When we told Shen Long what Knight had in mind, he agreed to change his lesson plans. "That is actually an excellent idea." He sent Archer to the stables to request the hostlers bring out the school's horses.

As Kit was not a horsewoman, nor up to training of any sort because of her injuries, she was sitting this session out on the bleachers. My singing had helped her somewhat, but her shoulder needed more time to recover completely. It seemed unwise to chance a setback when riding was not within her skill set anyway. The medics had made it very clear that shoulders were slow to recover even with magical assistance.

Archer returned with the hostlers leading a string of horses. The stable master sent skeptical looks Knight's way. "We don't have any tack for yon beast," he told me.

I smiled at him. "Don't need any," I told him, then grasped a handful of mane and threw myself up on the dark horse's back. Bridle-less. No saddle. I urged the big black into a gallop, then guided him in loops and serpentines with just the cues my body gave. As Epona, Goddess of Horses, had once told me, the tiniest shifts of weight, just the power of my idea 'we're going this way' guided the huge animal where I needed him to go.

To my surprise and great satisfaction, Loki stripped the saddle from a small buckskin horse, but left the bridle in place. "Normally I'd just use a jaw rope, but this is what they have," he said, then swung on from the ground exactly as I had.

"We're Native," I explained, at the stable master's skeptical look. "This is how we ride."

"Not always, sis." Archer had chosen a steady-looking grulla and left the saddle on. "Comes in handy when I have to hang off his side to shoot," he explained. His bow and quiver were slung over his back.

"You two are showing off," Hàorán pronounced as he mounted his own horse, a handsome gray. He sat like an accomplished horseman, completely at ease. Morien followed suit on the big bay I had ridden the first day of classes. He looked unconcerned as the horse jigged and fussed at being asked to stand. Herakles and Leonidas swung onto their own mounts, obviously comfortable with being on horseback as well.

Dub mounted up as well and jogged his chestnut gelding over. "This way, Archer. The targets are over there."

Shen Long rode up on a glossy black stud horse and handed out practice swords... swords that bore a strong resemblance to my own Fraegarthach. I doubted it was coincidental. Once again, he showed the technique with Hàorán first, then paired me with his son, and instructed Morien to work with Loki while Herakles paired off with Leonidas. As before, we practiced everything in slow motion; muscle memory was everything. Being able to react to an attack without conscious thought was the key to survival. Block, strike, whirl the horse away, urge the horse forward, reengage. Knight knew the dance, and as we brought our practice up to speed, he started injecting his own maneuvers... charging his heavy shoulder into Hàorán's mount, shoving the unfortunate animal back onto its haunches, giving me a clear cut at Hàorán. Spinning away or striking when I lost my balance, Knight held the dragon at bay until I could regain my seat, although one such spin tossed me to the ground. I could barely regain my sword before Hàorán was on me, slashing from above... until I cut through his saddle girth and sent him crashing to the ground. One advantage of riding bareback: no one can cut your saddle out from under you! He didn't stay down, but leapt to his feet and we were back to fighting: strike, block, counterstrike. His low strike had me jumping into the air over his blade and bringing mine down on his shoulder from above. He barely had time to block my strike. Then we locked hilts, facing each other inches apart, both of us gasping for air as we pushed against each other's blade.

"Enough!" Shen Long rode his horse at us, forcing us apart. "One would think you two were enemies instead of sparring partners!"

I dropped the point of my sword to the ground and dragged a forearm over my sweating face. "Not enemies, Dragon Lord. Just focused." My knees went wobbly, and I dropped to the ground on my rear. I was so tired...

Hàorán dropped next to me, breathing hard. I could feel his body quivering from exhaustion. "You... are..." He didn't finish that thought.

I sent him a questioning look from behind a curtain of hair dripping wet with sweat. "I am what?"

"Mad skilled for someone who has never fought with a sword on horseback before."

I scoffed. "It isn't me. It's my sword."

"It's a practice sword, Raven," he drawled, a frustrated expression on his face.

"It's Fraegarthach's skill. Something about it takes me over and informs my actions. Otherwise, I'd be toast. And Knight obviously knows what to do, too."

"Knight?"

"My horse. He's demon-spawned on a night mare. Deeply opinionated and sometimes unpredictable. But crazy talented."

Shen Long had dismounted and come over, offering a hand, which I accepted, puzzled. He levered me to my feet effortlessly. "You fight well, but too recklessly. Fine for a skirmish, but not sustainable for a longer fight. Let me demonstrate."

Hàorán scrambled to his feet and fell into his stance.

His father sent him a glance. "Her, this time." He looked around at my teammates. "Dismount and watch."

The hostlers took the sweaty horses away to care for them. Knight had wandered off to graze already.

I took up the ready position. What was the Dragon Lord planning? He slowly paced around me, forcing me to constantly readjust my stance. Minutes passed, until, unable to stand the tension any longer, I attacked. He dropped back, grabbed my sword arm, forcing me to stagger forward. The flat of his sword came down across my back, knocking me to the ground, breathless. A moment later, he had his sword point on my neck, ready to pierce my jugular.

"And just like that, you're dead, Light Bringer," he said. "I didn't even break a sweat."

Hadn't Hàorán said something very like that not so long ago? I lay there lightheaded from the sheer whiplash of it.

The sword tip left my neck, and he was pulling me to my feet. "Again."

Shen Long never repeated an instruction. Each time, he used a different approach. Sometimes attacking immediately and without letup, forcing me to play defense until driven to my knees. "Again." Sometimes toying with me, keeping me off balance, wondering what he was planning until sending me to the ground with a single strike or two, his sword at my throat. "Better. Again." He finally took pity on me and slid his sword into the sheath across his back. "You will sleep on what I have shown you today, and tomorrow, we will try again. You are skilled, Light Bringer, but still have much to learn. Dismissed."

He walked away. I stood devastated as my teammates came over to join me.

"That was seriously nuts," Loki declared, looking more than a little freaked out.

Hàorán merely hooked an arm around my neck and pulled me close. Placed a kiss on my temple. "Welcome to my world, Raven." He sighed. "It's nearly supper time, and I'm starving. How about you?"

Kit and Archer joined us as we headed for our rooms. We didn't talk about the day's activities; Mostly, the guys were catching up with one another. I didn't talk at all. Being "killed" that many times in a row renders you speechless.

Kit was admiring, though. "You and that horse, what you could do together? It was beautiful! Like poetry in motion. I am so envious!"

I sent her a crooked smile. "Thanks." I fell silent again, letting my friends' conversation ebb and flow around me. 'Too reckless,' he'd said. Too. Reckless.

"Are you OK, Raven?" It was Hàorán, whispering in my ear.

"No. Yes... maybe?" I brought my head up and stared into his eyes.

He chuckled. "Got your bases covered, goddess."

We'd reached our bedrooms. Everyone headed for their showers. Kit had disappeared into our room already, Loki reluctantly letting her out of his sight and heading for his own.

Hàorán and I remained in the hallway. "It'll take them a little while to finish their showers. We have time," he said. He caught my hands in his own, swinging them back and forth and smiling down at me. "I don't think there is a single expression you have that I don't completely adore, girl."

"Even the pain one?" I scoffed.

"That one just makes me want to kiss it away," he said, and pulled me close. Kissed me. "There. Now it's your 'why did you just kiss me?' expression. And that one just makes me want to kiss you again." And he did.

I sank against his chest, my heart melting, just letting myself enjoy the feel of his lips on mine, trying not to allow the thought that this would not be forever to intrude on our time together. But intrude it finally did, and I drew back.

"We need to go shower," I murmured into his chest.

"Are you saying I stink?" he joked, tipping my head up with a finger under my chin. But he knew what I meant the minute he saw my face. Ran his fingertips over my cheek and touched my lips gently. "At least we had this much, Raven. Some people never even have that."

I tried to smile for him, not that it worked, and saw the reflection of my sorrow in his eyes. "See you at dinner," I whispered, and turned away. I heard him draw a shaky breath as I left.

Dinner was a subdued affair. Afterwards, we went to the rec room, where we tried to follow our usual routines. Hàorán had brought his laptop down from his room and wrote an email to his empress, his face furrowed with concentration. Kit and Loki cuddled... how I envied them their far less complicated relationship! The others got out a Monopoly board and got underway building fake fortunes. I applied myself to the grimoire, still seeking a way to break the collar from Kellas' neck—and not finding one.

"You're huffing." Hàorán closed his laptop and laid an arm across my shoulders. "You're upset."

I closed the book and pried my medallion out of the cover. Slipped its leather thong over my head. "Not finding any help in there." I leaned into him, drawing reassurance from his presence. "How's Mèng yáo?"

"She's okay." He sounded distant.

"What happened?"

He hesitated. "She's asking me lots of questions about you. Wants to know if I have feelings for you."

"Oh." I sat quietly for a minute. "I hope you were honest."

He drew a deep breath. "I was. I think. Not sure how she will take knowing what you mean to me." He fidgeted a bit. "She told me about her flings. Said they meant nothing to her. She just wanted to make her parents angry."

I chuckled. "I bet it worked, too."

"Oh, it did." Another pause. "She wants to meet me, she says. Once we're done here. She says I interest her."

I looked up at him, but he was staring at nothing, frowning. I gave him a little dig in the ribs. "That's good, right?"

He scoffed. "I guess so."

"One step at a time."

He pressed a kiss on my temple and stood up. "Time to turn in. Practice will be brutal tomorrow, if today was any indication."

He wasn't wrong about that.

Six weeks went by in a blur. I would like to say I got more skilled, better at strategy, stronger, faster, but mostly I think I just got really worn out. I wasn't alone. Herakles was good to his word, helping me learn how to monitor my avatar's size and fury so that I could direct it and never lose control. My swordsmanship improved dramatically until I could occasionally match either of the dragons in a fair fight. They both had years of training on me, and that wasn't something I could overcome in the time we had available.

We were sitting at dinner, none of us particularly chatty, eating the way exhausted people eat—like it was duty instead of hunger that drove us—when the Morrigan strode in with our instructors in tow. They were carrying multiple bottles of red juice, which they distributed among us.

"Drink the entire contents of your bottle and then listen carefully to what Dub has to tell you," the Morrigan ordered. "It is ambrosia; it will give you back your strength. You are going to need it."

Obediently, we raised our bottles and drank... cherry juice. Nothing else added. Rather tasty, truth be told. But the effect it had on all of us was remarkable. Spines straightened, eyes brightened. Tension left shoulders.

Morien raised his empty bottle. "More where this came from? I feel incredible!"

"More of that and you'll be flying higher than a kite," Dub told him. "We've already given you the maximum anyone should have. However, you must know why you received a drink usually reserved for older gods." That brought every eye on him. "The Cait Sidhe's deception has been exposed. They know he has not been living up to his end of the bargain." The God of Darkness sent me a knowing look, and I startled, suddenly realizing just exactly what Dub was referring to. Kellas had somehow refused to be Dother's reluctant stud... though how he'd deceived the God of Evil this long was a puzzle. "They will send him to the Colosseum in mere hours. My young friends, it's time to save the cat."

We received instructions to arm ourselves with our weapons and armor of choice and to dress for hot weather. It didn't take me long to switch from evening clothes to tank top and stretchy shorts. There was no point in choosing any of the weapons on my wall; I carried my own across my back everywhere I went. The three daggers on my avatar's belt? Well, I hadn't learned how to wield them well enough, and as such, I would employ them only as a last resort. Kit took longer to get ready than I did, finally emerging from her closet dressed in a black, skintight tank top and shorts, with as large an assortment of daggers and throwing stars strapped to her as I'd ever seen in one place. She had pulled her hair back into a tight bun at the nape of her neck. She saw my loose hair and promptly sat me down, braiding my hair in two rows down my skull, then wrapping the ends into a tight knot at my neck. "Long hair is dangerous in a fight," she growled. "You should know better."

Indeed, I should, having had my hair used against me the last time I'd faced Dother. I'd forgotten. Stupid.

We met up with our teammates in the entry hall and walked out to the parade grounds together. Bright floodlights lit the area like a football stadium. And, waiting for us under the lights was my father. I broke into a run and threw myself at Dad, laughing and crying at the same time. "What are you doing here?"

"Same thing as you, fledgling," he retorted, catching me up in his arms and swinging me around in a circle like he'd done when I was little. "Going to save Kellas." He set me down at arm's length and studied me carefully, noticing every fading bruise, every healed mark not covered by my clothing. He scowled when he saw the faint scarring around my upper arms left by the repression cuffs but refrained from commenting. Instead, he focused on the positive. "You've gotten strong."

I glanced down at myself. "Maybe?"

He laughed. "You've actual biceps now."

I grinned and flexed my arms. "Yeah?"

He chuckled, slung an arm around my neck, and kissed my forehead again. "Showoff."

My teammates came over, and we went through the introductions. Restrained and deferential, all the boys greeted my father quietly and then quickly stepped back. Kit kept staring at Dad like she'd seen a vision, which didn't really register until she pulled me aside.

"When were you going to tell me your father looks just like Liam McIntyre?" she demanded in an urgent whisper.

I sent her a puzzled look. "Who's Liam McIntyre?"

"Only the cutest actor ever! My gods, the dimples! Now I know where you get them from."

Loki wrapped his arms around the Kitsuné, pulling her back up against his chest and whispering in her ear. "Careful, girl. You're making me jealous, and of an older man besides!"

"You'd be jealous of a stone if you thought I was making eyes at it!" Kit retorted, but let him pull her away.

I left them to their bickering, knowing this was how they related to one another. They were always teasing each other, but if one was threatened, they would fiercely defend each other.

Dad must have overheard Kit, because there was a tiny smirk on his face when I rejoined him. "Being compared to Liam McIntyre is a first for me," he whispered next to my ear as he led me over to a quartet of heavily armed men. In a normal voice, he said, "Time to introduce you to my team now, fledgling. Give you a bit of background."

"Oh? No more secrets?" I poked him in the ribs with an elbow.

He grimaced at me. "Don't hold that against me, Raven. I did what I thought was best. Just because it wasn't..."

"Shh, Dad. Just picking!"

He growled and wrapped an arm around my shoulders. "You know these guys as the A-Team, but now you see them as they really are." He pointed to an armor-clad blond giant first. "This is Siegfried. He's German. We met here at fight school."

I smiled up at Siegfried. "Greetings, dragon slayer." I might not know all my mythology, but I knew about him. "Maybe don't go too close to the Dragon Lord and Hàorán?"

Seigfried grinned, his blue eyes twinkling. "I only kill evil dragons, little lady. Your dragons are safe from me."

Dad sighed, like dealing with his buddies was a trial. "And I believe you talked to Cú Chulainn that night at the hospital." He gestured at a second man.

I remembered him. The Celt was short, beardless, built thickly, like a bull. He had cautioned me about young men who considered themselves irresistible to women. A tragic figure in Celtic mythology, he was also a Berserker, like me and Herakles. He just smiled and nodded acknowledgement, sad eyes ancient in a youthful face.

"Diomedes," said Dad, dropping a hand on the next man's shoulder.

The Greek king of Argos was tall, with curly brown hair that fell to his shoulders, a full beard, and lovely brown eyes—a very pretty man. He bowed as Dad introduced us.

I nodded hello, then frowned, puzzled. "You look familiar."

"He shouldn't," Dad said. "He was your bodyguard for a while. But he didn't stay as hidden as he should have."

I gave Dad the side-eye. "Bodyguard?"

"I monitored you for years, Raven," Diomedes said. "Instructed to do so from the shadows..." he sent a glare at my father "which honestly was not a simple task, Michael, so ease off! Raven notices when she's being followed, and I paid for it with a 2 by 4 across the kidneys." He sent me a rueful smile. "That hurt, kiddo. Took me a long time to recover."

OMG, Diomedes was the guy I'd hammered back in Kestrel? I had thought he'd been stalking me. Biting my lower lip, I gave him an apologetic grimace. "I was afraid."

He merely smiled and shook his head. "Would never have happened if I'd stayed hidden. As it was, it proved a valuable lesson. Don't underestimate teenage girls."

"I wasn't about to leave you and your mother without protection, what with her prosecuting sex offenders, Raven," Dad scoffed. "So, yes. Bodyguard. He sometimes posed as a homeless man."

"Whom you fed cookies, so thanks for that!" Diomedes added. "I was also a school resource officer, a carpenter, and a few other unnoticeable individuals," he explained. "I rarely serve from the shadows. Not my style, frankly."

I raised my eyebrows and took a deep breath. "OK!" Turned my gaze on the last fellow, who stood silently at parade rest, gazing at me like he was memorizing everything about me. It was… unsettling.

"And this guy is Diarmuid Ua Duibhne. He's also a Celt. And he bears the Love Spot, Raven, so beware. The ladies all adore him."

I could see that being a problem. The man was, in a word, beautiful. Tall, with tumbling blond curls and sparkling green eyes. Strongly built, like all Dad's men were. Somehow, though, I was unmoved. Maybe blond guys were not my type.

"Back home, you all look different," I said.

"Glamour, fledgling." Dad chuckled. "You think they could pass for mortals otherwise?"

I raised my chin marginally. "Hmm. And is it glamour you use to look like you're in your forties? Right now, you look more like 25. Not exactly old enough to be my sire!"

"I strive to appear age appropriate for your mother's sake, Raven," he retorted, flushing.

I bumped my head against his shoulder. "Teasing again, Dad." I gave them all a quick once-over. Clearly, all were warriors, all in armor, bearing an impressive arsenal of weapons. All here willing to fight for Kellas. "Thank you all for coming."

"Wouldn't miss it for anything," Diomedes said, and the others were nodding in agreement. "Like old times, right, Michael?"

I was going to have to quiz Dad about that if we made it out of this fight alive.

Hàorán drew near, now that introductions appeared over. "Please excuse the interruption. The Morrigan asks that we be ready for transporting."

Suddenly, it all seemed too much. I threw myself at Hàorán and wrapped my arms around his waist, looking up into his dark eyes. "I'm afraid," I whispered.

His arms closed tight around me, cheek pressed to my temple. "It's okay to be scared. I'm scared too," he breathed in my ear.

I heard Dad's sharp intake of breath. Then: "Morrigan!" he bellowed, furious.

"Not now, Michael. I'm busy," she snapped. A moment later, a swirling fog surrounded us, and the parade grounds faded from view.

The heat was the first thing that registered. Blinding sunlight forced me to squint. Smells hit next: a combination of blood, sweat and dead things rotting. I felt my supper rise in my throat and struggled to force it back down.

"Ugh!" Kit was nearby, pulling her tank top up over her nose, leaving her midriff bare. "What stinks?"

"Death, Kitsuné." Hàorán released me. "Welcome to the Roman Colosseum, where killing is all good clean fun and the common folk decide who lives or dies."

My eyes were adjusting to the bright sunlight. The stands stood empty. Heat shimmered from the stone surfaces.

Across from where we stood, a door opened and a single figure strode out into the arena, far enough away that I could not make out his features. He was a gladiator, though, clad in the light armor typical of the age, right shoulder bare, the left covered with a pauldron. Leather covered his chest; vambraces bound his forearms nearly to the elbows. Leather greaves reached from his knees to ankles. His only clothing was a loincloth partially covered with leather straps that dangled from the waist of his chest covering. He carried a short sword and a round shield. He had tucked his helmet under one arm. When he saw us, he hesitated briefly, then continued to the center of the arena where he stopped and faced back the way he had come. Apparently, what he knew he was going to be facing was far more life threatening than the unknown we presented.

A moment later, the Morrigan appeared by his side. He barely flinched and turned his head slightly toward her, listening. I saw him nod, then slip on his helmet, adjust his shield, and bring his sword up in the ready position.

Then the Morrigan was at my elbow, and I startled. "Kellas says there will be archers in the stands. A full legion is coming. Men on horseback as well. Call your dark horse and three more to mount the men I shall put to guard you."

Kellas. Relief that he was still alive flooded through me, and fear as well, for what we faced. He was too far away for me to call to him, though. I swallowed hard and nodded acknowledgement to the death goddess, then called for Knight, mind to mind. The horse responded immediately to my thought-call, joined by three blood-red horses with eyes red as fire. Demon spawn, just like Knight.

The Morrigan swiftly made her way around the group. Dad and his A-Team were to fight alongside Kellas. Dad sent me the briefest look, nodded slowly, blinked. I touched two fingers to my lips and then away toward him... the same air kiss I'd always given him at the airport, when I'd been leaving after our summer visits. The kiss that said *this is not forever. I'll see you soon.* A grimace of pain crossed his face, but he forced a smile, returned the air kiss.

The Dragon Lord and Hàorán received instructions to take out the archers. "And bust down as much of this unholy edifice as you can while you're at it," the Morrigan told them, an order greeted with dragonish glee. Archer and Loki were to protect Kit, who was to summon her warriors and bring them in behind the legionnaires once they entered the arena. Dub and Dian were assigned to find and eliminate the Cait Sidhe, Erin. Leonidas, Herakles, and Morien were to ride with me.

"Dub has confirmed Dother is now inhabiting the Centurion. Look for him. You know what you must do, Light Bringer. You must not fail," Death told me, her dark eyes fierce.

"All these warriors to fight one man?" I wondered.

The Morrigan grimaced. "Dother knew we were coming. He has his spies everywhere. I've long suspected that little snake, Eramos, but had no proof. None of this is a surprise to the God of Evil, my champion. Now, mount up and be ready when I say the word."

Morian, Herakles and Leonidas each mounted one of the red horses. I grasped a handful of Knight's mane and slung myself onto his back, then gasped as black scales edged in gold flashed into being across his glossy hide. Hard, titanium-like scales clambered over my legs, pinning me to his body, and covering him completely. My horse had armored himself.

He was not alone. My companions' horses had similarly become scaled in red and gold, pinning my companions to their bodies as well. The horses themselves changed also, their necks becoming longer, more snakelike; their heads less horse-like and more demonic. Their teeth became fangs. Smoke curled from nostrils and flickers of flame trailed from gaping mouths.

"What are these things?" Leonidas gasped.

'*We are demon spawn, warrior. We go to fight. And we never, ever lose.*' Knight's arrogant tones sounded in my head and must have resonated in my companions' as well, because I saw the shock that sped across their faces.

"Well, then." Morien recovered first. "Fight we shall!" He drew his long-sword. It made an evil-sounding hiss as it left its sheath.

We were moving. Dad and the A-Team had joined Kellas in the middle of the arena. Dub and Dian moved off to locate Erin. Hàorán and Shen Long went to opposite sides of the arena, giving themselves room to transform.

Kit remained well back, guarded by Archer and Loki. Archer had his bow in hand, an arrow nocked. Loki transformed into the largest coyote I had ever seen, nearly as big as a horse, golden brown and thick-furred. He stood next to Kit, a snarl lifting his lips back from sharp white teeth. Kit knelt and dug her fingers deep into the sand covering the wooden floor of the colosseum, her head bent, chanting something in Japanese—something that sounded deeply ominous.

The Morrigan transformed into her raven and flew above us, croaking as we rode up behind my father and the others. I sent Kellas an anxious glance, but he acted as if he didn't even know I was there. It would be best if I didn't let his presence distract me... but that wouldn't be easy.

Multiple doors opened on the far side of the arena, and a legion of Roman soldiers marched out, spreading across the width of the space, swords out, shields up. They'd left space in their center, which was soon filled with a small troop of mounted soldiers, arranged on either side of their centurion. He was resplendent in shining armor and a red cape that fell in liquid folds from his broad shoulders.

'Do not look directly at the Centurion, any of you.' The Morrigan's harsh croak echoed in our minds, a warning I knew only too well to heed. Dother could overwhelm your senses with fear, freezing your ability to defend yourself. *'Wait for them to attack. May the gods be on the side of the righteous.'*

What an odd thing for her to say. Most everyone on our side was a god, or at a minimum, a demigod. But perhaps that was her normal going-into-battle pep talk?

The Romans were moving in a solid line toward us now, shields up. Dother and his mounted guard paced along behind them.

"Are you ready for me?" I whispered to Knight and reached over my back to grasp Fraegarthach. Pulling it free of its sheath, I felt my body transform, matching Dother's size; felt Knight grow larger and thicker under my thighs. My armor formed over my body, encasing me in dwarfish steel.

I heard Herakles laugh softly. "You go, girl!" he encouraged, and transformed into his Berserker—larger, more muscular, and scary as hell. A far cry from the stripling he normally was.

Morien lifted his helmet over his tight black curls. Leonidas nervously adjusted his own.

In response to a shouted order, archers rose as one from behind the short walls in front of the stadium seats; arrows rained down on us in a deadly shower. Several thudded home in my shield. More slid off Knight's armor plating. I saw Morien sweep his broadsword over his shield, splintering off the arrows that had buried themselves there. I followed his example.

Above us, the archers reloaded.

Two massive blue dragons launched themselves into the air and flew at the archers, fire gusting from their jaws, hard, sinewy bodies crashing into the barriers the archers hid behind, smashing the rock to rubble, tossing men to their deaths on the arena far below. But there were archers arrayed around the entire colosseum. Our dragons could not attack everywhere at once. We were sitting ducks.

'Now, my heroes!' The Morrigan's voice croaked in our minds.

We charged, and so did the Roman foot soldiers. The mounted ones paced up behind, ready, but saving their strength. Not an option the rest of us had. The enemy outnumbered us.

Until they didn't anymore. The Roman soldiers shouted in alarm as Kit's warriors attacked from the rear. Gray men had risen from the sand-covered colosseum floor; samurai warriors who attacked silently and with deadly efficiency. Kit's warriors. Useful constructs, but one she constantly had to remake, as a single slash of a Roman blade reduced them back to sand. Still, they gave us a fighting chance of survival.

I pushed Knight onward through the melee, slashing at any soldiers who dared to impede my progress toward my target, the Centurion. Surrounded and protected, he alone remained unengaged amongst the clash of samurai and legionnaires. I kept my gaze on his horse, an enormous gray stallion, knowing only too well the danger of looking the God of Evil in the face. Morien, Leonidas, and Herakles rode beside me.

Then Knight rose on his hind legs, squealed a stallion's challenge to Dother's big gray, and charged. Fraegarthach met Dother's blade with a resounding crash, sparks flying in an explosion in every direction. Then we were past them, whirling, coming up behind the Centurion. I slashed at his ribs. He blocked my blow with his shield as Knight's impetus carried us past. Dother roared, a wordless threat that made my blood turn to ice as we disengaged and put distance between us. Knight pivoted on his hind legs, his powerful haunches bunching as he flung himself at the gray stallion again. His teeth bared, Dother urged his stallion forward on my left. Not good. His sword crashed down on my shield, but my return strike was cross-body. Weak. Ineffective. Knight threw his massive shoulder into the big gray's haunches, causing it to stagger, preventing Dother from following up on his attack... and then we were clear of them. Knight carried me past the centurion, cantering in place as he pivoted once again. Then he was rearing back, muscular haunches bunching like powerful springs. '*Ready?*' sounded in my head. I grunted affirmation before he launched himself at our foes. I had my sword couched like a spear, tip up. Not broadcasting my move until Dother swept close, then I thrust it forward at the god's throat. He barely knocked the point aside in time. Fraegarthach's tip scraped along his helm, sending blue sparks flying as Knight charged past, carrying me into the clear once again.

My focus narrowed to just the god and myself. The only sound we made were grunts of effort as we fought. Our horses' hooves thundered on the sanded floor. The sounds of battle around us receded—just the two of us battling for supremacy. My focus was necessary, but infinitely dangerous. Another could attack me without my being aware of the danger. But that was what my companions were there for. Just like the mounted guard Dother had surrounded himself with.

I do not know how long we fought, neither of us gaining the upper hand. It could have been mere minutes, or hours. My Berserker strength was fading. Six weeks was not nearly long enough to train. The Centurion had prepared for battles like this his entire life. My blows were losing strength. A grim smile widened on Dother's borrowed face as he realized what was happening. He turned his mount to face us again.

Knight's long neck slashed out with the striking speed of a rattlesnake, sinking his razor-sharp teeth into the big gray's throat. The Centurion's stallion screamed in agony. It threw itself back, trying to break away, succeeding only in tearing out its own throat. It crumpled to the ground, dying. Dother leapt clear, slashing his sword across Knight's shoulder. The Dark Horse shrilled in pain, stumbled, and fell to his knees, taking me with him, his scales still binding me to his back. There was no time to fear for Knight before Dother struck. I caught his blade on my upraised shield. Blow after blow rained on me. My shield cracked.

'*Let me go, let me go!*' I thought-screamed at Knight. With just my upper body to bring to bear, I did not have the strength to continue blocking Dother's repeated blows and had none to strike back. Oh, gods, could he even free me, injured as he was?

Dother and I locked blades, and he pressed down, the edge of his sword coming closer to my throat by a fraction of an inch at a time. His helm came closer also, red eyes gleaming through the gaps.

"Whoever you are, warrior, you fight valiantly." His voice was just loud enough for me to hear. "Yield, and I will spare your life."

"Liar," I gasped.

Eyes widening at the sound of my voice, he abruptly pulled back.

'Knight! For the love of the gods, release my legs!' I cried to my horse again.

"You're a woman!" the Centurion exclaimed. "A woman!" He grasped my helmet in one hand and ripped it off my head. Stared at my face, recognition immediate. Then he laughed, an ugly, humorless guffaw. "Well, if it isn't the tasty tidbit. How sweet is that?" He raised his sword and brought it crashing down. Fraegarthach met his attack, knocking the blow aside just as Knight released the scales that trapped me to his back. I fell to the ground as the Dark Horse staggered to his feet between me and the centurion, blocking Dother long enough for me to scramble to my feet. The Centurion dodged around Knight and attacked again. His blow sent me sprawling, and I fell under another horse's pounding hooves. I barely avoided being kicked, scrambled back to my feet... and felt a burning stab just under my armpit, above my armor. My strength fled. I staggered.

"That's for Erin, little tidbit." Dother's voice was triumphant.

Leonidas was suddenly there, throwing himself between me and the Centurion. He met the God of Evil's blade once, twice, and then the God of Evil ripped it from his grasp. I stared in horror as Dother skewered Leonidas on his blade.

"Now, goddess!" Leonidas screamed, as he grasped Dother's sword guard in both hands, trapping the God of Evil's blade in his own body. Giving me an opening.

I lunged, Fraegarthach foremost, screaming with rage and loss. My pain was dashed away by the horror of how Leonidas was dying. Driving my sword up through the bottom of Dother's helmet, I speared through his skull, cleaving the Centurion's brain in half. Fraegarthach's tip exploded through the top of the god's helmet in a shower of electric blue sparks.

The Centurion's blood sprayed over me in a revolting red cascade. He collapsed to the ground, dropping the dying Leonidas to the ground in a broken heap. Black smoke—Dother's life essence—was escaping, but Fraegarthach wasn't leaving this unfinished. Fireworks erupted from the Retaliator's blade, tearing Dother's darkness to bits. My sword still piercing the dead centurion's body, a magic fire surrounded us, burning away the god's essence until it was gone. Completely gone.

My Berserker's strength spent, I collapsed to my knees, unable to pull my blade free. Herakles appeared at my side, helped me free my sword. He pulled me to my feet, then fell to his knees next to Leonidas, sobbing.

Morien stepped close and steadied me. "We're done. We've won," he said. His voice was shaky, his face pale as he stared at Leonidas and Herakles. He spoke truly, however. The Roman soldiers, those still standing, had pulled back when their centurion died.

Knight stood nearby, blood sluicing from Dother's cut, his head swaying back and forth threateningly, looking for something else to fight, but there was almost no one left. The centurion's stallion lay dead, one of several. Dead men lay strewn about like broken toys. The wounded clutched their injuries, some keening in pain, some tight faced as they bore their pain in silence.

It staggered me. So much death. So much pain.

I knelt next to Leonidas and laid a hand on his chest. "Oh, my friend. What have you done?"

He looked up at me, face twisted in agony. "I saved you, goddess." He coughed, and blood trickled from the corner of his mouth.

"Sing for him, Light Bringer!" Herakles begged. "Save him!"

I shook my head in sorrow. There was no saving Leonidas. The Morrigan stood nearby, ready to take his soul to the next world, and there wasn't a thing I could do to change that. Death did not compromise, nor did she spare anyone just because they were noble. Like Leonidas.

"I will never forget everything you did for me," I whispered, tears tracking their way through the blood splatters on my cheeks.

"One last kiss?" His eyes were fluttering closed.

"Oh, Leonidas…" I pressed my lips to his. The blood did not matter. I poured my love for his beautiful soul into that kiss. Something to take with him to the next world. When I drew back, his life left him in a final shuddering breath. Next to me, Herakles sobbed. I laid an arm around his shoulders, pressed my face to his. Our tears mingled.

"We go now," the Morrigan spoke. "Look up, you two."

We did. Leonidas' spirit stood next to the Death Goddess, uninjured, clean, smiling through his tears at Herakles and me. He raised one hand in farewell… and was gone.

Herakles remained kneeling by his boyfriend's dead body, weeping inconsolably. "Where are the others?" I whispered to Morien as he helped me to my feet.

"Coming over now," he assured me. "How much of the blood on you is yours?"

I gestured vaguely toward my stab wound. "Just this. You?" It took too much air to talk, and now that the adrenalin from battle was leaving me, the pain was making itself known as well. My breath was coming in short gasps.

"Unscathed, by the grace of God," he said. I gave him a swift up and down glance. He was bleeding from a gash on his sword arm. He smirked. "This is nothing, Light Bringer."

Yeah, right. Knights and their crazy 'nothing.'

Dad hurried up, face pale. "You're covered in blood."

"Mostly his, but he stabbed me." I pointed at the dead centurion. "You?"

"Minor," he said. "Who died?"

"Leonidas." I gestured to where Herakles was bent over the body, sobbing. "He took the blow meant for me. Gave me the opening I needed. The others?"

"Cú Chulainn hovers near death. My men have already taken him to a hospital. They all need medical attention as well. I think the coyote and fox girl are okay. Archer took an arrow through his thigh, but it missed an artery. My guys took him back with them as well. The dragons are already healing themselves... must be nice to have fast regeneration like that. Let me see your wound."

"What about Kellas?" I hissed in pain as Dad turned my body so that he could see where I'd been stabbed.

He grunted. "He's a bloody mess, but he's still vertical. The gods only know how that's possible." He sighed heavily. "Raven, you have a dagger wound to your lung. Hold still. I'm going to put a blood plug in this to stop the bleeding. But you must not take any blow to the chest for at least a week. Longer would be better. There is a danger of pneumothorax."

"What's that?" I gritted my teeth against the hard pressure he was applying to my stab wound. I gasped in relief as he released the pressure. "Pneumo-whatever it was you said."

"Air between your lung and your chest wall. Your lungs could collapse. Breathing would be... difficult."

I nodded wearily. "What do we do with them?" I gestured at the gathered Romans.

The Morrigan landed on my shoulder with a heavy flapping of wings, returned from escorting Leonidas to the Elysian Fields—the Greek version of Paradise reserved especially for heroes like Leonidas.

'We shall be merciful,' she said telepathically. *'Tell them to gather their wounded, bury their dead. Go home to their loved ones. We bear them no ill will.'*

Dad started forward.

'Not you, Michael. My champion. But first, unbind your hair, Light Bringer. They must see you as the woman you are.'

I dutifully undid one braid while Dad undid the other. Shook my hair loose, kinked now from the braiding, and sticky with the Centurion's blood. I walked toward the gathered Romans, the Morrigan on my shoulder, Morien and Dad pacing a step back. Just behind them, Dub. And Dian, who was carrying a bloody sack. Kellas had not come over—I'd checked. I felt his absence like a hole in my heart. Why hadn't he joined us?

I stopped before getting too close. Fraegarthach remained drawn; my battered shield was on my arm.

"I am the Light Bringer." My voice echoed magically from the walls of the Colosseum. The Morrigan's work, as I had little enough breath to spare as it was. "We bear you no ill will. We came to reclaim one of our own." I paused, scanning their ranks. Sorely depleted, with many walking wounded. "A cruel god has deceived you." A gasping breath separated each short phrase, the best I could do. "Gather your wounded. Bury your dead. Go home to your loved ones. Be grateful we did not... kill you all." I may have sounded tough, but anyone trained in war would know I was not 100 percent.

"'Ware archer!"

I heard Kellas' warning shout, glimpsed the archer from the corner of my eye and used my remaining strength to point Fraegarthach at him. Blue lightning shot from its tip, blasting apart the parapet and the single archer standing there. I returned my attention to the soldiers. "Anyone else want to try?"

None did. Well, fancy that! With Dad supporting me, I walked away, sliding my sword back into its sheath. There would be no more killing today.

Twenty-Two

I wanted to talk to Kellas alone, but that would not happen. Not here anyway. My companions had arranged themselves in a protective group around me and Kellas.

He was bleeding from multiple cuts, none deep enough to cripple, but they must have hurt, nonetheless. We stood gazing at one another as if neither of us knew what to say. Until I reached out to touch his face.

Kellas drew back. "Don't." His eyes pleaded for understanding.

"What's wrong?" I took a step forward, following him.

The sorrow in his eyes was almost more than I could bear. "Erin cursed me. The last thing she did," Kellas whispered. "Any touch from you, any at all, will feel like torture."

I couldn't be sure if my loss of breath this time was from horror or the stab wound. "How do we stop this?"

"Remove the collar," he told me. His face twisted in sorrow and pain. "But you mustn't." I reached for him again. He backed away... again. "There's a catch, Brannaugh."

I waited, gazing up at the man I loved, aching for him.

He drew a deep breath. "If you remove the collar, even if I survive the pain, it will alter my memories of you. I will hate you. I cannot bear for that to happen."

My vision blurred. No, he could never hate me. Or I him. "If the collar stays, you will be trapped forever in this dimension. I cannot leave you here, Kellas!"

"Better that than lose my love for you."

Hot tears spilled from my eyes. "I cannot leave you here, Kellas. I cannot do that to you. To me."

"You must." His voice broke. There were tears in his lovely blue eyes.

I glanced at Dub and Dian. Cut my eyes from them to Kellas, who knew instantly what I'd decided, as did the two gods.

"Oh no, you don't!" he protested, but he was not fast enough to avoid the brothers as they grasped him by both arms and held him fast.

I stepped closer, meeting his steely gaze with my tear-glazed one. "Forgive me, my love," I whispered, touched the collar around his neck, pressed a fleeting kiss to his cold lips at the same time. My love magic was needed to break his bonds, but I hoped brevity would spare him the worst of the pain.

It didn't.

He screamed in agony as the collar crumbled from his neck. He sagged between Dub and Dian as he fought off the torture my kiss had subjected him to. A long moment later he regained his feet, and we stood staring at each other for the briefest moment. His gaze was unfocused, dazed, until awareness flooded back... and he was glaring at me with raw hatred in every line of his body.

"You filthy witch!" Using the twins' grip on his arms to support him, Kellas curled his knees to his chest and struck out with both feet, smashing into my chest, screaming in pain and rage. He struggled against the brothers, nearly breaking free. "I'll kill you! Do you hear me? I will find you no matter where you hide." He said more, but it didn't register as I lay sprawled on the ground, gasping for air.

Life devolved into vignettes as I struggled to breathe, the coppery iron taste of my own blood flooding my mouth, reeling from Kellas' cruel words. Why? *WHY?* Despair overwhelmed me. I rolled over weakly, spitting blood on the ground, gasping desperately for air.

"Get him out of here!" The Morrigan ordered Dub and Dian. I glanced up in time to see them gripping a spitting, struggling Kellas, and then they were gone.

Dad was on his knees beside me, talking urgently to the Morrigan. Something about my lungs. Air! I needed air... There was the swirling half-awareness, too familiar. Dad lifted me into his arms; I felt the strange suspension of dimensional travel, then the bitter cold as we returned to our world. Bright light glared down at me, and I smelled the sharp stink of anti-septic. Low voices. Gentle hands touching me. A cool cloth washing my face. Then oddly clear: Archer's sweetheart, the nurse Ian, his face inches from mine. "You're making a habit of this, girlfriend. You've gotta stop, hear me? The whole emergency department is going crazy with all your wounded friends."

I heard beeping—constant, continuing. Also a shushing noise, air pressing into my lungs, then releasing. Press. Release.

Darkness.

∼

I woke up in our spare bedroom. There was machinery clustered around me. I lay on a hard hospital bed, hooked up to multiple instruments... and I couldn't move my arms.

Panicking, I struggled. Mom appeared, her hands pressing my shoulders back to the mattress.

"Shh… it's all right," she soothed. I subsided, staring up at her, unable to speak because of the oxygen mask attached to my face. "We strapped you down because you kept trying to rip out the tube draining your chest." Mom straightened, crossed her arms over her chest and sighed. "You're on oxygen, antibiotics, and heavy-duty painkillers, so don't get any smart ideas, kid." Her face crumpled as she struggled to maintain her famous self-control. "You nearly died… again. That damned cat."

Mom never swore. The rage and pain on her face were clear, though. Her baby had been badly hurt, and apparently, she held Kellas responsible. Didn't Dad tell her the whole story?

I had lots of questions but no way to express them. Frustration caused my eyes to fill with tears.

She bent close again. "Are you in pain?"

Not like she thought, no. Not with the drugs they had shot me full of. Discomfort, but not pain. I shook my head slightly.

Her brow furrowed, trying to phrase her questions for yes or no answers.

"Hungry? Thirsty?"

No.

"What then?"

I twisted my right arm so my hand was palm up. Wiggled it, trying to point to the tattoo that graced the soft skin just above my wrist.

She glanced down, saw the small cat tattoo there. "You would ask about him? After what he did to you?"

I nodded and hoped my eyes could plead my case.

She huffed, and turned her head to one side, biting her lip. "He nearly killed you!"

I shook my head. No, he hadn't. He'd been cursed. He hadn't wanted me dead, Erin had. She'd weaponized him. She'd intended for Kellas to hurt me. Had planned for the possibility that she and Dother would die and wanted insurance that I would die, too. It was the only explanation that made sense. Unfortunately, the only way to confirm this was to ask Kellas. If he would even agree to answer.

Mom sighed heavily, knowing that not answering would not make my question go away. "At last word, the gods confined him to Dub's demesne. They are caring for his wounds. Despite his impossible behavior, they treat him well."

What consisted of impossible behavior? What was Kellas doing?

Mom couldn't read minds, but she certainly knew how mine worked. "He refuses to eat. Breaks things. Curses any offer of help. Impossible and unpleasant." She fussed my bedcovers straight. "And to think I thought him honorable."

I nodded. Sounded like Kellas was a very unhappy cat. I closed my eyes, impossibly tired.

"Get some sleep, honey," Mom urged. "You'll be up and around in no time, knowing you."

It wasn't like I had a lot of other options. I slept. Did my best to heal myself with dream singing, but it was going to take time. It takes functional lungs to sing, and mine were still a mess.

Dad and Ian removed my draining tube the next day with a nasty, sucking sensation. It felt like pulling barn boots out of deep mud, only this was my body, not mud. Gross! They encouraged me to sit up and move around to help my lungs recover. Fortunately, I no longer needed a mask constantly strapped over my face. Dad warned me I was a long way from full recovery, but the scary part was past unless I did something stupid. They allowed me visitors to ensure my good behavior. I was still very weak, so visits were brief.

Cú Chulainn came with Diomedes, looking somewhat the worse for wear, but alive. He'd lost weight, and haggard lines had been added to his already care-worn visage. Of all of us, he'd been hurt the worst, multiple internal organs pierced with swords. It was a wonder he was still alive.

He sank on the edge of my bed. "Hey, fledgling," he greeted me softly, using my father's nickname for me. "You look like crap."

I snorted, but it was with a shadow of my usual snarkiness. "You don't look so hot yourself, mister."

A crooked smile twisted his mouth up. "I'm alive. That's more than I had even hoped for. I wouldn't be, except for the fox goddess and her constructs. She had them guard me after I was struck down."

"Gods can't die, though. Right?" I struggled to sit up, and Diomedes slid a hand behind my back to help. "They just find a new body and come back." Like Dub had. Dear gods, did that mean Dother eventually would as well? Panic made my heart race and my breathing more ragged than usual.

Diomedes sank down behind me on the other side of the bed from Cú Chulainn. "Not always, kid. There are a few ways the gods *stay* dead... and you did one of them to Dother. Your sword killed his new body, but its fire also killed his essence. He won't come back, rest assured of that." Weak from relief, I sagged against him, and he wrapped a fatherly arm around me. Cú Chulainn took one of my hands in his own, a quiet gesture of reassurance.

"What other ways kill the gods?" I had to know. Just in case I needed to kill another god someday.

"Three that I know of," the ancient Celt said. "Beheading, having your body consigned to hellfire... and being forgotten by mortals. Those unfortunate ones fade away and disappear." Cú Chulainn shuddered. "Being forgotten is the worst of the three. A protracted, painful way to die."

"Then I will make sure no one ever forgets about you," I assured him.

He squeezed my hand, eyes shiny with unshed tears. "Thanks, kid,"

The two of them left soon after, warning me not to overdue, because they wanted me in one piece ...and feisty enough to join them at the gym for sparring lessons. OK, so that was their excuse, but their concern for me had been unmistakable, and that warmed me through and through. I had friends here, too.

Hàorán came with his empress, which surprised me—until I saw how she constantly touched his arm, leaned in to him. Laughed at things he said. It was obvious that she was totally into her fiancé... and making sure I knew she'd laid claim to him. I could see how her attention pleased him. When they left, it was with his arm around her waist, the way he had once held me close. He turned his head as they left, smiled sadly, and nodded. The only acknowledgement of what we had once shared.

I fought back tears. How is it you can be happy for someone else, and yet so devastated for yourself? Even though I had known from the start that Hàorán and I could never be together.

Kit and Loki came as well. She was bubbling over with excitement, doing her best not to let on about the silver engagement band on her left hand until I demanded she fess up and show it to me. Loki leaned against the wall, hands thrust into his jeans pockets like always, a crooked grin on his face as his lady showed off her ring. She was as giggly about it as the silliest teenager over an invitation to the prom. There was a soft look in his eyes as he gazed at her: deeply fond, tolerant of her over-the-top enthusiasm. I was happy for them and swallowed my own sadness.

It wasn't until Ian and Archer arrived arm in arm that I finally lost it. My face crumpled into an ugly mess and I started sobbing.

Archer rushed to my bedside and immediately pulled me into a hug. "Gods, sis! What's the matter?"

I shook my head against his hard chest. "It's stupid..." I swallowed hard. "Everyone is so happy... and I am so *not*." My throat swelled tight.

"It's Kellas, isn't it?" Archer asked, his voice gentle.

I managed a jerky nod.

Ian sat down on the bed on my other side. "Oh, girlfriend..." He stroked my hair as my brother held me close. "I'll make sure you have a kajillion handsome men all vying for your attention. Just watch me."

"Unless you want girls," Archer joked.

I scoffed. "Straight girl here, bruh."

"Guys it is, then," my brother chuckled.

Gay guys make the best friends. At least these two were to me. Archer was so certain Kellas would come around eventually, and Ian was determined to make sure Kellas regretted it if he didn't. They didn't leave until I was giggling helplessly over their elaborate silly plans, and promised to come see me the next day.

Exhausted, I slept... and immediately dropped into Dub's office. Despite my brother's best efforts, I was still seriously unhappy. The God of Darkness was at his computer, scowling at the screen, and did not immediately realize I was there. He looked worn down. Not defeated exactly, but close. He sighed, pushed his keyboard away and leaned back in his chair, cussing under his breath, then saw me. There wasn't even a flicker of surprise on his face. "Had a feeling you'd be showing up soon," he grunted. "Have a seat."

I hopped up to sit on his desk, close enough to touch him.

Dub's eyes narrowed, noting how close I was to him, and studied me quietly for a beat. "You healing up all right?"

I leaned back on my hands and sighed. Nodded once.

His expressive eyebrows lifted. "Feeling pretty low, aren't you?"

I grimaced. Nodded again.

He reached over and squeezed my knee. "Understandable." He leaned back in his chair again. "Give yourself time."

I had a pressing question for him. "Will Antaeus return?"

Dub growled, his anger surging to the surface in an instant. "Not likely." He gestured at his fireplace. "Demon fire. I threw him in it that very night. And Dian saw to it Erin's head ended up there too. Those two will never bother you again, rest assured."

I nodded, relieved. But I stayed perched on his desk.

He studied me thoughtfully. "Hoping to see Kellas? Because I'm not sure that's a good idea just yet."

I dropped my chin to my chest so he wouldn't see the tears start up in my eyes.

Dub cursed, stood, and gathered me off the desk into his arms. "You don't have to be alone, beautiful. I would be your everything if only you'd let me."

Gods. This was so unfair to him. "I know. But..." My arms had gone around him, clinging. I was a cruel wretch. I should have pushed away, but craved the comfort of his arms.

His breath sighed against my hair. "We were sweethearts once, Light Bringer. Long ago. In another of your lifetimes. Your given name was Skye."

Shock rippled through me. I looked up at him through my tears. "We were together?" Oh, gods, this was so awful. "I don't remember." It came out in the barest whisper. If we had been, that would explain so much of his actions right from the start. Also perhaps why I'd always felt drawn to him, even when he was being his worst self.

"You were my everything, and I lost you." He struggled to hold himself together, the fight within reflected in his face. When he spoke again, his voice sounded like he was trying to hold back tears as well. "One of those cruel tricks the Fates play. Some remember past lives. Others do not."

"But... there's Kellas." Tears slid down my cheeks. "I love Kellas."

He groaned, in pain. "I know. That's why I have worked so hard to make sure he doesn't kill himself. I was never able to deny you anything, Light Bringer. Come. I'll hide you in shadow so he won't see you. But I warn you: it's not pretty."

We walked out of his mansion and over a long expanse of lawn until we reached what looked to be ocean shoreline. A sandy beach shone white in the dim light of a million stars. There was no moon. A dark figure stood at the water's edge, feet dug into the sand, arms crossed over his chest, staring out over the waves as they rolled onto shore.

Dub stopped short of the figure. "You've got to eat sometime, Kellas." The Cait Sidhe merely grunted. "Sleep too."

"I'll sleep when I'm dead." Kellas' voice was rough-edged, like he'd been screaming. I still could not get his agonized scream out of my head from when I'd freed him. It haunted my dreams.

"You'll die if you don't," Dub persisted.

"Good." It sounded like Kellas thought it would be, too.

"What if I said you have a visitor?"

He scoffed. "Tell them to go the feck away."

"Kellas..."

He rounded on Dub, white teeth bared in a snarl. "Let me die, Dub! I don't want to live. Not without her."

I gasped, clamping my hands over my mouth to muffle the sound. No, Kellas. Don't wish for death. Fight back. Come home to me!

"What if she still loves you?" Dub sounded shaken, too. "Your death would devastate her."

A harsh laugh escaped him. "*You* should claim her. Take her back. She was yours first, anyway. I was just a mistake."

I couldn't breathe. What was he talking about?

Kellas continued. "*I* tried to kill her. She hates me. Her whole family hates me. And why wouldn't they? I hate myself!" He raked his hands through messy, overlong hair. "And even if she did still love me, I can't trust myself around her." The agony in his voice was palpable. "What if the curse takes me over again and I kill her this time?" He shook his head, his shoulders slumping in defeat. "I can't, I *won't* take that risk. She's better off without me."

What if the curse takes me over again... No. It wouldn't, it mustn't! He loved me, he would never hurt me if it wasn't for Erin's curse. Surely it couldn't last forever. But his words struck horror deep into my gut. I didn't hate him. I loved him. And it was killing me to hear him hate himself. I couldn't remain silent any longer. "Kellas..."

He went rigid at the sound of my voice and drew a deep, shaking breath. "Get her out of here, Dub! I swear to the gods, if you don't get her out of here, I can't stop myself." He groaned as though he was in the worst sort of pain, fell to his knees, and dug his fingers into the sand. Threw his head back in an agonized howl more feral than the wildest panther scream. "I will kill her!"

Dub spirited me away in an eye-blink. "Go. Now. Don't come back. If he ever recovers, I'll come get you." He gave me a shove, and I was gone.

～

Imbolc—the return of the light—came and went at the beginning of February. It was a time to celebrate the maiden goddess Brigid and new beginnings. I could not find it in me to celebrate when everything I'd hoped for, had fought for, was gone. Yes, we'd saved Kellas, but he suffered for it, and I... I suffered too. He'd been cursed, and because of it, my heart was shattered. Erin had won, even after her death.

February passed slowly as winter continued to hold sway over our part of the world. I healed and grew stronger, finally able to return to my bedroom under the domed roof. I spent a lot of time there, curled up in my armchair, my grimoire open on my lap, reading... memorizing useful spells and enchantments, learning new ways to set wards. Trying to learn everything I could about curses, especially the kind Kellas was suffering from. I looked up counter-curses. The trouble with those was they had nasty side effects. I was not enough confident in my abilities to chance any of that with Kellas. My only hope was knowing that curses lost their effectiveness over time, gradually fading to nothing—if they didn't get reactivated by the person who had cast it. Erin was dead. The only cure for Kellas' curse was... time.

Kellas would eventually recover, but I had to stay away from him. Completely. Utterly. And hope.

Hope was in short supply this winter.

I told my parents what I'd learned. Mom was unconvinced. Dad was supportive. "They have an expression for this in the army," he told me. "'Embrace the suck. The only way out is through.'"

One bright spot in my life: Mom moved back in with us. She said it just made things easier with me being injured, but in truth, it was because she and Dad had done the work and fixed where their trust had been broken.

I kept busy. There was a lot of schoolwork to catch up on, not that it took me long to do so. It was all too easy compared to fight school. My thought was that I would go for my GED and skip the rest of high school entirely. Take classes at the local junior college. I was questioning college entirely, too. Would it get me where I needed to go? And where was that exactly, anyway? I was a singer, a fighter, a magic maker. Was there even a college that helped train in that? Lots to consider.

The spring equinox came and went. The snow melted. Robins and bluebirds returned. On my daily hike, I discovered drifts of snowdrops hidden along my grandmother's favorite walk, the long trail that meandered around our property. When things warmed up further, peepers and wood frogs sang from the vernal pools that dotted the woodlands. Buds swelled on the trees. Daffodils and forsythia bloomed.

I alone was not thriving. Loss sat on my heart like a block of ice, cold and unrelenting. I lost weight. My black hair, normally lustrous, lost its shine. Even I could see the haunted look in my eyes when I looked in a mirror.

"Here," Mom said one morning at breakfast, shoving a pretty journal under my hand, then piling a handful of pens nearby. "Write it out. Take out the mental garbage. It's no good for you to have all those sad thoughts rotting in your mind. Put them on paper, then you can let go of them. It worked for me. It'll work for you, too." She tipped her head, smiled sadly. "Write three pages every day, Raven. You can't stay sad forever. It's killing your dad and me to see you so unhappy." Then she handed me a book. *On Death and Dying* by Dr. Elisabeth Kübler-Ross.

I read the book, not that it gave me any joy to discover that I was grieving a death of sorts. Everything the doctor wrote about—the anger, the bargaining, the self-recriminations—I recognized. Not that I could have done anything to prevent this all from happening. So, I wrote every day. It felt awkward at first. Some days it took hours to fill the three pages, but I stuck with it.

Dad dragged me along to his frequent gym workouts with his teammates now that COVID restrictions had eased. He said it made a handy half dozen so we could all spar, but I knew it was less that than making sure I didn't sit around feeling sorry for myself. His buddies easily embraced my presence in their group, teasing me, pushing my limits. Making me work to keep up. It felt good to be part of a team again.

But Kellas stayed gone.

Twenty-Three

One rainy morning in late spring, Diomedes and I were sparring with swords during our gym time. We'd just executed a sweet combination of strikes and parries. I was congratulating myself on my improving skills when a bystander spoke. "That last bit was sloppy."

I didn't bother to look over at him. Our workouts always attracted attention from others at the gym, and snide comments were not all that rare. After all, here were five big, muscly men and one petite girl duking it out with swords or fists like they meant business—and I clearly could hold my own against them. It wasn't surprising that it drew people's attention, and we had become adept at ignoring the inevitable comments. My companions would shut down inappropriate remarks in a hurry, though. A single level-eyed glare would quell most offenders, and the others? Well, they didn't hang around long when approached with intent to injure. I appreciated that.

I stepped back from Diomedes, and we saluted each other with our swords, ending the bout. The King of Argos scooped up the towel he'd dropped on a nearby bench and swiped his sweaty face with it.

"You got this one, Raven?" he asked, his gaze cutting toward the young man whose snide remark had interrupted us.

I retrieved my towel and slung it around my neck, still not bothering to look at the rude guy. "Got this." I sent the king a saucy grin.

Diomedes chuckled low in his chest. "Sic him, kid." He sauntered toward the men's locker room.

I started toward the women's locker room, ignoring the jerk who'd criticized my technique.

He followed. "You know I'm right."

I stopped, sighed, faced my detractor... and felt a shock of recognition. "Hàorán?" It couldn't be, though. My friend was busy getting ready for his over-the-top wedding scheduled for this summer. Or, more accurately, he was busy dealing with his empress as *she* went crazy about the dumbest details of their over-the-top wedding. I didn't know what was worse.

"Yǔxuān," he corrected me. "Wrong brother."

That same slow grin I'd so loved on his brother lifted the corners of his mouth. My heart stuttered in my chest. Oh, gods. Me and my nutty susceptibility to beautiful men! "What are you doing here?"

"Orders." He gave me an appraising look. "You have friends in high places who are worried about you."

"Really." I packed 'rueful' into that word. It wasn't a secret that people kept close watch on me. That Shen Long was keeping tabs on me as well didn't surprise me much, given our history.

That made his grin spread into a smile. "My father rarely takes such an active interest in mortals."

I scoffed. "There's where you're wrong, dragon."

He closed the distance between us. Loomed over me. Tall... over six feet. "I'm wrong?"

Crap. Why did every man I found attractive require looking up at? "I'm not quite mortal."

He smirked. "I know what you are. Think you can work your love magic on me... goddess?"

He unsettled me. I still hurt from losing not one, but two men I loved. I wasn't ready to try again. Even if Kellas never came back to me, there was Dub, who I know loved me. But Yǔxuān had quite the pickup lines! "You asking?" Gods. This was so crazy. He looked so like Hàorán.

"That depends."

"On what?"

"On whether you carry through, goddess."

I rolled my eyes. "Not wasting my time on wise guys, dragon!" I started for the showers again, then tossed a parting shot over my shoulder. "For the record, that sword work was not sloppy. You're just envious."

I heard him chuckle. "Catch you later, goddess."

Oddly, even though he'd been a smart-ass, I felt... lighter.

~

Warmer weather came. I took my driver's test and passed. Took the GED and aced it, too. As a graduation present, my parents gave me a car, a new plug-in hybrid, royal blue. I argued with them about it, but they insisted it would free them up from having to drive me everywhere, ultimately saving them money. Save them time as well... and time was not a replaceable commodity. My new car was super cute and sporty looking. I took to going places, just because it was fun to drive. Met up with friends I'd made at the gym to go for long runs. Went shopping for sneakers at the local running store and made friends there... and landed a part-time job as well. Hung out with Archer and Ian and their buddies, because they were easy to be around. Started going to local races with Archer and not doing too badly for myself. I'd gotten faster. Stronger.

I fared better in the longer races, where my endurance came into play. I out-lasted the speedsters.

I got pulled over while driving home from a local race one Saturday. The radio was going full blast: Kelly Clarkson's *"Stronger (What doesn't kill you)."* I didn't think I'd been going that fast—normally I was a certified member of the five-miles-an-hour-over club. But this time? I'd been going close to 70 mph. Crap. A speeding ticket was a waste of money. My job at the running store wasn't bringing in enough to spend foolishly.

The cop kept me waiting. I rolled down my window to let in the warm spring breeze and sat there, jiggling one leg as I waited for the cop to come over. He was taking his own sweet time about it.

Oh, come on! I flung open my car door and lunged to my feet just as the cop reached me. We stood face to face, practically touching.

"You aren't supposed to get out of your car," he whispered, a slow grin widening his lips.

I looked up... and up... at Yǔxuān. In a cop's uniform. "I'm not?" Why was I having trouble breathing? Gods, Raven. Get a grip!

"Nope." He touched my face. "But it makes this easier." His hand slid around to the back of my neck, then he leaned down and kissed me. Slowly and thoroughly.

OK, that was unexpected! And darned forward of the dragon, but... Oh. My. Gods. I felt hot all over.

He broke off the kiss and backed up a few inches. "Hi, goddess."

We stood looking at each other for a beat. "You're a cop." I'd found my voice again—in time to spew the obvious. I wanted to kick myself.

He barked out a laugh. "Well done, Sherlock. What gave it away?"

"Tsh!" I put my hands on his broad chest and shoved, putting some space between us. He laughed at me again. "You're insufferable." I told him. "Just give me whatever ticket you think I earned and go bother someone else."

"Did you earn yourself a ticket?" His dark eyes were twinkling.

"You tell me," I scoffed. "You're the one who stopped me."

He laughed again; a soft chuckle that made me feel that warm rush all over. Not fair! "70 in a 55 zone, goddess. Pretty zippy! However, I'm just checking on you for my father. Looks like you're doing better these days." He gave me the once-over look, noting my sweaty running clothes. "Getting out and doing things. That's good." He stepped back and acted like he was admiring my new car. "Nice wheels, by-the-way. Yours?"

I nodded. "Do you kiss everyone you pull over?" OK, so that was a dumb thing to say as well.

He sent me a grin as he started walking around my car. "Only the pretty ones."

He was a shameless flirt.

Yǔxuān finished his circuit of the car. Pulled out a pad and scribbled something on it. Tore off the top sheet and folded it up small.

Crap. He was giving me a ticket, after all! "We finished here?" I lifted my chin defiantly.

"You're free to go." Yǔxuān gave me the sort of slow, small smile that could melt hearts, and closed the remaining distance between us in two swift strides. His mouth was right by my ear. "Don't forget your ticket, goddess." Sliding the folded-up paper into the palm of my hand, he backed away. "See you around."

I rolled my eyes at him, reached for my car door, then watched as he sauntered back to his squad car, slid into the driver's seat, and pulled away, sending me a jaunty wave as he passed. I unfolded the ticket he'd given me. *Your fine for doing 70 in a 55: 6 p.m. Tonight. The Boatyard Grill. Be there, or else...*

One heck of a way to set up a date! But it made me feel good in a way I hadn't for a very long time.

~

I took time getting ready that evening, wanting to look nice, but not send the wrong message. I still wasn't sure I wanted anything more serious than friendship at this point. After deciding on a deep-red silky tank top over a pair of close-fitting white slacks, I even used a little makeup and put on earrings. Grabbed my favorite jeans jacket to take along in case we sat outside on the deck. It was still chilly enough by the water's edge that a jacket was necessary.

Dad looked up from his novel when I came downstairs. "Going out, I take it?"

"Got a date."

He closed his book over one finger. "Do I know the guy?"

I huffed in annoyance at his overactive parental attitude, patted his shoulder, then bent to give him a hug. "I can handle myself, Dad."

He chuckled and went back to his book. "Tell Yǔxuān I said hi."

Dad knew. Drat! Like I could keep any secrets from my parents. Between Dad's buddies and a few nosy gods, it seemed someone always had eyes on me. I wondered if Dub was still tracking me with his spy flies. I hadn't thought about that possibility for months.

Yǔxuān was late. Granted, I'd gotten to the restaurant a little early, allowing myself time for slow traffic, but he was a full 15 minutes late and I was getting antsy. When he finally arrived, he looked annoyed. His apology was short and gruff.

The hostess showed us to our table and left us with the menus. Yǔxuān opened his and was scowling at it. Not exactly how I'd visualized our evening together going! "You want to tell me what's bugging you?" I asked.

He huffed. "Nothing important." He continued to study the menu, avoiding my gaze.

I sent him an oh-really look, anyway. "Then why are you so grumpy, if it's unimportant?"

He drew a deep breath and set the menu down. "I'm getting the crab cakes. What would you like?"

Crab cakes were the most expensive item on the menu. Mom had coached me not to order anything more expensive than my date. His choice made that easy. "The chicken parmesan sounds nice, but listen, if you don't want to do this, I can grab a burger on my way home."

That got his attention. He straightened up in his chair. "No. It's fine. I'm sorry. It's just been a tough day." He finally looked at me. I could see the storm clouds roiling in his eyes. We were likely to get a downpour *inside* the restaurant if he didn't cool it pretty darn quick. Like his father and brother, he commanded the rain.

I tilted my head and gave him a stern look. "Maybe act like you want to be here, then?"

That made him smile ruefully. "You're a force to be reckoned with, goddess."

"Worth remembering, dragon."

Our date went better after that. He relaxed, joked around, acted interested in what I had to say. Shared a couple humorous things that had happened to him since he'd been in town. Made a wry comment about being the DEI hire for the year. But the sly boy who'd kissed me out of the blue earlier that day was notably absent. There was a stiffness to his bearing that confused me. I wondered what had happened since I'd seen him last.

He walked me to my car after dinner, opened the door for me. "I'll follow you to make sure you get home all right."

I'd started to get into my car, but that stopped me. I stood back up and leveled a narrow look at him. "Why?"

He avoided my gaze. "In case."

This was absurd. I gripped his shirt in both hands, gave him my 'don't mess with me' glare. "You've been acting weird all night. What's going on?" He still wouldn't look at me. "Yǔxuān?" The warning in my voice was unmistakable.

He growled deep in his chest and finally looked at me. "The Cait Sidhe's back. The God of Darkness decided he was safe to return. Kellas is at your place, and I'm worried."

Kellas was home? My heart leapt like a wild thing in my chest, but I forced my voice to remain steady. "If Dub thinks he's safe, why are you worried?" Or was it something else... like jealousy? Which didn't make sense, given how we barely knew each other.

"Maybe because the dude tried to kill you?" He'd kept his hands off me up to then, but now he wrapped large hands around my waist and pulled me close. "I've only known you a little while, but it would bother me if you died, goddess."

But... Kellas was back. "I need to go." I pushed on his hands. It wasn't wonderful of me, abandoning Yǔxuān like this, but Kellas was at our house and I couldn't wait to see him again.

He released me reluctantly. "I'll follow..."

"No!" That came out harshly, and I tried to fix it. "It's OK, Yǔxuān. Truly. I've got this. Thanks, though." I slid into the driver's seat and reached for the door. He was blocking it with his body. "Please?"

A muscle flexed in his cheek. He stepped out of the way, scowling.

I closed the door and started the car. I was aware he watched me until I was out of sight.

~

I pulled into the driveway so fast my tires sent gravel flying. Jumping out of my car, I ran for the house, gaining the porch just as the front door opened and Kellas stepped out. I stopped my headlong rush, barely in time to keep from crashing into him.

"Oh, hi!" I was breathless, my heart racing. I tucked an errant lock of hair behind my ear and bit my lip. Looked up at him from under lowered lashes.

He studied me, a curious expression on his face. "Good evening." He stepped to one side. "Going in?"

I stared at him, shocked to my core. "Kellas?"

He frowned slightly. "That's me. Have we met?"

Have we met? I couldn't breathe. *He didn't remember me?*

Dad came up behind Kellas and saw me standing there. "Back from your date already? I thought you'd be later." He shifted uneasily.

"Introduce us, please, Dad?" I felt faint. Kellas didn't know who I was.

"Kellas, this is my daughter, Raven. Kellas is an old friend of the family, fledgling. You met once, a long time ago. When you were little." There was a pleading look on Dad's face. *Just go along with this*, it said.

I nodded, unable to speak.

"Nice to meet you, Raven," Kellas said, all formal, detached.

I stared into his beautiful eyes, eyes that gave no hint of having any memory of me, and felt my own fill with tears. "Excuse me." The words came out choked, and I ducked my head before any of those tears fell. Pushed past the man I loved and ran for my room.

Not that my parents let me stay there. After Kellas left, Mom bullied me back downstairs and into the living room, where the God of Darkness and the Morrigan were waiting side by side on the leather couch. Dub rose when I entered the room. There was a look of dread on his face.

Whatever was ailing my Cait Sidhe was Dub's fault; that was immediately clear just from the way he was behaving.

I stopped in my tracks and glared at him accusingly. "You did something to Kellas."

Mom took my arm. "Listen to him, Raven. Don't judge. Get the facts first."

I shook her off and stalked toward Dub threateningly. "Kellas doesn't know who I am. Does he know anyone, or am I the only lucky one here who he doesn't recognize?" My voice carried a rough edge; The shock of Kellas not even knowing me had undone everything I'd worked for months to repair.

"I can explain." Dub looked awful. Shadows darkened his eyes, and his face was gaunt.

"You had better!" Hysteria tinged my words.

The Morrigan laughed, but there was no humor in it. "Sit, my champion. I assure you this sad turn of events was necessary to save the Cait Sidhe's life. You will give the God of Darkness your undivided attention. No interruptions."

When the Goddess of Death tells you to sit, you sit. I perched on the edge of a nearby chair and attempted to still my trembling limbs.

Dub eased back down on the couch. "Kellas attempted suicide," he said finally. His eyes pleaded with me for understanding. "He nearly succeeded."

I gasped and clamped both hands against my mouth. Suicide? He'd been serious about wanting to die, then.

Dub sighed. "I thought he was getting better, but I was wrong. The rages had faded to mere foul humor, but he'd gone quiet. Brooding. I was busy with other things. I wasn't paying enough attention. Quiet is easier to ignore than temper tantrums and smashing things." He shook his head, grimacing. "After months of him acting out, it was a relief. But then Kellas used his own dagger on himself. Dian found him. We got him to a surgeon right away, but it was a very near thing. If he'd had access to a gun, he'd be gone." He sent me a sad look. "After you chided me about allowing guns in my demesne, I cleared them out. It saved his life. Probably the lives of several of my visitors."

Morrigan gave his hand a subtle squeeze. He gave her a tight smile. He continued. "Kellas wasn't getting better. Whether it was Erin's curse or PTSD from the horrors he suffered while a prisoner, I don't know. But just waiting it out wasn't working. I had to do something."

I waited.

He groaned as if he were in genuine pain. "I hacked into his memories, Light Bringer. I shut them away behind a firewall. Not all of them, just the ones that hurt him the most, the ones driving his self-hatred. Unfortunately, besides his memories of the Roman Colosseum, those included all his memories of you."

"Will he ever remember me?" It came out as a whisper.

Dub exchanged glances with the Morrigan. "Maybe?"

"Or maybe not," the Morrigan stated.

Just the facts, ma'am. "I see." I stood. "Thanks." I headed for the back door.

Mom stopped me. "Where are you going?"

"Just for a walk, Mom. Don't worry. I've got this." No, I didn't—but I needed space to scream. I got as far as the lake before I sank to the ground and let the tears come.

I was unaware that, from a short distance away, a giant raven watched me. So did a very large black cat.

Twenty-Four

The moon had risen high over the lake before I stopped crying. I went over to the large flat rock where last summer I'd told Elias that I loved Kellas, and sat down. Pulling my lute around to my front, I ran my fingers over the strings and sang. Eric Carmen: "All By Myself." A sad song for a broken heart, of course, but it didn't stop there. Lewis Capaldi's "Someone You Loved" came next. Then Calum Scott's "You Are The Reason." That done, I let the notes fade away and sighed.

"Somebody hurt you," said a voice in the dark. "Terribly."

I gasped. As wrapped up as I had been in my sorrow, I had sensed no one nearby.

"I didn't mean to frighten you." Kellas stepped out of the shadows and stood between me and the lake, backlit by the moon. "You have a beautiful voice, but your songs are all very sad. Why?"

I stood up, unsure of what I could safely tell him. "My boyfriend and I broke up," I said at last, and slid my lute away in its hiding place.

His face was in shadow. "I take it he's an idiot."

I made a choking sound. "You're kidding, right?"

"Hmm. No. If you were my girl, I'd never let you get away."

His words stunned me. "You don't even know me," I whispered.

"Your heart shines through in your singing, girl. What more do I need to know?" He took a step toward me. I must have flinched, because he stopped, suddenly still. "I mean you no harm."

I was having trouble breathing. Kellas, who didn't know me, was treating me like a fragile thing he wanted to take care of. I wasn't sure how I felt about that. Would he be like this for any girl he'd found crying on the beach? Or was it my love magic? "I'm not sure I'm ready for this," I breathed.

"There's no rush. I've nothing but time." He sounded sincere.

I stood silent for a beat, then asked, "What's my name?"

"You've forgotten your name?" There was a humorous tone in his voice.

No, he'd forgotten. "Say my name, Kellas." I could hear the pain throb in my voice.

He hesitated before answering, as if this was a trick question. *Well, true that!* "It's Raven, isn't it? That's how your father introduced us earlier."

I sighed. "Yes."

"I'm confused." He meant it, too.

"Don't be." Despair was bringing the tears back. I blinked hard, fighting them.

He took another step closer. This time I didn't flinch. He closed the distance between us. He was so close. And still so far away... "What would help?" he asked softly. "What would push the pain away for a little while?"

I looked up at him and knew what I wanted, what I needed, no, *craved*, from him. Knew it was probably a bad idea, but I didn't care. "Kiss me?" I whispered.

His eyes widened briefly, surprised; his expressive eyebrows quirked. Then: "If that's what helps, I can do that," he murmured. And he kissed me. Gently, chastely... then with a rough groan, he pulled me up against his chest and kissed me again, this time deepening the kiss until my lips parted under his. He ran the tip of his tongue along my upper lip.

Was he *tasting* me?!

"Peppermint," he breathed against my mouth. Then he kissed me again... and yet again until we were both gasping for air. He finally drew back, laid his cheek against my forehead. "Why does it feel like I've kissed you before?" he asked, his voice hoarse, barely louder than a whisper. "Your touch, your smell, your taste... it's all familiar, somehow."

Because we had been sweethearts. Before Dub made him forget me. I was trembling all over.

"Your ex really is an idiot," he said after a while, his voice steadier. "And I intend to make sure you forget all about him. However, I suspect your parents are wondering why you haven't come back to the house yet. Plus, they might not be happy if they found out you were out here with the likes of me. I'll walk you back."

What did he mean by 'the likes of me?' He had used that line before, multiple times, in fact. I didn't dare ask.

We walked back up the lawn, not touching, but not far apart either. We didn't talk until we were on the deck outside the back door. Then he took both my hands in his and stared down at me like he was trying to memorize my face. "May I see you tomorrow?" he asked at last.

My smile was tremulous. "I'd like that." Oh, his beautiful smile! How I'd missed it!

"It's a date, then. 9 o'clock too soon? I'll call first." He raised my hands to his mouth and kissed them. He released me reluctantly and stepped back. "Tomorrow." He gave a brief salute and disappeared into the dark.

Dad met me as I came in. He'd been sitting in the dark waiting for me. Kellas Iend I would have been easily visible through the glass doors with the moon high overhead shining like a spotlight on us. He did not wait for my explanation. "I'm not sure this is such a great idea, fledgling. He's just gotten back. We still don't know how stable he is. Until we know more about his mental state, it's not safe for you to be alone with him."

"I love him, Dad." It was a plea for understanding.

"I know you do. But he's fragile. We need to be careful."

I was fragile, too. "He wants to go out with me tomorrow. Early."

Dad looked bleak. "Invite him to join us at the gym. Then we can step in if need be."

I sighed. Grimaced. "All right. But don't smother me, OK?"

He pulled me into his arms for a hug. "Thanks, kid. I appreciate it." He held me a while longer before turning me loose. "I know how hard this is for you. Like it was for me with your mom. Be patient. It'll be worth it in the end, I promise."

He'd waited ten years for her to come around. I would not be that patient.

~

When Kellas called the next morning, I invited him along to our training time at the gym. He was gracious about it, but it obviously wasn't what he'd had in mind. However, once we met up with Dad's teammates, it was apparent they had a long history together, that he *remembered*, and everyone was pleased to get reacquainted. Seigfried collared Kellas for a bout with swords before I paired off with him myself. I wasn't stupid. I knew that had been intentional on the German's part.

Being without a partner, I settled down on a bench to watch. It's not exactly a hardship watching good-looking guys with their shirts off, working up a sweat. Not for me, anyway. But the fresh scars on Kellas' upper body were a grim reminder of what he'd been through not so long ago. He was much leaner than he'd been last winter, far too thin.

Yǔxuān appeared suddenly, sliding onto the bench next to me and bumping my shoulder with his arm. "How are you doing?" he asked without preamble. He was wearing his uniform. Probably either working or headed there.

The awkwardness of our parting yesterday weighed heavily on my conscience. "OK, I guess."

"He came here with you." Stating the obvious, trying to keep our conversation going.

I nodded, not taking my eyes off Kellas as he executed a neat parry and attack that had Seigfried jumping out of the way like a scalded cat. I flinched, feeling the power of his fighting abilities almost as strongly as if he had directed it at me.

Yǔxuān huffed softly. "I never stood a chance, did I?" he murmured.

I looked at him then and saw the sadness in his eyes. "I'm sorry." It was the quietest of whispers.

He gave me a small smile. "Don't be. I can recognize the love of a lifetime when I see it. I just wish it were me you were looking at like that."

I felt my shoulders sag. "Please, Yǔxuān. I never meant to hurt you."

"You forget. I was the one coming on to you like a house afire. You just got caught in a weak moment." He laughed softly. "I don't blame you. It's my own damned fault." He patted my knee before standing up. "Gotta head to work before I'm late. I'll see you around, goddess."

I stood on tiptoe to kiss him on the cheek. "Thanks, dragon."

He did a finger gun at me. "I've got your back if you ever need me, goddess." He plastered a cocky grin on his face and sauntered off.

Ouch. I knew he was hurting as I watched him leave. Drat this love goddess crap, anyway!

A crash of swords and the sound of a falling body had me whirling, my attention yanked back to the contest between Kellas and Seigfried. Kellas was flat on his back. Seigfried's sword was at his throat.

No! Not Kellas!

Kellas' sword lay between me and the mat, where the two men remained in a motionless tableau. I reacted, snatching the fallen sword up in one fluid motion. Knocked Seigfried's sword away from Kellas' throat. Attacking the German like I intended to murder him. Moments later, I had the god backed against a wall, my sword tip at his throat. "Don't you *ever*..." I was trembling with rage.

Then Dad was stepping between me and Seigfried, grasping my sword tip with his bare hand and forcing it away from the god's throat. "Easy, fledgling. We're all friends here," he soothed.

The blood rage abruptly fell away. I staggered back in horror, dropping the sword. It clattered to the floor. "Oh, gods." I felt hot and cold at the same time. "I'm... sorry. So sorry." I swayed on my feet.

Then Kellas was there, his arms around me, supporting me, his breath warm on my cheek. "Hey. You're fine. Seigfried's fine. I'm fine. Easy, girl. You've got this."

I turned in his arms and wrapped my own around him, my face pressed to his bare chest. Shock had me shaking all over as I babbled nonsensically. "I would have killed him. He had a sword at your throat. I would have killed him..."

"For me." Kellas slid gentle fingers under my chin, tipping my face up so I was looking at him. There was the oddest expression in his blue eyes. "Why?"

"It's complicated." I forced myself to let go of him. Turned to Seigfried and my father. "I'm sorry. I lost my head."

Dad merely nodded and looked at the floor, hands on his hips.

Seigfried chuffed a shaky laugh. "Damn, girl. I'll make sure you never get really mad at me! Phew! That was as sweet an attack as I'd ever had leveled at me, and I've been attacked by some of the very best." He offered a fist bump.

I met his fist with my own, still apologetic. "Seigfried..."

He caught me by the nape of my neck, pulled me close and put his mouth next to my ear. "Don't you dare," he scolded, his voice pitched low so only I could hear him. "You have nothing to apologize for. I know your history." He released me. Nodded. A sad smile touched his lips. He knew what heartbreak felt like. Having lived as long as these gods had, it was impossible not to have experienced loss repeatedly.

It put a quick end to our workout session. When I exited the women's locker room, the A-Team and Kellas had already left. Dad remained.

"The guys went for a run together," he told me. "Gives them a chance to catch up. I'm due at the hospital. You OK getting yourself where you need to go?"

I checked my analog watch. "I start work in less than an hour. Should get home around 3 p.m. or so." The thing is, Dad knew my schedule. Why would he be double checking like this? "You don't need to worry about me, you know."

He gave me a wry smile. "Worrying about you is my job, Raven. Promise me, though. Take it really slow with Kellas. That little demonstration of yours made a deep impression on him. He's already questioning us why you came to his aid in so dramatic a fashion, when all he and Seigfried were doing was sparring."

"I reacted. I wasn't thinking." Like the Dragon Lord had hammered into me repeatedly. Muscle memory. Maybe it wasn't entirely that I was lovesick over a guy who did not remember me. Yeah. That was a lie.

"And Kellas admits Seigfried got the drop on him because he was distracted by you kissing Yǔxuān. He quizzed us hard about the dragon, what he meant to you." He shook his head before looking back at me, worry writ large on his face. "Be careful, fledgling." He pulled me in for a hug. "Just... be careful."

I went through my workday in a daze, going over the morning's events in my head repeatedly; trying to make sense of my reaction to seeing Kellas at the end of Siegfried's sword, and what Kellas must be thinking of my behavior. I walked out of the store at the end of my shift, not any closer to making sense of it.

Kellas was in the parking lot, leaning against my car, arms crossed over his chest. He pushed off the car when he saw me coming. "I've been waiting for you." He was still in his workout clothes: a tight black T-shirt, black running shorts, bright orange running sneakers. Smokin' hot.

I forced myself to act nonchalant. "Need a lift?" I unlocked the car and gestured at the passenger side.

He nodded. We rode in silence as I navigated the heavy traffic on Route 13. Once we were headed north on 89 by the lake, he drew a deep breath. "You want to tell me what that was all about?"

I pretended not to understand him. "What do you mean?"

"This morning's demonstration, Raven. You acted like I was in mortal danger, and you weren't about to let me die."

"Oh, that." I was in trouble for sure.

"Yeah, that," was his dry rejoinder.

I drew a deep breath. "That was me losing my head. It happens sometimes."

"Over me?" Now, his voice dripped sarcasm. "Not that I don't appreciate your concern, but we just met, remember? Or is there something I'm not being told?"

I didn't have an answer to that.

"Raven?" There was a warning note in his voice.

I heard the edge of panic enter my voice. "I can't tell you."

"Why not?" He sounded even more annoyed.

I shook my head, feeling my throat swell with emotion. "Kellas, what's my name?"

He huffed, his forehead wrinkling in a heavy scowl. "Not this again."

I chanced a glance his way, and my car chastised me for driver inattention. "You've lost a sizeable chunk of your memory, Kellas. You need to recover those on your own. We'll give you all the help we can, but..."

"Is that why you keep asking me what your name is?" he asked, suddenly quiet.

I held back the tears that threatened to fall. "It's key, actually. Your name for me. No one else calls me that, Kellas. Only you."

He blinked. "So, you think if I remember this special name, the one that only I have for you, then I'll remember?"

I nodded, unable to speak.

His scowl deepened further, as if he was battling the locks on his memory and failing utterly. "I'm the idiot boyfriend, aren't I?" he said after a prolonged silence.

"Not an idiot!" I protested, and now the tears broke free and slid down my cheeks. "Never an idiot!"

He sat still for a long beat. "So, you don't deny I was your boyfriend." Another silence, then "Did we break up?"

"Not exactly."

"What happened?"

"I can't tell you that!" My voice rose in dismay.

"Pull over." It was an order, harshly put.

I pulled over. He got out. Leaned in the open window. "I'm gonna walk the rest of the way," he told me, his voice flat, even, like he was holding his temper tightly in check. "Don't follow me; I'm not in danger. I just need some space to make sense of what's happened to me, OK? Now, go on, get out of here." He straightened up and slapped the roof of my car. "Git."

My heart splintered into pieces. All this time apart, and he *needed space?* Isn't that what people say when they want to break up, and can't quite bring themselves to say goodbye?

He had close to eight miles to walk to get home. At a three-mile-an-hour walking pace, he should have been back in time for dinner.

He didn't show.

Twenty-Five

Knowing how worried and upset I was, Archer went looking for the Cat Man and found him sitting on a bench alongside the Black Diamond trail. My brother told me later that Kellas had been staring off into the distance, so deep in thought, he'd not even been aware of Archer's approach until the last moment. This was not normal for Kellas. But since his rescue, nothing about the Cait Sidhe was normal.

Kellas didn't join us for dinner. He didn't come around the next day or even the next. My parents put him up in Dad's old cabin, so he would have more privacy—also to keep the two of us separated while he worked things through.

He avoided me, even though he wasn't avoiding anyone else, which told me I was the only one he was angry with. Archer reported that they got together for runs, but Kellas never asked about me. Otherwise, the Cait Sidhe seemed calm and in control of himself. He regularly joined the A-Team for workouts when I wasn't there, but if I showed up, he'd excuse himself and leave.

A week turned into two. Kellas didn't join us for meals. He didn't hang out with us in the evenings. It broke my heart all over again.

Diomedes pulled me aside after Kellas left for the locker rooms when I'd showed up at one of their workouts. "That's becoming a habit for the Cat Man, taking off when you show up. Something you'd like to share with me?"

I looked up at the King of Argos and managed a bitter smile. "He finds my presence galling, apparently."

"Too bad for him, then. Maybe you should pretend to hook up with one of us? Just to awaken the cat's jealous side?" He grinned and dropped a fatherly arm across my shoulder. "Siegfried, perhaps? He's the closest to you in age."

"Siegfried's blond. I like my guys dark," I scoffed, and threw an elbow into the king's ribs.

The king grunted in pain and grabbed me by my wrists, humor dancing in his brown eyes. "I'm dark. It's a tough job, but I'd volunteer to be your pretend boyfriend."

I tugged free of his grip. He released me, raising his index finger, warning me not to slug him again. "I don't play those games, Diomedes. You know me better than that." I sighed heavily and grimaced at him. "Besides, you all act disgustingly paternal toward me. Not exactly boyfriend material."

"It was just an idea. Anything to get you out of the doldrums." He sent me a sad smile and gave me a gentle shove toward the door. "Better scat. You'll be late for work."

I nearly ran into Kellas as I left. He sent me a dark, unreadable look, and deliberately stepped out of my way. It took my breath away. I spent the rest of the day fighting back tears.

I started going down to the lake in the evenings and playing the lute by myself. Orianthi rarely sang with me anymore. While I'd been away at fight school, she had made friends with a set of twins next door and spent most of her time at their house playing. I didn't resent her for their friendship; five-year-olds need five-year-old friends to spend their time with, not depressed teens. And frankly, I wanted alone time.

I filled the time learning new songs. Although I had never been a huge fan of country western music, I found ones that just seemed to fit what I needed: Nate Smith's "Fix What You Didn't Break." Muscadine Bloodline's "10-90."

Music helped. It always helped.

Hàorán's wedding was fast approaching. Earlier that spring, Mèng yáo had asked me and Kit to join her and four of her friends as bridesmaids. It was to be an enormous wedding... who needs six bridesmaids, anyway? But when you are unbelievably wealthy, this was practically a requirement. People would see anything less as stinginess. The wedding venue was on a private island in the Caribbean. We were guests of the Dragon Lord—whose island it was. An entire island. Holy shiz. My family was well off. Hàorán's family was filthy rich and so was Mèng yáo's. It was eye opening to see what that much money could buy, and the wedding was just one manifestation of that wealth.

A private jet flew Archer and me to the island one week before the wedding for last-minute details. Archer was one of Hàorán's groomsmen. My presence was required for fittings; my opinion on music was sought. We 'absolutely must' tour the wedding venue.

I needed a change of scenery, anyway; there had been no change with Kellas. His memories did not seem to be coming back... and he continued to avoid me.

Mèng yáo and Hàorán met us at the airstrip. He looked quietly happy, although a bit tired around the eyes. His empress was about five foot nothing;

a tiny, 90-pound dynamo bubbling over with enthusiasm and information. Our dressmaker had completed our dresses; we needed a last fitting. She had the entire week planned with fun things to do. Anything we wanted to eat or drink, all we had to do was ask. She chattered on and on as she led us toward a stretch limo parked nearby.

Hàorán leaned down and whispered in my ear as we followed the others toward the limo. "One word of advice," he told me. "Elope."

I burst out laughing, earning a puzzled look from the empress and Archer. "It's nothing!" I assured them. "Just thrilled to be here and see all this finally. It's amazing!"

Hàorán chuckled under his breath. "You're an amazing liar."

I gave him a gentle shove. "No! I mean it! This place is just... sheesh." Palm trees, azure water, silver sand... it fit the OMG description.

A pleased smile crossed his lips. "You like it?"

"What's not to like?" Now I was lying, just a little. I had noticed the military bearing of the private security men who seemed to be everywhere, the lethal-looking guns they held, the watchful, carefully neutral look on their faces. The island might be beautiful, the riches amazing—but the wealth came at a cost to freedom that I would not be willing to pay.

We met with Hàorán's groomsmen. Yǔxuān was his brother's best man. Herakles, Morien, and Loki had come too. I was so thrilled to see my teammates it didn't register that the dragon was a man short of matching Mèng yáo's six bridesmaids. We spent a lovely hour catching up with each other. Following a light meal, Mèng yáo introduced Kit (who had arrived on another jet with Loki) and me to the other bridesmaids and maid of honor—all pretty Chinese girls who fluttered about like a flock of brightly colored birds. Mèng yáo led us through the giant complex of buildings to a lovely, bright room overlooking the ocean.

A bevy of seamstresses awaited us with our dresses. Kit and the other bridesmaids greeted these with enthusiastic screams. I just stood and stared. We bridesmaids were wearing purple. That was fine: I liked purple. The thing was, these dresses showed off the feminine form in as sexy a way as possible. Our gowns were strapless. The stiff boning in the bodice held our breasts high, eliminating the need for a push-up bra; to top it off, the neckline plunged into a V. The skirt was floor length, but, like the red dress I'd worn the first night at fight club, it was slit up the thigh so that every step revealed leg. Gods. I was going to feel naked while fully dressed, and dared not say a thing to the bride, who was in orbit at how her bridesmaids were going to wow her guests. I would need to keep my love magic under tight wraps. It would be bad form to upstage the empress on her special day, and I had no desire to attract undue attention, anyway.

Three very efficient Chinese ladies stripped me to my panties, bullied me into my dress, and placed me on a pedestal for easier alterations. Mèng yáo fluttered around the room, visiting with each of her bridesmaids, finally reaching me at the far end of the assembly line.

"This is my singer," she informed the ladies, who were assiduously tucking and pinning my dress so it hugged my every curve. "See these stretchy bits hidden here, Raven? That's so you can draw a deep breath when you sing. The other dresses don't have that feature." Then she gasped. "What happened to you?" She touched my back. "You have scars all over!"

Until she'd fussed, I'd forgotten about them. Her concern made me self-conscious. "I had an accident in fight school."

"Oh." The empress drew back, a mix of emotions on her face. It made me wonder if she resented the connection her future husband and I had enjoyed while we were at the school together. "I suppose we could mask those with makeup," she said after a moment, then forced a merry smile back on her face.

"You look spectacular in that dress; it would be a shame to alter it to cover your back."

I'd have been fine with having my back covered. But the dress design was clever, and Mèng yáo was very pleased with it, I could tell. "I'm sure you're right," I told her, pressing down on my reservations.

Mèng yáo showed us her wedding dress while we were on our pedestals getting stuck with pins. It was stunning, although not nearly as revealing as ours, and made of heavily embroidered silvery fabric studded with pearls. It was not the only dress she would wear during the wedding, either. Apparently, tradition demanded the bride change five times into a wide variety of outfits, each meant to show her off to best advantage. She showed us all of them. They must have cost a king's ransom.

"We'll be doing a lot of the photography before the wedding," she told us. "That way, I can enjoy the party instead of endlessly posing on my wedding day."

She had given me a long list of songs she hoped I would sing a month ago, but now reassured me I didn't have to sing the whole time because she had a rock band. Phew. Less time singing meant less opportunity for my magic to slip into my music. Mèng yáo poked me and giggled. "These boys are very popular in China!" she assured me. "They will want you to join them on tour after they hear you sing. Hàorán says you have a lovely voice." She scowled just the slightest bit when she said that. Like maybe she didn't like her fiancé appreciating another woman.

With the hours of pinning and prodding finally over, I followed the others out to the beach where a party was set out for us: tables full of food and drink, shade shelters, lounge chairs... the works. I studied the list of songs as the other girls went into the changing tent where they ditched their scanty clothes... emerging in even scantier bikinis.

Mèng yáo trotted over, wearing a gold lamé bikini that barely covered the essentials, and gave me a rough push. "Why aren't you in your bathing suit?" she demanded.

"I didn't think to bring one," I admitted. The truth was, I didn't own one. I'd been too busy to go shopping.

"Didn't bring one? When you knew you were coming to a tropical island?" She threw back her head and laughed. Her laugh was infectious, rippling like a thousand little bells. "You are a funny girl. But I have a solution." She grabbed my arm and dragged me into the changing tent. "Pick one!" She showed me a clothes rack displaying a dozen itty-bitty suits on hangers. As I stood there, mouth open, she started picking them up one by one and holding them against me, then rejecting them. "Wrong color for you. Nope, not a nice cut for your build. Here!" she held the final one up in triumph: it was a lovely turquoise shade with a silver swirling print. "This is perfect. Put it on!" and she thrust it into my arms. "Hurry! We're missing out on the fun!"

Thank the gods it was a one-piece, not that it covered much even at that. The leg openings were so high they came up to the point of my hips. The back of the suit did not cover my butt cheeks at all... and the neckline was positively scandalous. But I had to put it on, because Mèng yáo stood there watching and waiting. I had no choice but to shed my clothing in front of her and slide into the swimsuit. Nakedness wasn't something the empress was shy about. It made me deeply uncomfortable, however.

The empress stood watching me through narrowed eyes as I struggled to adjust the suit so my breasts weren't hanging out in places I didn't want them to, at least. Unfortunately, there was nothing I could do about my backside.

"You have a beautiful figure," Mèng yáo declared, as I straightened up from a final adjustment. "Wonderfully tanned with no need of hours in a tanning booth. And so muscular! My gods, you are a sculpture. You should flaunt your body, girl!"

I flamed bright red. Flaunting my body was not something I was in the habit of doing, and given how my magic affected others, it was unwise as well.

She laughed out loud. "I mean it! You really are gorgeous! Go show what you've got to the boys out there." And she shoved me unceremoniously out of the tent.

I stepped into the sunlight and saw that Hàorán and his groomsmen had joined Mèng yáo's bridesmaids. I felt exquisitely, horribly naked as every head turned to look at me. Even the private security guards gawked. Gods... there was nowhere to hide. My teammates' expressions held a mix of surprise, even concern. They *knew* this was nothing I would choose for myself.

Somebody whistled. "Stunna!"

To me, it felt more like an attack than admiration. I couldn't bear facing anyone dressed like this! I whirled and tried to reenter the tent, but Mèng yáo blocked me. "Nope! You are going to stay out here and let Hàorán's buddies all get an eyeful. I have promised myself that every one of my bridesmaids will catch their future husbands right here at my wedding." She fixed me with a determined glare. "You don't want to disappoint me, Raven. I am not a nice person when I am disappointed!"

"Please..." I begged quietly, not that it got me anywhere. I didn't want to make a scene, but this was not my idea of fun. Not that Mèng yáo had any way of knowing how badly she was triggering me.

"Yǔxuān!" Her voice held a note of command. "Go throw this woman in the ocean. She is far too dry for this party!"

"I live to obey, empress!" Hàorán's brother appeared by my side, scooping me up in his arms before I could protest and striding toward the water's edge. At least it took me away from so many eyes...

I tried to twist free, but I was seriously worried my struggles would cause my bathing suit to slip in a not-so-wonderful way. It barely covered me as it was.

Yǔxuān waded out until he was waist deep. The water was a cool shock against my sun-warmed skin, and I shivered.

"Are you all right, goddess? It looked to me like you wanted to get the heck out of there," he asked. His voice was soft, but his dark eyes were sparkling with mischief.

I glared up at him. "I am not in the habit of dressing quite this scantily. And you are manhandling me, dragon! To answer your question: No, I am not OK!"

"Ah, but what a lovely armful you make, even when you're upset." His arms tightened around me, and he bent his face closer.

I struggled. "Put me down!"

Yǔxuān laughed out loud, his head tipping back as he crowed, "As you wish, goddess!" And he tossed me into the water.

I came up spluttering, dashing the water out of my eyes, to discover the others had joined us. Within moments, a water fight was in full progress. I had no choice but to fight back. I gave as good as I got, and, unlike some of the other girls, kept my bathing suit from getting washed off me.

I gradually worked my way to the edge of the splashing and squealing group and made my way up the beach to a brilliantly colorful sun shelter, where I found an enormous beach towel and wrapped myself up in it. I was trembling, but whether it was from being chilled or a reaction to Mèng yáo's idea of fun, I had no idea.

"They play hard, those dragons," an achingly familiar voice said behind me.

Kellas! I whirled, almost losing my balance, startled that he was here, and even more shocked that he was close *and* talking to me after all this time.

His hand shot out and steadied me. "Easy, goddess. You don't want to fall in the sand. It might not feel so good under that... swimsuit you're wearing." There was a concerned look on his face. "Something tells me it's nothing you'd choose for yourself."

I felt my face flush hot. Apparently, he'd been there when I'd been shoved out of the changing tent for all to see. And how was it even fair that he was completely dry, although clothed in nothing but black swim trunks? I tore my gaze away from his beautiful, tattooed chest. Tattoos I had inked him with last year. "Since when do you call me 'goddess,'" I demanded. "And why are you here?"

Kellas took his hand off my elbow. "Isn't 'goddess' what Yǔxuān called you?" he asked quietly, blue eyes narrowed. "And to answer your other question, I'm one of the groomsmen. Hàorán asked me. I was just a little late getting here."

"Yǔxuān's a bit much..." I did a hard double take. "Wait! Hàorán asked you? You know each other?"

"Ah." Kellas studied me thoughtfully. "Yes, Hàorán asked me. It surprises you I would be friends with the dragon? We've competed against each other a few times over the years."

I wondered how much he was remembering. "Being called 'goddess' makes me feel awkward."

A small grin quirked his mouth, but there was an undercurrent of something else in his voice. "Like that suit you're wearing obviously makes you feel awkward, or awkward as in, 'you feel all warm inside just being held in Yǔxuān's arms' awkward."

The Cat Man was jealous! I didn't hesitate for a moment. "Yǔxuān's not my type." I pushed my hair out of my eyes with one hand, causing my towel to slip, revealing more of the swimsuit in question—and me—than I should have liked. I swiftly tugged it back around my shoulders.

Kellas drew a deep breath, holding his gaze steady on my face. "He's not, eh? Didn't I hear you tell Diomedes that you go for dark-haired guys?"

He'd heard that? Geez. That cat's hearing was way too good. "Why aren't you out in the water beating up on the others?"

His lips tilted up in a lazy smile. "Deflection. Nice one, goddess."

Now he was trying to make me feel awkward. And I needed to stop staring at his beautiful mouth. "Please don't call me that."

He stepped closer. Inches separated us. Heat flushed through my body.

"What should I call you, then?" His voice was soft, caressing.

Our gazes locked. Held. Oh, gods... "That's not fair, Kellas. You know I can't tell you," I whispered.

"Maybe I can convince you to tell me," he whispered back—and kissed me.

My towel fell to the ground as I wrapped my arms around his neck and pressed myself against his warm body. Felt his arms go around me and hold me tight, kissing me until I ached in places I didn't know could ache.

He finally broke off our kiss. I moaned in protest. "Take pity on me, girl. Tell me my name for you, and I'll promise never to stop kissing you," he breathed against my mouth, his breathing as fast and shallow as my own.

I nearly did, then. But something stopped me. A deep, ominous note was growing louder by the moment. Alarmed, I broke away from Kellas and whirled to look over where the wedding party continued to play in the water.

Men wearing full-body diving suits and carrying spear guns were rising out of the waves, headed for the wedding party, none of whom were aware of the danger they were in.

Twenty-Six

I didn't think, just reacted—running toward the water's edge, drawing Fraegarthach and yelling a warning. I met the first man as he was nearly out of the water and swung my sword, slicing into his right arm. He dropped his spear gun and staggered to his knees, crying out in pain. I was past him and going after the next attacker as that man brought his spear gun up, aiming at me—before a bullet found his throat and knocked him back to sink into the water, blood staining the azure blue an unnatural red...

The attack was over in less than a minute. Alerted by my yells, the security force had come running, and they were shooting to kill. The only attacker left alive was the one whose arm I'd cut badly. He was unceremoniously pulled further up on the beach, and, judging from the sheer quantity of blood in the sand where they had dragged him, he was in imminent danger of bleeding out.

Sheathing Fraegarthach, I pushed my way through the circle of security guards ringed around the man. They were doing nothing to help him. I knelt next to him, but one guard grabbed my arm and yanked me back to my feet. "What do you think you're doing?" he demanded.

"He'll die if we don't stop this bleeding right away." I tried to pull away. He just tightened his grip, fingers digging painfully into my flesh.

"Who cares if he dies?" another guard scoffed. He bent and ripped the goggles and wetsuit hood from the man's head, revealing a young Chinese man. He was very pale, in terrible pain. Hàorán and Loki joined the guards clustered around the fallen man. Their expressions were hard, angry.

"Don't you want to know who's behind this?" I growled at the guard who was holding me back.

"Take your hands off her." Kellas had come up behind me. His voice was hard, cold. Dangerous. I could see the guard's reaction, and the fear that crossed the man's face was palpable. He released me as if I was a hot coal, practically jumping away.

"Touch her again and I'll rip your guts out." Kellas spoke, so close now I felt his breath on my cheek. A moment later, he was wrapping a large towel around me. "You OK?" he whispered. I nodded. "Good. Do your thing."

I dropped to my knees beside the injured man. "Hang in there. I'm going to fix this." It would have been better not to do my healing song in front of so many unfamiliar people, but the man was bleeding to death. My song welled in my throat, and I was murmuring the words.

"Everyone, give her space." Kellas knelt next to me, laying his warm hand on my back. "I'm here for you," he added quietly, for my ears only. His presence was reassuring. And bless him for bringing that towel.

The man's bleeding stopped in moments, his sword wound knitting together. His pain had diminished, the tension in his face relaxing enough he could open his eyes. He stared at me. "*Nǐ shì shéi?*" His voice was a breathy whisper: who are you?

"Bad news for you, I expect," I told him, my medallion translating my words into Mandarin. "You'll live, but I'm not sure how well your little gambit against us is going to serve you. Want to tell us why you attacked us?"

He closed his eyes, weakened by his injury. "*Wǒmen zūnzhào mìnglìng,*" he breathed.

"He was following orders," Hàorán translated. He straightened, his face a grim mask. "Put him in cuffs and take him to the guardhouse," he ordered the security team. "Gently. And bandage his wound."

The guards helped the man to his feet. I would not say they were all that gentle, but they could have been harsher, for sure. Kellas helped me to my feet, wrapping the towel more closely around me. The man sent me a last lingering look as the guards led him away. I wondered what would happen to him… not that I would have any say in the matter.

The rest of the wedding party clustered around us. The bridesmaids were talking a mile a minute, exclaiming over the suddenness of the attack, wondering why anyone would attack them.

Random attacks out of the blue were a regular occurrence in my life. I found their chatter overwhelming. Wordlessly, I pushed my way through the throng, headed for the changing tent, needing to rid myself of this bathing suit, get some clothes on. The man's blood was all over my hands. It felt horrible.

"Hey." Kellas had come after me and caught me by one arm. "You need to rinse off first." He guided me to an outdoor shower, adjusting the water temperature before taking my towel and gently setting me under the warm jets. "Here too," he said, touching my cheek as I rinsed the blood off my arms and hands. "You're a bit… splattered."

I huffed at that and put my face under the shower stream. "It happens a lot, sad to say," I responded, stepping out of the shower and reaching blindly for my towel.

He placed it in my hands, and I lifted it to my face. "It seems to, Brannaugh," he said quietly.

I froze, motionless. "Kellas." I could hardly breathe, slowly turned to face him, letting the towel fall from nerveless fingers.

"Brannaugh," he whispered, and drew me into his arms. "I finally remembered."

It was some time before I broke away from his kisses. "What did it?" I asked him. "What brought your memories back?"

He ran his thumb down my face and across my lips. "When you went into warrior mode," he said finally. "You acted like you heard something no one else could hear. It triggered a memory. I remembered seeing you go on alert like that before. Then you drew Fraegarthach and went on the attack like an avenging angel. And if I had any doubt, your compassion for the man you injured put an end to that. Only my Brannaugh can be that lethal and that loving in the space of a breath."

I hesitated before asking my next question. "How much else do you remember?"

Pain shot through his beautiful eyes. "I remember all the ugliness from the Colosseum." His voice broke on his next words. "I remember trying to kill you." He pulled me close. I could feel his body shuddering. "Now I understand why I was never allowed to be alone with you. Why you always seemed to be surrounded by your own security detail." He groaned. "Even when you sang by the lake, one god or another was always there, watching me watch you. They must have been concerned Erin's curse would take over, and I'd try to kill you again." He pulled back just far enough he could look into my eyes, whispered: "I promise you, that will never happen. The curse is gone. Even the thought of hurting you makes me sick. Before, when you were near, the curse's directive to kill you was... nothing I could resist." He brushed a stray lock of hair behind my ear, his fingertips lingering on my cheek. "You were right. Remembering your name was the key to unlocking my memories."

I hadn't been aware of being watched. I'd been far too wrapped up in my misery. "You avoided me. For *weeks*!" Sorrowful accusation tinged my voice.

A grimace flitted across Kellas' face. "I needed time to think. It was terribly confusing. I remembered some things, but there were enormous gaps." He sighed. "I knew you and I had meant something to one another. And for the life of me, I could not figure out how I could have forgotten you, when you responded to me like we'd been..." his voice broke on the next word. "Lovers."

"Sweethearts only," I whispered. "We were never lovers. You always told me I was too young."

"Ah. I was being noble, wasn't I? I'm a fool." He started tracing every feature on my face with his fingertips. I closed my eyes, just feeling his touch. He continued. "I remembered everyone else, knew our history together, knew we were friends. But you... a beautiful, fierce, unforgettable young woman... I'd somehow forgotten. And that just seemed impossible to me. Why would I remember everyone else, but not you?" He groaned; those weeks had not been easy for him, either. "So, I spent a lot of time trying to break down the walls I sensed around those memories. Listening to you sing, I could get glimpses, like a dream barely remembered, but it wasn't until you went full on Amazon that the walls around my memories completely crumbled."

I was trembling. It wasn't from being cold, but he was releasing me and wrapping me up in my towel like it was. "Let's get you into something a bit more your style, yes? This suit may be super sexy, but I know it is nothing you'd choose for yourself. Now I understand why, instead of just admiring you, I felt ready to gut the empress when she put you on display like that." He reached over and shut off the shower, then wrapped an arm across my shoulders and turned me toward the changing tent. "It looked like Hàorán about lost his mind, too. He wasn't best pleased with his empress. And Loki looked ready to commit murder. Why is that?" He led me to the changing tent and followed me in.

I was grateful to see that no one else was in the tent. "We were in fight school together," I said. "We were teammates. Kit too. It... got awful at times."

I rummaged around and located my clothes. Started to let my towel drop, then hesitated.

Kellas took my towel. "I promise I won't look," he said, holding it up like a curtain between us.

I shed the swimsuit as quickly as I could and slipped into my clothing. It was an immense relief. I must have sighed, because he spoke.

"All set?" he asked, still holding up the towel between us.

"Much better." I caught the top of the towel and drew it down. Smiled at him. "Thank you."

"Anything for you, Brannaugh." He smiled down at me, warmth in his gaze.

I wrapped my arms around his neck. "Then kiss me, Cat Man. I've missed you."

"With pleasure," he said, and did just that. I melted into him, let myself get lost in his kiss. Let myself feel everything: his mouth on mine, the strength in his wiry body, his arms tight around me. Then his lips left mine and started tracing delicate kisses across my face and down my neck, ending in a sensitive spot by my collarbone. I let my head fall back, sighing, losing myself in the moment. He groaned, and one hand came up and tangled in my hair before his lips closed on mine again, more insistently this time, until my lips parted and his tongue touched mine, sending a rush of heat through me. Hàorán's kisses had *never* felt this fine.

Guilt flooded through me in a dizzying wave and I pulled back. "Kellas, there's something I really must tell you."

"More important than this?" he grumbled, and tried to kiss me again.

I ducked away. "This is important."

He groaned. "Alright, if you say so."

"Knock, knock." Hàorán's voice called through the fabric curtain door to the changing tent.

Oh, gods. Worst possible timing! Kellas and I separated reluctantly, and I pulled the curtain aside to see Hàorán, Kit, Loki and Mèng yáo standing outside.

"May we come in?" Hàorán asked, his expression serious.

Silently, I stepped back, and they filed in. I kept my gaze down, a bit embarrassed, knowing how it must look. Surely my friends would know Kellas and I had been kissing.

"Are you alright?" Kit asked me, and her gaze cut to Kellas. She was asking about him!

I sent her a half-smile. Oh, yeah, I'm good. I'm more than good!

"Mèng yáo has something she needs to tell you, Raven." Hàorán sounded grim.

I sent him a quick glance, but he refused to meet my eyes. Oh, gods. He was upset with me. He had to be!

The empress looked a little green, but she stepped forward and caught my hands in hers. "I need to apologize for my behavior," she said, her dark eyes begging. "I am a very pushy woman! And I didn't realize I was making you feel so uncomfortable. Please forgive me! I promise I won't do it ever again."

"Until the next time," Hàorán growled under his breath. I chanced a quick look his way. Something in how he'd said that worried me, warned this marriage was a huge mistake.

She sent him a quelling look. "I heard that, dragon!" She turned back to me. "I'm a little wild. Sometimes I forget that not everyone is wild like me." She sent Hàorán another cross look before facing me again. "I'm sorry."

I squeezed her hands. "You're forgiven, empress. I know you didn't mean any harm." She hadn't. It was just that she had grown up in very different circumstances. Obviously she had always felt safe, unthreatened. On the other hand, I knew only too well the danger Native women faced, hyperaware of the horrifying statistics concerning murdered, missing, and abused Indigenous women. I'd grown up wary.

But Mèng yáo was speaking again. "Do we need to change your dress?" she asked. Her brow was knit in concern.

I pondered that for a beat. Yes, that dress was pretty over the top, but I had worn others just as revealing and survived it. And this was her wedding, her special day. I wasn't about to spoil any of it for her. "The dress is fine, empress. No need to change a thing."

The relief on her face was almost comical. She started jumping up and down, clapping her hands, her happiness infectious. "Yay! I'm so thrilled! You will look utterly amazing, I promise."

I glimpsed Hàorán's face: there was a small half smile on his lips, fond of his fiancé, but also guarded. Their relationship was still in early stages. Fragile. But perhaps they'd eventually pull it together. I hoped so, for Hàorán's sake especially.

He noticed my gaze and acknowledged me with a nod, but addressed Mèng yáo. "If we're good here, maybe we should return to our party, my dear. If you will excuse us?" He drew her out of the tent as she blew me a parting kiss.

Kit and Loki remained.

"You finally remembered." Loki addressed Kellas, offering a fist bump. "About damned time!"

Kellas scoffed, meeting Loki's fist halfway. "Does everyone know this?"

"You may have noticed the Light Bringer has a rather large fan club," Loki said.

That sounded like a warning. Tucking myself under Kellas' arm, I grinned up at the coyote. "Better late than never, dog boy."

That brought a smile. "If you're good, we're good." Loki relaxed and hooked an arm around Kit's neck. "Aren't we, sweetheart?"

She grimaced and transferred his arm to her waist. "You'll break my neck if you keep hugging me like that," she grumped, but sent me a wide smile. "As long as you're happy, Raven. This is what you've wanted, right?"

I looked up at Kellas, saw his blue gaze on me. "Absolutely," I said, and was rewarded with his beautiful smile. I smiled back, but couldn't help but wonder if he'd still smile at me when I told him about Hàorán...

Twenty-Seven

I was tired. The dragons had thrown party after party all week, and my practices with Mèng yáo's musicians had run into some long hours besides. The wedding was the next day. I just hoped I'd be ready.

Leaving yet another boisterous party, I wandered out onto a large deck overlooking the ocean. Moonlight reflected on the water's surface, glinting in a long silver path that led to the rising full moon. I leaned against the marble balustrade, rubbed my eyes, and yawned.

"Had enough of celebrating?" Kellas joined me at the balustrade and leaned against it, his posture mirroring my own. He crossed his arms over his unbuttoned dress shirt, his tattoos dark against his fair skin.

Oh, gods, that beautiful body of his... I schooled myself against the desire that flared every time I looked at him, and straightened. "I miss the quiet. It's always so noisy here."

That half-grin of his curled the corner of his mouth. "Walk with me?"

"Don't have to ask twice." I pointed to the stairs that led down to the beach. "Ready when you are."

He took possession of my hand and led me down the stairs, through the still-warm sand to the water's edge where the sand was firm and wet beneath our bare feet. The cool water felt good after the heat of the day; the moonlight a relief from the glaring sun. We walked in companionable silence to where a spur of land jutted out into the water. Trees were growing along the higher middle of the spur, but the water's edge remained sandy and easy to navigate. Someone had placed a bench at the point, just above the high-water mark. Kellas drew me over to it and sat, pulling me down next to him. I snuggled against him, my head laid in the curve of his neck and shoulder, my arms around his middle.

He wrapped an arm around me, holding me close. "I cannot tell you how often I've dreamed of doing this with you."

"Walking on a beach?" I murmured.

"Holding you." He tipped my head up, so I was looking at him. "Kissing you." Which he did.

I melted into his kiss, savoring every second of his mouth on mine.

"Dub told me what he did," he said, finally breaking off our kiss. "Why he took my memories of you."

Sensing he needed to talk, I straightened and turned to watch his face.

Kellas didn't speak right away, just took one of my hands in both of his, absently rubbing a thumb over my palm as he gazed out over the water beyond. Still studying the ocean, he took a deep breath. "Dub said I was suffering from PTSD and the after-effects of Erin's curse. And he told me not to blame myself for trashing his demesne like I did." He shook his head ruefully. "I was awful, made a terrible mess of things. But all he did was laugh when I offered to fix what I'd broken. Told me that looking after me while I recovered was the least he could do, after all you had done for him and Dian." Then his blue gaze turned on me. "I am in awe of you, Brannaugh. Of everything you did, just to come after me. What you did for two gods we thought were enemies, but were themselves trapped."

I shifted uneasily. "It took weeks before I could come get you, and you suffered horribly."

Kellas was shaking his head even before I finished talking. "Not as long in that dimension, girl. You came as soon as you could. Stop blaming yourself."

"But you suffered!" I protested.

He looked grave. "As did you, my beautiful bird."

I sent him a questioning look. "And how would you know that?"

Kellas' expression grew even more serious. "Dub showed me some of his videos this week, while you were off practicing with the musicians. The ones of you and me, and what you went through at the fight school before you came for me."

Oh, gods. Would that have included the ones of me and Hàorán? My face flamed. "There's something I really need to tell you." I'd tried repeatedly over the past few days to tell him about me and Hàorán, but we were always interrupted before I could get the words out.

A rueful grimace twitched at the corner of his mouth. "Is this the important something you've been trying all this time to tell me?"

I gulped, nodded, and steeled my spine. "At fight school, Hàorán and I..." I swallowed hard when he frowned. "We kissed."

He dropped his head to his chest and shook it back and forth before looking back at me with a disbelieving grin twitching his mouth up on one side. "This is what you've been so desperate to tell me these last few days? That you and the dragon *kissed*?" He started laughing. "Oh you naughty, naughty girl."

I hid my face in my hands. "There's more."

He choked back his mirth and turned his body so we were facing each other on the bench. "Out with it. Confess your sins, Light Bringer. I can tell they're tearing you up inside." A barely suppressed smile was twitching his cheek.

I smacked him. "This is serious!" I groaned, fisted my hands, then forced the ugly words out of my mouth. "We kissed, and... made out, and I really adored him, but he was engaged and I had you and it was just so wrong, Kellas, and I am so sorry." It tumbled out in a rush. I could not stop the tears anymore. "I'm ashamed."

Kellas sat quietly, gathering his thoughts. Maybe hating me.

"Say something, please," I begged.

He looked up at me from under his eyebrows, studying me for a little while longer. "You think I should be angry with you that you fell for the dragon? That I should tell you to get lost, maybe? That I would be so petty that I would disavow you just because you had a tiny fling with a good man who was looking out for you when you were scared and vulnerable and thrust into an impossible situation?" His chest heaved with suppressed emotion. "A situation you were in just so you could further your skills enough to come save me? You would think me *that small*, Brannaugh?"

Oh, gods. He was angry at me, but not for the reason I thought he'd be. "No! That's not it at all! You could never be small, Kellas. I was unfaithful to you, and you deserve better than that."

I wasn't expecting the next words out of his mouth.

"I don't deserve *you*, Light Bringer."

I gaped at him. "What?" The word escaped me in a gasp.

"If you need me to say 'I forgive you,' then I will say it. But I hold none of it against you. It pales in comparison to what I did."

"You only did what you needed to survive," I protested. And I hated that he'd had to do it at all.

A pained expression twisted his answering smile. "At least I left no child of mine behind." He closed his eyes and shuddered. "I only made those girls happy, Brannaugh. What teen boys call 'getting to third base.' And only with their consent. Only because we had to make what we were supposed to be doing seem real. I never once..." he groaned softly, like talking about it bothered him enormously, "...went all the way with any of them. Dother and Erin found out that I was not holding up my end of their 'bargain.' Which is when they sent me back to the Colosseum. But I promise you..."

I put a finger over his mouth. "Sh. I understand." I did, too, and was glad he'd told me. "But I was... I fell hard for Hàorán."

"If you want me to be angry with you, you're sadly mistaken. Look where you are now," he whispered. "Not with him, the rich godling. With me, a broke and homeless fairy cat." He raised my hand to his lips and kissed my knuckles. "Sure, if you made a habit of kissing every Tom, Dick and Harry, I'd be furious, but you don't."

And then there was that. "Kellas..." The guilt was overwhelming, and I bowed my head. "I also kissed Leonidas."

He scoffed. "You're kidding me. That big lummox? Why?"

I hung my head. "It was the only way I could use enough magic to break him free of his arm bonds." Then I glared at him. "And that big lummox, as you called him, lost his life saving mine."

He fell silent again, his dark brows drawn together in a heavy scowl.

I couldn't take it anymore. "Kellas, talk to me." When he remained silent, I hung my head and let the tears I'd been fighting slide down my face. Kellas shifted next to me, and I feared he was getting ready to leave. It made me cry harder.

"Hey." Kellas put a finger under my jaw and forced me to look at him. "The gods threw you into the deep end, and you needed someone to look out for you. Hàorán took my place for a little while, looked after you when I couldn't be there for you. I am infinitely grateful he became your champion. And Leonidas has my eternal gratitude for saving my beautiful Brannaugh." He drew in a deep, shaking breath. "As well as all the others, too. What a kick-ass team you pulled together in such a short time, Brannaugh. My biggest regret is that I should have been the one to kill Antaeus." His face darkened with impotent fury. "He died too easily."

"So, you aren't upset that I, that we… you know." I cringed at the memory: Hàorán's and my hands roaming all over each other, the intense kissing…

At least that pushed the anger away. "How can I be upset with you when you're here with me, not him. *Me.*" He fell silent for a long moment, then surprised me with his next words. "How did Hàorán make you feel, Brannaugh? Be honest."

I was silent for a long moment, considering. "He made me feel safe," I said at last.

He accepted that with a quiet hmm. "And me? How do I make you feel?"

There wasn't a single moment of hesitation before I answered him, looking him straight in the eye. "You make me feel alive."

That made his eyes glisten. "Alive is way better than safe." Then his hand was cupping my face, and his mouth was on mine. And for a long, wonderful while, the world and its troubles went far, far away.

$\sim$

The morning of the wedding dawned cool and bright, then heated quickly. Like any wedding day, there were some last-minute disasters and a few tears and hissy fits by the bride, but those were quickly and efficiently handled by the maid of honor, a young woman hardly bigger than Mèng yáo herself. By the time the afternoon wedding was to take place, we bridesmaids and the bride had our dresses on, our hair and makeup flawlessly done by an army of professionals. The groomsmen had seated all the guests. While we bridesmaids waited around a chapel corner for the wedding processional music, I felt the first ominous low tone signaling impending disaster. Thankfully, I was at the end of the line of bridesmaids, so I went looking for the source. When I didn't find it, I rejoined the others just as the processional music began, feeling distinctly uneasy.

I was the last bridesmaid up the aisle, doing my best to walk like I'd been taught, my stiletto heels forcing me to watch every step. The chapel was full to overflowing with people, some even lined up against the walls. Every eye was on me, an uncomfortable focus I did my best to ignore, all the while smiling sweetly and trying not to fall on my face. Weddings. Ick. Hàorán was right: elopement was the better alternative to this spectacle. Two cute little kids followed me with the rings and a basket full of rose petals. Last up the aisle was Mèng yáo on her father the emperor's arm.

The whole time, that ominous low undertone continued, and went on even after the processional stopped and the clergyman at the front of the chapel started in with his "dearly beloved" speech welcoming the guests to the holy matrimony of Hàorán and Mèng yáo, blah, blah, blah. I tuned him out and instead made a thorough search of the audience, looking for the source of the threat. It wasn't until my gaze reached the back of the room, where a man in severe black had just stepped in, arriving late—and with him the ominous undertone, clearer now. That guy was trouble.

He was massive: tall and broad, his face chiseled with cruelty. Flaming red hair fell to his shoulders. And he was wearing a full-length duster coat in temperatures that had other attendees fanning themselves with their wedding programs.

I dropped my bouquet and stepped out of line. Kellas was immediately on alert, moving toward me, a question held in his eyes. I pointed, he nodded, and we met in the middle of the aisle.

The man in black stood watching us, a small smile on his face. "You're a little out of proper order, aren't you?" he commented. That brought confusion to the mumblings that had already started among the guests—and put a stop to the ceremony.

"You're a little unusually dressed for the occasion," I retorted, raising my voice to be heard clearly by everyone. "A duster in this weather? What are you hiding?"

His smile widened, and he drew back his coat to reveal a gun holstered at his hip. "Not hiding anything, moon witch." He let his coat fall back over the gun again.

I heard Kellas draw a deep breath. "Your manners need improvement, mister," I told the man. People were rising in the audience, the brush of clothing making shushing sounds as individuals made their way to the aisles along the sides of the chapel. Someone touched my arm.

"We're here, goddess." It was Dub, speaking in an undertone. From the corner of my eye, I saw Dian flanking Kellas. "Say hello to Ares, God of War."

Just my luck! "Are you looking to start a war here, Ares?" I said as evenly as I could, given how badly my heart was hammering.

The Greek God of War crossed his arms over his chest, a self-satisfied smirk crossing his lips. "Just here to observe. When two powerful families join forces, it is useful to pay attention."

"And for that, you require a gun at your hip." I put as much skepticism into my voice as I could. My 'gun at your hip' comment drew gasps of fear from the guests, some of whom were now urgently trying to leave.

"It's a part of me. How could I leave that behind?" Ares' gaze raked me from neck to knee. "You look good in that dress, witch. It's almost as revealing as the red one you wore at fight school."

Kellas gripped my elbow as a warning. I felt Fraegarthach hum at my back. "And you would know that how?" I replied as evenly as I could.

His eyes went all lazy, settling on my chest. "I was there."

Ick. He was disgusting. "No, you weren't."

"Maybe you'll recognize me as this?" Ares shimmered, then reformed as...

I gasped. "Eramos." The red-haired, mean-faced, back-biting little monster who had been on Leonidas' team with Herakles and the Rooster.

"The same." The God of War changed back. "Not my favorite form, but useful in certain situations where I need to be underestimated."

Suddenly, the pieces fell into place. That ominous undertone I'd heard from the beginning of fight school had been him. I'd just never had put the two together in my mind.

"Did you know this?" I demanded of Dub in a whisper.

"No," he responded. "But I should have." He stepped in front of me, joined by Dian, using their bodies to protect me and Kellas. "War is not welcome at a wedding, and especially not this one, Ares. You should leave."

"Make me," Ares sneered.

"I don't have to," Dub scoffed. "The father of the groom will ensure it."

Behind Ares, Shen Long's large blue dragon head and neck snaked around the doors of the chapel and loomed over the God of War, giant maw open, long, viciously sharp teeth bared.

Ares must have felt the dragon's breath, because he disappeared in a swirl of dark smoke an instant before Shen Long's jaws closed over where he'd been a moment before. The Dragon Lord roared his fury, gusting wind and rain over the wedding guests. He withdrew immediately, and Dub and Dian raced after him. I would have gone too, but for Kellas' grip on my arm.

"Let the gods handle this one," he urged. He escorted me back to the front of the chapel, and we rejoined the silently watching wedding party at the end of our respective lines.

I picked up my bouquet and faced the bride and groom, who were looking at me with alarm. "Please continue," I said in a bright, cheerful voice that had nothing to do with how I was feeling inside. "I apologize for the interruption."

I fixed a bland smile on my face, but my mind was in turmoil. Ares. Was he the one behind the attack at the waterfront last week? My gods, what next?

The rest of the ceremony continued without a hitch. Dub, Dian, and Shen Long rejoined us at some point. Ares had left—the ominous undertone that had haunted me for so long was gone. After the exchange of vows and the wedded pair left, I linked my arm through Kellas' as the recessional music played.

He leaned over as we reached the doors and spoke in my ear. "Have I told you how beautiful you look today?"

I caught my lower lip between my teeth and sent him a sideways glance.

He laughed softly. "You're blushing."

I side-bumped him with my hip and stumbled on my stupid heels. He pulled me back upright. "Easy, girl. You need a bit more practice on those stilts before you get physical with me."

Drat this bouquet! I couldn't punch him with both hands occupied. I just sent him a demure look. "Lucky for you I am currently hobbled, Cat Man."

He smiled and tugged me closer. "*Neach-strì colganta beag*: my fierce little warrior. Come on, we've a party to go to." I groaned. His answering chuckle warmed my heart.

An hour and thousands of photographs later, we were driven the short distance from the chapel to an enormous dining room where the wedding meal was underway. We were seated at the head table and served many fancy Chinese delicacies, most of which I did not know what they were, nor cared to eat. I didn't particularly like seafood, and most of the dinner consisted of whole fish, their dead eyes staring sightlessly at the ceiling, as well as squid and octopus.

Kellas leaned over and speared the calamari off my plate. "Not your favorite, eh?" he stuffed the chewy morsel into his mouth. "Yummy." He leaned over like he meant to give me a kiss.

I recoiled. "You will brush your teeth before I kiss you again, Cat Man. Ew!"

He just chuckled and helped himself to the rest of my serving of squid. "This is the best calamari I've ever had. You're missing out."

I just rolled my eyes at him.

Darkness fell as we finished up the wedding meal and wandered over to the dance hall. Kellas accompanied me as I sought the musicians, then stepped away to lean against one of the tall columns supporting the high arching roof of the ballroom. I walked out in front of the band and lifted the microphone to my mouth.

"Welcome everyone, and thank you so much for attending the nuptials of my friends Mèng yáo and Hàorán. I hope you are having as much fun as we all have been. The dragons certainly know how to throw a party!" I clapped my fingers against the heel of the hand holding the microphone, then waited for the applause to die down. "Let me introduce your musicians for the night, who I know you will love; they are very popular in China. Ladies and gentlemen, I give you the Jaguars!"

That brought cheers from the younger set and a few disgruntled expressions from the older ones, who then shrugged and moved further away from the black speakers hanging from the rafters.

"Tonight, I will join these lovely young men for a few songs, then they will continue with the music while I join the rest of you on the dance floor." I turned to the lead singer. "Shall we get started?" He nodded, and the opening notes of our first duet began. Half an hour and several songs later, everyone was still up and dancing, even the older guests, who seemed pleasantly surprised the band was not knocking them senseless with excessive volume.

"One last song from me," I crooned into the mic. "This one is for a very special man in my life." I sought out Kellas where he had remained lounging against the pillar the whole time, and started singing "Kiss Me," as Sixpence

None the Richer sang it. As the song continued, I walked slowly toward him. He straightened up from his pillar, hands at his sides, a small smile just touching his lips. "Kiss me," I sang as I leaned against him. And yeah, he did. Four times, each time as I sang the last words. I clicked off the mic and handed it to the musician who'd followed me out onto the dance floor to retrieve it. Then, Kellas took me by the hand and led me through the clapping crowd, out of the ballroom into the dark that had fallen outside. Backing me up against the side of the building, he kissed me thoroughly indeed. Well, I had asked him to, hadn't I? In a very public manner, too. Not that I objected—I dug my fingers into his shaggy mane and returned his kisses with enthusiastic abandon.

We did eventually come up for air, clinging to each other and allowing our hearts to slow down and resume a more normal rhythm.

"Brannaugh, there's something I'd like to ask you."

I opened my eyes and looked up at his face, mere inches from my own. "Yes?"

That lopsided grin of his nearly undid me all over again. "I haven't asked yet. How do you know what you're agreeing to?"

I scoffed, and that made his grin widen. He fumbled at his neck and undid a chain, sliding something off it. A ring. I stared at it and then up at him. "A ring?"

"It's a *fáinne Chladaigh*... a Claddagh ring. A promise ring." He explained. "The hands symbolize friendship, the heart love, and the crown loyalty. The best ones are handed down through family." He paused, taking a deep breath. "This was my mother's. I've had it for centuries, waiting for the right woman. On the left hand, it signifies a woman is engaged or married, depending on how it's worn, heart toward the wearer, or away." He smiled. "On the right, it can mean the wearer is looking for love, or in a committed relationship. I am not asking you to promise me anything yet, *mo chroí*. But if you wear it on your right hand with the heart facing you, I would be honored and blessed."

He was asking me to commit to him, then. I did not take the ring from him, but laid my hands over his, looking at the delicate silver design, the two hands clasping a ruby cabochon carved in the shape of a heart. "It's beautiful," I breathed.

"May I?" he whispered.

I could only nod, too overwhelmed. Relief flooded his face, and he kissed me before sliding the ring onto my right-hand ring finger, heart pointed at me. Committed.

We did eventually return to the reception, and danced with others in the wedding party, but I was never so happy as when I was in his arms.

Life would never be simple. It would likely never be easy. But was it ever, for anyone? All I knew, with Kellas by my side, and my friends and family at my back, I was ready to take on whatever the world was planning to throw at me next. And if my recent history was any kind of predictor of what was to come, that would be plenty.

~

I fell asleep curled up in Kellas' arms as we sat together on one of the big white sofas in the Dragon Lord's private living room, where the wedding party had gathered after the reception. I was exhausted and just wanted my bed, but everyone else still seemed too keyed up to rest. Kellas knew without asking just how worn out I was and had drawn me over to a quiet corner. He snuggled me close in his arms and bade me rest. I had no trouble following his instructions.

I fell asleep immediately, and dreamed I was peering through a partly open doorway at a beautiful female Cait Sidhe. She was tall with long, wavy hair black as jet, her eyes as blue and sparkling at Kellas' own. Her expression was the sort you'd wear if you found some kind of bug swimming in your soup.

"I cannot believe our son picked a mortal woman to bond with. All these years waiting for him to decide, and what does he go do? Falls for a mortal!" She paced up and down in frustration. "Really, Fionn, our son is a tremendous disappointment."

A tall, fair-haired Cait Sidhe stepped into my narrow field of vision, clasping the woman by her upper arms and drawing her close. Both Cait Si were beyond beautiful… and far too thin. Like they didn't have enough to eat. "Aoife, you fuss too much, and you oversimplify. The girl is anything but mortal…"

"Her dam is!"

"And her sire is anything but," Fionn added gently. "We must trust Kellas' judgment in this."

Wait. What? Kellas? My Kellas? Were these two his parents?

The female Cait Sidhe—Aoife—scoffed. "A lousy love god. And his little girl is a love goddess? How lame is that? How do we know she didn't just charm him with her abilities?"

Fionn laughed at that. "I'm fairly certain her abilities *did* charm him. But not in the way you suggest. There was no artifice there, from what I can make out from his communications. Aoife, please give our boy a chance to show us his choice is wise, before you attempt to smash them apart."

"Tsh!" Aoife pushed against Fionn's chest, but he didn't let her go.

"Promise, *mo ifreann beag,* my little hellcat. Give our boy the benefit of the doubt this once."

"Fine!" she exclaimed, but her tone showed she felt it was anything but fine. "I give her one year to prove to me she has what it takes to be his mate. After that, the gloves are off."

He kissed her. "That should be adequate, mo ghrá. Do you even know what the gods are calling her?"

She snorted in disgust. "No. Should I care?"

His mouth curled in an echo of Kellas' own sneaky grin. "They call her the 'Light Bringer.' She bears the sword of Nuada. We Cait Si have been waiting for her all these years, and our son has found her for us."

Epilogue

Kellas cradled the sleeping girl close, listening to her breathe, watching how her eyes moved behind closed eyelids, dreaming. She was so trusting, so beautiful; vulnerable in her sleep. Love embodied, a deadly weapon wrapped in the most alluringly feminine package he had ever met in his thousands of years of existence. And she loved him. Him! A lowly Cait Sidhe. He brushed a gentle thumb over her parted lips, saw how, even in sleep, she responded to his touch with a slight smile. It made him ache with longing, and something else: shame. Shame at what he had done to win her, to tie her love so closely to himself. Not that he hadn't tried to warn her against caring for him many times. 'You shouldn't be here with someone like me,' he'd said often enough. He'd even dumped her cruelly, once, hoping to protect her. Despite being dreadfully hurt by his actions, she'd defied time itself to save him from Dub's arrow. That selfless act had been his undoing. He'd loved her, then, truly loved her, not just valued her for what she could do for his people. But she didn't know him, even though she thought she did. He was a Cait Sidhe. Liars and thieves, every one, capable of deception, bad bargains (only for the other guy) violence and murder. And worst of all, betrayal of the worst sort: that of the heart. And he was preparing to do just that, if that was what it took to save his people. It made him sick to think about it, but it was the only way his people would ever be free again. He'd told her there were only a few of his kind left in the world. That was true... to a point. For their transgressions, the

Cait Si people had been trapped by the god Lugh in an in-between dimension, along with the witch Carman. They had been forced into servitude to her in her own banishment. Cait Si were not servants. They were a proud, independent people. His people. And if legend was to be believed, the only one capable of freeing them was the Light Bringer.

He'd guessed what she was almost from the beginning. Since she'd come to him hundreds of years ago, he'd made it his mission to find out what she was, had combed the world to discover how the Light Bringer would be reborn. Then he'd manipulated her father to make sure Michael mated with the right woman to create her. Had guarded the girl from the shadows as she grew, ensuring she remained safe, even as her father put his own men to watch over her after Margaret had thrown him out. He'd killed more than a few trolls and wicked men who'd stalked her over the years, including some that had pursued her the day she'd come into her magic. He'd expertly played on her affections, teasing, tempting, frustrating her, until she was well and truly hooked, then moved to ensure she would love nobody but him. Sure, it had nearly cost him his life more than once, but he was a cat, he had more than one life. The closest to disaster was when Erin had nearly ruined his well-laid plans by clamping a collar of compulsion on his neck, convincing him it was the only way to save the Light Bringer's life... but even that had worked to his benefit. This girl, this precious life, had fought the epitome of evil to save him, and against all odds, had won. Now, he adored her and couldn't get enough of her. And yet, here he was, on the brink of betraying her for the one thing that meant as much to him as her love. His parents. His clan. Thousands of Cait Si, trapped in a never-land for millennia, waiting for the one creature who could free them: the legendary Light Bringer, reborn to mortal woman and Celtic god. Totally unlikely, yet here she was. Alive, in love, and in his arms.

"Cait Sidhe." Hàorán spoke in deliberately quiet tones so as not to wake the girl. The dragon had approached silently.

Kellas looked up at the Dragon Lord's son and felt a surge of jealousy. He'd nearly lost his Light Bringer to the young god. He nodded, putting the question on his face instead of into words.

"I know what you are deep in your soul, even if she does not recognize it," the dragon said. "If you hurt her—if you betray her like your kind always seems to do—you will have me and my entire family to contend with. Understood?"

"I have no desire to hurt her." That was the truth.

Hàorán saw through his prevarication. "No desire to, but shall. The fable of the Light Bringer is familiar to me. I believe you intend to use her to free your people. Although I understand your desire to do so, you play a dangerous game, and her life could be forfeit." He glared, blue-green reptilian eyes glittering. "She dies? You die. And that's a promise I will keep."

Kellas nodded. "Fair enough," he said. If Brannaugh died, he had no desire to live, anyway.

All the wonderful people who have played a hand in helping my books come to fruition:

...My readers, because without you all my efforts would be in vain.

...My grand-girls, who act as my first readers. If you feel there isn't enough kissing in my books, blame them. The violence? They never flinch. Weird that kissing would be more cringe-worthy than taking a magical sword to a fictional character.

...My beta readers, who point out weak points in the story.

...My editors, from whom I have learned so much about style, technique, and substance, as well as what makes for just plain good writing.

...My husband of 47 years, who tolerates my disappearing into my workroom at all hours to pound out my stories, but who also makes sure I get out and do things instead of living in my head all day long.

...Our youngest son and his wife, who sell many copies of my books at their ice cream shop. Yes, an ice cream shop is my best sales venue. Go figure.

...All those great writers of fantasy fiction whose books I devour multiple time over, studying how they string words together into a gripping story.

...My friends and family, who, whether they understand my obsession with writing fantasy or not, support me in any way they can.

...My fur babies (pony, dog, and rabbit) who, by their live-in-the-moment examples, help me retain my sanity in these uncertain times. And to my cat, Eli. May you rest in peace. I love you.

...And the world outside my front door: the fields, the woods, the yet-to-be-explored distant lands whose siren call to come explore is not to be denied any longer.

A call to action:

Earth is a magical place. I hope the ones who are hellbent on destroying our peoples, ecosystems and planet don't succeed in doing so. Sadly, the God of Evil lives on in many different iterations of awfulness. It's up to all of us to deny him repeatedly, in any way we can.

Never give up, never give in.